PENGUIN BOOKS

BURNING BRIGHT

Helen Dunmore is an award-winning poet and novelist. Her poetry collections include *The Sea Skater*, winner of the Poetry Society's Alice Hunt Barlett Award, *The Raw Garden*, a Poetry Book Society Choice, and *Secrets*, winner of the 1995 Signal Poetry Award. Her first adult novel, *Zennor in Darkness* (Penguin, 1994), was awarded the McKitterick Prize in 1994 and her third novel, *A Spell of Winter*, was winner of the 1996 Orange Prize for Fiction. *Talking to the Dead*, her latest novel, has recently been published by Viking.

Helen Dunmore was born in Yorkshire and now lives in Bristol with her husband and children.

HELEN DUNMORE

Burning Bright

PENGUIN BOOKS

The author gratefully acknowledges
an award made to her by the
Authors' Foundation in 1992

PENGUIN BOOKS

Published by the Penguin Group
Penguin Books Ltd, 27 Wrights Lane, London W8 5TZ, England
Penguin Books USA Inc., 375 Hudson Street, New York, New York 10014, USA
Penguin Books Australia Ltd, Ringwood, Victoria, Australia
Penguin Books Canada Ltd, 10 Alcorn Avenue, Toronto, Ontario, Canada M4V 3B2
Penguin Books (NZ) Ltd, 182–190 Wairau Road, Auckland 10, New Zealand

Penguin Books Ltd, Registered Offices: Harmondsworth, Middlesex, England

First published by Viking 1994
Published in Penguin Books 1995

One

Last night Sukey came back. Her poor head was bleeding. *You know how scalp wounds bleed,* Enid told herself. The cut was only perhaps an inch long, but the blood welled and welled and would not clot. And Sukey looked at her and said, 'What a nuisance this is, darling. I can't seem to do anything about it,' while Enid wiped the blood off Sukey's forehead as it sprang sparkling on to her dress and arms. Sukey's arms were bare and brown. She turned them over, holding them out, exposing the white flesh with fine blue veins beating in it. Blood spray hazed against her dress, though she was upright, smiling. But in the back of Enid's dreaming mind there was a shadowy knowledge that all this blood could never have come from so small a wound. Even in her dream she knew what had really happened.

Maybe if I'd seen her dead, thinks Enid for the thousandth time, turning over and brushing the light-switch. Sukey, cold and stiff as the inside of a trussed chicken. No more smell of her hair. No more secret door. Her hair all matted with blood and flies and bits of bone. You can't make murder pretty. Sukey's skull blue inside like chicken bones, and all in slivers.

She's here with me now, in this room. Sukey's eyes, her breath, her long bright fleece of hair spread like a tent around us both. She never went away at all.

Everything returns, thinks Enid. There wasn't an inch of Sukey's body I hadn't touched. More than touched: loved. Perhaps Caro was right, that's where it gets you, wanting everything. Where did it get you, my darling? Who would ever have dreamed it would get you there, sprawled out on the floor of that small closed room, your head askew on the fender? There was blood drying slowly from the outer rim of the stain on the dull red Turkey carpet. It dried inward, darkening. The slow tick of blood became silent. There was so much blood. And the fly still kneaded the window with its legs, trying to get out, crisping against the glass. By the time men with big boots came tramping round the cottage, you weren't even Sukey any more. 'The body.' 'The victim.'

'Darling,' murmurs Enid. She'd never have thought it would be so much worse not to have seen, and to go on and on imagining. She has imagined through fifty years.

'I wasn't there,' says Enid. 'I didn't do anything. I never came.'

'Enid, sweetheart,' says the Sukey in her head, 'you'll have to find me another handkerchief. This one's soaked through.' And she holds out her white handkerchief stained with her bright blood.

Downstairs Jenny's baby howls. Jenny will be walking the floor again, to and fro, to and fro, missing out the board that creaks. There's something wrong with that child of hers. It can't be right for him to scream and scream like this, every night. But what a life for a ten-month baby, going from one squat to the next, one step in front of landlords and social services and bailiffs. The last place Jenny was in there wasn't any glass in the windows, and it was winter then. Jenny boarded them up, but then she had to keep the electric light on all day, and she was sure it wasn't good for the baby. She thinks this place is paradise by comparison, never mind the stairs and the fact there's no proper kitchen.

The buff official letter stands on Enid's mantelpiece so she won't forget it. She does forget things. Long-hidden memories rise, new rinsed. Decades of adult life are like a dull tide which is going out fast, leaving bare the landscape beneath. The letter tells her that the house has been sold again. Well, that's nothing new. Buying and selling, buying and selling; they don't seem to be able to think of anything else to do with this house. Certainly, nobody ever does any repairs. Well, Enid's protected. A sitting tenant. They've explained her rights to her at the Law Centre.

It'll be the end for Jenny, though, and the baby, and the others who drift in and out, half living here, drying their laundry in the bathroom and cooking meals at midnight on a Calor-gas stove. Some of them are quite nicely spoken too. If the new landlords are the ones Enid watched over the banisters, then Jenny has no chance. A precious pair, thinks Enid, I wouldn't like to meet either of those on a dark night in a dark alley.

One was a big, powerful-looking man with curly hair. She'd listened but she hadn't caught his name. It sounded foreign. He'd called the other one Tony, the one with a face like a knife-blade.

They'll sell up the house and move on fast enough, once they see there's no money in it. And Enid's not going to take a cheque for a thousand pounds and move out to please them. She knows her rights, and she knows that rents are sky-high outside. Here, her rent's fixed.

'We shall not, we shall not be moved . . .' quavers Enid, beating time with her heels on the rumpled cotton sheet. The baby in the room beneath is silent, then there's a gasp and another roar of outraged breath. How the noise carries. The baby might as well be in Enid's bedroom.

'Terrible jerry-builders, those Georgians,' says Enid aloud. She knows the history of the house. The fine façade hides some Georgian jiggery-pokery all right. Rubble inside the wall cavities, and there's a long crack down the side of the stairs. Oh, the house is beautiful, if you don't know what's behind that honey-coloured stone which splits in the frost. The days of one hundred per cent conservation grants are long gone. They'll get a lot more than they bargained for, those two, buying this house.

Enid shuts her eyes, feeling for the delicious warm entry into half-sleep. The baby's crying recedes, and instead she hears the far-off noise of a ship's hooter in the docks. 'All gone . . . all gone . . .' says the hooter. Enid breathes the warm smell of herself under the blankets. Wool prickles her chin. She's wearing

3

her jumper still, so she must have forgotten to undress. Did she go to the pub last night? She can't remember.

She sleeps, and there's Sukey, standing by the edge of a lake and shielding her face from the sun. She's about to dive. Her long beautiful body is flexed, her weight balanced on the balls of her feet. The rock she stands on is black and glistening. 'Basilisk,' whispers Enid in her dream. Sukey's bare white toes curl, gripping the rock so as to launch herself from it. Below her the dark water is tense. Sukey's waiting for something before she dives – what is it? She glances at the thick green bushes and calls, 'En-id! En-id!' but no one answers. 'She's waiting for me,' says Enid, and she struggles to answer but cannot speak. Suddenly she is not behind the bushes any more, but high up on the rocks opposite, much too far away for Sukey to hear her even if she was able to call out. She can hear Sukey, but Sukey can't hear her. She can see Sukey poised on the rock with the thick frame of the forest behind her. And then, out of the frame steps Caro. Her red hair sings against the green. Red for danger. Sukey hasn't seen her; she calls again, 'En-id! En-id!' on two notes, high and clear ones which echo around the forest. Enid's tongue is thick in her mouth and no sound comes out. Caro walks very lightly up behind Sukey, keeping directly behind her so that Sukey won't catch even a flicker of movement out of the corner of her eye. She creeps up on Sukey like a cat, light but stealthy. The dark water waits for Sukey. And behind her Caro is climbing the rock, ready to spring.

'Sukey!' screams Enid, bursting her lungs, tearing her throat, but the sound is no more than a whimper. Sukey hears nothing. She drops her hands to her sides and bends her head forward as if she is laying it down on the block, and Enid screams again, rustily, and wakes.

She scrubs tears off her face and struggles out of her blankets. This time she presses the light-switch and looks at her clock. Quarter past four. The baby's not crying any more. Jenny will have an hour of peace before the dawn wail begins. A lot of time has passed. She must have been asleep.

4

'No wonder you had a bad dream, going to bed in your clothes,' she scolds herself. She must be more careful. The distinction between night and day is an important one, especially with new landlords coming. From the look of those two they'd have her put away in a home before you could say knife. Enid is good at watching, and at finding out what people are like before they've even seen her. People don't realize how voices carry up a house. Enid's door is usually ajar, and no one guesses that she's just inside it, standing still, listening. You have to keep on the look-out. That's what Sukey didn't do, the dream said so as plain as plain. She didn't see Caro coming. Miss Danger.

Two

A midnight-blue BMW sits in the clot of traffic moving up the East End's Commercial Road. It's not a ministerial car, and there are no police outriders to clear its path. Paul Parrett doesn't want them today. He's with the rest through the filthy air of the Blackwall Tunnel, through Tower Hamlets and Limehouse. The long file of cars is the only wealth in these streets. Banks have closed, shops are boarded and drifts of uncollected post bulge back through letter-boxes. Metal shutters the colour of mercury fillings cover *Pizza Perfect*. A row of derelict factories shows jagged teeth of broken glass braced by razor wire. Two Bengali road-menders stand laughing inside their tent of red and white road tape, then crouch over their drills. Paul Parrett's car passes the drills very slowly. Their squeal bites against the thick metal of the BMW, and he sees that the men aren't wearing earmuffs. Young men, they never think ahead. He knows this part of London well, with its sweat-shops, its missions, its disastrous housing where walkways cook in diesel fumes and tiny balconies drip washing. His round, toffee-brown eyes glisten with attention while his hands deal automatically with gears and steeringwheel. The day is muggy. The sun's already high but invisible in a pale haze of pollution. He winds down his window and rests his elbow on its frame. Just then a woman on the pedestrian refuge screeches after her child, who swings out off the rail, looking for a second as if he'll somersault as a Transit van swerves close enough to shave his forehead. She's wielding a double buggy and she can't catch hold of him. Suddenly the child's eyes dilate with fear as he sees the van and his game is stripped from him. He shrinks back against the dented steel railings which hold off cars from the refuge. Paul Parrett looks straight into the mother's face, scored with fear, tiredness, the weight of the buggy, the breaking wave of traffic noise against her body. The little boy stares back at the big car with TV eyes. The babies' mouths are level with the exhaust.

No one in the world knows that he's here, in a traffic jam on the Commercial Road, bonnet to bonnet with the sweaty drivers of Hondas and Toyotas and Audis. He could be anyone. He could do anything. He flexes his hands on the steering-wheel and looks in the mirror. He sees the bored face of a commuter, talking to himself or to his car telephone. A traffic jam is a good place to be alone. Who's Paul Parrett to that gaunt young man in a green parka who feels a winter wind blowing even in July? That woman on the refuge won't have seen the latest cartoon in the *Guardian*. He's hard to caricature anyway. The thing about Paul Parrett is energy, so much of it that you have to wonder what would happen if he ever used it all. His dark perfect clothes are neutral. No eyebrows or catchphrases.

St Anne's on the left. Soon he'll be nosing into the City. Everything's packed so tightly together in London. Between one street and the next you move from world to world. If the traffic wasn't so bad he'd glide from metal-sheeted shops and desolate housing projects to the canyons of the City in three minutes. It's beginning now. Money starts to whisper through the car windows. There's the first secretary in immaculate taupe suit, stepping out of a smoked-glass lobby and hurrying up the pavement to the next entrance. A dispatch rider jerks his Yamaha off the pavement.

Paul Parrett loves the game of anonymity, just as long as he can stop it any time he wants. There's a telephone on the left of his dashboard, and he keeps the codes in his head. He's about six minutes late. They'll be waiting for him. He presses a button.

'Five-seven.' He's through. 'John. I'll be another quarter of an hour or so.'

A small fluster. John knows the car hasn't been sent for him, doesn't know what's going on, has been fast-footworked by his minister again.

'Relax. Just have the messages ready.'

Instantly John is calm, ready for business. He'll be annoyed with himself because he has betrayed surprise. His role is to be ready for anything Paul Parrett chooses to do. John gives a précis of the papers which have arrived for the morning's meeting. He is lucid and to the point. The best briefer in the business: the sort who can make any minister feel it's all due to his own grasp of key facts.

'Well done. That's excellent,' says Paul Parrett warmly. He's always known about stroking people.

He presses another button, cuts the connection and leans back against the seat. The air's just a little too warm, but not unpleasantly so. Nearly there now. London's all around him, like an animal in its lair, still potent in spite of everything. It smells of money the way a fox smells of fox. He smells it through the open window. He loves it. Those cliffs of glass are charged and humming. There's not a door he passes that he can't go in. It is his own choice to shunt past them in a traffic jam which is loosening up now, breaking into its component cars which stream off right and left as the drivers accelerate, thinking of the next meeting, of money, crisis, gain and loss. They may not think of the Commercial Road but it's there somewhere, lodged in their minds like grit which they pearl into profit. They are allowed to see but not to suffer, shielded in their central-locking cars, guided by traffic signals, linked by emergency contact to AA, RAC, police. But the sight of what's on offer along the Commercial Road frightens them deep down, way below the stories they tell themselves. They race up their office steps boyishly, where a boy would take the lift. They pour a cup of freshly brewed coffee, lift a telephone, set the screens humming and pick up the rest of the world.

Paul Parrett sits inside his expensive suit, and feels the remembered itch of cold winds through clumsy clothing. He remembers standing for hours at bus-stops for buses which never came, listening out for cars so he could cross the roads in London smog. He remembers chilblains and chapped knees, dressing in unheated bedrooms, icy lino, underwear washed once a week, the black bits cut out of potatoes. He remembers meagre fires and margarine. He doesn't need a guide to the Commercial Road. He's made his own maps to get out of it, and now he's here in his car, after a bowl of coffee and French bread and on his way back from a place he'll never visit again. A complete waste of time.

He is a GI baby: one of the ones whose mother never got the chance to go to America. He is a bit of the war. By the time she found out about Paul, his father had already been shipped across to France. And that was that. His father might have died in France, or returned to the States. He might be alive still; he could very well be alive still. His mother is alive, he knows. He has checked it. One of the advantages of a ministerial position is that all sorts of small barriers fall away. The social security system is usefully comprehensive, and old people live a long time these days. She is in receipt of a supplementary pension, and she lives alone in rented accommodation. He has never seen her.

Perhaps his adoption could only have happened just then, immediately after the war when there were so many children to be had. Bombed-out children, evacuated children, refugee children. A river of children whose parents had lost touch with them or with life. All these displaced kids to be slotted back into some sort of home. This is what Paul Parrett hopes. He hopes that a woman like Mrs Parrett wouldn't find it quite so easy to get hold of a child now. In 1946 she got her hands on a six-month baby with no trouble.

His adoptive mother never disclosed to the adoption society that the reason she had not been able to have a child herself was that she had never slept with her husband in fifteen years of marriage. Mr Parrett said nothing and died two years after Paul was adopted. Her dislike of sex extended to those who practised it and to those who were obviously the result of it. Paul was clearly in the second category, as the product of sex which must have been undertaken for pleasure rather than endured for the satisfaction of a wedding ring. Such an attitude was inconceivable to Mrs Parrett. She foretold bad blood. When Paul was a baby she would watch him, as if to see through his transparency the sexual act which had engendered him, going on and on, endlessly repeating itself, endlessly unforgivable.

She was a big, firm, righteous woman who stood alone outside the infant school gates, not speaking to the other mothers, the ones who had toddlers clawing at their skirts and huge moon-faced babies who sucked on dummies and smelled of shit as their mothers smelled of milk and menstrual blood. Her mission was to protect Paul from himself. She believed in swooping into the boy's room at night and switching back the covers to ensure that he was not playing with himself. He never was, after the first couple of thrashings with Mrs Parrett's wooden egg-whisk. Even in childhood his sense of timing was excellent. She would find him lying on his back, as instructed, hands crossed over his chest, his lustrous eyes following Mrs Parrett as she tweaked the bedspread back into place. She could not hide her disappointment from him. He hated her and knew that he hated her, but she gave him pleasure too as he grew older. She made him laugh. And he learned quickly. Soon he would get the better of her. By the time he was eight he knew he was stronger than her and that she was making a fool of herself. He was half American, he told himself in the night. Mrs Parrett was a foreigner to him. He invented a language which she could not understand, and spoke it to himself under the covers. American. He laughed quietly in the darkness, knowing that she was stupid. Soon he would grow up and never see her again. She was not his real mother.

But Mrs Parrett never knew that she had had the last laugh. When Paul Parrett grew up he found that his penis, always so receptive to masturbation, his best and most eager friend, wilted completely at the touch of a naked female body. Nor did he want men. It took him quite some time to discover exactly what it was that he was after, but by his mid-twenties he had it all worked out. The problem was that his sexual needs were unfriendly. There was nothing in them for anyone else, except money. He made up his mind that he'd never find a woman willing to put up with them on a long-term or unpaid basis. Once that was decided he could get on with arranging things. It meant having money. That was all right, it was part of the plan anyway. It meant employing intermediaries, which he didn't like. There was bound to be a risk in it, especially while a young man from nowhere was moving from research for an MP to money-making and back to politics. But he was always good at judging risk. There was a tight web of calculation under the wild surface of his money-making. Sex could be made the same.

Luckily he knows he's not cursed with the desire to take risks for their own sake, to court exposure and degradation in order to increase his sexual excitement. He knows men who are. He's seen some get away with it, and he's seen others caught. For some of them the frisson of idling the car engine round King's Cross is part of the game. They pretend it's a necessary evil, but he perceives their pleasure. He's seen enough of indiscreet telephone calls, the use of an official car for unofficial business, the semi-deliberate, dangerous mingling of two worlds. He isn't like that, and King's Cross is no place for a minister of the Crown. Paul Parrett believes that those who are caught want to be caught. They may not be aware of it, but deep in themselves a desire for punishment wells up to meet the punishing world.

And he has never made the mistake of thinking that the editors of tabloid newspapers are stupider than he is. He requires a service, therefore he must deal with intermediaries. He makes sure that these intermediaries are professionals who want to stay in business, and also that they have no links with major organized crime. He wants people who can be frightened when necessary.

He has one of the newer, secure car telephones. He presses another sequence of numbers and listens to the ringing tone. It answers, and he presses another security button.

'Tony,' he says 'It's Paul. How's business?'

'Terrific. And yourself?'

'That last consignment was way below your usual standard. I'm really not happy with the way things are going. I don't want to have to find another supplier, but –'

'No need for that. You say there's a problem, we sort it out. No worries. Give me a window while we get you fixed up. Two weeks?'

'Excellent. I'll be in touch.'

Paul Parrett changes down and shoots into a side-street. Not many drivers know this rat-run. He picks over the conversation in his mind. Something niggles. Yes. He enjoyed playing the game just a little too much that time. He plucks up and identifies his own small flicker of gratification. Stupid. Once you start liking codes and secrecy for their own sake, it's time to think things over carefully. Never kid yourself you're getting away with anything. Never kid yourself you've got things taped. Or, like many before you, you'll find that they've got you taped.

It's getting too cosy. Tony and Kai are reliable and they're building up a reputation for dealing with specialist clients, but if they don't get it right with the next girl it'll be time for a change.

That's settled. He drops the thought, cuts neatly across a stream of traffic, turns west and lets details of a tricky briefing rise to the surface of his mind.

Three

The house waits. Jenny and her baby are gone, as well as the other squatters. Enid saw the men who came to get them out. They weren't the men who've bought the house. Those two are keeping out of the way until all the dirty work's done. That Tony and Kai. She knows both their names now. They don't take any notice of her, they know they can't get her out. And they don't look like the sort who'd want trouble, not with respectable tenants. With squatters, of course, you can do what you like. Enid'd be straight to the Law Centre if they tried anything on with her. The men who came to get the squatters out were heavies, hired men, not owners. Enid watched and listened and then at last it was all silent again. Now Enid is waiting too. She's waiting to know why they have bought the house.

It starts to rain. Thick warm drops drum on the van's roof. Water runs down the windscreen, dislodging the bud-silt which clogs the wipers. Kai turns the ignition and starts the windscreen wipers. The left one doesn't work: Maddeningly, it skims the windscreen without cleaning it.

'Do turn them off,' says Nadine.

'I need to see out.'

'Why? There's nothing to see. It's much nicer in here.'

He looks round the inside of the van, at the cracked leather seats, threadbare mats and rust-blotched chrome. Nadine's sweet-papers lie on the floor. She's eaten a quarter of a pound of sherbet lemons. The ashtray is full, and it doesn't close. The rain beats harder, a squally wind rises, and the chestnut tree under which they've parked the van thrashes its branches until immature conkers drop and bounce off the windscreen like small green mines. In front of them a big empty field stretches. Neither of them would be able to identify the crop which is growing in it. They are city people.

'We can't stay long,' says Kai. 'With this rain we'll get stuck in the mud going back up the track.'

Nadine listens to the rain on the roof. The sound makes her feel safe. She doesn't know where they are and she doesn't care. She's here with Kai and they don't need to go back yet.

Kai watches the raindrops running sideways, joining, puddling. He reaches across the gearstick and puts his hand on Nadine's thigh. She is wearing her school uniform; a plain white shirt and a short dark blue skirt. Her shirt collar is limp, her skirt is not new. He traces the shape of her knee, round and bony, then he slips his hand under it into the soft angle between thigh and calf, and strokes her skin.

'We can't,' says Nadine. 'I've got my period.'

Kai continues to stroke. 'Never mind,' he says, as if consoling her. 'Never mind. It doesn't matter.'

'It does to me,' she says. The van is small enough, their acrobatics tricky enough as it is.

'OK,' he says, and pats her thigh, then bends down, collecting the sweet papers, stuffing them into the overfull ashtray. Kai hates dirt, and mess. Nadine tenses slightly. Kai takes up so much more space than she does. It's warm and airless in the van. She turns and unwinds the window. Fresh wet air blows into the car, drops spatter her bare arm. He wipes the rain off her skin with a finger, then licks it.

'All right,' he says. 'Never mind. We'll go back.'

As soon as he says it she wants to stay. Why can't they just sit here and talk? But Kai never wants to do that. Sometimes his practicality melts her: the way he put a towel under them, that first night in his flat, and told her to drink a glass of water before she went to sleep in case she got cystitis. Sometimes it chills her. *Nothing's happening, we might as well go back.* It is really quite cold now, and she hasn't got a jersey. Kai starts the car and puts it into reverse. The wheels skid and whine, then grip as he reverses much too fast back up the track. They've left the gate open, so the van bumps back easily on to the road. The wind and rain have torn off bright green leaves and scattered them on the road. They are soft and tender and they tear easily, then they crush into slime.

'Aren't you going to shut the gate?' asks Nadine. The gate had been fastened and tied with twine. Kai shrugs, puts the van into gear and accelerates down the road. He has no intention of learning the language of the English countryside.

'Don't worry,' he says. 'We'll get you back to school by two o'clock.'

'Second lesson,' says Nadine. 'I'll have to say I've been in the library.'

Kai concentrates on the road, his eyes narrowed to peer through the badly wiped, streaming windows. Their tyres slosh through surface water, kicking up mud and spray. Nadine crosses her arms and rubs her cold elbows as she watches his hands on the steering-wheel, casual and assured. He's been driving for eighteen years. Two years longer than she's been alive.

'Where are you going, back to the flat?'

'No, I'm going down to stay with Tony. Some business's come up.'

'When're you back?'

'I don't know,' he says, as if it doesn't matter. 'Wednesday. Or Thursday if I have to go on to London.'

Wednesday. That's five days away. One hundred and twenty hours. Or if it's Thursday, one hundred and forty-four hours.

'It's getting stupid, all this travelling,' he says, yawning. 'It'll be good when the house is sorted out. I must talk to Tony, get him moving. It's all too fucking slow.'

She stiffens. His voice is as easy and casual as his hand on the wheel. 'You mean you might be going soon?' she asks.

At the sound of her voice he turns and looks at her briefly.

Small extinguished pale face, dark hair blown about by the window draught. All her small round softness hidden under the clumsy shirt and skirt. No one else knows it's there yet: only him. He looks back at the road, takes his left hand off the steering-wheel and runs it round the shallow curve of her face, from temple to jaw-bone to chin. Then he rests his warm hand against the side of her face. She rubs her lips into his palm, shuts her eyes, kisses his skin and tastes metal. The taste of money: small change.

'You'll come down,' he says. 'Once you've passed your exams.'

What does he mean? A visit – or to stay? She won't ask.

'It's too long,' she says. 'I've got another year after this one.'

'You're sixteen,' he says. 'Old enough to leave home.' He turns and looks at her, smiles suddenly, too close, his eyes slitting. A real smile, a smile from the eyes. Distracted, he's let the van drift to the crown of the road. Luckily the distraction has also made him slow down, so there is just time for him to wrench the van back to the left as a grey Volvo packed with children rocks round the corner in a cloud of spray. The Volvo horn blares. Nadine turns and through the rear van window she sees three children staring back, their round cosseted faces agape. The school run, neatly livened by near-death. Kai says nothing. Nadine looks at her watch.

'The bell will have gone,' she says.

'Say the rain made you late.'

'Not very convincing if I'm supposed to be in the library.'

He laughs. It's easy for him, thinks Nadine, all he has to do is drive away in his van.

'I've always thought libraries were sexy,' says Kai.

'Maybe they are where you come from. Not here.'

Kai is Finnish. He's always telling her how unusual it is for a Finn to speak English as well as he does; a Finnish Finn, that is, not a Swedish Finn.

But he's been here ten years, and he's in business. In business you've got to learn fast or you might as well get out. His language is loose, colloquial, easy. Only rarely is it skewed by something else: interference coming through from a foreign language she doesn't speak. Kai knows about communication. When Nadine goes to his flat the answerphone is always loaded, winking with messages. Tony phones most nights, and the two men talk for a long time. Kai takes calls in the other room. It's all business. It would only bore Nadine.

'You'd better not drop me near the gates.'

'You'll get so wet, darling.'

She shivers. *Darling.* He doesn't say it too often, so each time it's fresh and delicious. It's not easy for her to trust the word. She's heard it too often at home, passing between her parents as part of a complicated exhaustion of emotions. But from Kai it goes straight to her stomach every time, with the weight of Kai behind it, his age, his rough hair with a bit of grey at the front, his warm, heavy, muscular body, his sexual confidence, his directness. It goes straight to her heart. She keeps it there and never tells anyone. And perhaps it helps that 'darling' is a word in a foreign language to Kai. He reaches out and flips the stereo button. In this decrepit van the only thing of quality is the stereo. He slots in a new tape and a second later the van is flooded with a mournful tango. The voice quality is radiant.

'What's he saying?'

'Oh,' he shrugs, reluctant, wanting only to listen. 'The usual stuff.'

'What usual stuff?'

'It's about a dream place he wants to go to, deep in the forest. He'll build a house for the girl he loves, and if she doesn't come to him then he'll kill himself. Typical Finnish song ending.'

'I like his voice.'

'Yes, he's very famous. He has to sing this song wherever he goes – they always ask for it. He hates it.'

'How do you know?'

17

'I used to know him.'

Kai makes her feel as if she has no past. Only being a child.

'Does she go?' she asks.

'Who?'

'The girl. The girl he loves.'

'No, of course not. That's the point of the song.'

'So he kills himself.'

'Not straight away. Not while he's singing.'

'All your songs are about the same thing,' grumbles Nadine, but the flood of the song has gripped her too. She yields to the luxury of sadness, nostalgia for places she has never seen, dark whispering forests and falling rain. Kai rewinds the tape so they can hear it properly. His hand is back on her leg.

They are coming to the outskirts of the city now. In his old van Kai gets through it faster than anyone else. He knows all the rat-runs. In the back-streets, in early afternoon, the first prostitutes are out on the corners. They look tired. Young white-faced girls in jaunty little lycra skirts, bandeau tops and frail sandals, they stare through the van as if it's not there. Kai and Nadine are of no interest. These are short-cuts for business-men traversing parts of the city where you keep your windows wound up and lock your doors at traffic lights. Unless you are after something. If you are, it doesn't take long to get it. Since she was eleven Nadine has walked home from school and seen what happens. Slowly it's swum into focus and become something she understands. First the slowing car, then the sauntering girl glancing quickly up and down the street before she leans in at the car window and assesses its driver in the same second as she asks him the ritual questions and puts her hand on the doorhandle. Kai doesn't give the girls a glance. He buckets the van down a one-way which brings them out near the school, runs it along the road a short distance, stops. It's not quite at the gates, but she knows it can be seen from the windows, and the staff-room's on this side of the building. She opens the door and clambers out, then with deliberate bravado she leans back in again, bends over so her short skirt rides up her thighs, and kisses Kai.

'See you soon,' she says. 'Darling.'

Four

The phone rings, and Paul Parrett takes the call without looking up from the papers on his desk.

'Tony.'

'Yeah. Just getting back to you about your query. You know, yesterday.'

'Yes.'

'Thing is, can you wait? I mean, I can fill you in for the meantime but there's something really special coming up which might be just right for you.'

'How long would that be?'

'Well, could be six weeks, two months.'

'That's ridiculous.'

'Yeah, I know what you mean, but this is once in a lifetime stuff. Is this line OK?'

'Yes.'

'Right,' says Tony in a burst of candour. 'Sixteen. Really classy. And looking for her daddy all right. This could be it.'

'Sixteen,' says Paul Parrett. A faint, responsive sweat tingles in his armpits. 'Really sixteen?'

'Yeah, guaranteed. No kidding. I wouldn't mess you about. I mean, it's wasting my time as much as yours, isn't it?'

'Six weeks.'

'Could be as much as two months, I got to be honest with you. But it'll be worth it. We could be talking long-term here. And, like I said, Vick'll fill in for the time being –'

'No. No. We'll leave it like that. You let me know when.'

'Soon as I can. The only thing is –'

'What?'

'If Kai gets in contact with you –'

'Kai's not in on it?'

'Yeah, 'course he is, he's my partner. But not till it's all ready to roll, just in case there's a problem.'

'No funny stuff.'

'No, this is straight.'

'Isn't it always?'

The safe line goes quiet. If it's safe, of course. Paul Parrett takes off his jacket, walks to the window. Night-time London blossoms beneath him. The smoky, reinforced windows don't open, but he leans his cheek against the glass for coolness. The glass is rainy. Amplified bubbles of it roll down towards his eyeball. He can smell his own sweat.

The service station hums and glows as if it's been dropped from Mars. Nadine stumbles as she gets out of the car, shivering. Cold night air wraps round her legs. Kai clicks the central locking. He's got rid of the van and she misses it, in spite of the rust, and the springs sticking into her buttocks. It felt like home. The hired BMW doesn't smell of anything except air-freshener. She'd thought it was Kai's at first, when he picked her up at the end of the street with her suitcases. Ten o'clock, they'd agreed, and his car radio was giving the news as she climbed in. But they hadn't left the city straight away. He'd had to call in at two or three addresses, to leave messages, to see people. It was all business and she'd stayed in the car listening to the radio. She wasn't looking where they were going and suddenly there was her school, a dark ghost of itself, with one security light burning over the main entrance. Nobody home. She looked back: she'd never see it again. Have a nice life, Nadine Light, eight GCSEs taken a year early, one of our high-flyers. Nadine Light, half-way through her A-level course when she suddenly stopped being able to read. But they didn't know that. Only the essays coming in late and the coursework not done and the lessons missed. Nadine Light standing in the staff-room, face sullen, averted. A disappointment. 'After all we've done for you,' said their eyes. '*Not university material,*' said the headmistress's report. A BTec maybe? What that girl needs is six months behind a shop counter, then she'll appreciate all we've done for her. Five years on an assisted place and nothing to show for it.

It was past midnight by the time they got on the road, and the night was clear with a rind of moon. Kai accelerated on to the ring-road and the city shrivelled behind them. At the blue motorway turn-off they'd shot across the path of a lorry spangled with lights, carrying its freight of darkness, then they were on the slip-road. Kai put his foot down, the car leaped, then steadied, and the miles started to fold away behind them. She lay back in her seat. She was away, she was safe.

Behind her, in the past, a tree was flowering in her parents' garden. It was the orange-blossom. There was one in the front garden, and one in the back. The scent taunted her, brushing her face, then retreating into dry dusty caverns of leaves. She had loved it so much. She had sat inside the bush, cross-legged, longing, teasing her lips with white flowers. No one knew where she was.

She had stood under the mock-orange, waiting for Kai. She pushed her bags into the shadow of the hedge in case anyone passed who recognized her. There was a bus-stop near by so it wouldn't look strange if she stood there, waiting. She looked up through the flowering branches. The street-lights smudged them but they were more delicate in dusk than they were in the sun. At the last moment she saw how beautiful they were.

Four lads in a car went by, shouting and whistling at her out of the windows. A bus slowed for her, but speeded up when she didn't put up her hand. Five to ten. Five more minutes. Behind her, in the house, Lulu would be deep in dreams. They were hers and no one could touch them. Not even their mother could follow Lulu there, interpreting, moving her lips as Lulu moved hers. Lulu would moan and gargle or lie still in the shadows of the night-light which was always on, because Lulu hated the dark.

Their mother was making lists again. They were selling everything, going away. Away over the sea to the centre which could help Lulu. For months they had been studying brochures and calculating their finances. If they sold the house they could do it. Nadine would be fine. She'd transfer to the tech and get a room with a nice family near by. The centre was a village of pale wood, lost in vegetable gardens, orchards and pinewoods. Here Lulu would live. Here were the kitchens where her mother would work. And her father spoke German, he could work in the office. It was all arranged. There was everything Lulu needed. Conductive education: repatterning, intensive speech therapy, hydrotherapy, music therapy, art therapy. One to one, two to one, three to one. All for Lulu, grunting and rolling in her wheelchair, fighting free of the world which pinned her down.

Nadine blanked out Lulu's cries, the smell of tonight's sausages, her mother scrabbling under the sideboard to check for woodworm, her hair tied up with one of Daddy's socks. She stood still under the tree with her suitcase ready and thought of nothing. A glossy car peeled out of the stream of traffic and pulled in at the kerb. She frowned, looked away, tugged her bags closer so it was clear what she wasn't waiting for. Men coasted these roads all night. The car hooted and she flicked a glance at it. It was Kai.

There are oily puddles on the service station forecourt. It must have been raining here, though it was dry at home. She saunters over to look at a bucketful of carnations while Kai fills the petrol tank. The flowers are giftwrapped in foil and cellophane but some of their petals are brown. Not worth the money, she decides, though it would be nice to put flowers on the table when they arrive.

'Do you want coffee?' calls Kai.

'No, let's get on.'

She's glad when they are back on the motorway. If they could go on for ever, with the traffic thinning and the road wide and black in front of them like a strip of liquorice. When they're driving they seem to belong together. Kai opens the glove compartment and pulls out a bar of fruit and nut chocolate and a bag of toffees. He must have bought them in the service station. She feeds him chocolate piece by piece, and dissolves a square on her own tongue, rubbing the raisins clean of chocolate and then biting out their plump hearts. For once Kai doesn't put on a tape; he hums to himself a growly little tune on five notes. In the back are her bags with her clothes and a few books and her building society savings book into which her grandparents have been putting money each year since she was born. She has nearly two thousand pounds. Her dowry. It was to help her through college. It doesn't matter, since she'll be getting a job. The road is dry and the tyres hold firmly as Kai pulls out to overtake. On the digital display his speed flickers to the late nineties, then down.

'Go to sleep,' says Kai.

'I'm not tired. Put some music on.'

'It's all crap. I forgot to bring any tapes.'

'It doesn't matter. I wish we could go on and on, just driving through nothing.'

He looks round at her and smiles, then begins to whistle his song.

'When I was a kid,' he says, 'that's just what I wanted. Sometimes I'd walk to the edge of our village and stare down the road going south. You don't know what they're like, our Finnish villages in the middle of nowhere. One day I'll take you there, then you'll see what I mean. There's nothing like it here in England. Little places scattered in the forest. Fishing in summer. Tiny farms miles apart. No tourists because it was too far from anywhere. People came into the village to the dance hall once a week to dance tango and drink in the car park. Get drunk, throw up, go home. All the respectable people inside going round and round and round. Maybe it's changed now: I don't know.'

Nadine smiles in the darkness. Kai is lit up for her by the soft glamour of midsummer nights she's never seen.

'When I was fourteen I'd go and drink in the car park with my friends, because we didn't dare ask the girls to dance. Boys are boys.'

This is one of Kai's sayings. He has several and she knows them well. Life is difficult. Boys are boys. He uses them ironically but he uses them.

'My grandmother had a story she used to tell me,' Kai went on. 'Where I grew up was close to the sea, on the north-west coast, you know?'

She nods. She's looked it up, of course, in the City Library atlas which shows the tiniest village, the most fragile serration of international boundaries. And there it was, north of Vaasa, north of Kokkola, way up the coast. Her face flushed in the reference library as she lighted on its name.

'She told me about a woman who lived in the snowstorms. A kind of spirit, I suppose. My grandmother had a name for her, but I've forgotten it – I was only about six when she stopped telling me stories. All the old people believed in spirits, but they never talked about them except to the kids. My mother would have been angry if she'd known.

'The snow-woman was the most beautiful woman in the world. If you were out alone on the ice you might hear her singing, and if you listened or called to her, she'd come. She had gifts she gave to human children. You'd go to her, thinking you were going to get one of those gifts, but as soon as she touched you, you belonged to her.

'She'd rock you in her arms until you fell asleep. Next morning your parents would find you frozen on the ice. All us kids knew about it. We used to whisper the spirit stories. My grandmother told us that each winter as the sea froze near our village, the snow-woman came closer. On a windy night when snow was coming from the north my grandmother would put her finger to her lips and make us listen, and she'd whisper: "Shh. Can you hear her? Can you hear her calling?"

'I always wanted to find the snow-woman and get her gifts. I knew I was cleverer than my grandmother. Maybe I was cleverer than the snow-woman, and stronger too, no matter what my grandmother said. I'd trick her. I'd snatch her gift and run off with it. I kept pestering my grandmother. "What's the gift? Where does she keep it?" I thought it must be toys or something to eat. But she wouldn't tell me. She sat drinking coffee and saying nobody knew. I wanted to knock her off her stool against the stove and keep her there till she told me.

'But I couldn't. I wasn't strong enough. So I decided to find out for myself. I didn't tell anyone, not even the other kids. I put on my snowsuit and my skis, and buttoned my cap over my ears and skied away from my grandmother's house. By the sea the snow was rough. I took off my skis and walked. The ice was hard and crusty and it hurt my feet through my boots. It was all white in front of me, and there was a noise of wind, just like my grandmother had said. But there was no snow coming. I knew how to tell. I walked and walked.'

'On the ice?'

'Yes. I kept listening. I'd never been alone like that before. I knew if she was going to come, she'd come now, when I was all alone in the middle of the ice. When I looked ahead the air seemed to dance. You don't last long in that cold, if you get lost. My face was hurting. I cried a bit, but that hurt too because my snot froze on my cheeks. Then I got angry. The snow-woman was supposed to be looking for children. Why the fuck didn't she come? So I started yelling for her, the way I used to yell at my mother when she made me mad.'

'Did she come?'

'No. Nobody came. I kept on shouting. I didn't know how to go home. Luckily a man heard me, who'd been fishing on the ice. You know, they make holes. He was going back to shore because it was getting dark. He couldn't believe there was a kid out there, alone. Later my grandmother told me what I was shouting. "Come here, you fucking snow-woman! Devils and

Satans take you, you bitch!" All the words I'd learned from my grandfather when he was alive. This man wasn't from our village, so I didn't know him. He carried me to shore and into our village, and asked whose I was. I kicked him with my boots all the way home. I was lucky he didn't leave me there on the ice.'

'So you never got your gift.'

'No chance. My grandmother cried and my mother pulled off my snowsuit and beat me with a wooden spoon. She was so ashamed of my bad language. "*I don't know where he's picked it up,*"' he mimics savagely. 'And my mother shouted at my grandmother, later on, after everybody else had gone. She never told us spirit stories again. That was thirty years ago. Everyone was moving to the cities, away from the country. They were afraid people would think they were peasants. If it was now, people at Helsinki University would be chasing my grandmother with a tape-recorder, to get her stories for their archives. But she's dead. She couldn't live in the city. My mother wanted to take me south. My grandmother was nearly eighty: she was forty when my mother was born. Nobody wanted to hear her stories, except us kids. My mother hated all that old stuff.'

A sign flashes by, too fast for Nadine to read it. 'How far is it now?' she asks.

'Another hour on the motorway. Try to sleep.'

'It's nice to talk.'

But Kai's silent. He's never talked to her about his childhood before. Surely that means they're getting closer? But it's so hard to know with Kai. There are so many things you can't say. Things like 'I missed you. I want to be with you.' But she's going to be with him now. She's got nothing to worry about. Of course he's busy – all those telephone calls and trips. That's the way business goes. It takes time to set up a deal. Kai's in property, mainly, and it's not a good time. He has other interests as well, and he and Tony are partners. It's not like her father's working world with its neat salary and deductions every month. It's much more exciting.

She's going to be with Kai, in Kai's house. The deal's gone through. Tony'll be there too, and she doesn't know Tony that well. He's a lot older than her, like Kai. But he seems all right, and besides he's a friend of Kai's. He's known Tony for years.

The car cruises on. She's never understood why people talked of cars cruising before, but the word matches this car. She slides down in the seat and curls herself sideways. Maybe she will sleep, just for a while. She is nearly asleep when she hears Kai laugh once, softly. He's remembering himself when he was little, she thinks drowsily, that boy in the middle of the ice, swearing and screaming, not knowing how near he was to death.

She jerks awake with light on her face. She shields her eyes and cowers back in the seat, blinking. The car is stopped. It's a policeman, big and square in the nearside window, an Alsatian on a short chain beside him, its front legs splayed and braced. The Alsatian looks at Nadine and rolls out its tongue. The policeman looks beyond Nadine, into the car.

'Don't say anything,' Kai murmurs. He opens the car door and gets out, leaving the door open. There's a lot of noise, shouting, shrill continuous whistles, cars revving, horns, chanting – and can that be a mouth-organ? It sounds as if there are thousands of people out there. She peers behind. They're still on the motorway, just by a service station slip-road, but all the traffic is stopped and dark shapes are running between cars, vaulting bonnets and blowing their whistles. Kids. Younger than her even. They bob in and out of the lights, grinning. Torchlight spills and dazzles, crossing beams of blue police lights. Sirens from stopped police cars whoop quietly to themselves. She presses the window button and Kai's conversation with the policeman slices cleanly into the car.

'Rave party . . . clear it in half-an-hour. Road-block –'

The Alsatian is right by Kai, its muzzle nearly touching his hand. Kai seems not to notice it. The heavy expensive flank of the hired car is at his side: lucky they aren't in the old van. The young from the stopped convoy of cars mill across the motorway, on to the hard shoulder, scrambling towards the service station slip-road. One tattered boy juggles four clubs as he runs. His head is back and he's laughing.

'Won't do them any good breaking through there. The service station personnel have orders not to let them in. We try to stop them using the telephones, though the leaders carry portables . . .'

'It must be difficult,' agrees Kai.

The policeman drops his voice, confidential. 'We're not making arrests at present. Once we know the venue we can do something. They're waiting for the signal now. There's always a lot of hanging about. Funny sort of way of enjoying yourself, but they can afford it. No jobs to go to in the morning – they've all the time in the world, this lot.' His tone is observant but uncritical, as if he's talking about a herd of cattle which has got on to the road.

Kai laughs. 'What it is to be young,' he comments. The policeman smiles politely, but his automatically assessing gaze flicks to Nadine in the car, as if noting for the first time the twenty years between Kai and her young, pale, upturned face.

He's no fool, thinks Nadine. For God's sake, Kai, don't say any more . . . get back in the car. . . .

Spidery bodies race back down the motorway embankment. There's a flash of light, an outburst of whistling, cries, the sound of reversing engines. The policeman stiffens. His dog smiles, showing teeth.

'Right, sir. Best get in your vehicle and wait here,' he says and sets off at a steady half-run.

'Look! Those cars are going through the gap. They're doing a U-turn – they must be heading back north.'

Tyres screech, two police cars rock towards the central barrier, find the gap and nose through. Hands reach down and bang the roofs as they pass. Then they're through and chasing off up the motorway. A nearby policeman talks urgently into his radio, then lopes off along the verge. More and more cars swerve into the gap and away. There are sirens hawing in the distance, reinforcements coming up from the south, their blue flashes miles off. Everywhere kids pile into cars and vans which are already moving away as the last body hurls itself through the door. There's a frenzy of car horns, flying crests of hair, shoehorned bodies. Faces gape at windows. The hunt turns, streams and flattens down for the race up the motorway.

'They've gone,' says Nadine.

Behind them lorry-drivers get back into their cabs and over-night salesmen put coats back on hooks in the backs of cars. Law abiding, the remaining traffic hovers, waiting for the off. Engines start and turn over, but no one goes forward until a police motorbike comes up alongside, going slowly along the line of stopped traffic as its rider speaks to the drivers.

'Right, sir. The road's clear ahead.'

The knotted traffic stirs as vehicles edge into position. A few minutes later they are humming down the motorway again, each car or lorry a separate pencil of light. The incident's over.

'Just as well we were in this car,' says Nadine.

'Money's the one language every policeman in the world speaks,' says Kai.

'You didn't try and give him money!'

'No need. He only had to look at the car.'

'He might have thought you'd stolen it.'

'Do I look like a thief?' Kai turns to Nadine and smiles, then flashes his lights to make the car ahead pull over. The soft, supple, leather jacket. The shoes. The heavy hand-made cotton shirt. The old-fashioned gold watch. None of it too new, all of it living on Kai as if it had been born there. Money might not be Kai's native language, but he certainly speaks it well. Nadine lifts his left hand off the steering-wheel. She rubs her cheek against the jacket, breathes in. The smell of leather, the smell of money.

'I love this jacket,' she says.

'We'll get you one. You'll look good in leather.'

Five

The scrubbed floorboards are scabby and cool under Nadine's feet. Kai said the whole house smelled of cat's piss. It was all coming from this room. He scrubbed the boards with a bristling wooden-backed scrubbing brush, then he bought a yellow plastic mop and bucket and swilled the floor with boiling water and washing soda. The planks are swollen and the grain of the wood is raised. Later they'll sand down the wood, seal it, make it smell of clean pine and resinous varnish. She slides the soles of her feet gently backward and forward while her bare body cools until it feels dense as marble. Behind her the bed is a warm, sweat-damp heap of expensive linen and Liberty covers. It smells of sex and new goods, and it's too hot to lie there through hours of summer twilight when she can't sleep. Kai can always sleep. He's asleep now, behind her, on his back in the centre of the bed, one arm flung up and crooked behind his head, palm open.

There was a cat in this room when they first moved in. Nadine saw her streak across the landing, followed her, found the nest of torn newspaper and ginger kittens. She would have shut the door on them and gone away until the kittens were full grown. There were plenty of rooms. But Kai and Tony were close behind her, going through the house room by room, deciding what had to be done. They opened the door and there was the cat, back arched, legs stiff, covering her kittens, spitting and showing her teeth. She was a feral cat, Kai said, who must have got in somehow when the door was left open. She'd been looking for somewhere safe to give birth.

Kai got rid of her. He did not want animals in the house. The carpet stank of cat piss and cat shit, so he and Tony rolled it up and it went into the skip along with the sodden underfelt and the litter of newspaper. The kittens were half grown. Kai baited a box with mackerel and trapped the mother in it, then it was easy to drop the kittens in after her. They were straggle-limbed writhing creatures with needle-sharp teeth: even Nadine couldn't make herself want to touch them or tame them. A kitten twisted in the air as Kai half lifted and half threw it into the box. A narrow red thread of blood zipped down his arm. He stopped, holding his arm, looking at the small bright beads of welling blood.

'Have we got any disinfectant?'

There was nothing but bleach. Kai poured salt into water and swabbed his arm.

'Filthy creatures. God knows what they're carrying.'

Kai hates sickness. He does not like blood or dirt. When Nadine has her period she flushes the toilet twice so that he will not be disgusted by small floating cardboard tubes, tipped with red at one end. Yet he'll want sex during her period.

Now, after five weeks, the room is habitable. Floor by floor, room by room, they are occupying the house. Until two nights ago Nadine and Kai slept downstairs in the drawing-room, with its marble fireplace covered in liverish paint and its floor-length windows. Their bed was a raft of new, expensive brass. They can do what they like in this house. The spaces are vacant, unmarked by furniture, waiting for the word.

'Let's have this as our bedroom. What about this for you, Tony? It's nice with the plane tree outside the window.'

The four-storey house is as fluid as a child's brick playhouse. Anything might happen here.

Nadine stands up. She is naked but for the ghost-haze of last year's suntan bikini. She steps out quietly to the brocade chair, beached on pale boards, where Kai has slung his jeans and his heavy cotton sweater. The sweater cuffs brush the floor, nearly hiding Kai's gold watch. It looks careless, this arrangement of cloth and gold, but by now Nadine knows that Kai is never really careless. Blindfold, he could trace the ticking of that watch as easily as the beat of his own heart. It is valuable. It represents a past which he doesn't yet possess, just as this house does. Kai's slim heavy dark gold watch with its old-fashioned face and inscription on the back in minute flowing cursive: *To Captain Robert Denville on the occasion of his marriage, 28th September 1924.* The watch and its history have nothing to do with Kai, but it's not out of place on his wrist, the strap pushing flat the dark hairs that grow there. Nadine bends and touches the sweater, then stops. The jeans' legs are buckled where Kai has stepped out of them. They hold the shape of his body so strongly that he's bound to wake if she touches them. She glances round. He's still sleeping. For once he's vulnerable. It happens so rarely that she stops to enjoy the quiet-breathing room, the sleeping man, her own power. The only other time she feels like this is when Kai strips off his clothes at night, his back to her, and then turns and walks to the bed where she lies propped on her elbows, reading. She turns, looks up and sees his erection. It's part of him, but at the same time it's apart from him. It's like a present which can't be wrapped up or hidden. What if nobody wants it?

Often Kai comes home even later than she does, and she's late enough after the evening shows at the Warehouse. He smells of night air, tobacco, drink. He's lit up and triumphant. Things are going well, he tells Nadine. Another deal's firming up. She is naked. He holds her tight against his jacket. The cool supple graininess of leather moves against her skin. It is like being enfolded by an animal. She rubs against the leather and her legs part.

Kai sleeps on safely. Her thin-boned brown hand slides into the fold of his jeans, searching for the pocket slit. Kai lies like a dead man, like a man buried in sleep. But he might open his eyes any minute. When he does he's awake at once, wary and alert. He doesn't wake up bleary like Nadine, burrowing back into the bed's heat. He snaps out of sleep between one second and the next. His features tighten. There's no tenderness in the mornings with Kai, no blurred moments of murmuring and dozing. He's up and off.

I must have a cigarette, Nadine excuses herself, feeling deeper into the pocket. Kai doesn't like her smoking, but when she's run out of cigarettes late at night he'll always find a new packet in a drawer somewhere and give it to her, the cigarettes snug in their wrap, fresh and moist. If he sees her going through his pockets she'll say she was looking for cigarettes. She risks another glance round. Kai has turned away on to his side. Deeper and deeper into his pockets her hand goes, her narrow hand which he so admires. She draws out a packet.

New banknotes are just as fresh and moist as cigarettes. She eases them over the lip of the pocket. The money is dense but pliable, and surprisingly heavy. The band around the notes is unbroken and it's too tight for her to slip them out or fan the edges of the notes and count them without the risk of the band tearing. Then he'll know she's been in his pockets. The notes smell of new books with a touch of metal. They have bent where Kai shoved them down into the bottom of his pocket. Nadine fingers the edges. Fifty-pound notes. Three thousand, perhaps? Probably more, carelessly stuffed into Kai's jeans. What's the difference between a naked woman holding three thousand pounds and one with empty hands? She smiles. It's not so much what you can do with the money; it's what can't be done to you once you've got it. Money's another kind of cover.

Kai always has money. If he's got a bank account she's never seen him use it, and he doesn't use credit cards. No electronic spider can trace Kai through a web of his signatures on credit card blanks: a tank of petrol bought here, a meal bought there, an overnight stay, air tickets. Easily traced. His transactions don't show up on any maps. It's Nadine with her casual wages who has a smart grey cheque-book and two cards in plastic folders and a monthly statement addressed to the house. Tony has money too, but she rarely sees him use it. Tony has 'arrangements', a system of exchanges which works without cash. For Tony the city is like one of those tourist maps where you press a button to light up YOU ARE HERE. The people and places where he does business are brilliant and the rest are blanks. Asda and Sainsbury can wink and glisten, Marks & Spencer can open a new wing, Tesco can crowd itself with special offers, but none of them affects Tony's economy.

Once Nadine went with Tony to buy wine from a warehouse down by the canal. Tony was acting big. Money was on its way, and you could hear it coming. Things had to be done in bulk, in style. There was a snap in the air like the first frost. Yes, the money was so close now that you could nearly smell it.

And now she can. She sniffs the wad of notes. It is cool and reassuring in her hands, like good luck. That day Tony had got hold of a white Transit van and parked it by a peeling garage door at the back of the warehouse. Nadine got out and stood in the sun. There was honesty flowering in one corner of the yard. Buddleia burst its way through the beaten-up roof. Tony knocked at a side door and a man let them into a cave-like concrete warehouse. It smelled of earth and air which had been closed in all winter. There were no bottles, no labels, no descriptions. It was cold too. The man saw Nadine shiver and fetched a two-bar electric fire which mottled her legs as she waited. Lists were spread out on the desk. Tony leaned over them, ran a finger down, pointed. They talked in Italian and Nadine stopped trying to follow. At last the men shook hands, coffee was brought with grappa, and by the time Nadine and Tony went out into the sun Tony's boxes had already been loaded into the back of the van. No money, no signatures.

Nadine went to London with Kai. They took taxis everywhere and kept them waiting outside shops, clocking up time. It didn't matter. The whole weekend went by in a soft noise of money. They went to shops where girls of her age drifted and fingered and giggled, not dreaming of buying. Nadine and Kai were borne past on their wave of money. She was different now, not free to loiter and spray expensive perfumes on to her wrist until the smells blurred and cancelled one another out. She had to make choices. When Kai bought the brass bedstead he paid in cash, peeling off notes from his calfskin wallet. He stood there in his battered deck shoes on his raft of money. He knew what he wanted next: linen sheets, plain white.

'Feel these, Nadine,' he told her. 'After all, you're going to be sleeping in them.' He only ever used her name now. Never *dear*, never *darling*.

'Superb quality,' the shopman murmured sacramentally, tweaking a pillowcase. Superb, thought Nadine. One of those words nobody uses in real life. Around them people lifted and looked and felt, not buying. An invisible chapel of money surrounded Nadine and Kai and the shopman. Inside the chapel there was a holy echo of money and voices talking about money without ever saying the word aloud. Kai didn't ask the price of anything.

'Will these do?' he asked Nadine.

Her voice was small and cool as she answered, 'Yes. But we'll need three sets. We can't wash linen at home. These will have to be sent away to the laundry.'

He smiled at her approvingly. He liked her to display such knowledge, but she had so little of it. She had never touched linen sheets in her life, though she had read a book on household management – Mrs Beeton perhaps – one rainy caravan holiday in the Gower when there was nothing else to read. Rain on the roof, a bible of housekeeping on her lap (all those things she was never going to need to do), the taste of chocolate – Mars bars cut into slivers so they'd last – Lulu wasn't there. She must have been in respite care.

The house was a cash sale too, dirt cheap. How many inches of money had it cost? She wasn't there to see. No trips to estate agents with the two of them clearly a couple, no lists of particulars or young men in cheap suits ushering them through carefully tidied sitting-rooms. Buying this house was like buying a ship which had been wrecked at sea, towed into port and sold off at auction. The shipwreck had left the structure and some surprisingly intact detail – a cornice, some exquisite moulding, a frieze of nursery-rhyme characters in an upstairs room with barred windows, one porcelain cup hanging on a hook in the kitchen. But tides of dirt and neglect had beaten over the hull year after year and it was barnacled, stripped by crabs and nibbling shoals of little fish. The whole creaking structure of it, laced with parasites and dependants, was knocked down to Tony and Kai. It had all been under the water for years.

The banknotes are springy against the tips of Nadine's fingers as she shoves them back into the soft white cotton lining of Kai's jeans pocket. Jeans, sweater, gold watch, roll of money: Kai's equipment. In the mornings Kai dresses and is gone. Some nights it surprises her to find him home when she gets back late from a second showing. His departing back looks so final. There's no promise of return in it.

Did he stir just then? Is he pretending to sleep, testing her to find out if she will take his money? No, he is still as a stone. She only asks questions of Kai when she knows he is asleep.

'All that money,' she whispers. 'All that money, Kai! Where does it come from?'

She slides back into bed beside him, her bare cool skin prickling with anticipation, as it does whenever she touches him. After a minute she lifts her head to look at his face. Under his eyes the skin is pulpy. He has a weak chest and last winter he had bronchitis so badly it frightened her. She hadn't known him long then. She can hear his breath creak inside the narrow tubes of his chest when she lays her head against it. It sounds as if there's a bird's nest in there. He ought to lose weight, but she likes him as he is. His colour is bad tonight, as it was just after his bronchitis. That might be just the light filtering in through the dirty lace curtains and dirty magnificent windows. The windows haven't been cleaned for years. *ANGIE 4 DICK* someone has written, and *BAZ WUZ YER*. There's been no one living here properly for so long, unless you count Enid upstairs. Seven years, Kai says. Seven years of dust silting in curtains which are held up by tacks because the brass poles were the first things to go, seven years of blistering paint, newspapers rucked and yellowing under doors, mouse droppings in the kitchen, crisp spider-wrapped packages of flies. The house has had five owners in seven years. The property market has never come right. Prices don't go up as they used to any more. Each new owner waited a year or so for the sudden rise, like beautiful fireworks signalling the sell-off. But nothing happened. The market stalled or crept up or down by an inch. They cut their losses and sold without doing more than stir up the dust, sell scrap metal from the backyard, try to bully the sitting tenant out of her attic.

Kai can't bear dirty things to touch him. The new sheets, bluish-white like skimmed milk, are tangled into ropes where Nadine and Kai have tossed and sweated and kicked and twisted. A new duvet with a Liberty cover swells over the bedstead. They are buoyed up on brass and rust and rose and bronze. They have two pillows each and a bolster which he took from an apartment in Rouen. He might have bought it, paying off the concierge in French notes as immaculate as his English ones, or perhaps he just walked out of the building with the bolster under his arm like a corpse. No one would have stopped him, because Kai always looked as if he had a right to do what he was doing.

'Feel how firm it is!' said Kai, thumping the ticking stripes. Nadine smelled shuttered French rooms.

Nadine has polished the bedstead until its brass knobs wink at her. The bed is a promise of what is going to happen, in this bare room with its streaky wallpaper, its damp patches on the plaster, its thick hook set in the ceiling as if for you to hang yourself there. The curtains don't fit. Lace roses make maps of lighter and darker grime. The curtains are slung up on a plastic washing-line which dips in the middle, showing a few inches of glass. Outside, the grubby sky is changing to violet. Where the sash cord has rotted, Nadine has wedged the window open, and warm petrol-laden air blows in.

Kai rolls, pinning her shoulder. He is heavy and when he is asleep he spreads out to claim the bed. She braces herself on her left elbow and shoves him away. Kai is always warm, and now the steady pulse of his body heat has settled for the night. He'll be fresh for tomorrow. Things to do, people to see. The soft July light will last for an hour or so yet. She sniffs for the thread of jasmine perfume which comes into the room at about this time, from the bush below their window. It seems as if the jasmine has been flowering for ever, just as the summer has been going on for ever. When it's dark you'd never know that its stems are lodged in builders' rubble, and its starry flowers are coated red with brick dust.

Kai's arm lies crooked and exposed. The underside of his arm is white, but heavily muscled, invulnerable. Nadine's little sister used to sleep like that, both arms braceleted around her head. The only time Lulu looked like other children was when she was relaxed by sleep, eyes shut, limbs sunk into the mattress. Nadine knew the names of all those muscles once. She did them at school. The hair in Kai's armpit is straight and silky. She's been staring at him too long. He's beginning to make no sense, like a name repeated too often. He is almost frightening.

She wants to bury her face against his arm, but it would wake him. She wants to lick his skin and breathe in the burned smell of him, like the skin of a child who's been playing in the sun all day. No. There's nothing at all childlike about Kai. He just smells burned, that's all.

Her parents have left England. They took the van that had been adapted for Lulu's wheelchair, and clothes, and passports, and maybe they took with them some old photographs which show Nadine squinting against sunlight in the back garden. She phoned the empty house and there was a long, low, flat sound, the sound of nowhere. She phoned again and a bright female voice answered. The new people. The back garden must be ashy with all the things her parents have burned: Nadine's school exercise books, reports, certificates, a stack of winter clothes. Her parents have gone but she knows where they are. They know where she is too. One phone call.

'I'm fine. Really fine. Staying with friends. And I've got a job. Yes, I'll write. Make sure you send the address in Germany, and love to Lulu.' Lots and lots of love to Lulu. They didn't come after her and she knew they wouldn't. She's had her turn.

'We've got to think of Lulu now. This might be her chance.'

She imagines her mother's face, transparent and ugly with hope. This might be Lulu's chance. Sell anything, go anywhere. Nadine'll be fine. It's so respectable you could put it in a Christmas circular letter.

'Nadine's fine. Not very academic after all, as it turned out. Those GCSEs were a bit of a false dawn. Still, she's got a job and a room in a house with friends. Oh, yes, we're in touch. She phoned us just the other week. Nadine's always been old for her age. Independent. You wouldn't believe she was only sixteen.'

No, thinks Nadine, they'd leave out the last sentence. Even an unbelievable sixteen is a bit much, a bit much to ask people to swallow. Well, she's not sixteen any more. She's nineteen at work and nineteen with Enid and anyone else she meets. Nineteen is fine.

Six

Above, the plumbing wheezes. Someone's running water into the bath. It's deep, claw-footed, and it takes ages to fill. Water gushes and then coughs in the pipes before it trickles into the geyser and out again in a thin boiling stream. It takes for ever. Nadine wants a bath or she'll smell all the next day, of sweat and semen and her own vaginal juices. She likes all these smells when they are fresh, but not when they are stale and masked by a quick squirt of deodorant before work.

'Nadine! Nadine! Are you there, dear? Have you got a minute?' Nadine flips out of bed, runs to the door, calls up softly, 'I'm coming!'

At least Enid's not deaf. You don't have to bawl around the house to make her hear. So it's Enid in the bath, her wispy hair damp round her face. She always runs the water too hot. She can manage the geyser as nobody else can. With a flick of her wrist she keeps the balance between a rush of cold and a trickle so hot it makes the geyser blow back and shut itself off. But then Enid ought to know, because Enid's always been here.

The geyser is huge, dangerous and stained with verdigris. Enid likes the smell of hot water, she says to Nadine, 'Oh, hadn't you ever noticed it, dear? Put your face over a basin of hot water, then – it smells quite different from cold.' She's right, it does. She likes to simmer, slowly reddening her skinny calves and thighs. Getting in is a gradual immersion, staged with small pained lip-pursings and a hiss of indrawn breath.

'I . . . KNOW *that my redeemer liveth*,' hoots Enid from above. Nadine pads up the uncarpeted stairs, past the dirty windows on the stairway where three pigeons sit plump on the ledge. Warm used-up air moves deliciously against her, while the insides of her thighs catch as she walks, sticky with Kai's semen, her body leaking with Kai, her nipples dark and swollen from his sucking. The big bare house echoes as she goes up through it. '*And that He-ee-ee-ee*,' sings Enid, her voice thinning as it spreads through the sun-warmed cavern of the house. All day the tiles have been baking until they shimmer, and now they pump back stored heat into the upstairs rooms. You can scarcely breathe up in the attic, where Enid lives. Flies die of heat, and toast on the window ledges. Nadine pulls her baggy t-shirt on over her head.

The bathroom door is off its hinges and propped up against the door frame outside, leaving a gap through which Enid and Nadine can slide with ease, although Kai and Tony have to manhandle the heavy door aside each time they want to go in. Enid doesn't mind the lack of privacy. She likes company when she's in the bath. She calls out again, hearing Nadine, in a hesitant old-lady voice which she knows Nadine will not be able to resist. 'Are you there, dear? Just come in a minute, would you?'

As soon as Nadine is through the gap and into the bathroom, Enid's voice deepens and firms to its usual tone. 'Nadine, just look behind the toilet a minute. The soap's down there. The bugger slipped out of my hands when I was getting into the bath. And you know I'm not supposed to bend down.'

Enid claims that the doctor has told her never to take a bath on her own. Since flu last winter, and pneumonia after it, she ought not to risk it. 'Dr Govind says it's affected my heart,' she tells Nadine now, as she tells her every bath-time, fixing her with small peremptory eyes in which there is also a trace of genuine fear. 'After all, what if I fainted? Who'd hear me in this mausoleum? I've got to think of that.'

'We'd break down the door. And then Kai'd give you the kiss of life.'

A small discriminating grimace from Enid. 'No, thank you, dear, it would scarcely be worth his while, would it? With an old woman like me.' And Enid pats the wicker dirty-linen basket beside the bath, leaving a wet hand mark on its satin seat, inviting Nadine to sit there. Nadine stoops behind the pedestal, locates the soap and rinses fluff off it before handing it to Enid and sitting down. Enid soaps the small pouched purses of her breasts. These breasts fascinate Nadine. They are empty. They have outlived their purpose, as if Enid has metamorphosed into some new and unexpected creature, reborn into sexless innocence. Is this what everything comes to? Enid has voyaged through decades of being a woman and come out on the other side. Now she doesn't bleed, she doesn't fill and empty each month. Her buttocks are hollow and she is breastless. It's not so long since Nadine was breastless too, and she remembers it clearly. A white ribby sheet of chest, and two nipple pimples. The freedom of swimming in a pair of cotton pants, to the indulgent smiles of adults. Then the first warning signs: small burny triangles lifting themselves from her chest, like the symptoms of a disease. And someone whispering that it was time that child stopped running round in her pants.

Enid smiles and hands Nadine her special Castile soap. Frail ropy muscles move on Enid's arms. Nadine worries that Enid is frighteningly thin, but then she is the only old woman whom Nadine has seen naked. Perhaps under their layers of brown and fawn and washed-out blue all old women are like this. Enid's grey groin looks innocent as a child's. It's hard to believe that a baby has fattened inside Enid, has pushed his way out through those concave thighs, has blissfully petted Enid's breasts through a trance of milk. For Enid breastfed her child for a month before it was adopted. 'He was like a tiger for milk. I had a lovely figure, dear, and he didn't spoil it. Two weeks after the birth my stomach was as flat as a board. Not like these girls you see sagging along. There's no need for it.' Enid has told Nadine the whole story. She couldn't keep the baby, because in those days if you weren't married there weren't any of these benefits. You had to crawl to officials, and then all you got was a few shillings from the National Assistance, if you were lucky. No chance of a flat either. You'd get the door shut in your face. In those days they could do as they liked. But Nadine wonders. If Enid had wanted to keep the baby, a hundred officials wouldn't have budged her. Enid's tough.

Enid never wears old-lady clothes. Fawn and beige and stone are anathema to her. From behind, in her black reefer jacket, beret and ski-pants with a strap under the foot, she looks like a skinny bold twelve-year-old who's pretending to be grown up. Her ankle socks are scarlet.

'Is your Kai at home?' she asks.

'Yes, but he's asleep.'

Enid nods, satisfied, and puts out her hand for the soap again. Her sharp glance takes in Nadine's body, knows what it has been doing. That sort of thing doesn't bother her at all, she's made it quite plain. And besides, Nadine keeps Kai sweet. Enid is wary of him, and Nadine isn't sure if it's just because he's the landlord or not. If only Enid wouldn't leave the bathroom in such a state when Kai was around. And she ought to get properly dressed in the bathroom, not just wrap a little towel round herself which falls off as often as not as she clambers back upstairs to her attic. She doesn't know how puritanical Kai can be. An old woman should not have a body, let alone risk its being seen. Enid disgusts him. He'd be well pleased with an Enid subdued in fawn and stone.

Enid never cleans the bath after using it, because Dr Govind told her not to stoop. Often she does not flush the lavatory after using it either. The cistern is erratic and Enid is afraid it may affect her blood pressure if she stretches up and hauls on the chain. Nadine flushes it after her when she's at home, releasing the roaring brown waterfall which it takes the cistern ten minutes to collect. Nadine wipes around the bath and rinses it too, before Kai or Tony can come upon Enid's soap scum, Enid's small curled grey hairs beached on the ring round the tub.

Enid lies back, eyes closed, her weightless body bobbing. Her eye sockets are deep and sunken. They are filling up with darkness. But it's only the way the light falls that makes her face look like a skull, not a living face at all –

'Enid!' cries Nadine, suddenly panicking.

Enid opens her eyes. 'What is it, dear? Is something the matter?'

'You looked awful. Are you OK?'

'You mean you thought I was dead. Oh, no, I'm not going to die in the bath, not with you here. Very upsetting all round. You needn't worry about that,' says Enid and stands up, so that water divides over her hip-bones and her small shrunken stomach, and puts out her hand for the towel Nadine gives her. Then the careful patting and drying and powdering, the gathering of the Castile soap into its special soap-box and Enid is ready, towel trailing, arms bundled with clothes and soap.

She squeezes her way around the door, leaving the bathful of water rocking gently and puddles of water and talcum on the floor.

'There you are, dear. Now you can have your bath. Just give that geyser time. It blows back if you rush it. Come up and say goodnight later on if you like, I shan't be asleep, I'm going to do my jigsaw.'

'How's it going?'

'Terrible, you never saw so much sky in your life. It's like one of those day-trips to Lincolnshire to see the bulb fields. Still, I *have* just put in the top of a chimney-pot, so things are looking up.'

She goes out, across the landing, up the winding carpetless stairs to her attic room. No one comes up here. Enid does not find it stifling. She likes the heat soaking through to her bones. She stoops and picks up leggings and t-shirt. She's never worn leggings before, but there was a pair in the Oxfam shop, so she decided to give it a try. Perfect for sleeping in, she finds. Warm and elastic, like a second skin. She pulls her WOMAD t-shirt over her head – Cancer Care – and looks at the sky spread out on the table. The jigsaw has one thousand pieces. Enid likes a challenge. Sky isn't all the same anyway. It deepens and darkens, and there are clouds. But jigsaw sky is an even mid-blue all over. You have to forget about colour and go for shape. The best thing is not to stare too long. Catch a bit out of the corner of your eye and it fits. You have to take a jigsaw by surprise. It's all instinct. The sky is on the table and the grass is on the floor. Enid leans down, stirs the pieces, pounces. There. That bit goes on the corner. The brown house bits are still jumbled together, not even spread out. It's a dull jigsaw, but they are much the most satisfactory. A house, grass, sky. No clues, but everything you need. She sniffs the Johnson's talcum powder smell settling round her.

I wonder if you can still buy that powder Sukey bought. Rose Geranium. Sharper than roses. I used to dredge myself with it as if I was a sponge cake, till I saw the price in John Lewis one Saturday. Sukey didn't care. I saved for weeks and bought her some, but it was no more to her than if I was delivering the milk. 'Why, Enid, darling, that's sweet of you.' She always had things like that around her, so it meant nothing to her. A smell like that takes you back. You couldn't get Floris powders in the war; you couldn't get anything. It must have been years later I went past the perfume counter, not even thinking. Years later. And I was back there in her green bathroom, with the soap in cold glass shells and the water rocking. I never knew people had bookshelves in bathrooms, and fires, and plants so tall they were nearly trees. And the bath standing on its own feet, out in the middle of the room, so that when the fire was lit you could see the pattern of the flames on your wet skin. The flames would run up from the coals like flags. It was best coal, Welsh coal. It burned with a clear flame and no smoke. She had big Turkey towels, put away with lavender bags between the folds so you could smell it when you shook out the towels. And a low window with a window seat in it and the chestnut tree growing outside, making the light green. Sukey would sit naked in the window seat after her bath and I'd see the chestnut candles lit up behind her head. White candles. That spring we saw the hands of the chestnut leaves spread out against the window, touching it. It was the greenest thing in the world. Sukey had iris in the bathroom then, tall purple and brown iris. I sat in front of the fire reading out of a book with red covers, rough, not nice to feel. It used to catch on my nails. *A Fairy Tale Treasury*, it was called. Sukey had had it when she was a little girl.

We needed the fire. It was April and April's cold in Manchester. We didn't often see sun coming through the leaves. The sky was grey, grey behind green. Long grey afternoons with the fire burning. It was everything I'd ever wanted. 'No point going out in this, darling,' Sukey said, and she turned the hot tap on with her toes. The hiss of rain keeping us in, the fire burning up, me on the hearthrug reading *The Red Shoes*. Clara danced through the forest. *Dance, dance, she must keep on dancing.* The only way they could stop her was to chop off her feet. I've never forgotten Clara's red, bloody feet. I can see them as clearly now as I can see those green leaves. That was what you got. It was the price you had to pay. Not that I cared then, with the heat of the fire on my back.

She looks like a dancer. Nadine. I would never have thought she belonged with those two. When I saw her come I thought for a moment she was his daughter. She's young enough. Nineteen! She's no more than sixteen, if she's that. But then I saw the way he touched her. I saw her glance up at my stairs, as if she wanted to climb them and find out what was up here. I knew then she'd come and see me.

The first time was, she didn't know how to work the geyser. Could I show her, she asked.

'There's only me at home,' she said. Oh, yes, she's quick. She'd guessed I wouldn't have come down, not if her Kai and that Tony were about. I don't ask people up here. Jenny never came up, it doesn't do. But there was something about the way Nadine looked up the stairs and said, 'It must be nice up there, away from everything.' It made me feel different. We'd run the bath and it was waiting, but I said, 'Come and have a look if you like.'

She didn't say much, didn't touch anything. I had bunches of peppermint hanging up to dry, and she did ask what they were, but not in that way people ask as if they're laughing at you inside themselves. I said I'd make her some mint tea if she liked, and so she sat down. She wasn't bothered about the bath cooling. So we sat and talked for a bit. Nothing much, but it was nice.

She knocks most days. 'Enid, I'm going out to get the milk. D'you want some?' 'Enid, I'm sure there's mice in the kitchen. Have you ever seen them?' I don't tell her I've seen worse than mice here, till Jenny got the cat. 'Course her Kai's got rid of that.

Nineteen! If she'd any sense she'd put on a bit of make-up and not cut her hair so short. But I suppose he must like it. Some men are funny that way.

I like having her here.

Seven

The bathroom is clammy with steam. Nadine pushes up the window. She won't bother to have a hot bath, she'll just pour cold water over herself. This is the only sash window which still works. Freshening night air flows in, carrying the city's gabble. Police sirens flee downhill towards the docks. Each night Nadine lies awake long past midnight, listening, unable to sleep. She hears fights, cries, groans, high heels clipping past alone, much too late, much too fast, alone and frightened. When everything's gone quiet a baby always starts to howl through an open window. It doesn't matter how far away it is, the sound pierces her like a needle. Nothing seems to join up. She can't read what is going on here. And Kai sleeps and sleeps. It's as if she's the one with the bad conscience. She can't put her finger on what keeps her awake. There's just this faint threatening sense of tension, as if something bad is about to happen. If she keeps awake she'll be safe. It's been hot too long, that's the trouble, one flawless day following another. We need rain to wash away the dried dog shit on the pavements, the burger litter and the dust.

It's the end of July, and the weather's changing. The spell is beginning to break. Quick wings of cloud are moving from the west. The leaves are dark green and drying to crisp edges. Soon it's going to matter that there's no heating, and many of the tiles are missing. She hasn't got any warm clothes, only the summer stuff she came with. On the top landing there are dusty plastic buckets to catch the rain when it falls. Better not think of that now. She'll just fetch a clean top and her jeans and go down to the kitchen and make coffee. No, not coffee – it'll keep her awake even more. Something to eat. That tin of ravioli – has anyone eaten it? She won't put on the kitchen light, because it's nice in the kitchen in the half-dark. The electric lighting in this house hasn't been touched since the twenties, Kai says. In the kitchen there's a brass chain to pull down the big light-globe from the ceiling. Its brilliance scores your eyes and stains your retina so that even if you shut your eyes you see the same patterns pulsing red behind your lids. There aren't any side-lights or table-lamps in the house yet, because they would overload the circuit. Even as it is the fuses blow regularly. But it's summer and it doesn't matter.

She's got to have something to eat. Her stomach's growling. There's Enid's door shutting with a squeak and a click. She must be going to bed. Often she leaves her door ajar all evening, drawing voices and music up her attic stairs and into her room. Perhaps she's lonely and likes to listen out for the sounds of the house. Hers is the only door which closes properly, the only one which still has its brass doorknob. The rest have gone in the steady stripping of the house over years of shifting owners and disappearing tenants. Only Enid has been here all the time, the sitting tenant, riding out long silent nights in her room, lighting fires in her grate with coal which she buys in blue plastic sacks and wheels through the city streets on a buggy frame. She collars the postman to help her lug the sacks upstairs. 'I can't lift anything, dear. It's my heart.' Enid has kept her doorknob. Nadine wonders if Enid ever woke up to hear the mouse-like sounds of a screwdriver working away at the plate which secured it to the door. Did she wind herself up in her sheet and go out to tell the kneeling young thief that he might take every other doorknob in the house, but not hers?

'I live here, you see, dear.'

So much of the house has disappeared. The lead flashing, the downstairs cloakroom fittings, brass curtain rails torn out of every room, leaving holes in the plaster; the wrought-iron balcony railings sawn through and sold. Georgian cast-iron is worth money. Now the balcony is just a narrow unguarded ledge from which you step off into space. It faces south and gets the sun most of the day, so in spite of the sheer drop to the pavement Nadine still sunbathes there with one foot drooping over the void. If she kicks she touches the overgrown branches of lime and plane trees tangled together in the air. Leaves brush against her toes. No one has pollarded the limes for years. The square is a communal garden and as derelict as the houses which share it.

A whole marble fireplace has been hacked out of the back sitting-room, but whoever took it missed the matching one in the front of the house. They must have been in a hurry, and besides, the second fireplace is disfigured with dusky red paint, mould-spotted like salami. They might not have seen that there was marble underneath. What was Enid doing while thieves hauled a six-foot wide marble fireplace through the hall and down the front steps? Did she shut herself away in her attic room, or did she peer down over the banisters and encourage them: 'Up a little, dear! Careful now or you'll do yourselves an injury.'

Now the house has passed to Kai and Tony in its time of weakness and nakedness. They walk round it, plumbing its flaws. They are the possessors. Even Enid in a way belongs to Kai and Tony. That is why Nadine is so quick to clean the signs of Enid from the bathroom before the men see them. They have power, and Enid has none.

The kitchen is at the back of the house, facing north against the steeply rising terraced hill and its criss-cross of fire-escapes, backyards and walls shaggy-topped with broken glass. The kitchen is cool and shadowy. The shadows hide dirt which is beyond any cleaning Nadine knows how to do. It needs industrial machinery to shift it, not human strength. The dirt is organic, rusted and sooty and earthy, oozing out of gaps between walls and skirting boards, growing upward between red tiles which haven't been scraped or waxed for years. There is black fungus around the sink. When you bend down a thin acrid smell sets your eyes stinging. One set of tenants kept ferrets in the basement, years ago, says Enid. Congealed grease coats the plates of the Aga, which has a damaged flue and can't be used. A man is coming to take it away. The gas cooker is more or less usable. Kai poured two bottles of cleaner over it and left the paste there to penetrate layers of burnt-on fat. He scraped the mixture off the next day, and, though the cooker surface is dull and scratched, it is now clean. But even Kai failed with the sink. A whole packet of washing-soda and a bucket of boiling water hadn't cleared its sweetish smell of decay. A sour blob of water and fat went round and round in the plughole.

'What's the problem?' asked Tony. 'Is it blocked?'

'I'll have to take the U-bend apart. There's some crap in there blocking it up. We'll have to get shot of it. Yes,' he repeated, relishing the idiom, 'we must get shot of it. And the rest of this so-called kitchen,' and he allowed his gaze to sweep scornfully over the three cream-painted 1930s cupboards which no longer had doors, over the scored Formica table and the enormous gas refrigerator which opened to reveal a minute cave of ice.

Nadine takes a tin of ravioli from the cupboard, opens it and glops its contents into a saucepan. Every sound rings hollow in this kitchen. It's too high for its area and has too little furniture in it. Nothing absorbs sound. Her bare toes curl up against the sticky cling of the tiles. Apart from the ravioli there's a loaf of rye bread, a piece of Parmesan which Tony got from Paolo's where he eats, and six bottles of wine. Otherwise the kitchen is bare of food. And yet she's earning a wage and she has her building society book. Kai has three thousand pounds in his jeans pocket. Why don't they have nice food? Why don't they sit down together?

She'll have a glass of wine. There's another bottle open somewhere, from last night. Yes, here it is, wedged in the snow which nearly fills the fridge, half a bottle of white Burgundy.

'They could use our fridge for the Winter Olympics,' Tony had said. 'For making snow on the ski-slopes. It's unbelievable.'

There's the front door now. It won't be Enid, who never goes out after she's had her bath.

'Tony?'

He comes in with carrier-bags slung on both hands. He puts them down on the table, wedged so that they won't keel over and spill their contents. Food, thinks Nadine, peering into the bags. But the top of the largest bag is full of knives. Tony takes them out. There are four. A carving knife, a cook's knife, a vegetable knife and a knife for which Nadine can't imagine a use. It's long and thin and flexible, made of the same dull steel as the others. Like them it has a matt-black handle. The knives are sealed in bubbles of plastic. Nadine picks up the slender knife and weighs it across her hand. It's beautifully made.

'What's this one for?'

Tony removes it from her. 'It's a boning knife.'

'Boning?'

'For getting flesh off the bones. Like this.'

With his knifeless hand he sketches a gesture so graphic that Nadine flinches. She turns over the other knives, looking at the prices. '£28.99! Tony! Or is that for all of them?'

'You're looking at quality here. Real lifetime stuff. See that edge. You get what you pay for with this sort of thing.'

'Shame we haven't got any food to cut up.'

He points to the other bags. 'Here, have a look.'

Nadine delves. Veal. Flour. Oil. Cheese and herbs in transparent wrappings. A net of tight-skinned peppers, red, orange, yellow, purple. A fat scented cantaloup melon. A thick bar of expensive plain chocolate, and a dozen eggs which are slightly too big for their cardboard box. White briny cheese, and a jar of plum tomatoes. Plump olives, a mophead of endive. And more. She spreads out the stuff on the table and breaks off a piece of chocolate.

'I've had enough of eating out. It's always the same,' says Tony.

'I thought you liked it. You're always saying –'

'Yeah, well, it gets boring. Anyway, I'm a good cook.'

Tony always eats out, usually at the same restaurant: at least, he has done so in the brief *always* which is all she knows of him. The restaurant he goes to is Paolo's, which is what everyone calls it, although it has *La Dolce Vita* scrolled on the awning. They cook family food, low-key and strongly flavoured, and the wine is sent over from a family vineyard. Paolo still has land at home, and cousins work it for him. At weekends the restaurant is packed out with Italian families celebrating weddings, baptisms, first communions, confirmations. Tony has an arrangement there too. He eats late. Sometimes Nadine sees him walking up the road to Paolo's when she's already on her way back from the pub with Enid. He goes alone, but often he eats at the family table, and the daughter, Clara, stops work for a few minutes to talk to him. That's the pattern Nadine knows. But, after all, she hasn't known Tony that long. Perhaps something's gone wrong. Paolo likes Tony, you can tell. He's always calling Clara out of the kitchen to have coffee with Tony after the meal. Maybe that's the trouble. You can't mess about with Paolo's daughter. Tony'll have to be careful.

'Have some more chocolate, Nadine,' says Tony, snapping the bar in half. It's beautiful chocolate, dark and silky. Tony grins. He has a narrow wedge-shaped face and very short hair, black and shiny as wax. He's ugly, most of the time, but he has a warm Manchester voice and when he smiles his face matches it, lighting slowly from the eyes. 'You'll get fat,' he says now. 'Here, chop up these peppers for me.'

You think you see a pattern, you call it normality, but it's when you've known people well for a short time that you know them least. Better not to think of that. Better to think of Tony and Kai drinking round the kitchen table when she gets home from work, pouring another glass of wine for her. Tony always grumbles about the music Kai puts on the stereo. Peasant music, he calls it. She's always tired after hours in the cinema's headachy darkness, and she can't be bothered with anything but beans on toast. Sometimes Kai makes it for her. Once he scraped ice out of the fridge, packed it into a clean tea-towel and put it on Nadine's forehead because her head throbbed after hours of stuffy cinema darkness. They were like a family.

Tony takes off his jacket, eases out a pair of gold cuff-links, rolls up his sleeves, unwraps the veal and spreads it out. It glistens on the brand-new chopping board. Tony unzips the meat knife from its plastic shell with a razor-blade, and rinses it under the cold tap. Nadine puts out her finger.

'Here, what you doing? You don't want to touch that,' says Tony. He dries the knife on a paper towel, then he unrolls the veal, flattens it with the back of the knife and begins rapidly to slice it into fine, almost translucent ribbons of flesh. The meat is nearly bloodless. It doesn't looks like flesh at all. Her mother would never have veal in the house, because it was cruel. Nadine watches the small muscles moving in Tony's forearms as veal ribbons peel away beautifully from one another, then spread out fanwise on the board. They look like the gills of oyster mushrooms. Certainly this meat doesn't look as if it was ever part of anything as warm and sweet-smelling as a calf. She's fed calves from a bucket on a farm holiday, and let them suck her fingers after with their warm rasping tongues.

'Is Kai asleep?'

'Yes, he was tired. No point waking him up to eat.'

'Tired!' Tony sweeps the veal into a pile and begins on the sauce. 'What you been doing to him, eh, Nadine? You'll wear him out.'

He looks up from the meat and smiles. The smile is much too intimate, with a spice of contempt in it, as if he's been watching them from the foot of their bed. Both men are so much older than her. It's not surprising Tony's got some funny attitudes, she thinks. Tony's known Kai for years, ever since Kai came to England. She was a little kid then. To him she's someone of Kai's and he'll be nice to her as long as she's going out with Kai. He's never mentioned other girls of Kai's, the ones who

55

came before her. Tony doesn't need to score easy points. His attitude to women is to do with the way he was brought up, Nadine reassures herself. He grew up in a close Italian web, that's what Kai says, even though his parents have lived in Manchester for thirty-five years. He has two ways of thinking about women: girls you fucked and girls you married. One way for a woman like Clara, another for me. He'd never dream of smiling at Clara like that. He knows there'd be consequences. Girls like Clara are chaperoned even when they go with their fiancés to talk to the priest about their wedding.

She's seen Tony talking to Clara. The three of them were at the restaurant one Saturday night: Tony and Kai and Nadine. Clara was going out with her aunt. Clara worked in the restaurant all week, but now she shone out in her midnight-blue dress and her gold jewellery. The customers stopped eating to look at her, but they didn't stare. That wasn't the way. She progressed through the tables, stopping to talk to favoured customers. It was a Saturday night ritual. Tony stood up and pulled out a chair for her and there she sat for a few minutes, talking to him in Italian, her small lively hands smooth with cream and manicure, betrayed only by a nick at the base of her thumb. She nodded to Kai, but she didn't take any notice of Nadine.

Clara, a girl going out from her father's house, accompanied – no, chaperoned – by her aunt. But also a girl who more than earned her own living, who was not afraid of hard work and who helped to build up the family business. She had new ideas, and they worked. Her parents watch her with concealed vigilant satisfaction. Are they even a little afraid of Clara, who did so well at school and could easily have gone on to college if she'd wanted? Clara, whose English is the perfect English of a child born here, and yet who chooses to speak not only in Italian but in the dialect of her parents? One day she'll have a fine wedding, with embossed cards for the nuptial mass. She'll organize the catering and God help anyone who tries to put anything past

Clara. She'll be back in the restaurant with her apron on the day after she returns from a magnificent honeymoon in New York and San Francisco. There are branches of her family in both cities, but naturally the young people will stay in expensive hotels.

Clara doesn't waste her time on Nadine, who has no family, no apparent qualifications, and who works in a job with no future. She lives in a house with two men and a crazy old woman who also has no family to look after her and who sings in the streets on Friday nights on her way home from the pub. Eccentric, eh? You could call it that. Nadine's here today, but who knows where she'll be tomorrow? You don't waste time on her. Once she's gone you'll never hear her name again, and you'll never know where she went.

It's completely different with girls like Clara. They know where they're going. No matter how short the journey, they give destinations and times of arrival. They are met by uncles who wouldn't dream of letting them carry any luggage but a handbag. They are kissed on both cheeks by aunts who cry a little at the sight of them, and exclaim that they're much too slim, they need feeding up. Clara knows where she belongs. She's never going to disappear.

Tony's sauce bubbles and thickens on the stove. The kitchen smells of basil and vaporizing wine and new bread. Nadine lays two places. They'll put some of the meat sauce in the ice-crater of the fridge for Kai to eat tomorrow. Tony stirs in the ribbons of veal until the meat whitens and loses its translucency. He turns the mixture once more, then reduces the flame. He throws two handfuls of fresh pasta into a panful of simmering water. The water swells up the sides of the pan and he calms it with a few drops of olive oil.

'Two more minutes,' he warns Nadine. 'Give me the plates. But what the fuck's this?' He takes the lid off the small pan which holds Nadine's congealed and cooling ravioli and peers into it. 'Has the old bitch been in our kitchen again?' he asks.

'You'd better speak to her, Nadine. She's pushing her luck.'
And with a flick of his wrist he shoots the tinned ravioli into the
open bin.

Eight

'I can't bring myself to do it. I just can't, that's all. It makes me go all goosey thinking about it.'

'Yeah, well, you're not really trying, are you, Lila? A bright girl like you. You've just got to make the effort. This is a really big client we're talking about.'

'I know he is, 'course I know that. I've seen him on television. I pretend I don't recognize him, though – I'm not stupid. It's not the client, Kai –'

'It'd better not be. He's the kind we want.'

'I've got nothing against him. I didn't even mind that other stuff, I mean, I'd rather do it straight but there's no harm in it, after all, is there? That whip's just a toy; the worst thing is trying to keep a straight face. But if he wants more than that, there's girls that specialize aren't there? I mean it's like in the magazines. Some of them would make you sick. Girls doing it with donkeys. It's just not my cup of tea.'

'Did you tell him that?'

'Well – I did, sort of. But he kept on it was me he wanted to do it. He's got this thing about tall girls, and then me being blonde as well is just right, apparently.'

'Listen, Lila. We can't afford to lose him. Just what did you say to him?'

'I keep telling you, I didn't say anything. I just kept thinking, what if my Rosie was to come in and see me doing it. I mean, I know she's at the nursery and she can't, they would never let her out, but I just can't stop thinking about it. After all the trouble I had getting her to use her potty, if you get me. What's it going to look like? Him lying there with his mouth open and me weeing into it sort of thing? It's not what you'd want a child to see her mother doing.'

'That's all he wants? Nothing else?'

'Yeah. Would you believe it? I mean there's girls you can go to for that kind of stuff.'

'I can't see the problem. He's taking the risk, not you. What with AIDS – still, it's not for us to say. He's the client.'

'Is that all you can think of? Him getting AIDS? What about *me*?'

'Lila, there's just no risk. OK, it's a bit childish, but why let it get to you? You didn't use to be like this.'

'Yeah, but what's he going to want next? I mean, you don't know what he might move on to. There's no telling, is there? Where's it all heading?'

'You ought to read the newspapers more, Lila, then you'd find out. He's going places. We need more clients like him. That's the way to get contacts. You want to read the City pages. Anyway, that sort of client, it's the one thing they want, nothing else. They don't change. They're stuck, you know, like a record going round and round.'

'Yes, well, all the same. What I really wanted to say was, could you pass him on to one of the other girls – maybe Vick, she's done all that S & M and she doesn't mind –'

'Lila. Is Vick five foot ten? Has she got long blonde hair? Is she twenty-two? What'm I supposed to say, I chopped your legs off? This is business. If a man goes into the greengrocer's for apples he doesn't want turnips. What's your problem? It's a piece of piss. Don't you know science, Lila? Every single human being is ninety per cent water. You girls go to the toilet all day long. All you do is flush it away, nothing gained but extra work for the sewage pipes. And here's one of our best clients, brilliant future, going to pay well because you're special. *You*, Lila. Not those other girls. He likes you. There's no question of passing him on to Vick or anyone else. Either you think it over properly or we lose a lot of money. And you know how I feel about that.'

'It's Rosie I'm thinking of, really. I know it sounds silly. If you had kids of your own you'd know what I mean. It's not just me I've got to think of now. I mean, there's standards.'

'Rosie is nice and safe in her nursery, Lila. Safe as houses. And that's the way we all want to keep it, don't we?'

'*Kai!*'

'Life is difficult, Lila. Sometimes we all have to do things we don't want. What about me? Don't talk to me about "standards". People doing what they're paid to do, that's standards. They know me at the nursery, you know. It's nice the way Rosie calls me Uncle Kai.'

'*Kai, you wouldn't —*'

'So what you'll do is put on the gear – yeah, the black stuff – and those stockings and all the rest of it, and get Mr Famous Client flat on his back on the bed and spread your legs and piss right down his throat. And try and look as if you're having a nice time. You can think of little Rosie while you're doing it. And put a plastic sheet down on the mattress first. Your other clients won't like the smell.'

Room 7 in the Sports Hall smells of sweat. The room isn't big enough; the circus skills course was oversubscribed and even though they've had to turn people away there are still twenty people in here, juggling with balls and clubs and scarves. Cathy, the group leader, has two assistants with her who are working at full stretch. The bald white walls echo to encouragement and dropped balls. Here's Dacey who makes unicycles out of old bike frames; here's Sal who studied ballet for eight years before she gave it up and learned to fire-eat. Every move Cathy makes has the brilliant definition and larger-than-life quality of something done on a stage. She's teaching juggling basics again, patiently, to a couple of big-framed sixteen-year-old lads in singlets and tattoos. Almost all the circus skills clients are unemployed.

Cathy watches, moves, intervenes. She wears dusty red baggy trousers and a washed-out black vest. Her skin is deeply tanned and against it her eyes are pale, clear and restful. She's the full-timer, the professional. Born and raised in a tepee in Wales, she is twenty-one now and has been earning her living since she was fourteen. She travels, but not all the time. She'll be there at Glastonbury, or WOMAD, earning her living at the summer-long round of festivals. One season she was at Covent Garden; another at Edinburgh. She'll work with anyone, as long as they don't mess around. Either they want to do something, or they don't. On Saturdays she's down the Ring, juggling ball after ball into the air until she's hidden by a ripple of colour you can't follow, a fine fast blur of red and orange and violet and gold. She makes her juggling balls herself. Cathy fire-eats too: she loves fire. It makes money: there's something about a woman swallowing flames or passing them over her body so that they seem to lick the taut glistening skin which acts like a release-button on men's wallets. They don't see the sober careful business behind the thrill.

Cathy's patient with clumsy beginners, not so patient with smart-arses who want to stick to what they know rather than learn the new, the next, the more difficult trick. She likes Nadine. Nadine's got the right body to begin with, light and flexible and not too tall. A good sense of balance too, from years of ballet as a kid, like Sal. Lots of people come on to circus skills from dance. They can earn money. You can't busk on a couple of arabesques and a *pas de chat*.

The place is full of kids. Fees are cut if you can show a UB40, and most of these can. Leggings, baggy t-shirts, shaved heads with a little slender plait making its way down the nape of a neck. You don't get the crusties here, though. These are the kids who still think there's some hope, and it's worth learning something new. Lots of them'll learn for a bit, then head for the resorts where people are in holiday mood with a bit of money to throw away.

Yeah, Nadine's all right. She's got the makings. Well

coordinated, and she can concentrate. Amazing how many people can't. And she looks right too. That's important, though it's got nothing to do with ordinary good looks. It's the way someone can make you watch *her*, not any of the others. That part's not so easy to teach.

Nadine's damp hair spikes up off her forehead. It's hot tonight. She's slower with clubs than balls. Can't get the rhythm right today; too slow. It's all a question of rhythm. Relax, says Cathy. Relax and keep your eye on the clubs. A trickle of sweat inches its way across Nadine's forehead.

After the class Cathy stops Nadine on her way to the shower. 'You done any busking yet?' she asks.

'No,' says Nadine.

'Want to try?'

'All right. I'd like to.'

'OK. I'll take you down the Ring one Saturday.'

Nadine nods, smiles, recognizing privilege. She rests her arms on a windowsill and leans her weight on them, cooling off, watching the room sideways. People are stopping now, packing away balls and clubs into the wicker hamper. Some bring their own stuff. A couple of kids laugh and fool, juggling their way across the room. The balls go up sloppily into the air.

'Give them here,' says Cathy.

As they throw the balls to her, she catches them and sets them spinning. First they make a tight fast loop around her head, then they fluke higher and one's behind her back to be flipped up again and set sideways, over arm, under arm, the balls free and thoughtless as birds that always want to fly back to Cathy's hands. As suddenly as she started, she stops. The balls pour up under one raised leg, fly into her right hand and are neat in the basket. It's over. The kids lean against one another, watching, hoping she'll do more. But she doesn't. Cathy's timing is perfect.

Nadine strips off leggings, singlet and pants, and steps into the women's communal shower. A woman with a tiny girl at her knees presses the shower button beside her. The kid jumps in and out of needles of water. The mother is big-thighed, big-breasted, reaching up to soap herself, shutting her eyes to the spray of water. She is four or five months pregnant. She is lovely as she stoops awkwardly, legs straddling, picks the child out of the soapy water that swills in the shower stall, and rinses her off. The little girl squeals and flips her head back, mouth open, small perfect teeth showing. The mother smiles at Nadine sidelong, a proud, apologetic smile. 'Shut it,' she says tenderly to her daughter. 'Shut it now.'

'Sukey, it's gone far enough. Too far.'

'What can you mean, darling?'

'This business with Enid. It isn't fair to her.'

'Isn't it? I don't see why not.'

'You're encouraging her. Putting ideas into her head. Having her here all the time. What about her job?'

'Enid has a perfectly good job, Caro. She *is* allowed a day off occasionally. Those brutes owed her some holiday. Poor lamb, she works like a slave.'

'She'll lose her job, and then you'll be stuck with her. And you'll get bored, you always get bored. You know what you're like.'

'I'm afraid I *don't* know what I'm like, Caro. Have some of these dates: they're fresh. Basil sent them from Egypt in the diplomatic bag, can you imagine? Lots of date-y documents for the diplomats. I must just go and telephone –'

'Sukey, don't go! I've got to talk to you. It isn't a joke, it's serious. Why do you turn everything into a joke?'

'Caro, darling, be reasonable. We're going to the cottage next week. We'll have all the time in the world. We'll sit in the garden and you can tell me anything you like and I promise I'll listen. There won't be any interruptions . . .'

'Oh, Sukey, darling, I can't believe it's ever going to happen.

I can't wait to be there, just the two of us. Can you, darling? Aren't you awfully impatient?'

'Awfully impatient, Caro. I'll telephone, then we'll talk about it some more. Ring for some iced tea, you look so hot . . .'

Nine

A bell drags Nadine out of sleep.

Our room. The bell's still ringing. If I wait maybe they'll go away. Could be Tony, if he's forgotten his key. Nobody else'd come this early. Feel on the floor for t-shirt, clench it between my toes, get hold of it, shake it out and over my head. And run downstairs, combing my hair with my fingers. It'll be Tony for sure.

No. A tanned woman with hair pulled back in gold and silver streaks along her scalp, expensive sunglasses on a chain, gold chain, gold earrings. Make-up, tight smile and a row of perfect teeth. She stands there immaculate, looking at me. The sun makes me blink.

'Sorry, I thought you were Tony . . .' I apologize, and tug the t-shirt down my thighs.

'Having a lie-in, were you? I don't blame you, I'd do the same myself if I had the chance.'

No, she wouldn't. This one would be up at dawn whatever happened, face-packing and leg-waxing, telephoning and doing her nails. Her fingers are perfectly manicured, her polished nails are curved ovals with an extra-long claw on the thumb. It must be nearly an inch long. She's like a Chinese nobleman, letting one nail grow so everyone knows she doesn't work with her hands. She'll have spent hours plumping the tiny wrinkles around her eyes with cream made from human placentas. Her hair's so perfect it looks like thin metal with a slick of gel. Then she'd have to floss and rinse and spit till those big teeth were free of plaque. It's a serious business, looking like that.

'I kept on knocking but no one came, so I pulled the bell-rope. I don't know how you can stand the noise. You might as well be living next to a church. Not that they let them make that

66

row these days, do they, churches in a residential area like this? People complain. And quite right too. I mean to say, I've nothing against religion –'

'It was here when we came. Part of the house. I quite like it.'

'Oh, well, tastes differ, don't they? Kai about?'

'He's away.'

'Any idea when he's likely to be back?'

'Tomorrow, I think. Unless he rings.'

Less of the teeth shows now. A rim of white glistens, balked. What does she want? Why's she come to see Kai here, at this time?

'Tony in?'

'No.'

'Gone off with Kai, has he?'

'He might have done. I don't think so. He's probably around.'

Another blast of smile, woman to woman this time. She opens her handbag and scrabbles through it.

'Oh, knickers, I haven't got a pen. I'm not doing very well, am I? Can I pop in a minute and leave a message for Kai?'

I don't want her in our house, with her hard snooping eyes, but she steps into the doorway and I have to move back.

'Mind where you tread with those heels. The boards are loose. Tony's been checking the gas pipes.'

'Tony's a wonder, isn't he, the way he can turn his hand to anything? I've heard ever such a lot about the house. Kai was really keen. Potential, he said it had. And you can tell, can't you? That plaster moulding must be the original. Very classy.'

'I wouldn't know. I'm not really interested in architecture.'

'Well, not *as such*, maybe. But it's different when it's your home, isn't it? You must be Nadine, have I got it right?'

Oh, she's got it off perfectly, that look of inquiry as if there might be any number of girls in here, all shacked up with Kai.

'No, I'm Suzette. Who's Nadine?'

A really sharp look this time, then an unwilling smile, the

67

teeth again, and, 'I've heard ever so much about you from Kai. In here? Oh, *very* nice. You must get the sun all day long in here. Now this would have been the morning-room, am I right?'

'You seem to know a lot about houses.'

'Oh, well, you get to, don't you? You pick it up. You can't go anywhere without people wanting to tell you about their houses. You ought to go to Prague. 'Course it'll be spoiled soon, once they get more money. Miles to walk to the bathroom in the hotels, but if you want style that's where to go. There's one good thing about these countries that used to be Communist, they don't get mucked up. I remember one bloke had a castle — not in Prague, mind you, it was over here.'

'What, a real one?'

'Oh, yes, it was a real castle all right. He'd got the lot: sieges and cannon and boiling oil. But it was only small. Not famous or anything. In fact it was a bit rough on the outside. But he'd made it really nice inside. They'd turned the dungeon into a disco, with a light show. There was a band later on, and they put them in a sort of cage where they used to keep the prisoners. You'd never guess how they used to kill prisoners in the olden days, down in the dungeons.'

Why guess when you're going to be told anyway? Look at that bracelet going round and round on her wrist. She's getting excited. I can tell what kind of shivers it gives her.

'No.'

'Well, you have to imagine the dungeon down there, and a sort of chute from the tower above it. All dark and smelly then, not at all like it was when we were there. He'd done wonders with the place. What they'd do was they'd throw down animal carcasses — pigs and cows and so on, after they'd taken off most of the meat for the kitchens. Then they'd leave them to rot with the prisoners. Well, you can imagine they niffed a bit. The prisoners used to suffocate because the air was too bad to breathe. And then there'd be flies and maggots, and rats. They chained the prisoners to the walls so they couldn't move. Not even if a rat ran over them. It was this bloke's ancestors that did it all. If you were a guest at the castle you'd be brought to look down at the prisoners, just like going to look at a room someone's done up. And then go off and have your dinner. Well, I suppose people were different then. It makes you think, doesn't it?'

'You'd think it'd be easier to hang them.'

'Yes, but it was a deterrent. And the thing was that they died without a mark on them. Charlie explained the whole thing. You could say they'd died naturally, of plague or something.'

'Well, perhaps not plague. It might put the guests off their dinner.'

Impatient shrug. Narrowing of eyes. She thinks I'm taking the mickey.

'I've always taken an interest in history, I'm funny like that. You can learn a lot if you keep your eyes and ears open, Nadine.'

'You must be a friend of Kai's. I haven't met you before, though, have I?' I'd never forget those teeth.

'No, but that's Kai, isn't it, he likes to keep things separate. So he went off this morning, did he?'

'Yes, very early. He never wakes me up in the mornings.' There. Just so you know.

'Yes, you need your beauty sleep, don't you? All those late nights.'

'I'm ushering down at the Warehouse. They have late shows on Wednesdays and Saturdays.'

'Oh – you work at that arts place? Not that I've ever been down there. How long've you been down here now – three weeks, is it?'

'Four.'

'So you're not really in the business yet? I must have got it wrong.'

'Well, no,' says Nadine. 'Not as such. But this is only temporary. I'm thinking of starting something on my own later on.' There. Let her work that out.

'Oh. But surely there's no need for that? Not with Kai to look after you. He could easily fix you up. Though you have to think ahead, I can quite see that.'

Ahead to the time when Kai's chucked me out, that's what she means. She's so sure of it. She knows how it goes. All that gold jewellery. At least she's got something to hang on to.

'But there's the question of capital —' I go on. Her face warms, brightens. For the first time I'm talking sense.

'Oh, don't talk to *me* about capital! I know exactly what you mean. Setting up on your own is no picnic. Everything's tied up with forms. I was at my insurance adviser's last week to talk about a little PEP plan for my Donna — but the fuss they make you wouldn't believe, contacting your tax office, loads of forms. And they've even changed the name of the scheme. Well, I turned round and told him I might as well keep my money in a sock under the bed.'

Really animated now. Warming to me. I'm not such a fool as I look. Not such a fool as I look standing here in my baggy t-shirt, thinking I'm young, I'm OK, I don't need to bother with make-up or good clothes. One curve-clawed hand fastens on my arm. She's not as tall as I am so she has to look up. She makes me feel clumsy and big. Confiding flower-like eyes, only I'm pretty sure they're tinted contact lenses. Fixing me with those eyes she coos, 'And then there's security. That's such a big worry.'

I lean back a little from the lipstick smell of her mouth. I haven't brushed my teeth yet this morning and I'm sure my own breath smells of last night's garlic. 'But for now, I'm happy enough at the Warehouse. It's not hard work. I'd pay to see the films anyway, and you get some interesting people.'

'Oh, I'm sure you do. That's what it's all about, isn't it — contacts. Mind you, so does Kai. Meet people I mean. Very interesting, some of them. Have you got a bit of paper and I'll just write my little note? But maybe you don't meet many of them — Kai's and Tony's friends? Business contacts, I should say — it comes to the same thing with Kai and Tony, doesn't it?'

A cat-like look turns her mouth into a muzzle. She's watching me intently, very close, wondering how much more she can play with me. Wondering how much I know.

'Is this pad big enough? I can get you an envelope if you like.'

'Oh, it's nothing *private*. Just a little note. An arrangement Kai asked me to confirm. I am being rude, aren't I? I know your name, and you don't know mine. I'm Vicki. Vick. Bugger this bracelet. It's my wrists, really. Can I find anything to fit in the shops? Can I Christmas. Not even in Bond Street. Too slim, they all say. No, it has to be Hatton Gardens and custom-made, and you know what *that* costs.'

'It's very pretty.'

'I suppose it's not bad. A lot of people don't know quality when they see it, do they? They think everything's paste. Just as well, with all these muggers about. This area's gone down a lot. They're quite good stones apparently. You have to be careful with diamonds, you can get taken for a ride. But perhaps you're not very interested in jewellery? You look more the natural type of girl. Green. Your hair's lovely, though. I like the style, it's very unusual. And you can get away with it at your age.'

'You could write your name on the window. Don't diamonds cut glass?'

'Quite a lot of people have already, haven't they, from the look of it? I can't bear dirty windows myself. I have to get going with a wash-leather, even in someone else's place. I'm funny like that. A bit like Kai, really. You know what he's like about dirt. Don't get all worried, though, Nadine, I'm not going to start having a go at *your* windows. I can see you're all upside-down still. A place like this is an investment, isn't it? Not like a home. Do it up and move on. I don't know that I'd fancy it myself, not knowing what sort of people were here before me. I like new houses. I mean, you wouldn't wear someone else's old clothes, would you? And a house is much more personal. A bit like underwear. Nearly done. There, now if I give that to

71

you, you can pass it on to Kai for me, can't you? Just say Vicki popped round. He'll know what it's about. Well, see you again, Nadine. Now we've got to know one another, we can have a real chat next time. My daughter's got her Grade 3 violin exam this morning and she's a bag of nerves, so I've got to get back to take her to the examination centre. Silly, really, 'cos she's ever so talented. She's had a very good teacher. You've got to be prepared to pay if you want to get anywhere. Do you ever go to the sauna at the Swift Health Club?'

'No.'

'Oh, I thought you would. Kai's ever so keen on saunas. I suppose it's to do with him being Finnish. You ought to come along one day with me and Lila – she's another girl I know. She's in the business too. You ought to meet Lila, I think you two would get on. She's got a lovely little girl. Rosie. Have you got any kids yourself, Nadine?'

'Well, I have got a little boy. But I put him into care – it seemed the best thing to do, considering.'

'Did you? Well of course you know best. I know it can be tricky when a girl's on her own. But you're not on your own now, are you? Kai's very fond of kiddies, you'll find. You ought to talk to Lila. The toys Kai's bought for Rosie! Uncle Kai, she calls him. How old is your little one?'

'Six. Nearly seven.'

'Oh, my God, you got started early, didn't you, Nadine? How old are you now, if you don't mind me asking?'

'Nineteen,' I lie, as I've lied at work.

'Oh, that's terrible. Oh, you've really upset me now. You must have been the same age as my Donna when you had him.'

She is really shocked. I've touched a nerve under the year-round crocodile tan.

'Sorry, Vicki. I was only kidding.'

An explosion of teeth. 'Lucky I didn't go and tell Lila. She's got no sense of humour at all. I'll give you a ring about that sauna, then, shall I? I've got your number. Nice to meet you, Nadine.'

I shut the door behind her, open the window to let out the dark smell of her perfume. Enid is calling. How long has she been calling? Her voice sounds little and lost and old.

'Nadine! Nad-eeeen!'

Enid trembles on the landing in her sunshine-yellow pyjamas.

'Oh, Nadine. Oh, Nadine. Oh, I've had such a terrible dream.'

I put my arm around her. She is vibrating. Maybe it's shock?

'Come and lie down. You look really ill.'

'I can't go back in there. I'll get that dream again. Let me just sit down here a minute and get my breath back.'

She sits on the landing, small and shrivelled, her knees drawn up to her chin, her wispy hair disarranged so that looking down I see pink bald patches on her skull. I put my arm round her shoulder and smell her bird's nest smell.

'I'll be all right in a minute.'

But she's very pale and her mouth is open a little, panting. Her colour is bad. I wonder if I should get Dr Govind.

'You ought to lie down, Enid. Shall I ring the doctor?'

'No. No.'

'Come into my room. Kai's not here. You can lie down on our bed. It won't bring your dream back in there.'

'I couldn't go in there. Your Kai wouldn't like it.'

'Enid, don't be silly. He's away. He won't know.'

'He'd find out. He's the sort that finds out everything.'

She won't move and she doesn't want a drink of water, so we sit there while the trembling settles and her colour becomes yellowish again rather than dead white. Or is it just the reflection of her pyjamas? I can't be sure. She ought to see the doctor but she won't. Someone else fetched Dr Govind when she had pneumonia. She's frightened they'll put her in a home, though I keep telling her they won't do that, they're only too glad if people can manage at home. And she believes that the body can look after itself if it's not filled with drugs to upset the balance.

73

Dr Govind gave her sleeping tablets and she's never touched them.

'If you feel better tonight, we'll go out to the pub. A couple of ginger wines will warm you up.'

Enid pulls her shoulders back and sniffs. She's really looking better.

'Thank you, dear. I shall be able to go back into my room in a minute. Did you have a visitor? I thought I heard voices.'

'Yes, it was someone Kai knows.'

'I thought it was. I knew I'd heard that voice before.'

'No, you must have mistaken her for someone else. It's the first time she's been here.'

'I don't want to contradict you, Nadine dear, but she has most definitely been here before. Wait a minute. It'll come back to me.' She stares down at her knees, then up at me triumphantly. There's even a hint of colour in her face now. 'Blonde woman, big teeth. One of those voices that goes through you like a saw. I've heard her laughing. She looks like a horse when she laughs.'

Maybe Enid was looking down over the banisters when Vicki and I went across the hall. She likes to know what's going on. Often when I look up from the hall or the landing I can sense she's there. No – she can't have seen Vicki this morning, because she's only just woken up from a nightmare. And she can't be faking that because she really looked ill. Or could it have been something else which frightened her, not a dream at all? Vicki can't have frightened her. So Vicki's been here before. No use asking Enid about it now.

'I wouldn't trust that one, Nadine. Not if I was you. She may pretend it's the first time, but she *has* been here before, and more than once. I remember one night I heard her laugh. I looked down but it was dark.'

'You're imagining things. I'm here every night.'

'Yes, but sometimes you don't get in until late, do you, dear? Not when they have those late-night shows. But you know me,

I'm always here. I shut my door and put on my music. I don't want to hear anything.'

'It's just a business thing.'

'I'm not saying any different. Business is business and it's got nothing to do with me. I don't want to know about business. I'm only saying, she's been here before. I'm not saying what or why or when or who.'

Enid's here all the time. You get used to her, like you do to a bird which has made its nest in your chimney. That's how Kai thinks of Enid, I'm sure. He'd like to poke her out of the nest she's made, then fetch a brush and sweep out the nest itself and every trace of Enid would be gone. He'd do it if he wasn't afraid of the mess she'd make. She wouldn't go quietly. She'd scream and shout and cry in the square and all the neighbours would know. Someone might even call the police, though I don't think so, not here. Kai doesn't want that.

Kai doesn't know Enid, not like I do. He thinks she's stupid, a stupid, dirty, awkward old bird who came with the house, one he can't get rid of, not yet. He had the lawyers look into it, but they told him she had her rights as a sitting tenant. He knew that anyway, when he bought the house. I don't know why he bothered with the lawyers. He must have pretended to himself that she'd just disappear when we moved in, leaving another empty room in the attic. But Enid isn't a stupid old bird. Enid thinks. She's here, and she thinks and she listens. The doors don't close properly in this house, with all the doorknobs missing. Does Kai ever think about what Enid hears, or what she sees? She's got enough sense not to let anything slip in front of Kai and Tony. Anyway they never talk to her. It's their way of pretending she's not here. If they don't notice her then she doesn't exist. But Enid will tell me. She trusts me . . .

'I should forget it, Enid.'

'You're a good girl, Nadine. And I'm good at forgetting. But you don't want to go making a friend of that one. Not even if your Kai wants you to. I wouldn't trust her. She's got a look in her eyes like someone I used to know.'

'Kai doesn't know anything about it. He didn't even know she was coming this morning.'

'Didn't he? Well, you know best. But when you're young you shouldn't need to be forgetting things all the time. You need your memories when you get to my age.'

She hauls on my arm to stand up, then straightens herself carefully and swings one knee back and forth, testing the joint.

'Just a silly turn,' she says, suddenly buoyant again. She pats my arm reassuringly. This is always happening with Enid and me. One moment she's leaning on me like a small bony child, the next she casts me off as if I'm the one who needs her. And the door shuts, like my parents' bedroom door shutting on me when I was little.

'Time I got dressed,' she says briskly and scuttles up to her room, closing the door firmly. And there I am in my stale t-shirt at the top of the stairs.

I go back to my room and pick up my tapestry, squat cross-legged on the bed and begin to cross-stitch the back of a kitten. I'm angry with Enid. There are three kittens in the tapestry, one arched across a rug, digging in its claws, another savaging an apple, a third running off after the mother cat whose tail is just flicking out of the tapestry frame. Why does Enid have to keep on about things? OK, we all know Kai and Tony aren't Marks & Spencer. But if I can live with it, why's she got to keep on asking questions? These kittens are lovely. They are real kittens, not cute at all. Lulu will like them. She will keep the tapestry on her knee, stabbing at it with her wild hands, cuffing the frame. She will go to bed with it at night until she has worn it out.

'Oh, look, Lulu, a present from your sister.'

Lulu will make throaty noises of excitement and lunge forwards in her wheelchair, but the safety strap will hold her. They don't take any risks now, not after Lulu fell out and gashed her head on the corner of the fridge-freezer.

'Lulu, look. Kittens. Your favourite. Nadine made it for you.

Deenie!' Deenie. It sounds so intimate, the kind of nickname you'd give to a child who couldn't say her own name. Then you'd hold on to it out of love long after everyone had forgotten where the nickname came from. But they only made it up for Lulu. To make things easier for Lulu. That cry of pain which means Nadine. My sister. But they mustn't get her too excited or she'll start screaming. Three black and white kittens on a background of red. Lulu will like the red.

'For heaven's sake, Nadine, leave your mother alone. Can't you see she's worn out. She's been looking after Lulu all day. Have some sense.'

I shrink back across the long unkempt grass, back into the shadow of the mock-orange blossom. Mother has been exercising Lulu's legs on a rug in the sun, bicycling them up and round, up and round, like daisy wheels in the sun while I blink and watch. Lulu loves it. It's so exciting, she's choked with it. Mr Gargoyle looks over the fence and frowns. Lulu screams.

'Oh, hello, Mr Garrigle, oh dear, I'm so sorry about all the noise . . .'

She isn't sorry at all. Her fierce face flames at Mr Gargoyle. She's angry. Lulu's legs thrash weakly, the sun pours down, I want a drink.

'For God's sake, Nadine, what is it now?'

'How many times have I got to tell you to leave your mother alone? All the other children are playing out. Off you go, out into the lane.'

Pick, pick, through the strong linen goes my needle, piercing an eye for a kitten, a chewed segment of apple. Why should Kai be blamed? It's not his fault Enid was here first, and he's never done anything to her. He's not trying to get her out, and plenty of landlords would. There are ways. Enid doesn't know how lucky she is. You can't afford to be sentimental in property.

I keep thinking about the banknotes, and the smell of money. It has a safe smell. I know Kai's into some stuff. I'm not stupid. And I don't particularly want Vicki here, any more than

Enid does. But you can't be that rigid. You have to let her in. Pass, friend, pass, business associate. Kai keeps saying these are difficult times. *Life is difficult, Nadine.* You raise money on property you've bought with money you've raised on property you've bought with money you've – It's like defying gravity on a fairground ride that pins you to the wall by centrifugal force. It whips round faster and faster, and then they take the floor away and you look out level with the weathercock on the church tower. The thing is not to look down. The money'll keep on balancing as long as no one realizes there isn't anything underneath. Why should Enid keep going on about it? Why should anyone?

And one thing I do know is that Kai's clean. That used to worry me, because of all the money. I thought he must be dealing. But I know there's nothing like that. That one time I scored some dope from Chris and I was in here smoking a joint when Kai came back. Never again. I was amazed – why make such a fuss? After all, everybody does it. I'd have thought Kai would have known that. But he made me promise, never again. Never anything. Never in the house. It was easy to promise. All I wanted it for was so I could lie and listen to music when Kai was away and time could come apart and loop and loop and loop like someone drawing big circles freehand. I'd had enough of time jerking from minute to minute and me having to watch it. But it always seemed to end up making me feel sad. So I didn't mind not smoking it any more. I started doing cross-stitch and it worked nearly as well. And I've never touched anything else. I didn't really mind that Kai was so angry. It made me feel safe. Looked after . . .

. . . like I felt when I first met Kai. When he had that old blue van, and he used to meet me out of school. I don't know what he was doing up in the Midlands – business again, I suppose. I thought he lived there, I thought that little flat by the park was his home, not just one of the places he stayed in. Every day I walked through the school gate, and under the laurels, and down to the tunnel, and there was Kai. He'd always have something for us to eat. He said I wasn't eating properly. He brought food in white paper carriers from the delicatessen: tunafish sandwiches with mayonnaise, chicken tikka, gherkins, fat black olives. I was worried in case the gherkins made my breath smell, but Kai didn't care. And always cakes. Greek honey cake, and a cake with poppyseed paste in the middle, and small bitter-chocolate cakes with almond slivers sticking out of them. Once we had fresh dates – the first time I'd tasted them. I liked the white papery shell round the stone. We ate in the van, or in the street, or in the park. And we drank polystyrene cups of coffee, and vodka. It was all right to drink vodka, everyone said, because no one could smell the alcohol on you afterwards. I used to meet Kai in school dinner-times, so it was important not to smell of drink. But I'd stretch the time out, invent a library period, say I was practising for my French oral ... I don't know if anyone noticed. I don't think they cared. I'd stopped caring about marks, or what they thought of me. Books made my head ache. If I looked hard at the blocks of black print little bits would change back from black cross-stitch to words, but only a line at a time and by the time I'd laboured through one I'd forgotten what came before. And I could never join it up to what went after. It was like doing one of Enid's jigsaws where all the pieces are sky. Little, even-shaped pieces, prickling on the page.

The van always smelled of oil. I didn't mind, I like smells of oil and petrol, and cigarettes when they've just been lit. It was old and the seats were real leather, but cracked and crazed so that the stuffing was leaking out of them. And you could feel the springs when you leaned back. I used to shut my eyes and feel the sun on my face and Kai would drive and I wouldn't even know where we were going. Only the sun behind my eyelids and a dark shadow when we went past a building, or a slow tilt at a roundabout, and then a long road, gathering speed, the van roaring and the heat spreading out all round us while the wind pulled at my hair. I could give up everything. I didn't have to think. If I could have chosen I'd never have gone home. Once I heard Kai laugh and I knew he was looking at me. I felt so safe with him.

Ten

Paul Parrett turns off the video, rubs his eyes, swivels and looks out of the window. Dawn has come since he last looked round. He's been awake all night. It doesn't matter. It's Saturday and he'll catch up with a couple of hours' sleep in the early afternoon. It's going to be a quiet day. The House is empty. Times are jittery and no one can afford to sit back for a four-year ride, not the way things are now. Back to the constituency to attend Red Cross summer fairs, village donkey derbys, Polish ex-servicemen's dinners, surgeries, tenants' association meetings on draggled estates where you get lost and reverse furiously between Skylark Crescent and Goldfinch Gardens. But not too furiously. There are no votes in running over your constituents.

He has a safe seat close to London and an excellent agent who judges to the second when and where a personal appearance is called for. The newspapers are always there when Paul Parrett comes. The crowds doughnut eagerly for TV newsbites. It's not just to do with him being a minister either. His constituents actually seem to like him. How does the bugger do it, his fellow MPs grumble as they struggle into cabs to Paddington, Euston or King's Cross on Friday nights.

It is a fucking depressing video and he's going to have to watch it again. But he's hungry for something sweet first. He'll make pancakes with real maple syrup. He's been hooked ever since that first fact-finding tour to the US, when was it? Twelve years, it must be. He dumps eggs, flour, melted butter, milk into a blender and whizzes the mixture while he greases the pan. He flips down the button of his kitchen CD player and Cajun music floods out. The Alley Boys of Abbeville. Terrific. For a heavy man he's light on his feet as he shimmies sideways, ladles pancake batter to fall hissing against the frying pan, puts a plate to warm and opens another bottle of syrup. Someone brings it over from Vermont for him. He remembers apples heaped against red barns, fat lolling squash, the smell of frost. But the music takes him south and he goes lightly across the kitchen, turns and *chassés*, playing an imaginary fiddle. The surface of the pancake pales as it cooks through. He slips the edges loose, hesitates, tosses. It goes up and lands in a crisp bubbly brown circle. Perfect. He waits a minute for the other side to cook, then dances down the kitchen again, frying pan in hand, and tosses the pancake in mid-turn. It turns twice in the air but flips down on the right side. His hands just can't do wrong. He turns up the volume and trickles maple syrup in a thin stream, making lattice on the pancake. Then he rolls it up, swallows it in half a dozen bites and drops another half-ladle of batter on to the circle of hot heavy iron. Something to drink too. After all, it's five a.m. Not brandy – Armagnac. There's some somewhere, there's some of everything somewhere. He finds the long wooden coffin they pack it in, pours the drink into a glass, pours more over the cooked pancake and sets light to it. It flares up and he eats it the second the flames go out, buttery, crisp and soaked in booze.

Now for that bloody video. He runs it back, finds the place, leans forward feeling for the pad and pen by the side of his chair.

'His wife has brought up the four boys on her own,' says the commentator. An image flashes up, a still. She mustn't have wanted them to be filmed. Four boys, twelve, fourteen, fifteen, sixteen. All the bottom rungs of the ladder are missing: the kids she'd have had if her husband hadn't been in prison for eleven and a half years. They had both loved kids. A voice-over tells the thin factual tale of the solid wall of justice coming down on this family like a tidal wave, smashing it flat. One of the boys had cancer. He'd had a bone-marrow transplant and he seemed to be doing well. She'd coped with that on her own, along with everything else. The woman was thirty-five and she looked fifty, though maybe that was the lighting and the dark plain jumper and her hair pulled back like that. She'd look different in the film of her husband's release. She'd have her hair done and she'd be wearing something new and somebody'd have told her to put on some make-up, for the cameras if not for her husband.

But that film hadn't been made yet. Paul Parrett goes back again, replays. The usual story. Contradictions in the forensic evidence, allegations of police brutality, a time-gap which no one's explained, an alibi which might stand or might not depending on who was looking at it. It had been the kid's birthday, the eldest one.

'He was there. He lit the candles. He'd never've missed Paul's birthday.'

Paul Parrett feels the small flicker at the sound of his own name. Evidence has been built on less than such a small flicker, he knows. He can't help a moment of empathy for a father who would never miss the birthday of his little son called Paul. Evidence, evidence. He knows about evidence.

'Why are you lying there looking as if butter wouldn't melt? I know you've been up to something. I know what you've been up to.'

'Don't pretend you don't know what I mean. I can see right through you.'

'If it wasn't you done it, then why are you looking at me so innocent?'

The past's a great place, he thinks, as long as you don't have to live in it. The way that family's had to. The forensic expert's dead and dodgy, the two detectives from a well-known squad have admitted fabricating evidence on another case. Yes, he decides, that film's going to be made, the one where the wife buys a new red dress which doesn't suit her and has her hair coloured as well as permed, and wears lipstick which all comes off because she can't stop biting her lips just in case, at the very last moment, it's all going to be snatched from her. And the boys'll be wearing their jeans and huge trainers, hair gelled into place, eyes wary. They know about cameras and what newspapers can do. And there'll be a crowd of well-wishers, campaigners, family members, hangers-on, surging around the court gates. They'll look angrier than the family and maybe more joyful. The well-wishers haven't gone through these gates a hundred times.

Yes, the film's got to be made. It needs research, production, costing. The budget is going to be enormous. Appeals are getting slammed back these days. There's a reaction after the wave of appeals which ended in men and women walking out of the dock into the world. In these cases there are all kinds of costs to be taken into consideration. Public confidence in British justice, for instance.

But the film will be made. He already knows some of the actors. The programme researchers and the presenter he's just watched will be in it. Miscarriages of justice are their field. They know the score. Judge and lawyers are variables. The family have already got their parts. They live in role. And the man in prison too, and the three men convicted with him. The Manchester Four, they call them now. Safe casting: they aren't going to run away.

'Fuck it,' says Paul Parrett aloud, writing notes on his pad. The things that happen in daylight, under the camera's eye – they're not the point. The point is kids lying awake in bed at night, wondering what the fuck is going to happen to them now.

Eleven

As the credits start to roll, Nadine pulls back the door and fastens its hook, letting in the light from the corridor outside. Then the auditorium lights go up, small orange bulbs in the comfortable gloom, and people pick their way over one another, commenting on the film. They've all seen it before. The point of the film season isn't to go to films new and naïve and ready for enjoyment. This is the Warehouse's Icons of Sexuality season: Monroe this week, Garbo next, Mae West the week after. Talks at seven o'clock, before the screenings, drinks afterwards. Tonight there was a discussion on glamour and feminism, but Nadine wasn't ushering for that. It's the third time Nadine has seen *Some Like It Hot*. She listens to the comments of the departing patrons, as they move along to the complex's café which overlooks the water. Now they'll sprawl at fragile metal tables, drinking expensive bottled beers and tiny cups of overboiled coffee. Stumbling and blinking, they brush past her. Chris, the usher from Cinema 2, pushes his way in against the tide. His show ends about ten minutes before hers.

'Coming for a drink, Nadine?'

She shakes her head. 'No, I got to get back. I promised Enid I'd see her. Kai and Tony are away again.'

Chris has never met Enid, Kai or Tony, but he knows who they are. There are lots of dead hours with nothing happening, when Chris and Nadine talk.

'Just a quick one? I've got something to tell you.'

'Well . . . ' Nadine hesitates. But Kai's away – he won't look up and frown as she comes in and say that he thought the show finished at ten this week. And Enid is awake until all hours, night after night. She won't mind what time Nadine comes, as long as she comes.

'OK, then. I'll check the auditorium and lock up. Be down in about five minutes.'

'There's no rush. I'll wait here.'

They go along the corridor into the smoky café. A soft dull roar of conversation folds around them.

'And her arse when she walks down the platform . . .'

'Yes – those amazing buttocks.'

'But she's so *lovable!*' cuts in a girl's voice, 'Don't you see – it's not just a sexual thing. I mean, it makes *me* want to take her home and look after her, and I'm not gay or anything. It's sort of innocent.'

'That cotton-candy hair.'

'Did you see that film they found, from *Something's Got to Give?*'

'Amazing.'

'Of course she'd lost a lot of weight.'

'Fifteen pounds.'

'Yeah – she *was* a bit overweight in *Some Like It Hot.*'

'That just shows how your ideas about female beauty have been conditioned by fashion models.'

'Did you see the autopsy photos?'

Chris winks at Nadine. Everyone's seen the autopsy photos, they're the thing to talk about. Marilyn Monroe with her face pocked in death. Bruises, splats of decay. Her jaw fallen, her cheeks pouched, her hair flat and stringy. Less beautiful, at last, than any of us.

Soon they're tucked into a corner by the bar, drinking. The wine is very dry, just like drinking stone, Nadine thinks.

'How's Mark?'

'Oh, he's fine. Except I never see him – he's working late on a commission every night, then he's away to the studio again before I wake up.'

'It must be big business, jewellery,' says Nadine, who has none.

'Well, it is, once you start making serious pieces,' agrees Chris with eager vicarious pride. 'This is for a Nigerian client. He came into Mark's exhibition and took three pieces straight away. The neckpiece and gold bangles. And now there's this commission as well. You've got to ride the wave.'

Nadine swills her wine round in her glass and stares into it. She and Chris sound like children boasting about their parents. The big people: the people who do things. Kai's done this. Mark's done that. Only she's more subtle than Chris, knowing that he'll gladly swallow every hint from her secret world.

'So what was it – what you wanted to talk about?'

Chris gulps his wine and answers, 'There's a job coming up here. A proper job.'

Yes, there it is again, his childhood in his voice. Echoes of mothers, of 'standards'. *A proper job*. All the things he's supposed to have grown out of.

'Where?'

'Programming assistant. You must have heard about it?'

He is looking at her sharply. He's been here much longer than she has, and no permanent vacancies have come up in that time. She's temporary, casual labour, and so's Chris, even though he knows everything about how things work here.

'I didn't know anything about it. Are you going to apply?'

'I might. What about you?'

'Me? How could I? I don't know anything about it.'

'Of course you do. You know quite a lot about films. You could read. There's loads of good books. You'd soon learn how to build up a programme. How do you think Richard started? He hasn't got a masters in film studies, that's for sure.'

Nadine drinks before she answers. Chris isn't really talking to her: he's persuading himself. It's obvious that he wants the job. Anyway she can't apply. She'd never be able to hide the way words dazzle and won't do what her mind wants. There'd be an application form, national insurance details. They all think she is nineteen.

'No, I don't want anything permanent just now. I don't want

to tie myself down. I might go to a few festivals with Cathy. I'd like to do that.'

'How are you getting on?' He knows about her juggling, and approves. Everybody's doing it now, even in serious theatre. Circus skills. Tumbling and juggling and swallowing fire and hustling for pound coins. If Nadine gets really good, all sorts of things might open up. Film companies are always looking for people. Look at those Angela Carter films.

'Cathy's going to take me down the Ring.'

'You must be getting good. I've seen her there.'

'Yes,' she says, stretching in her chair, feeling the new suppleness Cathy's building into her muscles. 'Yes, I like it. It feels good.'

'I'm thinking of going for it myself,' says Chris and swallows wine. 'The job, I mean.'

'You should. Mark's doing so well now –' She doesn't go on. She shouldn't have said anything. Chris has tensed up, and no wonder. Mark is beginning to get clients, to travel. There's talk of a one-man show, a big one this time. And there's money coming in, money which Chris can't match. People at parties talk to Mark first, then turn politely to Chris. 'And what do you do, Chris?' 'Oh – I work at the Warehouse.' If he's lucky there are no more questions, and they leave it that he might be a photographer, a video-maker or an exhibition organizer. If they cut to the bone Mark's suddenly there, casually close, casually sexy, making it all right. But that can't last for ever.

'Anyway, I shan't be applying,' says Nadine. 'So the field's clear for you.'

'Veronica's bound to – and she's tough, she'll talk her way into anything,' he says gloomily, staring across the café at Veronica, her glossy wedge of hair slipping forward as she points out something on her clipboard. She's talking to Richard again. Veronica likes working in public. She's never self-conscious, only perhaps a trace more focused and professional when she senses eyes on her. Nadine watches Chris watching

Veronica. Yes, he's right to be worried. She's a winner, and he isn't. Chris turns back to Nadine.

'I like your hair. Where did you get it done?'

'It was somebody Tony knew. She doesn't work in a salon, she comes to the house.'

Nadine's dark hair has been cut short so that it waves around her head and curls in at her nape. It is even shorter than she wore it at school and much better cut. A disturbing look: boy/girl, yes/no. It was Tony who shaped out the cut in the air for Francesca, Tony who flipped over style books and scooped Nadine's hair off her face to judge the effect. Kai was away at the time. It was going to be a surprise for him, Tony said.

'It looks good,' says Chris. 'Androgynous. Very sexy. Does Kai like androgynous girls?'

Nadine blushes faintly, remembering how Kai had reacted to the haircut that night when he got home. She thought Tony'd wanted this too. It had been part of the pattern he'd sketched in the air for Francesca. Tony made you feel naked to him. He was there in the bedroom shadows, noiseless, waiting and watching for what he already knew was going to happen.

'You can't go on ushering here for ever. What about going to college? You could easily get some A-levels,' says Chris.

'I like it here. Where else could I see all these films without paying? And it's Garbo next week. My heroine.'

'Is she? Lots of women go for Garbo, did you know?'

'Mmm. I can see why.'

Nadine thinks of Garbo's eyelids, faintly vaselined, gleaming, and the star's face turning into camera, breaking into movement. She stops listening to Chris. Besides, she ought to get home. She's said too much. Why does she always tell Chris things?

'I owe you a drink,' she says. 'I'll get it, but then I've got to go. Enid likes to chat – you know how it is.'

That was safe ground. Never, never had she heard Chris admit that he did not 'know how it is' about anything. She bought him another glass of Muscadet and watched him cross the room towards Richard and Veronica as she made her way out of the café. They did not look up or seem to notice him. Chris would be running over his opening line in his head as he approached.

The rear lights of the bus wink triumphantly as it moves off just as Nadine crosses the green. It rumbles away uphill, tauntingly slow at first, then gathering speed.

'Have you got the price of a cup of tea?' asks a voice from the ground. He is sitting in a pool of shadow under a lime tree. He does not ask for change; he has no dog or musical treatment, no baby in a pram. He has been asking for the price of a cup of tea for twenty years, and he will not change his begging now to fit in with these young ones. Long-haired, deeply weathered as he aged in public, often reading, he was unique in the district and known by name, Samuel. Little children pointed at his nest of beard and coiled greying hair, and sometimes their mothers put ten pence into their hands to give him. An object lesson. But you can't encourage children to do that sort of thing now, when there are hundreds of beggars all over the city.

This long uphill street is still Samuel's patch. He's usually on the green at night, under a tree, even now when the new rash of homelessness has queered most of the pitches. Nadine always gives him something. Remembering the price of the wine she has just drunk, she feels for the dead metal of a pound coin in her purse and drops it into his raised hand. A stink of burnt fat rolls from the open door of the Burger Bar, and the doorman at Club Suzie shifts his feet and looks at Nadine, but she goes past. A couple eat, spotlit in the window of a trattoria, looking intimately into one another's eyes as if they are being paid by the hour to do so. Nadine goes by within six inches of them, on the other side of the glass, not disturbing their gaze. She can walk faster in the dark, swinging uphill, breasting the warm night and the pulse of music and beery gusts from pub ventilators.

She turns off into tall silent streets where the lamps don't work and the trees are overgrown, tapping windows, scratching heaps of builder's rubble in skips. A retaining wall bulges towards her. She steps off the broken pavement and walks in the middle of the road. She passes a street light which works and her blunt orange shadow trails out behind her. She doesn't like it when her shadow is behind her. If someone steps on your shadow they possess your soul.

No, I'm not frightened, she thinks. Come out, come out, wherever you are, she sings softly as she chanted in the play-ground once, but no one answers. Black summer leaves hiss above her head. The honeyed smell of waste land buddleia drifts past like someone's perfume, then there's a burning smell of fox. There are foxes all over the city. She has watched them from the balcony in the early mornings, walking down the street with their heads up, long claws ticking on the pavement. Their ears are big and pointed. They have the perfect self-possession of actors. They map the city secretly, at odds with published maps of roads and footpaths. Their routes are tunnels through allot-ments and rows of garden, through steep-hanging ruined gardens above the docks, in and out of timber yards and upriver to the restaurant bins of the city centre, back to safe suburban gardens where the covers may have been left off the rabbit hutch, where the fat pedigree guinea-pig shivers in his straw-packed corner and smells fox.

She's almost home. Past the stained-glass lights of the Prince and Pauper, past the clang of the bin-lids where Clara shovels in uneaten bolognese, past the bakery where blue fluorescent lights will be humming again at four a.m., past the corner of the graveyard and through the alley, dark and slender with its one Victorian lamp-post shedding a pale ring at the blind corner. The blind bend in the alley where someone could hide. It's empty. Safe again. The square. Home.

The stairs are dark.

'Nadine! Nadine! Is that you, dear?' Enid's voice, nerveless and commanding. 'Come on up, dear.'

As Nadine climbs the last stairs to Enid's attic, the door opens just a crack, enough for Enid to peep round and wrinkle up in welcome. She opens the door a little wider and Nadine slides in.

'You ought to get a bolt fitted,' says Nadine. 'Then no one could get in.' There is no lock on Enid's door.

'No one has ever troubled me,' says Enid, looking at Nadine with sudden severity. 'Never trouble till trouble troubles you. Those squatters were perfectly nice young people. Once they realized that this room was my home, they didn't try to come in. They respected my privacy.'

'I didn't know there'd been squatters here.'

'Well, there weren't, not once your Kai and Tony had bought the place. They were gone as if the hag was after them. Why that should be, I can't imagine, seeing that your Kai and Tony are both so nicely spoken.' And she gives Nadine a sharp look.

'Did you know them?'

'Well, you get to know people, don't you, dear? Not like I know *you*, of course. There was Jenny, a very nice young person but taken up with the baby. Still, that's only natural, isn't it?'

'If she had a baby, I suppose she could've got on to a housing list.'

'Oh, yes, very likely she could. So that's all right, then, isn't it? I expect they found her a council flat,' adds Enid satirically.

Enid's small fire burns in the grate, making the room stiflingly hot. The windows are closed. A big bunch of buddleia droops on a table, overpoweringly sweet at first, then half forgotten like an infusion in the air. Enid painted the room herself two years ago, in brilliant Monet blue and pink, lavishly streaking the walls and ceiling. The paint is too heavy for the wallpaper and it has begun to peel away from the plaster. Enid does not believe in wasting money at launderettes, so she washes her sheets in the bath and hangs them perilously out of the window, where they leave long runnels in the grime. A small clothes-line dips above the fireplace, where two or three pairs of woolly knickers and vests hang, stiff as card. Just now the floor is covered with rushes. Enid was taken on a river trip two weeks ago. While consuming tea and scones at the riverside tea gardens, she spotted a bank of rushes, and, after begging a sharp knife from the proprietor, she cut herself pretty near a bin-bag full, saying that it was for church decoration. She brought them home and strewed them on her floor. 'As they did in medieval times, years ago, dear, to keep the air pure. It stopped the plague. And we shall be having the plague again, if they don't do something about the sewers round here. They're crumbling away inside, you know. And the things people put down them these days. Nappies and I don't know what. One of these days there'll be a collapse and a bus will go down into the sewers and then something will be done, once it's too late. The greatest gift of our ancestors thrown away by foolish neglect. Sanitation, dear.'

The rushes lie limp in the extreme heat, streaked with yellow. They smell unpleasantly.

'If you open the window, they'll dry out properly,' remarks Nadine.

'Oh, no, dear, I can't have all that dirty air in here. I can taste the fumes right down in my throat. By rights we should all leave the city in summer, but what can you do? Perhaps you could go and visit your family, Nadine?' Enid's small face peers inquisitively from behind the line of knickers. This is not the first time she has set out to discover a little more about Nadine. 'It's nice to know a little bit of background, isn't it, dear?' And why not, thinks Nadine. All these secrets. I'm getting as bad as Kai. Enid's so out of the world, who would she tell?

'It's too far,' she says. 'I can't afford the fare.'

'Surely *Kai* could give you something? He's always going here, there and everywhere himself. Money doesn't seem to be much of a problem.'

'My parents live a long way away. In Germany.'

93

'In Germany! Well, that does come as a surprise to me. I should never have taken you for a German, with your beautiful English.'

Nadine laughs. 'I'm not German, nor are they. They moved to south Germany. They're living in an Esseler Home there.'

'I seem to know the name. Very German − some sort of philanthropist, wasn't he? Of course they have a lot of those over there. Are they quite *old* parents, dear?'

'The home is for my sister. She has cerebral palsy − you know what that is? The home runs a programme for people with cerebral palsy. My mother works in the kitchen, and my father works in the office and on the farm, and so that pays for Lulu's keep there.'

'That sounds rather hard work for them, I must say,' says Enid, all her sympathies at once engaged by the thought of two elderly people doing heavy manual labour. It's refreshing, thinks Nadine, to find someone who doesn't immediately start to question and sympathize about Lulu.

'They're quite young, really. Early forties. They do get time off, and there's plenty for them there as well. Singing and meditation groups and so on. I had a postcard from them showing the place. It's above a lake and there are apple orchards all round. *The work is tough, but this place is wonderful for Lulu, and that's what counts. It's her turn now,*' quotes Nadine expressionlessly. 'That's what they put on the postcard. That's about all I know about it. They did send me some brochures and things.'

The little black kettle over the fire lets out a quavering warble and a puff of steam.

'There now! She's singing already!' exclaims Enid delightedly. 'Now we can have a nice cup of tea, and you can tell me what *your* turn was.'

'My turn? Oh, being clever was my turn. Being able to do things. Passing exams. Going to university and having chances nobody else had had, that was going to be my turn.'

'So what happened? I mean, this is a very interesting house

and I'm sure you're learning a lot here that you couldn't learn at the university, but it's not quite the same thing, is it, dear? Bugger these rushes. Nearly had me down then.'

'I don't know. I'd have a book in front of me and I'd be reading it but I couldn't understand what it was saying, not even the words. They weren't like words any more, just like black things I had to put in the right place. Only I couldn't. The words weren't like words any more. They felt so heavy, I couldn't get through them. Once I read one page and then I realised I'd put a tape on at the beginning and it had finished. And I hadn't made sense of a word. It wasn't even a difficult book. It was just a page of a novel. I got frightened.'

'And then you met Kai.'

'No, I knew him already. I met him when I was doing GCSEs –' She stops. Enid registers the slip, but instead of commenting or questioning further, she goes off at a tangent. Thank God, thinks Nadine, old people's minds don't stay long on one thing.

'I often wonder about this business of turns, if you like to put it that way. One day, when I was in Manchester, not long before the war it was, in 1937 –'

'Were you living there?'

'Not exactly. I was a business girl, living in Warrington at that time. But I'd seen a little of the world by then, even though I *was* only twenty.' She shoots Nadine the small coy glance of a woman who is lying about her age. Twenty in 1937, calculates Nadine rapidly, even that would make her about seventy-seven now. Can she be older than that? She'd have to be nearly eighty.

'Oh, yes, I've moved around a bit in my lifetime. But I'm staying put now,' Enid adds quickly, remembering that Nadine is not just any young girl, but one who lives with the landlord, and that the landlord would like to be rid of his sitting tenant. 'I don't believe you'd be able to guess where I came from originally, now would you? No, I thought not, dear. Well, I had come up to Manchester after an opening, very promising it sounded, I had to meet a Mr Albion at the Exchange Hotel. I thought it was a funny name even at the time, but then people do have funny names, don't they – like your Kai. I can't say his surname to save my life.'

'I expect it's perfectly ordinary in Finland, like Smith or Roberts.'

'I daresay it is to them. But not to *us*, is it, dear? Now where was I? So I waited for nearly three quarters of an hour in the hotel lobby and Mr Albion never turned up, and I could see the hotel staff were starting to look at me sideways – very suspicious they were in those days if you didn't have a man with you, you've no idea – so I went up to the desk and said very à la posh, "If a Mr Albion asks for me, tell him I was unable to wait," and out I swept into the street before they could say anything – there was a *very* saucy-looking boy by the lift.'

'So didn't you ever meet Mr Albion?'

'Oh, Mr Albion was nothing, he doesn't really come into the story at all, he was just the occasion of it, so to speak. Oh, no, I was delighted never to hear one word from *Mr Albion* again. An alias, you may be sure of it. But I wasn't going to go straight back home to Warrington with my tail between my legs. What a waste of the fare that would have been. It was only midday, and I thought I would go and look round the shops, and then have my tea. But when I went down the steps it was pouring with rain. You don't know Manchester rain, not as it used to be. It would leave black streaks down your clothes – you *never* wore white or cream when you went to Manchester. I was wearing a very nice costume, navy-blue, my best for the interview. I had my umbrella with me – you always did in Manchester – but I knew that I should be soaked through in no time even so, with the rain coming down the way it was. So I set off walking, thinking I would get something to eat in a tea-shop. Then it began to tip down just as if someone had emptied a bucket over me, and water was running down the street so I could see my best shoes would be ruined in a minute. I'd have taken them off and walked down the street barefoot only it wasn't respectable. I had to take shelter. I saw a shop entrance, so I hopped up a step and stood against the glass. It was a jeweller's shop. There were two or three of us waiting – everyone had scuttled off the pavements and the rain was still bouncing up and hitting my face even in the shelter of the shop doorway. Then I heard a voice say, "Come in a little farther, you're getting wet," so I did, even though it meant I was pushed right up against the lady who had spoken. It was a voice you'd notice, even in the midst of a rainstorm. Low and clear; what we used to call well modulated, though that's not an expression you hear these days. And the voice sounded as if the person speaking was smiling. I noticed the voice more than I noticed her, just at first; we were all crushed up together, and I could smell lilacs. We said one or two things, I can't remember what, about the rain, I expect. There was a car which went past slowly with a wave of water parting at the wheels, and I said it reminded me of the Red Sea. I always liked that story, from a child: the thought of the sea parting, and the floor of it bare. I used to wonder what happened to the fish. Were they swept up in the wave, or did they lie there floundering? She laughed – she had a lovely deep laugh, it went with her voice, and said she wished we were Israel-ites.

'The rain didn't stop and didn't stop. There was a cab coming – the rain made it look quite white for a minute. She looked at me and she said, "I'm going to get that cab. Can I drop you?" and I said, stupidly, "I don't really know where I'm going," so she laughed again and said, "Then you'd better come with me. I can take you somewhere out of the rain." She leaned out and signalled to the cab – it saw us and turned in towards the kerb. But I wasn't sure if I ought to go with her. You heard lots of stories in those days – white slave traffic and women in taxis with syringes. She must have seen it, for she said, "It's all right. It's a Ladies' Club." You couldn't look her straight in the face and think she was white slave traffic, so we both got in the cab. She pulled off her hat and shook her hair out – it was wet at the ends, like mine. She seemed very worldly and sophisticated to me, so I thought she must be quite old; I knew later that she was just thirty. I liked the way she signalled to the cab, and it came wheeling round, and the way she told the driver where to take us. Then she leaned back against the leather seat and said, "*That's all right.* We're out of the rain. Oh, this Manchester rain! Can you believe it? It's like some awful film." She hadn't a Manchester voice, but then I hadn't a Warrington one, or no more than a touch. I was looking at my shoes. "Suede, aren't they?" she said. "Don't worry, they won't spoil. We'll get them seen to."

'It wasn't very far, then the cab stopped in front of a little entrance, so close we had just a step to the door. She paid the cab. I had a shilling in my hand, though it was meant for my dinner, but she wouldn't take my money. It looked a dull place, and I was a bit disappointed. I'd thought it would be somewhere special. There was just a small door with a brass handle and a little plaque beside it: THE MILLICENT SOWERBY ASSOCIATION FOR LADIES. "Dreadful, isn't it?" she said as we went in. "No one calls it that, of course. We call it the Manchester Ladies." I didn't think that sounded much better, to give it a name like a public convenience. But in we went. The entrance was narrow and brown and old, the way these buildings are, then it suddenly swelled out into a big entrance hall, one of those geometric shapes with six sides, you know? There was a plain green carpet, and big seats to wait in, but "We'll go straight in," she said and pushed a big swinging door – doors led off the hall in all directions, and there we were.'

'Where were you?' asked Nadine, sipping tea.

'I couldn't quite take it in at first. It was a big silvery room, as if sunlight was coming in from somewhere. That was the mirrors. They ran from ceiling to floor on one side of the room, so that everything shone back on itself and you couldn't tell how big the room was or how many people were in it. There was a fire with big clean-looking flames leaping up in the grate.

Then there were plants, nearly as big as outdoor trees, growing right up the walls. They had an orange tree in a tub, I remember, with little oranges growing on it. You could smell the oranges. It had white waxy flowers as well as the fruit. How I wanted to pick one of those oranges! I'd never seen such a thing growing before. There was a dark blue and rose carpet, like an oriental carpet. And all round the room *chaises-longues* and women lying on them. Two were playing cards: there were three white five-pound notes crumpled on the floor between them. There was a woman in a kimono writing in a notebook; she looked up when we came in, as if she'd been thinking of something and we'd interrupted her. I thought perhaps she was a writer. She was my idea of what a writer ought to look like. She went out by another door. And there was a red-haired woman stroking a cat – stroke, stroke, stroke. I can see her now. That was Caro. It made me shiver to watch her. She looked up and saw us and said, "Darling! Who's your friend?" "My name is Enid Shelton," I said quickly, not wanting the lady I came with to let on that we didn't even so much as know each other's names.

'But I could see the red-haired woman wasn't really interested in my name. She put the cat down and came over to us. She touched my lady's shoulder, and then her hair. "Sukey, you're wet through. Come and take your things off."

'We went into another room – this time it was quite plain, with wooden panelling and a couple of beds, and a big carved wardrobe with more kimonos hanging there. Sukey took one and held it against me. "Yes – that suits you. Would you like a bath?"

'A kimono was quite enough. I certainly didn't want a bath. But Sukey did. She held out her foot so we could see the mud spots on her stockings. Beautiful stockings they were: silk. We didn't have nylons then – it was silk or cotton, and mine were cotton. Nylons came in the war, with the Americans. They gave us nylons.

'"I'll scrub your back," said the red-haired one. Sukey just nodded. But she hadn't forgotten about me, as I thought she might once her friend started fussing over her. "But will you be all right, Enid?" she asked me. "You ought to sit near the fire and get warm. Find a novel from the shelves. I shan't be long."

'I felt shy going back into the big room with all the mirrors, in case anyone asked me what I was doing there. But then the two who were playing cards stopped their game and talked to me. They weren't like Caro – they were quite friendly. They even seemed interested in me. I told them about Mr Albion and how I had met Sukey. I wanted to ask more about the club – whether it was just for professional women or might anybody join? They looked clever, as if they might have been doctors, or teachers. "Oh, no," they answered, "Nothing like that." "It's just a private club for women, that's all." "No restrictions." "Certainly no black-balls or waiting-lists." "It's not exclusive in any way." I looked round at the orange tree and the pile of new novels and the five-pound notes thrown on the floor, as if they were rubbish. They saw me looking. "Only it's a little tricky to find." "We don't advertise, naturally." "Members bring their guests along, and then *they* become members." "The entrance puts people off." "So shabby – it's deplorable, really, isn't it, Paula?" "And the name too. Poor Millicent Sowerby." "Shocking. But now you *have* found us . . ." "People usually do . . ." "You'll come again." "Of course she will." "Won't she?"

'They ordered tea, and we were just drinking it when Caro and Sukey came back in. Caro was very flushed, from the steam I supposed. Sukey looked younger in the kimono than she had in her black coat and skirt. Her hair was damp and it was curling round her forehead. She dropped to the floor and tucked the kimono round her ankles. I wondered if that was how Japanese ladies sat – it looked very graceful.

'"Whisky," she said. There was a sideboard with bottles on it. Caro got up and poured a stream of very pale whisky into a big heavy glass. It didn't look at all like the treacly stuff I'd seen in bars. "Heaven," said Sukey, drinking quite half of it. "What a haven this is." "Heaven-haven," said Paula. "Out of the swing of the sea," said April. "Except that we aren't nuns," said Caro. "Oh, why not? To stretch a point," said Sukey lazily, drinking off the rest of her whisky. "More heaven, please." "Will you have some, Enid?" Caro asked me. "No, she won't. She wouldn't like it. But she'll have a little brandy to keep out the cold, won't you, Enid?"

'So I did. I thought I shouldn't like it, but I loved it – first the taste of it puckering up my mouth, and then the heat of it fanning out right through me till the last of the rain and Mr Albion disappeared. But I could tell Caro was annoyed. She wanted to be alone with Sukey, anyone could see that, but Sukey didn't want to be alone with her. Then Sukey took a little comb from the kimono pocket; tortoiseshell, very expensive; and said, "I'll comb your hair for you, Enid. If you take it down it'll dry in front of the fire." For I still had my hair long then. Father wouldn't let us cut it when we were at home, and then I was told it was my best feature, though you wouldn't think it now.'

Nadine looks at Enid's sparse tufts of white-grey hair. Artfully deployed as they are, they scarcely cover her skull.

'It was down to my waist when I unpinned it. Nut-brown, they called the colour, like the nut-brown maid. That was what Father said when he got sentimental. I always washed it and brushed it and took care of it, so I wasn't ashamed when Sukey unpinned it and the whole lot fell down my back. "What slippery stuff!" she said. "And such quantities of it. I wonder why we ever cut our hair?" "Because we prefer it short," said Caro, who had her red hair beautifully shaped and no longer than a boy's. Now I come to think of it, Caro's hair looked a bit like yours, Nadine, apart from the colour. It suited her, but I could see Sukey had it in for her. "Enid's doesn't feel like hair at all," Sukey said. "It's like putting your hand under the tap. Soft water. It's marvellous, you ought to feel it," and of course I was pleased. "Put your head in my lap," she said. "And I'll comb your hair for you."

'Caro made a sharp movement, as if she was going to say something or do something, but Sukey smiled at her and she said nothing. I put my head in Sukey's lap. I could feel the warmth of her body through the kimono. She spread out my hair over her kimono and began to comb it in long sweeps from the crown to the ends. I shut my eyes. I felt as if Sukey was my mother, and I was long ago at home, being looked after. Except that my mother never did anything like that for us – she had no time. I could hear the fire bubbling, and the long hiss of the comb through my hair. Nobody said anything. It made me feel happy, but sad too, as if I would cry if she went on combing and combing. "There," said Sukey. "Perfect." I lifted my head from her lap and sat up without opening my eyes. She twisted my hair up and put in the pins. My hair was so fine that it never went up easily, but when I looked in the mirror Sukey'd got it just right, waving a little round my forehead, with a heavy knob shining at the back of my neck.

'April was smoothing one of the five-pound notes between her fingers. "I promise to pay the bearer on demand . . ." she said dreamily. "Do you think they would still give you gold for it?" "Why not try? Then you could bite off bits to pay for your dinners." "And where do you work, Enid," asked Caro. "In one of the mills?" "Don't be more of a bloody fool than you can help, Caro," Sukey said to her. "Enid is training to be a surgeon." April's face glowed. "Really? How splendid! Was there much opposition? Do you find there is still a great deal of prejudice against women in the medical schools?" "Now, April, remember, this is our haven. Enid has enough to do with training for a difficult career and battling against constant discouragement. Of course there's opposition: there always is. Now she needs to relax. That's why I brought her here. You have a lecture at three, haven't you, Enid? I shall put you into a cab." "Oh, yes, you mustn't be late for a lecture. You mustn't give them any excuse to call women students unreliable. What's the subject?" "Anatomy today, isn't it, Enid?" asked Sukey. Caro was crisping the five-pound notes between her fingers. She looked as if she would like to tear them up. I murmured something, hoping to God Sukey wouldn't say anything more. It didn't matter to her – she wasn't the one who was going to look a fool if anyone asked questions. I still don't know why she had to lie like that. It came out later that I wasn't a medical student, but Sukey made it all right. She made it seem as if I was very clever and had always wanted to be one, but it was too expensive. So April was more sympathetic than ever. But that was later. Sukey quite often told lies.

'It was half past two and I knew Sukey wanted me to go. I went into the wood-smelling bedroom and changed back into my clothes. My suede shoes had been brushed and shoe trees had been put into them to keep them in shape. That must have been Sukey.

'She was waiting outside. Paula and April and Caro nodded and waved. They didn't say goodbye formally – they seemed to think I'd be coming again. It was one of those places where people went in and out and melted into whatever was happening. But I wondered. If Sukey had meant me to come again, why had she said I was training to be a surgeon? I could never keep up the pretence. Or perhaps I could. Perhaps it was just a game and I could play it too. Why should everything be serious all the time? That delicious sound in Sukey's voice changed everything – even lying seemed like a game. I looked at all the other doors off the entrance hall, the ones Sukey hadn't opened. I wondered where they went. More rooms with women sitting reading and playing cards? Dining-rooms, perhaps? Libraries? It was silent but it was a warm humming silence. A private silence, not a library hush. Perhaps there were bedrooms behind the doors. Sukey had her arm around my waist. She drew me to the narrow brown club entrance.

'"Here we are. Yes, your cab's outside waiting. Don't worry about paying him – it's on my account. Now, darling, let me look at you. Perfect. And the shoes? Did they mark?" I held out my foot to show her the unstained suede. "Lovely. Now off you go. Till next time, darling – remember, Manchester Ladies."

'She drew me closer, put her hands on the sides of my face and kissed me, two kisses, one on each cheek. Her irises were striped when you got close to them, grey and black. Then she moved back and they began to sparkle. She gave a little wave and turned away before I did, to cross the green carpet while I went down the narrow strip of brown lino to the street and the cab. And that was that.'

Twelve

The story's over. The pink-skulled storyteller sips her cool tea as Sukey and Caro and the Manchester Ladies recede, folding in on themselves until they are no more than pinpoints in Enid's eyes. Like Japanese paper flowers dropped into water they have expanded and taken on flesh and colour. Drained, they are nothing but a smear on glass. *That was that.*

'No, I'm sure it wasn't,' says Nadine. 'There's much more, isn't there? I can tell.'

'How do you mean?'

'Something else happened afterwards. Something important, to do with Sukey and Caro and the others.'

'I told you I met them again, didn't I, dear? But I'll tell you the rest of the story another time,' says Enid, smiling over her teacup, her voice cosy and pacifying.

'I wish you'd go on with it now. I'm dying to know what happened to them. The Manchester Ladies. It *is* all true, isn't it? It really happened?'

'Of course it did! Why would I want to make up a thing like that?'

'It sounds quite bizarre, a place like that behind a door in an ordinary street in Manchester.'

'What about this place?' responds Enid sharply. 'I daresay people'ud be a bit surprised if they knew what went on behind *our* front door.'

Nadine is silenced. Satisfied, Enid goes on. 'I only wish you could have felt that carpet. You don't get anything like it these days. You'd think you could spread out your arms and swim away on it. It was like moss to walk on, though I don't suppose that means much to you city girls. And quiet – it soaked up all the sound. Oh, yes, I saw Sukey again. And Caro.'

The room is very quiet. Enid's head is framed by the semicircle of hand-painted plates on the wall. She has painted them herself, splodging fat-petalled scarlet daisies on to cheap white plates, binding the flowers into a pattern with trails of woodbine.

'Nobody could help seeing Caro,' says Enid. 'Even if they didn't know her. There were pictures of her all over the newspapers. She didn't do herself justice in the photographs. But then I suppose it was the circumstances. No one could look her best. And then in black and white you lost her colouring. I don't care for red hair myself, but she was very striking. Red hair, white skin. Not green eyes, though. They were brown, golden brown. And she would stare straight at you and never look away. It was as if there was no one behind her eyes. I can still hear the newsboys calling out her name. They'd got it scrawled in black across the front of all the news-stands.' The teacup is arrested in the air. Enid's eyes narrow. Nadine whispers so as not to break the spell again. 'Why? What did she do?'

Enid leans forward. Her small fierce fingers grasp Nadine's wrist, and she pulls Nadine towards her. Nadine's never been so close to Enid before. Her face dissolves into a crazed map of wrinkles, brown splodges, patches of skin incongruously milky as pearls.

'What colour do you think grass is?' she whispers.

'Why – green, of course,' says Nadine, annoyed. What's Enid playing at now? Can't she just tell the story through from beginning to end?

'No!' says Enid, her dry fingers gripping tighter. 'No, not if you look at it. It isn't at all. If only I could make you see her.'

'Who, Caro?'

'No. Sukey.' Enid pauses, sighs, says again, 'Sukey,' with slow, caressing love. 'That's how I know grass isn't always green. 'Course I was a town girl then. She was coming across the field towards me and all the grass was moving. It was a hill farm, high up, so there was always a wind. Not yet eight o'clock in the morning. All the shadows lying sideways, and the dew dried already, for it was June. The grass was purple and grey and brown and silver, all moving. None of it was green. And the grass shivered against her as she walked. There was Yorkshire fog and cocks-foot and fescue. It lapped up her legs and her skirts. Skirts were longer then. She was smiling at me. I could see her smile from a long way off, from the other side of the field, long before I could really see her face. She moved lightly and held herself very upright – Sukey always did. The wind made lines in the grass so it seemed to bow down and rise up around her.'

Nadine sees it: the pelt of grass, purple and silver-tipped, dipping under the stroke of Sukey's skirts.

'Then I saw Caro,' continues Enid. 'She was over in the far corner of the field, by the gate. The grass seemed to knot itself round her legs: she couldn't make her way through. She looked as if she was trying to run in a nightmare. She couldn't get to Sukey. And her mouth was open, wide open like a hole in her face. I watched her crawling over the field. She was like a red stain in the grass.'

Enid looks down. She is rocking herself very slightly, side to side.

'Don't get upset,' says Nadine. 'It's a long time ago. It's over now. I shouldn't have asked you to tell me.'

'Like blood,' says Enid. 'She looked like blood.'

'Don't think about it any more – I'll make us another cup of tea –'

'It isn't over, it's never over,' whispers Enid. But below them the big house booms like Jack's castle in the clouds when the giant comes home. The clouds crowd together, bruising one another, while the beanstalk leading into the sky begins to shake. The front door slams, the hall echoes, feet strike the bottom step –

'It's your Kai. Quick. You don't want him finding you up here.'

Nadine leaps up, slips on the rushes, grabs at the mantelpiece, misses, catches her temple on its black corner. For a sick second her head swims, the gas hisses in her ears, the line of knickers lurches towards her. Then Enid's got her and is steering her back to the chair.

'She needs a glass of water – now where's the bugger –' Then there's a chink of glass and a mineral smell of cold water under her nose. She breathes in, sips, eyes closed. She breathes in the dry nannying smell of Enid. But that banging and pounding is not just in her head any more. It's footsteps. She opens her eyes and sees Enid frozen, suspended, one foot on the rushes, listening to the rising clomp of Kai's footsteps, knowing now that she'll never get Nadine out of the way in time.

'Don't let him come in here,' she pleads, seizing Nadine's arm with her knuckly little hands as if Nadine carries magic with her to baffle Kai into seeing a fence of blossoming thorns where the door once was.

'Nadine! Nadine!'

Up and up, winding the starlit stair to the attic. He's close. He's just outside on the landing. The two women can almost hear his breathing. His footsteps stop. 'Nadine!' he bellows. Now he's bound to come in. Nadine might as well answer him. She opens her mouth.

'She's just coming,' screeches Enid, but it's too late. The knob turns, the door opens and there is Kai, tired and rumpled, a big green and gilt carrier-bag in his hand.

'What are you doing up here? I thought something had happened.'

'She only banged her head getting up, that's all it was,' says Enid, waving a damp wodge of cotton wool in the direction of Nadine's head. Nadine feels Kai's hands take the two sides of her temples. His hands aren't tender but they are firm and warm. They hold her so she can close her eyes and feel the pain go.

'You poor kid,' he says. His big warm body shuts out Enid. 'It's OK. Do you feel sick? Can you see OK?'

She nods, holding back tears.

'You poor kid,' he says again. 'How did it happen?'

'Hit my head on the shelf. I slipped.'

'It gave her a shock when she heard you calling,' says Enid.

'You mean this crap made you slip?' says Kai, stirring the rushes with the point of his shoe. A faint smell of decay rises where he bruises them. 'What's it doing on the floor?'

'Rushes,' mumbles Nadine. Talking makes her head hurt.

'It keeps the air pure,' says Enid.

'Jesus,' says Kai. 'Jesus. Come on, Nadine, let's get you downstairs.'

He won't talk to Enid. His eyes avoid her as he looks round her room with its piggled washing, its heaps of bedclothes and newspapers, its bunches of herbs drying from the ceiling, blodges of paint and spread-out jigsaw skies. He breathes in the smell of rushes, damp washing and old flesh. 'Get it cleaned up,' he says. He puts his arm round Nadine. They are two and Enid is one. Enid is small and wispy and worthless in her dirty nest. She's worse than a bird. Even a rickety old jackdaw won't foul its own nest. She'll be bringing vermin into the house next.

'Besides, it's a fire risk,' menaces Kai casually, as he steers Nadine towards the door. She goes with him, saying nothing. Her head hurts. She'd like to cry. It's the shock, she needs support. *You poor kid,* she says to herself, tasting the words. It's OK not to say anything to Enid. She's going to let herself go, leave the room and the story and let Kai take care of her.

Nadine yields. They walk down the stairs slowly, side by side, through the quiet blue darkness of the stairwell, with a cool breeze blowing through the open landing windows. The house is a ship again, creaking as the wind fills its sails and it tugs hard at its ropes, turned to the open sea, ready to leave behind the complications of land. Only now does Nadine realize how hot it was in Enid's room, how stuffy, claustrophobic even. And surely there was something odd about Enid's story. The Manchester Ladies. There was probably a grain of truth in it, but Enid must have made up the rest. It was just like a fairy story. Of course she makes up stories because she's lonely. Old people look back to the past. Enid's so proud of her memories. There's nothing magical about her. Only when you're with her, listening, the story floats like egg-white in water, transparent at first, then solid, white, whirling you round in its circle.

You need your memories when you get to my age.

Yes, Enid needs them; but I don't. I've got other things.

The carrier-bag crackles expensively as it bumps against Kai's leg.

'What have you got there?' asks Nadine.

'Don't talk, you'll make yourself dizzy. Wait until we're down-stairs.'

She wishes they could be forever descending the stairs together, touching the walls lightly, putting one foot down on the next wide shallow tread, then the other, then a pause, and again down. Nadine would never tire of it. Their heels sound soft and firm in the silence of the house. Down they go, down and down, half-circle by half-circle, fitted to one another, side against side, breath matched to breath, the breeze gently flattening their clothes against them. They are two and they are one. This is like the old days, before they came to this house, when she used to meet Kai in places which belonged to neither of them. They met in parks, in underpasses, in restaurants, in other people's flats, in country pubs where they left together to surge down country lanes in Kai's old van. The verges were white with cow-parsley, heavy with the weight of new leaves, insects, sap, nests. All the weight of summer. The old days when they were always just on the point of leaving for somewhere else. When she was glad to feel that Kai's silences held something that he knew and she did not. When it was such a simple matter for Kai to say goodbye and go, and leave her in his bare little flat where the telephone was always ringing. She didn't wonder where he'd gone, or how long it would be before he came back. She was unsuspicious. You can't get it back once it's gone, that stupor of trust.

*

In their room Kai switches on the light. The green and gold carrier-bag spills pale tissue on to their bed, and he guides Nadine's hand into the folds. Surprise. Don't look. See if you can guess what it is. The material feels like skin. She knows that touch: washed silk. The dress is creamy white, not pure white, and sleeveless, with a plain round neckline, short, shaped to skim breasts and waist and hips.

'Put it on,' says Kai.

Nadine peels off her top and leggings and kicks them into a heap. She lifts up her arms and the cool heavy silk slithers into place. She moves and the dress moves with her, caressing shoulders and thighs, coming close, swinging out. Her arms and legs feel as if the silk has polished them. Kai looks.

'You need tights. Those fine lycra tights. Or if you tan your legs more . . .'

'I could try a sunbed. Maybe there's one at the sauna. Vicki said –'

He tenses. His eyes flick from the dress to Nadine's face. 'Vicki? How do you know Vicki?'

'She called round this morning. She left you a message. It's downstairs somewhere. I wonder whether you can wash this, or does it have to be dry-cleaned? White's awkward . . .'

He puffs out his lips impatiently. 'Don't fuss about that. Do you think I can't afford dry-cleaners? What did she say – Vicki?'

'Nothing, really. I just thought of her because her tan looked like a sunbed tan. I could ask her,' says Nadine, looking straight at him. *Don't make me know things, and I won't ask about them.*

'I don't want you treating your skin like Vicki does. She's going to have a neck like a tortoise in a couple of years. Florida's full of women like that. Look at her skin when you see her.' He reaches out, traces the fine knob of bone on Nadine's wrist.

'We're going to go for a sauna. And I'm going to meet a friend of hers – someone called Lila.'

'My God, well, make it a short sauna. Lila'd bore the pants off anyone. Gab gab gab about her kid all the time.'

'Oh, it's only a sauna,' says Nadine lightly. His right hand is playing with the winder of his watch. Fiddle, fiddle, fiddle. 'I might not bother,' she says, walking around the room for the pleasure of feeling the dress move against her legs and breasts. He smiles, stops fiddling. So he didn't want her to meet Vicki. No need to think about that now.

'With a dress like that you need jewellery to set it off,' says Kai.

'A serious dress,' mocks Nadine.

'Plain gold. Nothing flashy. Though you can almost get away without anything. Turn around.'

Nadine turns like a statue on a plinth. At this moment she knows she's beautiful. Her beauty burns into Kai and leaves him weaker than she is. For once. She looks at him. He laughs at the sight of her, his mouth half open as if he's in pain. The way animals look when we say they're laughing.

'Do you like it?' asks Nadine.

He doesn't touch her. She has the power now. If she lifted her finger . . .

'Do you like it?' she asks again.

'You look –' he says, and the moment breaks. His attention snaps away from her, to the door. He's heard something.

'There's Tony,' he says. He goes to the door and calls down, 'Tony! Hey! Come up here!'

And there's Tony coming up the steps lightly, so much more lightly than Kai, and the sound of footsteps isn't frightening at all now that she's in her own room, not Enid's, dressed in the silk dress Kai has bought for her. Tony stands in the doorway, his eyes quick and sharp, going over her. This is how he likes a woman to look.

'She needs something with it,' he says finally. 'A necklace, and maybe a bracelet? Something heavy, you know? And different earrings.'

'Yeah, but it's fantastic, isn't it?' urges Kai.

'It's really classy. I always thought you had class, Nadine, but you don't make the best of yourself. It's the haircut does it as well. You could be anyone.'

She could go anywhere. She could be anyone. The dress slides over her body as intimately as a pair of hands. It's alive with changing light and it takes its curves from her breasts and hips. But it's subtle. It plays at making her unavailable and then she moves and there's a ghost of a chance.

'And shoes,' says Kai, considering the dress again.

'Yes. Nothing fancy. Her feet are a bit big, but in a classic style no one'll notice. Princess Di's got big feet.'

The two men look at one another. There's a charge in the air, but it's not the same charge as there was between her and Kai before Tony came in. She was in control then. She was making him feel things.

'Yeah,' says Kai. 'She could go anywhere like that. She's got style. I should've seen it before.'

Nadine wants to strip off the dress and put on the old leggings and singlet top she wears for juggling. Neither Kai nor Tony can juggle. But she also wants to wear the dress. She wants to find out more about what it does to her, and what she can do in it. It turns her into someone else entirely. She feels it herself, in the dress that is white but not too white, so that its folds hold a suggestion of candleglow, the dress that is short and sexy but also virginal, the dress that reveals the shape of her flesh for a moment at a time, so that each time it's as if they've never been seen before. It must have cost a lot of money. No two human beings could have sharper noses for the presence of money than Kai and Tony. It not only costs money, it suggests money. It suggests that Nadine herself is a polished container into which money has spilt all her life until it overflows and leaks out through her pores.

All this time she's been wearing jeans and leggings and sleeveless cotton dresses and they've never picked up the scent of money and style. Kai must have had some idea, or else why would he ever have bought the dress for her? Unless it was part of a deal. This immaculate thing might have come straight from a beaten-up warehouse, like the wine. But it fits. It fits perfectly. To put it on is to walk straight into another life and find that she's at home there. She's been given the code which opens security gates and gets you past doormen at clubs and parties. The guards are to look after her, not to keep her out. Nadine sits down on the bed. The dress makes her sit in a quite different way from usual, with her legs pressed lightly together and poised to one side. Kai and Tony smile.

'That old bitch up there in the attic, and Nadine here,' says Kai. 'What were you doing up there?'

She shakes her head. 'Nothing.'

'She's made for money,' says Tony. 'It's a crime she hasn't got any.'

'She's got everything she wants,' says Kai, and turns to Nadine. 'Haven't you?'

'No,' she says. 'I'm hungry. Bugger off, Tony. I'm going to get changed, then I'll cook us something.'

Later, as they lie tangled together, Kai rocks her gently.

'My baby. My baby. Go to sleep. My lovely one. My baby.' His hands cradle her skull, his fingers run through her feathery hair and touch her temples, smoothing lightly over the bruise which is forming there. 'How's your head now?'

'Fine,' she mumbles, 'I'm fine.'

'You must take care of yourself,' he lulls her, and his arms tighten. 'My baby, my lovely one.'

Drunk, Nadine closes her eyes. His endearments pour over her like oil, soothing, healing, melting into her ears while she feigns sleep.

Thirteen

The InterCity diesel glides past the photograph booth, past buckets of plastic-wrapped roses, past a mail-trolley and a skinny girl waving her baby at the train. It picks up speed as the engine runs clear of the platform into the early evening sun. The sun is full in Nadine's face. She shuts her eyes and leans back against the first-class seat. Just then the brakes come on hard. There's a harsh *wheeee* of metal and a stink of asbestos as the force of the brakes pins her back to her seat. The carriage bucks and judders, then stops. There's a second of silence. Everyone looks out of the windows. Someone starts to shout outside, a woman screams, 'Oh, no. Oh, no. Oh, no.'

A man in a suit gets up and strides down the aisle to the door. They hear the window go down, then more voices. The screaming sinks to low bubbling moans. A guard races past the window. The man in the grey suit comes back and looks down the train at the rows of faces, all turned to him. He knows the score.

'A girl tried to jump off the train while it was moving. Thought it was going to Penzance and panicked when she found she was on the wrong train.'

'Is she all right?'

'Was that her screaming?'

'Why didn't she speak to the guard?'

'No,' says the man. 'It was a woman who saw it happen.'

'Jesus,' says someone.

'She could have got off at the next stop.'

'It's only ten minutes to Bath.'

'How long are we going to be delayed? Did they say?'

'There've been all these deaths recently, people falling out of train doors. They've got to be careful.'

'Was she hurt?'

'Did you see?'

'It was a bit of a mess,' says the man, and he sits down, unfolds his newspaper and disappears behind it. A woman half rises from her seat, gropes behind her for her handbag, says, 'Oh, dear. Perhaps I ought to go and see . . .'

'Why? Are you a doctor?'

'No, but I've done my Red Cross.'

'The train door swung back and caught her head. I doubt if Red Cross is going to help.' The man in the grey suit rattles his newspaper into shape. He is very pale. 'They've sent for an ambulance. More harm's done by unqualified people interfering in these situations.'

The woman flushes. 'Well, I know *that*. It's the first thing we're taught.'

Tony catches Nadine's eye and the corners of his mouth turn down in a quick grimace.

'I'll get us coffee. This is going to take for ever.'

But it doesn't. A few minutes later they hear the ambulance. Heads poke out of doors all down the train. The buffet window mirrors the ambulance's revolving blue flash.

'They'll be taking her straight to the Infirmary,' says the Red Cross woman confidently. Grey suit taps his newspaper. Further down the carriage a young man with a ponytail goes on talking into his portable telephone. It's the same call he's been making right through the accident. His voice is loud in the silent carriage.

'Yeah, just a hold-up. Go on giving me the figures back to March. Yeah, yeah, give me March again. I lost week two.'

The train squeaks, groans and begins to slide mousily along the platform. Nadine holds herself braced. Finger by finger, she makes her muscles relax until her hands are heavy as stones in her lap.

'It's the driver I feel sorry for,' says Red Cross.

Tony returns with a bag of plastic cups, plastic stirrers, small vials of milk, sugar sachets, coffee, brandy miniatures and a cartwheel chocolate-chip cookie. He lays the drinks out on the table between them, and folds Nadine's cookie into a paper napkin for her. He pours a small bottle of brandy into his own black coffee and offers one to Nadine. She shakes her head.

'Yeah, better not,' he says. 'You'll only go to sleep.' Nadine picks up her cookie and bites. It explodes into crumbs all over her black linen coat. She stands up, wriggles, and the crumbs shower on to the carpet. Grey suit watches as she sits down again, spotless, smoothing out the coat behind her so as not to crush it. The black linen coat is her own. She bought it two days ago from an antique clothing shop, the day she got paid. It is cool and heavy and has the natural glassiness of linen. The collar is wide and embroidered with thick black corded silk and tiny jet beads. It's an evening coat, thirties probably, to judge from the buttons. If she sits carefully it doesn't crease too badly. Anyway, creasing is part of linen. Under it she wears the white silk dress. Tony's taking her to a business dinner with one of his clients. They'll dine late, and stay at an hotel overnight. Tony has a business meeting in the morning, and Nadine's going to buy shirts for Kai with cash he has given her. Her hair is newly washed and shiny. The big collar of the coat loosely shadows her neck. She wears gold studs in her ears, and a plain round gold necklace, both bought by Kai two days ago. They are made of old dark gold. She's spent most of the day getting ready, fixing elastoplast to her heels where her new shoes pinch, laddering tights and buying more, following step-by-step instructions in this month's *Vogue* on the natural summer face. It has taken her more than an hour to achieve the effortless look of a woman who wears no make-up. She's dredged her face with loose powder, then buffed almost all of it off; she's lined her eyes with grey kohl and smudged away all but a trace; she's plucked her eyebrows and thickened them with pencil. Her lashes are slicked with transparent lash-gloss, because mascara is too obvious. Nadine feels like a stranger to herself. She much prefers the kind of make-up Cathy wears when she goes to the Ring: a deliberate, dramatic mask.

Tony wears a very plain charcoal suit. But he doesn't look good today. He keeps yawning. His skin is waxy, faintly glistening with sweat. Still, he's being nice to Nadine. He likes the look of her opposite, upright and elegant. He can talk to this Nadine as if he doesn't know her, yet the whole thing's spiced by the number of times he's seen her stagger downstairs in the mornings to make coffee, rubbing sleep out of her eyes. It excites him to sit opposite her and know other men are looking at her, and also to know what her legs and arse look like in that big droopy t-shirt Kai has to put up with in bed at night. He can just see a slip of white in the neck of her coat where she's unbuttoned it. Perfect. Dark and severe outside, virginal inside the coat, and underneath that a hint of sexiness which is a lot more than bridal. It's going to work like magic. Nadine makes you think of money. The kind of girl you could take anywhere. She's not his type. But he's known for weeks that she'd be perfect, if he could only get the two of them together. Seeing her in the bedroom, in that white dress, he knew he'd got to move fast before someone else did. Kai's been giving definite signals that it's time Nadine started to pay her way. Of course it's much better if it doesn't come from Kai. Let Tony break the ice. Kai doesn't have to spell it out, not after all the time we've been together, thinks Tony. Yeah, I can read him like a book.

Tony believes in fate. Or why would Nadine come to the house, just when Paul Parrett was getting restless? He'd known they weren't keeping him happy. He wants a lot more than they've been able to come up with. He'll be off elsewhere if they don't watch it. Janine's a nice kid, but that face of hers gets you down. Blank. Ready for anything, OK, but that's because there's nothing much there in the first place. There's something a bit frightening about Janine, when you come down to it. You could tell her to do *anything* and she'd do it. Clients think that's what they want, but two or three sessions is the most they can take of Janine. Who did he have before Janine? Oh, yeah, Susie. Susie was just starting off then, and she'd done very well. Very nicely. That portfolio of hers was mindblowing. She knew more about bondage than anyone in the business. Trouble with Susie was she had no imagination. To get a man like Paul Parrett really interested in you, you got to have a bit of imagination. A bit of mystery. He looks across at Nadine. She is looking out of the window, showing the pure line of her profile. God knows what she's thinking about. He bought her a magazine, but she hasn't opened it.

There's got to be something special about the girl, something that makes you watch her and not anyone else. It's not really looks, or not just looks. Something that makes you think about her when she's not there, till you're hooked. And Nadine's got it, whatever it is. He ought to know. So take the risk. Take Nadine. She doesn't know anything – or not much anyway. This'll be her first time. She'll be able to give Paul Parrett something that just won't be there in a couple of years. He's seen it happen before. They go dead. They get like Janine.

'Thanks for the coffee, Tony,' says Nadine.

He looks at his watch. 'Nearly made up the time,' he says, 'should do it by the time we get to Paddington.'

'Jesus, Tony!'

'Don't talk like that, what's the matter with you?'

'That girl nearly got killed, that's all. So what if we're ten minutes late?'

Tony shrugs. But it's quite nice, really, the way she says things like that. That's the sort of thing some clients like. Class. He looks at his watch again. Just like the way she went racing upstairs to show the old woman what she looked like all dressed up, while he and Kai waited in the hall. Paul Parrett ought to have seen that.

'We'll get a taxi straight to the restaurant,' he says.

'It'll be quite late, won't it, by the time we eat?'

'We're meeting Mr Parrett there at ten. If he can get away

from the House . . . or else he'll join us later. Have something now if you're hungry. I'll get it.'

'No, thanks. But I'd like a drink.' A tiny pause; then, 'Right.'

Nadine holds up her gin and watches the landscape through it. Evening light slopes richly on the bare Wiltshire Downs as the train flees eastward. Kai's been right across Russia by train. Day after day of it, drinking tea in a compartment, sleeping for hours because there was nothing else to do. He didn't say much about it, but then Kai's no good at describing things. But one thing stayed in her mind. He said that one morning they'd stopped very early at a little wooden station in the middle of nowhere. Siberia perhaps, but it wasn't winter so there was no snow. There was grass blowing by a fence, and blue flowers growing through the platform planking. And he'd wanted to get out, he said. It was strange how strong it was, suddenly, the urge he had to jump down from the train on to the low platform, and to walk off, just to keep walking through the long grass until the fences dwindled away and there was nothing but grass and a low scrub of silver birches and the soft moving of the wind around him. When was it that he'd talked about it? It must have been in the van one day, when they'd stopped the engine and the space between them was slowly filling up with heat. And she'd thought, one day we'll go there.

The farmland flashes by, every inch of it owned and tended. She drinks. Gin smells of childhood. She remembers the clear stream of it running into the grown-ups' glasses while Lulu flopped on the floor, tired out, ready to go to sleep soon. Six o'clock. Mother never had a drink until six o'clock.

'Once you give way . . .' she said. But at six o'clock it was allowed. Daddy was home with his smell of trains and cigarette smoke. He would put Lulu to bed. Mother kicked off her shoes and hoicked her legs up on to the sofa. Her tights rasped as she crossed her ankles, and Nadine shivered. Mother put up a hand and eased off her spectacles so that she couldn't see Nadine or Lulu or anything any more.

'You're all just a blur,' she told Nadine. But Nadine could see Mother's face clearly. It was white, like a crumpled-up orange blossom from the garden, and there were dug-in red marks on her nose from the spectacles. Daddy took Mother's hand and rocked it through the air, backwards and forwards.

'What a day. What – a – day,' said Mother faintly, sucking gin.

'My poor baby,' said Daddy, taking hold of one of her feet, caressing the shimmering tights Nadine hated.

The ticket-collector sways down the aisles, printing data on to tickets. The Red Cross woman lays an arm on his sleeve, whispers questions. Nadine turns away, not wanting to hear his answers. The man's face is pale, but probably it is always pale. His light-lashed blue eyes don't meet anyone's as he hands tickets back to Tony.

'I might as well keep mine,' says Nadine. 'You know how they sometimes stop you in the corridors.'

Tony unfolds his wallet again, hands the OUT and RETURN tickets to Nadine. She looks at the price and thinks of what she could have done with the difference between the first-class fare and a cheap day-return. But no, they're staying overnight. Still, on her own she'd have caught the last train back and saved the hotel too. Kai and Tony don't think like that. Even though the client's not coming anywhere near Paddington, it's important to travel first class.

The gin's making her feel wonderful. If only it was Kai sitting opposite instead of Tony. It would be like when she first knew Kai and they sat opposite one another in pubs and talked. Pubs were new to her too, because she was only fifteen then. They never seem to have any time now, except in bed, and there they don't talk. Or was it really the same then, only I didn't notice so much, because I was younger? I didn't have any idea about what to expect.

The train goes faster and faster, bucketing on its long straight line to London. Grey suit is asleep now, the newspaper drooping from his hands, his head yawing as the train leaps and plunges. Red Cross has slumped down in her seat, and the portable telephone is silent. Only Tony sits relaxed and upright, looking out of the window. Nadine leans forward, buoyed up by the clear stream of gin in her veins. If only the windows would open – she'd love to have the wind rushing in through her hair. But everything's sealed, and the carriage smells of bacon rolls and brake linings. They're beginning to slow down. There's the first reddish stain of London. Grass grows paler and scrubbier. Nadine thinks of the fields Enid talked about, with the long summer grass swaying, and Sukey and Caro wading through it. Enid loved Sukey, you could tell. She talked about that field of grass in the same way as Kai talked of the blue flowers pushing up through the grey planks of the station platform. Lost and long ago. Or maybe you never had it anyway. Why did Caro get her name in the papers? What did she do? She must ask Enid for the rest of the story.

These fields aren't really fields any more, just sites waiting to be built on, with sale hoardings facing the train. The straight line from the west complicates itself into a maze of silver rods which cross and flicker as they run off into the suburbs. The train canters into London, clicking over the points.

The station is packed with foreign students butting everyone with their back packs. The students lower their heads and manoeuvre like a ballet of bulls. Their strong bare arms and legs glisten with tan, sun-oil and sweat. Nadine walks through them, keeping close to Tony to avoid being buffeted by red and orange nylon. A young blonde girl waving a plan of London laughs, so close that Nadine can look down her throat, then turns back to her gang.

It's nearly dusk as their taxi accelerates out of Paddington. Nadine pushes down the window. It's warm. The air's turning navy and lights are springing on everywhere, yellow and white, spilling out like the shaggy petals of chrysanthemums. Neon signs needle the air and laser lights ripple sculpture above the doorways of the big shops. London's just like a foreign country tonight, warm and glowing. Café doors open on to pavements. People lounge over beers which sweat with cold through the glass. The taxi swoops round a square where a party's going on in the private communal gardens. Golden lanterns burn against heavy-leaved plane trees. Nadine glimpses a small red-striped tent, a long table covered with a white cloth which touches the grass, and then the taxi bowls on. Cries and laughter follow them like the sound of a plane which has already passed overhead.

Everyone's out in the streets. There can't be a soul left in the big dark houses with their open windows. They're out on the streets in the soupy heat of evening, when the pavement is pulsing back the day's sun, but there's no glare and you can walk through blue intimate dusk for hours. The city is more alive than it ever is in daytime, and Nadine's skin prickles as she sits forward on the edge of her seat, tasting the smells of beer and burgers and dust and flesh, drinking in the beat of light and movement. Tony is a shadow at her side and she doesn't have to think about him. He's just there, taking her somewhere, leaving her free to think of nothing but each moment as they fly through it. People stroll four abreast on the pavements dressed in t-shirts and scraps of skirt or shorts. A girl walks fast, her face tilted up and her eyes inward, shutting out the street, thinking only of where she's going. Faces loom to the taxi window as it slows at crossings, then shrink back into the crowd as it gathers speed. The crowds thin as the roads become straighter and faster. Tony leans forward and the taxi-driver nods.

'We're early,' says Tony. 'We'll go and have a drink first.'

The taxi stops by a dull small door. A flicker of cash, and they're out in the street while the taxi pivots and disappears.

'Here we are,' says Tony.

'Is it the restaurant?'

'No, it's a club. We'll just have a drink here. If that's OK?' he adds, fractionally too late.

The club is a small room, darkly wallpapered, with little spindly chairs and tables and a small stage at one end on which nothing at all is happening. Three men in dark formal suits sit at one table, keeling forward slightly towards the empty stage. It's one of those rooms where something has just happened, or is about to happen, but it won't happen as long as you are there, waiting. Although there's a fan in the ceiling the air is heavy with smoke and whisky. A solid fortyish woman in black sits in the corner, adding up figures. She looks up and nods at Tony. Tony and Nadine sit on the uncomfortable chairs and a few minutes later a bottle of champagne is brought to their table in a bucket of ice by a sleepy-looking girl in red lycra. The three men at the other table gape across for a second at the dull thud of the cork, then the wine foams dutifully over the rim of the bottle as if it understands the stern need to give an appearance of pleasure. It gets its due second of attention, no more. Tony sips the champagne with a neutral expression, calls the girl back and asks for whisky.

'It's a sort of rule, I suppose, buying this stuff,' says Nadine.

There are six cashews in a sea of elderly peanuts. Nadine picks them out. Not bad, not too stale.

'Don't eat those – we'll be having dinner soon,' says Tony.

'What's this restaurant like?'

'Nothing like this, don't worry. I just come here sometimes. To see who's around.'

'Or who isn't,' remarks Nadine, looking around the room.

'Yeah, you're right, but then that's the point. Trisha's got a good business going. Nothing flash,' he says, nodding towards the woman in black. 'You got to respect her. She's made something of herself. Like my client, the one you're going to meet. You'll like him. 'Course he gets stressed out, all these politicians do. Well, they're watching their backs all the time. That's why he likes to relax. I want you two to get to know each other, that's why I brought you along.'

'I've never met a politician before,' says Nadine. She watches red lycra sluice whisky into the three glasses opposite. The slow men in suits come to life a bit, like lions in the zoo at the approach of meat. But they are lions who are too jaded by regular meals of dead flesh to do more than pantomime the instincts they've lost long ago.

None the less the whisky disappears fast. The three men relapse into silence and the whinging of the fan becomes the loudest thing in the room. The air's extraordinarily dry – or perhaps there simply isn't enough of it. Nadine licks her lips.

'Yeah, you're going to like Paul Parrett. Kai wants you to get to know people.'

'Oh, come on, Tony! Kai's not interested in my friends, you know that. That's why I don't bring them home. I mean I can understand it, he's tired, it doesn't bother me at all. I can always see people at work.'

'Nah, it's got nothing to do with people at work. This is Paul Parrett. You won't meet someone like him hanging around the Warehouse counting his money out of a little black purse. He's made something of himself. That's the sort of people you want to meet. People with ambitions. You're not going to spend the rest of your life taking cinema tickets, are you? You'll be seventeen soon.'

'Well, it's a job,' says Nadine.

Tony taps his glass. 'You're wasting your time. All you are is an usherette.'

'We're not called usherettes, Tony. That'd be sexist.'

'Oh, yeah. Because it's an arts centre and they're all artists, really, aren't they? Or going to be. Like that Chris you talk about. Always next year, when he gets a grant, when he gets a break. Only it never happens. He'd be better off learning to cut hair properly, like Francesca. I've got a lot of respect for her. She doesn't go round calling herself an artist. She cuts hair.'

'What's the matter with you, Tony? You don't even know Chris.'

'I want to make you see you got choices. A girl like you. You can go where you want.'

'You make it sound so easy.'

'Yeah, because it *is* easy!' He's leaning forward now. 'Most people don't have the guts to try and get what they want. In case they don't make it. They'd rather kid themselves they could have done if they'd wanted. But that's good. It makes it easier for us, because we know what we want.'

'That's you and Kai. Maybe I'm not like that.'

He sits back, sips whisky, looks at her. The black sheath of linen, the white sheath of silk. The stubborn sideways face he'd slap if she was a couple of years younger.

'You don't know what you're like, Nadine,' he says, dropping money on the table. 'All you let yourself think about is juggling and that old woman. Make sure you don't find out when it's too late. When nothing's on offer any more.'

A shape stirs by the doorway as they go out of the club. A hand comes up and a voice says, 'Got any change?'

Only a kid. He looks fourteen, and he's shaved his head, but a blondish fuzz is beginning to grow. There's a blue tattooed rose on the crown of his skull. His eyes are big and fixed on something just behind Nadine's shoulder. He's pale and the street-lights cast odd shadows under his eyes, but his face is still beautiful.

'Got any change?'

She fumbles in her bag. Tony waits. Mid-step, on his way. Then he looks at the boy's face. Nadine tries one zip compartment, then another. She hasn't brought her purse, because it's too heavy for this new evening bag, so her money is loose. Tony looks down at the boy, at the forehead, the lips, the tired blue eyes. He touches Nadine's shoulder, says, 'Wait here a minute,' turns, and goes back into the club.

She's caught. She can't just drop the pound coin into the boy's hand and move on, because she doesn't know where she's going. The boy's looking straight at her now. They can't stand here staring like this until Tony comes back. One of them is going to have to speak. She gives him the pound and he puts it carefully into a buttoned pocket of his army-style shirt.

'You ought to go to a hostel,' she says. 'It's dangerous. You're really young to be sleeping out on your own.' A flicker of glee crosses his face. 'Go on, how old d'you think I am?'

'I don't know – sixteen?' she flatters, remembering how kids always want to be taken for older than they are.

'I'm thirteen and a half. Everyone thinks I'm older.'

'Why don't you go to a hostel? You could tell them how old you are. They'd have to find a place for you.'

'Yeah, right, they'd find a place for me. They'd put me straight into care, wouldn't they? You don't know what it's like. I can handle myself. I got friends.'

The little street suddenly looks dark and threatening. The boy's cocky white face in the club light is all wrong – he ought to get away . . . When the light shines on him like that you can see he's just a kid, a beautiful kid. And it's not safe being beautiful out here on the streets. His thighs show through the slashes in his jeans.

'Where're your friends? You ought to be with them. It's dangerous on your own. There're all sorts of people around . . .'

'I know that. I'm not fucking stupid. But if you're on your own, people give you money. Like you and your boyfriend. You wouldn't of stopped if I'd been with a gang. Has he gone back to the gents?'

And then there's Tony behind her again, and behind him Trisha, and two of the whisky-drinking men.

'He's just going,' says Nadine quickly. 'I've told him he shouldn't hang around here, not outside a club.'

But Trisha's in no hurry to move the boy on. She moves up to him, scrutinizes him in the lamplight.

'You on your own?' she asks him.

'No. I got my friends. They're just round the corner,' he says quickly.

'Are they now,' she says, looking up the narrow deserted street with its black warm shadows falling so heavily they blot out everything. 'Just around the corner? Well, they're none of my business. But I might be able to help you, if you're a sensible boy. It's not safe out on the streets. You ought to get one of those Alsatians . . .'

'I'd like a dog,' the boy admits eagerly. 'This bloke I know's getting me a lurcher pup.'

'Not as good as Alsatians, though, are they? For keeping people away. I've got a dog of my own, as it happens. If you like we might be able to come to an arrangement.'

The two men, having looked, melt back into the doorway, back to their whisky.

'I'm a bit short-handed at the moment,' confides Trisha. 'One of my girls hasn't been well. I need someone to walk the dog for me – do a bit of work in the kitchens once we get you cleaned up.'

'Like a job, you mean? What'd you pay me?'

'We'd have to come to an arrangement, like I said. But there's a room with it – and your three meals.'

Her dark, wheedling, curiously insistent eyes are fixed on the boy's. He wriggles a little on his mat of cardboard.

'Come on, Nadine,' says Tony. 'We got to be going. It's nearly ten.'

'No, wait –' says Nadine, but the boy turns a repelling blue stare on her. Does she think she's bought him with her pound coin? Is this any of her business?

'It's not the sort of thing you want to talk about out here on the street,' says Trisha. 'There's no privacy, is there? Come inside.' Tony touches Nadine's arm.

'I don't want to keep him waiting,' he warns, and reluctantly she yields to the soft pressure of his hand. They start to move off down the street. She wants to say something, to call back to the boy even if it's only goodbye, but there's no one to say goodbye to. She doesn't know any of them. She doesn't know the boy's name.

'We can pick up a taxi at the end of the street,' says Tony.

Fourteen

Enid hums as she skirts the side of the square, swaying slightly, her face silly with pleasure. They don't know a real song when they hear it these days. Michael Desmoulins's 'Surprise' glides through Enid's head, perfectly on the beat in each bar. It must be years since she's heard it. These young girls like Nadine don't know what they've missed. '*Allons . . .*' chunters Enid, knocking into the iron railing, bouncing off, renegotiating the pavement corner. Just across here now. Ooops. Lights on. So you go quiet, Enid girl, quiet-as-a-little-mouse. Got to get the key in, though. Where's the bugger? Ooh, scrabble, scrabble, how I hate this bloody lock. I ought to put a bit of wire round this key, then it wouldn't slip in too far. There's a trick to it. There's a trick to everything.

There. No one about. So *up* the stairs we go, making sure to hold on to the handrail except somebody's yanked it off the wall. Good girl. And up on to the landing, have a little rest before going up the next flight. That's right, have a nice little sit-down, you deserve it. Now if Nadine was here, we could have a chat.

But she's not. Gone to London with Tony, the silly girl. All dressed up. Dressed to kill. Though it was very plain to my mind, black and white. But stylish, you've got to admit. And it's the sort of style they'd like, Tony and Kai, being foreigners. People get the wrong idea about Italians, they think they like the flash look. But they don't. Look at their own women. Finns I wouldn't know about – if he *is* Finnish. How would I know? I only go by what Nadine tells me.

Oh, he looked *very* pleased with himself tonight. I wonder why? When the cat's away . . . But she did look lovely. No wonder they say youth is wasted on the young. If I looked like that you wouldn't catch me wasting it on Tony's trips to London. Right, come on, Enid, time to get moving. Can't spend the night here.

That laugh. It's her again. *She's* here. In their bedroom too; well, I did try to tell Nadine. But no one listens when they're young. It'd be me she'd blame for telling her, not him for doing it. Oh, they think themselves safe enough in there. Nadine's away in London, Tony's away in London. Not that Tony'd care what Kai got up to, from what I've seen of him. Very much a business point of view, Tony's. You get to recognize the type.

Only me here. And I'd better make myself scarce before one of them comes out. After all, she's flesh and blood in spite of appearances, that Vicki. She'll need to go to the toilet some time, she'd piss bile, that one. They won't hear me, not with all the laughing. Cackling's more the word for it, and a very ugly sound if she wants my opinion. Not a peep out of Kai, though – it's all her. They'll have been drinking. She's the sort who gets noisy when she's been drinking. Look who's talking. What gets me is the way he acts so holy and gets Nadine to do his dirty work for him. Oh, she *was* embarrassed, but she thought she'd got to say it. '*Enid, do you think you could be a bit quieter when you come back from the pub? You see, Kai's got a bit of a thing about people drinking – it upsets him when it's people in the house. I mean, I know you only have a couple of ginger wines . . .*'

Well, as long as he's not such a b.f. as to let her stay the night. Nadine'll know, she's bound to. You can't hide the smell of another woman. And it always looks fishy when a man starts changing the sheets after you've been away. Except Kai's supposed to have a thing about clean sheets anyway, which is handy in the circumstances.

'*Kai can't bear to wear things twice. He has to have clean clothes every day. He's so fastidious. I suppose quite a lot of people are like that really, aren't they, Enid?*'

I should think quite a lot of people would be like that, dear, if they went where Kai goes, and did what Kai does. You've obviously never read *Macbeth*. But I don't say anything. I've no proof, and anyway, what's the point? It's no good telling people things until they're ready to hear them. Let her believe all that stuff about sheets and her Kai being fastidious.

It'll be a miracle if those two in there don't hear my knees cracking. My joints go off like pistol shots, even when I've only been sitting five minutes. Now up we go, one at a time and take it steady. Pity there's no carpet. If we had a bit of carpet no one'd ever hear me. I might as well not be there at all. That carpet at the Manchester Ladies. Nearly there. That's the way. I'll have another sit-down before I make a cup of tea. Just a small cup. You don't want to be washing out sheets again, do you, Enid?

Lucky I didn't tell Nadine what happened to Caro. But she's bound to ask. Why did I tell her any of it? I should have kept it to myself, the way I always have, till it's just words you can say over in the night when you hear noises going on downstairs. Or that woman laughing.

'*Manchester Ladies. Manchester Ladies.*' I say it over to myself, and I see Sukey's sweet smile and I feel her combing my hair like she was my mother. No, much more than my mother. I don't think of what happened after. What's the good? And who's to say that terrible things are any more real than good ones, just because they get into the newspapers? I know what was real. The cab and the rain and the Manchester Ladies. And Sukey in her kimono, then me in her arms. That's the sort of thing that never gets wiped out, no matter what happens after.

'*Till next time, darling.*'

Darling, she always called me that. And *sweetheart*. No one'd ever used those words to me before. Nor afterwards. All the Americans called us honey. 'Hon', Clyde used to say, but it didn't mean much. There wasn't any feeling in the words. You can always hear it if it's there, like something alive in the voice. When Sukey spoke I used to melt inside. When I talked to her on the telephone, it was, 'See you tomorrow, then, darling. Good night, sweetheart.' Next time. Come again. And I did. Again and again and again. There was never a time like it. She bought a tobacco-brown silk dressing-gown for me, because it went with my hair. 'You look marvellous, darling. If you went out on the streets like this you'd stop the traffic.' But we weren't out on the streets, we were on Sukey's bed and I was curled up in the silk dressing-gown and it slipped open over my legs and then she was touching me *there*. I didn't even have words for the places she touched or the things she did. *Down there*, that was what mother called it. *Make sure you keep yourself clean down there, Enid.* We had to hide our sanitary napkins so Father and the boys never saw them. We'd slip past with our brown paper packets like thieves. It was a crime to be a woman. Never with Sukey, though.

'Oh, darling, you're just exactly like silk. I can't tell which is silk and which is you.'

She taught me all the words. I used to wonder how she knew them. And she'd talk straight out about things I'd only ever heard whispered about. She'd had a baby – just one. She knew how to stop having them. I didn't know anything about things like that. People thought it wasn't decent.

Sukey's bed was a world of its own. Once I was there I'd forget everything, even what time of day it was. Except suddenly I'd notice things more sharply than I'd ever noticed them before. The colour the sky really was at dawn. There was a blackbird in a quince tree below her window, and I got to know every note it sang. I could have written it down, if I'd known how to write music. The only way you knew time was passing was when the sun came round to the window late in the afternoon. Sometimes it woke me up and I'd feel it on my face. I'd look up and Sukey would be there.

One week she had a bowl of Kent cherries by the bed and we ate them all day long until there was a heap of dry white stones piled up like a volcano. There were things I'd never tasted:

melon, and white peaches, and crystallized ginger. Then we'd bath. We were always going to get up and go out somewhere and have dinner, but it never seemed to happen. I wasn't hungry anyway. Sukey would walk about naked – at first I was too shy even to look at her, then after a few weeks I was doing it myself. I'd tie my hair up so it wouldn't get wet, then after the bath I'd powder myself all over – Sukey had a bowl of Floris powder by the bath and a big powder puff. I loved the smell and I'd always use far too much so that it flew out in a cloud round me - then I'd let my hair come down over my shoulders and sit cross-legged on Sukey's bed and she'd look at me and I'd smile at her. What a change. A changed girl, that's what I was.

'Darling. Sweetheart. Keep still – let me –'

And I would.

Then it all went wrong. She was such a silly girl, Caro. Yes, that's the word for her. Silly. Though that's not the word they used in the newspapers. They called her evil. But it was silliness to be jealous of Sukey. Sukey wasn't the kind of person you needed to be jealous about. It didn't matter what she gave, there'd always be plenty left. She was a bit like the sea – if she went out, she'd come in again, you could be sure of it. Of course she was naughty. Poor Caro, really, you had to feel sorry for her. Even I did. But she fooled herself. Sukey had never pretended Caro was the only one for her. She wasn't going to be either, no matter what she did, no matter how much she raged and begged. I suppose what I saw was Caro realizing it. Caro couldn't pretend any longer that she was going to have Sukey all to herself, the way she wanted. Sukey was never going to draw the curtains and lock her door with Caro inside and be glad that the rest of the world was shut out. It wasn't in her nature. I could tell that straight away, so why couldn't Caro? She wanted all of Sukey. But Sukey wanted all of everything.

That's what it was all about, the Manchester Ladies. I don't think Caro understood when they started up the club with April and the others. She thought it was going to make them more of a couple because they had created something together. But that wasn't the way it turned out, and it couldn't have been, ever. It was a place for people like Sukey who wanted everything and didn't mind where it came from. And the thing about Sukey that made her different was that she gave everything too. Nothing was held back. Caro would have glanced at me in that shop doorway and put me straight out of her mind. But not Sukey. She brought me back out of the rain in her cab. That was what the Manchester Ladies was for; at least, that was Sukey's idea of it. But not many people would've thought like that, if they already had a warm place of their own to go back to, and friends, and someone to love them. Fires, that thick green carpet, tall lilies in jars, brandy . . . she had everything. Tea that tasted like smoke in cups so thin you could see your finger through them. I had to learn to like it. Lapsang Souchong. Sukey had everything already, according to Caro – what did she want with more? But Sukey had to open the door, never mind if it let in the wind and the rain until there wasn't any warm place any more.

She showed me the secret door and then she opened it. You'd never believe how beautiful it was inside. I'm not talking about the Manchester Ladies now. It was Sukey herself; her body, her heart. What she was. Oh, she used to make me laugh. Laugh and laugh – we didn't care who heard us. But she could be so gentle. Some people would say bad things about Sukey, because she was older and she had all that money. And I know I was lovely then, though no one else knows that now; not a soul in the world. But what does it matter? Everything goes away. Sukey knew that, but Caro didn't. Sukey never made use of me.

Caro was always watching us when the three of us were together. You're cruel when you're young, you don't think. You don't care for anyone else when you're happy; it's one rule for you, and another for them. Or else no rules at all. I was happy. I didn't mind people seeing I was happy. I wanted Caro to feel that she was outside, just people, and that I was – well, what? Inside. With Sukey. I was as bad as Caro, really, only I couldn't feel jealous of her. Perhaps that was the worst thing I did to her, not being jealous of her. If we're talking about cruelty. And when it comes to a murder trial, you've got to talk about it.

That description in the newspapers. Those things they put in, they never think of the people who've to read them. I suppose you can't blame the newspapers. I'd read plenty of murders before and forgotten them five minutes afterwards, because they were just stories to me. But when I read those newspaper reports about Caro and Sukey and what Caro had done to her I felt like I was drinking something down so cold there's a part of me that's never been warm since. Not even when I was pregnant. It turned into another sort of loneliness, that was all. People say having a baby changes you. I thought it would change me and make me stop loving Sukey and hating Caro. After all, it had been seven years. There I'd be at those bloody clinics they used to have, sitting there with my knickers down. It wasn't very respectable then, being pregnant, even if you were married. And I wasn't married. Girls these days wouldn't believe how they used to talk to you when you weren't married. I was a fool not to buy a ring from Woolworth's and say my husband had been killed on D-Day. But I didn't. I couldn't be bothered, really. I didn't care enough about what people thought. I'd got a bit of money saved: we earned plenty in the war. And I knew it would be over soon, and I'd move away and no one would know. Trail trail trail back to my room, pushing my shopping basket on wheels, wondering if the butcher would be able to let me have a kidney with my mince. Lucky the house was nearly falling down with bomb damage so that the landlord didn't kick me out. He was glad enough to get any rent. Offal was said to be good for you. You couldn't get anything: it was worse than the war. Austerity, that's what they called it. I was always hungry. I didn't know if the baby was growing properly. They didn't bother telling you much at the clinic in those days. They knew what was good for you. I can't really remember what it was like having him. I've never talked about it to anyone. Perhaps that's why it doesn't seem real. I like to tell Nadine about him, just so someone else will know when I die. It doesn't seem as real as me being young and on my own, outside the Manchester Ladies and thinking it didn't look anything special, feeling a bit disappointed even though Sukey was there at my side. And here I am in my little room on my own, just like I was then. You can't escape from things. You can never get away.

'*The body had lain undiscovered for two days and the severity of the head injuries added to the difficulties of identification. Dental records showed . . .*'

They knew it was Sukey. They must have known, even though they said she'd given a different name at the farm when she rented the cottage. I don't know why she did that, but Sukey loved secrets. She gave her grandmother's name, so it was easy enough to trace her once they put their minds to it. And someone like Sukey has always got things with her: jewellery, cheque-book, letters. *Lain undiscovered for two days*. I felt sick when I read it. When she was at home Sukey always had to take the telephone off the hook when we wanted to be alone, otherwise it'd be ringing all the time. And telegrams, and people coming with flowers. And in those days the post came I don't know how many times a day, and there were always letters for her. She used to leave them lying about open. Anyone could read them.

Sukey, do come . . . Sukey, darling, we're absolutely dying to see you . . . Sukey, you were a fiend not to come, I'm awfully cross with you . . . Sukey, will you be at Eloise's house-party? We're absolutely dying to see you . . .

That was the way they wrote, the kind of people Sukey knew. That was a long time ago, though, I expect things have changed. All the letters would be pushed together on Sukey's writing desk until some of them slid off and fell down the back. I don't know if she bothered to pick them up and answer them.

Two days undiscovered. It was almost the worst thing. I just couldn't believe it. Not Sukey. I kept thinking, what if she hadn't died straight away, what if she'd been crawling round, crying out, going in smaller and smaller circles till she couldn't move any more. I'd seen a dog do that when it was dying. They would have found her less than an hour later if she'd been at home. But she was away, in the little cottage she and Caro had rented in the Lake District.

'It's not even on a road, Enid. You have to walk up a track, about two miles on from the farm where we get milk and butter. They bring the luggage up from the station on their trap and Mrs Garside has got the most angelic daughter who comes up and cleans when we're not there. Exactly like Puck. It's absolute heaven. No servants, no bells. All you hear is the birds, and the sheep on the hills. No telephone, no callers ... You'll have to come, Enid. You'll love it. I can't wait for you to see it. And there's the most adorable pump in the yard, like a toy pump. I can't squeeze *one drop* of water out of it, but Caro got the knack of it straight away. You've never felt water like it. It's just like silk. Caro wants to grow vegetables – there's a bit of garden with a wall round it. I can't imagine ever leaving here. I could spend my whole life in a cottage like this.'

I didn't mind that Caro was there with her. Caro had said she wasn't going to sleep with Sukey any more, until she stopped sleeping with me. Well, now I can imagine what it must have cost Caro to say that, how hurt she must have been. Because you could see her wanting to touch Sukey all the time, wanting to put her arms round her and hide her so that no one else could even see her. Perhaps she thought it would bring Sukey to her senses, and she wouldn't want me any more if she couldn't have Caro. But it didn't work like that, not with Sukey. She just said that if that was how Caro felt, then she wouldn't argue with her. But she was always there if Caro changed her mind. At the time I thought Caro was lucky that Sukey was so generous. Now I'm not so sure.

Caro could have escaped after it happened. She had money,

she could have gone abroad. But you'd know she wouldn't, if you knew Sukey. Caro wouldn't be able to leave her, even though she was the one who'd killed her. They found Caro in a barn just a few fields away from the cottage. She'd been writing and writing and there were sheets of paper all round her, mostly about Sukey. Then she'd swallowed some sleeping-stuff she took, and left a note to say why she'd killed herself. But she was still alive. She'd taken too little and it had only made her sick. After that she was too weak to move, and she hadn't anything else to kill herself with. They said in the paper she was too weak to escape, but I don't suppose she even wanted to. She must have seen the men coming over the fields through the barn door. Perhaps she tried to run then, but she couldn't.

I saw those fields, when Sukey and Caro had both gone. I went up there the next summer, after it had all died down. It was late on in June, and there was clover in the grass. The grass was tipped with red and purple and silver. I stood by the bank and smelled the grass and the sweet air blowing. We were so high up. There were short, steep little fields, and sheep. That was when I saw them, Sukey walking through the grass as if she was walking on water, smiling at me, walking and walking as the grass rippled around her, but never coming any closer. And Caro down by the field-gate, crying after her, her feet trapped in the grass. And then it was over and Sukey never reached me. That was when I knew I'd have to go away from everything that reminded me of Sukey and Caro. Keep my head down, not read the newspapers, start a new life. But it never works, not really. Some things burn themselves into you; you can't lose them even if you want to. I could close my eyes now and see them again. But I won't, not now.

I hope they didn't try to make Caro identify Sukey. They must have had to carry her back over the fields – she can't have been able to walk. Still, in a way Caro'd got what she wanted. No one else was going to get Sukey now, ever. It was summer, and there was a heatwave in Manchester. Even in the Lake

District it must have been warm. I remember counting the days, thinking of the green fields, and Sukey's pump, and the little garden. Her poor head was all caved in. There'd've been flies buzzing round . . . They got worried down at the farm when Sukey didn't come for the milk. They'd have taken it up to the cottage for her, but she'd told them she liked the walk. She loved that walk in the early morning, on her own. It was like the beginning of the world, she wrote to me. And then she'd asked them at the farm to bake extra bread in the next batch, because she was expecting a visitor. Maybe that was what did it.

'Oh, Caro, darling, Enid's coming on Saturday, just for a few days. I can't wait for her to see the cottage, can you? Perhaps she'll help you with the vegetables.'

What Caro did next I still don't want to imagine. It's not so much the way she battered Sukey, but her going and fetching the poker to do it with. It means that she must have thought about what she was going to do, and yet she still did it. But perhaps it wasn't like that. Perhaps it was all very quick and Caro just snatched up the poker. I'd rather think that. Sukey wouldn't have known much. She'd have thought it was a joke, just for a second.

'Why, Caro' – smiling and trying to calm Caro down, the way she did – 'don't be silly, darling.'

But this time it didn't work. I suppose Sukey might have had a second or two to know that, to know that it wasn't going to work. But I've never seen Sukey frightened, so I can't picture it.

I didn't go to her funeral. It was delayed, because the police had her body. And Caro was coming up for trial. Her family and the doctors and lawyers they paid tried to make out she was off her head and couldn't stand trial, but that didn't wash. It was very quiet, Sukey's funeral, it said in the newspaper. *Family flowers only*, so I didn't send anything.

If you want the truth, I was frightened to go. What if Caro said something? What if she tried to make out I'd been there in the cottage? That I'd had something to do with it? Even though the police thought Caro was a murderess, she was still more the kind of person they'd believe than I was. I wouldn't have put anything past Caro. And I thought that me going to the funeral might be just the thing that would start her off thinking about me, if she got to hear about it. The police go to funerals, don't they, when someone's been murdered? Just to see who turns up. So I never said goodbye to Sukey. I still can't believe that they put her in a box and under the earth and left her for the rain to fall on her. It's ridiculous, when I know more people who are dead than alive.

Anyway, Sukey's family wouldn't have wanted me there. I'd've just been part of the scandal as far as they were concerned. She had a sister who lived in Scotland, with three tiny children. The Honourable this and the Honourable that. She'd have come, but not with the children. I expect they kept it all from them. I wonder if they know now? Or won't anyone know, once I'm dead?

Nadine knows. I must tell her all of it.

I did go to the Manchester Ladies one last time. The bombing had started. An incendiary fell flat in the street in front of me one night when I was going home. That was before I got called up and they put me in the Land Army. So I did live in a little cottage in the end, just like the one Sukey rented, though getting up at dawn is more like the end of the world than the beginning when you have to do it every day. I wasn't hurt by the incendiary. I stood looking at it as if it was a coal that had fallen out of the fire, then a warden ran past shouting at me, and shoved me into a doorway.

It was curiosity that made me go back. I didn't expect to find anyone I knew. Sukey was dead, and Caro's trial was over by then. They didn't hang her, though they might have done. They still hanged women. Ruth Ellis was the last, and she was a long time after Caro. It sounds terrible when you say it flat out like that, doesn't it? Hanging. You can't think of it in connection with a person you know. Even when it's a person you hate. All sorts of doctors gave evidence. Caro's family would have paid for them. I think they thought they'd get her off completely, or get her put into some sort of rest-home, but they didn't. The prosecution made out Caro had dragged Sukey into a life of vice and then murdered her. Then the defence said the exact opposite: it was Sukey dragging Caro, who was younger than her, and impressionable and easily led. I remember every word of it. I bought the newspapers each morning and evening, and cut out the account of the trial and put it away. I've still got it. Evidence. But even the defence and the doctors couldn't manage to make out that Sukey'd murdered Caro. So what they agreed in the end was that Sukey and Caro had both dragged each other down, and so in a way the murder was a sort of punishment for both of them. They made it sound as if Sukey deserved to be murdered. And the jury swallowed it, or most of it. It was obviously a crime of passion, and they didn't really want to look too closely at what kind of passion it was between two women. It all had to be written up in a very roundabout way in the newspapers, so that you had to guess at what was meant. It made Sukey and Caro sound quite different: sordid and furtive. You could hardly tell when they were talking about Sukey and when they were talking about Caro, because they said the same things about both of them. *Good family, sheltered upbringing, beautiful, popular, high society . . . dragged down to a life of vice . . .* The hint was that they'd both become what used to be called 'sex-slaves'. It was easier for them to look at it that way than to believe that Sukey was happy. But I won't think about that now. And as for what they wrote about the Manchester Ladies – it would have made a cat laugh.

Caro was imprisoned for manslaughter. She came out in the end, then she went abroad. Oh, yes, I always followed her from the newspapers. She's dead now.

When I went there in the war there was still the little plaque outside the club, THE MILLICENT SOWERBY ASSOCIATION FOR LADIES, but the door was all boarded up. You couldn't see through into the building, but I'm sure there wasn't anything there any more. No mirrors or bathrooms or *chaises-longues*. No laughter or games of cards and five-pound notes on the floor. All vanished like a genie's palace. Just space. With the war and the bombing, clubs were closing down everywhere. But I think the Manchester Ladies had gone before the war started. There was such a scandal – you wouldn't credit it these days. It might even've got closed down because of the court case. I don't know. The police were always closing places down then, for vice.

Caro didn't name me. My name didn't come out in the trial at all. For a long time I wondered why: she could have had her revenge if she'd wanted it. Everything else came out. You might think that was because she didn't want to drag me into it – me being so young – but I don't think that was the reason. I've thought about it for a long time now. It was because she didn't want anyone else to know Sukey'd loved me. She didn't want to make it seem as if I'd been important to Sukey. That was one word they never wrote in the newspapers: *love*. It would have made a quite different story.

So I just stood there and looked at the plaque. It wasn't raining that day, for once. It was quite nice, with soft small clouds in a pale sky. I thought of Sukey in the taxi, then I said, 'You've won, Millicent Sowerby,' and walked off, because I didn't want anyone staring at me. But they had better things to stare at, with the war on. The trial was a nine-days' wonder, and a couple of years later if you'd said 'Manchester Ladies', no one'd've had any idea what you were talking about. There was the war, so we soon had other things to talk about.

It's still not the full story, though. I'm as bad as the newspapers. They wanted everyone to hate Sukey and I want everyone to love her. Sukey cold and stiff. Sukey on her back on the carpet on the stone floor, with her head in the fender. But her arms and feet were perfect. Caro never touched her body.

You can't make murder pretty. Perhaps Caro was right, that's where it gets you, wanting everything. I can still feel Sukey in my fingers. Soft and warm and quick. But she was hard too.

There she goes again. That one downstairs with Kai. Laughing. Out loud, she doesn't care. Why should she? She knows Nadine's not here. And I'm nothing. She reminds me of Caro. Maybe she's right and it doesn't matter if I hear them. I'm not much of a witness. If she looked at my record she'd feel she was safe enough. *Knows when to keep her mouth shut.* That's me.

'Oh, Caro, Enid's coming on Saturday. Poor darling, it'll do her good to get out of Manchester for a couple of days. I'll get some cream from the farm – we'll have to feed her up a bit. I expect she's frightened of cows, wouldn't you think, darling?'

I know that little bubble of laughter, laughing at me, at Caro, at the rain, at the whole world. I still want to scream out and warn her, though she's been dead for more than fifty years, '*Sukey, don't laugh!*' I don't know if I'm really trying to warn her, or if I want to scream at her because I'm angry too. I'm still angry. Then Caro's shadow crosses the room so fast Sukey doesn't even see it. The last thing she hears is the poker hissing down on her head. And Caro laughing. It was easier for the jury to think Caro was out of her mind, but I don't believe it.

Let that one downstairs laugh. I shan't say anything to Nadine. You can't make murder pretty and you can't tidy it up either, any more than you can tidy up love. I'll tell Nadine that.

Fifteen

The cottage, morning, June 1938. The early mist's clearing – look, it's nearly gone. A few streaks of it wisp up and dissolve as I watch. The fells look like a horse after a gallop, with steam coming off its flanks. I wonder if we could ride here? Caro would like that. What a day it's going to be. What bliss not to be in Manchester, or London, or anywhere but here.

Caro's left the bucket under the pump. I plunge my arms down into it, lift handfuls of silky water to my face, sluice my arms. Nothing matters here. An old cotton dress, my hair brushed back, my feet bare. Yesterday we sunbathed naked in the shelter of the wall. Caro had to lie in the shade, with her white skin. Her special redhead's smell comes out when her skin's hot. She had her eyes shut against the sun. Coral nipples, blue-white breasts, deep-dented navel. Her hair is exactly the colour of the fronds of a sea-anemone. Moving in and out, sucking . . . poor Caro. I ought to find a sea to put her in – a cool green sea with caves and seaweed where she could hide from the sun, flicking her tail. She shouldn't have been left here on dry land where there isn't any shade.

Look at my arms! But I don't care if I go brown as a gypsy. I would hate to burn, like Caro does. I want to soak up the sun until there's no winter left in me. The air here smells of hay and sheep-droppings, and warm stone. But the inside of the house is always dank and dark, even though it's so hot. You can smell the meat-safe. And there's too much polish on everything.

My little Enid is coming. I nearly told Caro last night. And then I thought I would wait. As soon as she knows, she'll watch me to see if I'm thinking about Enid, waiting for her, wanting her. Enid would think nothing of walking up from the farm carrying her own suitcase. She's like a little pony, with her long hair flapping and her funny little dusty brown face. And those eyes, light as water. She doesn't wait and watch me . . .

Caro's never had a child. Imagine a baby being born out of Caro. What a fight that would be, and who'd win, I wonder? Odds on Caro any day. But no baby's ever going to get the chance, I know that, darling. You don't need to give me one of your fierce looks. She doesn't like it that a baby's been where she'll never be, no matter how hard she tries. Actually inside me. It's different, making love to a woman who's had a child. Everything's been used. Ralph noticed the difference after I had Johnnie. 'Not so snug any more, Sukey darling.' I know what Caro thinks when she sucks my breasts. *Someone's been here before me*. Well, it was a long time ago, darling. The nurse used to bring Johnnie in much too late, after he'd been screaming for hours. Such nonsense, all those rules. She said it would spoil him if I fed him before the four hours were up. Poor Johnnie would be so angry with me. Dark red in the face, sweating, eyes tight shut. He'd crowd my nipple into his mouth, then he'd break off for one last sob. He'd stare up at me with those big wet navy-blue eyes. But it was the nurse's fault, not mine. Johnnie always smelled of potatoes when they've been boiled too long and they fall to pieces and the cook tries to push the bits together. And you have to send them back.

Silly Caro. What difference does it all make anyway? She's always asking questions. Do Ralph and I still sleep together? Does he ever come into my bedroom? Ralph has his own life, I tell her, and I have mine. I couldn't manage the spare, but I did produce the heir. And that was the end of that.

It wasn't quite, of course. Nothing ever is. It'll happen on a summer night when it's too hot to sleep and Ralph comes home after a party. I like him black and white and tanned and just a tiny bit rumpled. He might ask me to help him with his cuff-links because he can't manage them. I might suddenly notice his wrists. Ralph has nice wrists. He sways and we laugh. I smell champagne, and whisky, and something else.

'You smell of one of your girls,' I say.

'Speaking of girls, how's Caro?' he asks, freeing one hand, sliding a finger down my spine.

Caro says that Ralph is a monster. Isn't it true that he knows the Mosleys? He goes to their house, doesn't he, Sukey? I daresay. I don't know where Ralph goes. House-parties, trips to Bayreuth and Venice, weeks and weeks in London. Everyone laughs when I say I'd rather be in Manchester. And now I have my Enid, my pony, so strong and so silky. Ralph always goes back to his own room afterwards. The bed's suddenly cool and I hear the curtains flutter. I stretch out my legs and lift up the sheet and let it billow back down on me. Bliss.

Evening. 'Caro . . .' I say. She looks up. We're in the parlour. When two people sit in the ugly little tapestry chairs their knees almost touch. The sun never comes round to this side of the cottage. The windows won't open and the room smells stale. But Caro wanted to come in out of the sun because she had a headache. She'd had too much sun. Her face is puffy and her eyes are red. There's a fly by the window, kneading the pane with its legs, trying to get out. It doesn't know that the windows don't open. I ask Caro if she'd like to go upstairs and lie on the bed with the curtains drawn to keep out the light. But she says no, it's stifling up there under the roof. It'll be cooler outside, I say, what about putting chairs under the apple tree? No, she says. No. The fly rasps against the window. I want to walk up to the hayfield.

She lies back, shuts her eyes. I know she wants me to touch her. I stand and say, 'I'll just go and get things ready . . .' not thinking about what I'm saying. Caro's eyes snap open.

'What do you mean, get things ready?' she demands. 'I've peeled the potatoes. There's cold lamb in the larder. I've put muslin over it. There's no need for you to do anything.'

I can't imagine eating cold lamb. Fatty, congealed stuff. I hate the way meat smells on your breath in summer.

'I'll go up and look at the spare room,' I say. 'To see if Hannah's dusted it. Perhaps the bed needs airing . . .'

'Why?' she cracks out at me like a pistol-shot. Both eyes are fixed on me now, reddened and wary.

'Well, darling, I've asked Enid if she'd like to come up for a couple of days. On Saturday. I thought it would be such bliss for her to get out into the country. You know how hard she works, and it's awfully unhealthy for her to be stuck in Manchester all summer. She's looking pale.'

The eyes glare. 'If she comes, I shan't stay.'

'Oh, Caro darling, *really*. Don't be absurd. We can't have all this again.'

Caro heaves herself up in the chair. A clumsy movement – it must have hurt her head. A dull red tide creeps up her face, and her eyes go slitty. Where have I seen that look before?

'She can't come,' shouts Caro, and her voice cracks but she goes on. 'I absolutely forbid it!'

The fly is frightened. It beats wildly at the pane of glass which is never going to give way. I drop down on my knees by the side of Caro's chair.

'Caro, darling!' I remonstrate. I take her hand. I look at the flush and rage on her face and suddenly I see it. Why, she's like Johnnie! She's like my baby, pulling back from my nipple because he was too angry with me to feed. And I feel my face shiver with laughter as we look at one another and I open my mouth to tell her about Johnnie. Even Caro will see that it's funny, and then she'll come out into the cool sweet garden with me . . .

But then there's a jerk as she pulls back. I can't hold her. Her head lurches over the side of the chair as if she's going to be sick. She reaches down, scrabbling on the floor. I can't see what she's doing.

'Why, Caro!' I say and just then she rears up above me and I feel the rush of her arm coming up and the air shudders, then splits over me, but I'm still laughing about how much Caro looks like Johnnie as Caro's face flares like a torch, roars up in light, goes dark.

Sixteen

Carborundum and knife flash in the air. Dull and bright steels scissor against one another. Nadine shivers, though the dark-panelled restaurant is warm and a wide colonial fan turns just above their heads. The waiter swivels his meat-trolley like a small stage, presenting it to the table. On the carving tray there is a sirloin, pure meat, bloody and muscular but bred for tenderness. The waiter poises himself, adjusts angles of knife and carving-fork, and addresses himself to the joint like a bullfighter, his dark face serious above his work. He cuts a slice across the joint and it falls juicily across the plate he has laid ready. The slice of meat laps over the plate. But that's the point of this place. The vegetables are good but mundane. New potatoes, shelled peas, sliced carrots. There's horseradish sauce made with freshly grated horseradish, and English mustard. The beef is of the finest quality, properly killed and correctly hung before being roasted in the huge joints which permit a unique combination of flavour and juiciness.

Paul Parrett hands the horseradish to Nadine. She smiles, takes it and smears a dab on to the side of her plate, where it turns red from the oozing meat. Tony cuts his meat rapidly into narrow strips and swallows them efficiently. This is not Tony's kind of restaurant at all, even though Nadine's gathered that he's paying for the meal. And even Tony can't possibly have an arrangement here. There'll have to be money put on the table. She half smiles, thinking of it, and Paul Parrett catches her eyes. His moist, incredibly quick dark eyes flicker about the table as if the whole thing is a private joke which he's just about to share with Nadine. Nadine warms to him. He's extraordinarily attractive, for someone who shouldn't be attractive at all, with his round eyes and fleshy face. His photographs don't do him justice. It's the energy in him – you can almost hear it humming. And when he switches his attention to you the force of it stops you thinking whatever you were thinking about him. Since they've come into the restaurant she's never once caught his glance sliding sideways towards the other tables, where there must be more important people he knows.

He was at the table waiting for them when they came into the restaurant. Paul Parrett doesn't need to make a point of arriving late. He knows what he's worth, and so does everyone else. He's shorter than Nadine expected. She's seen him on TV, read the interviews and the gossip, seen the photographs and the cartoons. His face on the news was part of her coming into adolescence. He was always being given new jobs and smiling in Downing Street. Images stick in her mind: Paul Parrett going in and out of important doorways; Paul Parrett walking alone down a long white beach towards the camera, his dark body brisk against the waves; Paul Parrett speaking fluent German to his German opposite number, Paul Parrett on election night.

Then there was the early life of Paul Parrett. Illegitimate war-baby, adopted into a small terraced house in the outskirts of Manchester, rising through scholarships, fast footwork and the assumption of public schoolboys' effortless assumptions. Even someone who wasn't interested in politics couldn't help knowing about Paul Parrett. He took up space. He was still on his way up. Even before she met him, he took up space in Nadine's mind. She'd thought he'd be tall, but when he stood up to shake her hand he was an inch or so shorter than Tony. At once, that was the height to be. He was powerful all right, and although he was heavily built you could see how quickly he'd move if he had to. He was almost bald, but then he'd been bald since his twenties, she'd read in some profile or other, and so it didn't seem to age him. He hadn't compensated with a beard or a moustache. His eyes melted and twinkled at her as they shook hands and she smiled back.

All this meat is going to send her to sleep. If she eats the whole plateful she'll spend the rest of the evening in a stupor, digesting it. Nadine pushes her plate to one side.

'What's the matter? Don't you like it?' asks Paul Parrett, leaning forward to scan the barely touched slab of sirloin and the small blood-sodden potatoes.

'I'm fine,' says Nadine. 'I'm not very hungry, that's all,' and she picks up her glass and drinks off the dark red wine which seems to taste very faintly of blood as well. Tony says nothing. Nadine's never known him so quiet. He's simply eaten his slice of meat and crossed his knife and fork very definitely on his plate. How on earth could Tony and Paul Parrett have got to know each other? Business, of course. But what? Paul Parrett's on a different level completely.

The wine tingles deliciously in her veins, right down to her fingertips. The heavy silver glitters and the white napkins are glossy under the lamps. One napkin has a tiny exquisite darn across its corner. It appears more luxurious than a perfect napkin, for who can pay for such darning to be done these days – and who knows how to do it? Nadine fingers the stiff linen, her head bent. She feels her body dispose itself in still curves, with soft flattering light breaking on the surface of her skin. Both men are watching her. It's back again, that power she possessed in the bedroom with Kai, when she put on the dress. It floods her body. Or is it just that she's had too much to drink? Paul Parrett mentions a film he has seen lately. *Jesus of Montreal*. Not a new film, it's a few years old now. But he doesn't get tired of it, because the photography is so good. All those shots looking down over the city. And the magic – had she realized there were so many magicians around then? Has she seen it? Nadine begins to explain about her job at the Warehouse and the chance this gives her to see films seven or eight times and really get to understand how each film is constructed, but Tony breaks in, interrupting her so crudely that it's quite funny. He hasn't seen *Jesus of Montreal* – what's it about? Paul Parrett and Nadine both start talking at once, then both laugh and fall silent. But it doesn't matter, because he is one of those people you can be silent with very comfortably. Being in his physical presence feels like doing something. He's not having this effect on Tony, though. Tony is really on edge tonight. What's the matter with him? She's really making a big effort and paying a lot of attention to Paul Parrett, and she knows that's what Tony wants. A few moments later the head waiter comes to Paul Parrett's side with a note on a tray, and murmurs into his ear. Paul Parrett excuses himself, says it's a bore, but it won't take long. Now she can ask Tony what's going on.

'What's the matter with you, Tony? We were just getting talking.'

'Nadine, for fuck's sake, you don't come here and talk about usheretting in a cinema. Look at the people.'

'Ushering,' Nadine corrects him automatically, then looks around. A wall of dark backs, white shirts, discreet, rumbling, authoritative voices. Dashes of colour: a bow tie here or a cummerbund there. The clientele is overwhelmingly male. The atmosphere is one of serious eating and talk, and it's a little intimidating, but also a little absurd. However, Tony wouldn't see that.

'He doesn't want to talk about your job,' pursues Tony doggedly. 'He wants to talk about you.'

'He doesn't even know me.'

Tony crumples up his napkin and drops it on top of his knife and fork.

'People can get to know one another, can't they?'

Suddenly and for no reason, she thinks of the boy in the alley. One minute he was alone, the next he had a job to do, a home, someone taking an interest in him. He was taken inside to where there were lights and warmth and proper meals, not a padding of newspapers, a hamburger and cans of lager. And look at the way she'd met Kai. If anyone'd been looking at it from the outside, they'd have thought it was a pick-up. But from the inside, you know how things really are.

Paul Parrett's dark-suited arm brushes her bare shoulder as he comes back to the table. He looks refreshed, like a man who's slipped in an extra couple of drinks while pretending to go for a pee. But she doesn't think he's a drinker. He likes wine, but he's left his glass a third full for over half an hour now.

'Time for pudding,' he announces, his eyes glistening. Even Tony brightens, but one look at the trolleyful of treacle tart, bread and butter pudding and jam roly-poly and he slumps back in his chair, clearly itching for a cigarette. Paul Parrett scans the trolley and asks, 'Isn't there any summer pudding?' and then to Nadine, 'The summer pudding is wonderful here. You must try it.' The waiter frowns with mortification at being caught with an empty dish. He sends an acolyte off to the kitchen to fetch another pudding and it arrives whole and perfect on a plain white plate, moulded and pressed into shape.

'They put an iron weight on top of the plate overnight,' says Paul Parrett with satisfaction. The first slice is for Nadine. It comes out in layers of red and pink, the bread almost jellied with seeping fruit juices, the raspberries and redcurrants and blackcurrants crushed, releasing their fragrance into the bread. There is special cream to go with it, so thick it has to be cut with a knife. Nadine tastes the pudding. Tart fruit, sweet juices, bland bread, a coating of cream. It is almost too good to swallow. Then it's gone.

'Would you like some more?' asks Paul Parrett.

'Yes, please. It's wonderful. You ought to try this, Tony.'

'You're hungrier now,' says Paul Parrett, as the second slice slithers on to her plate and Nadine cuts into the cream. The wine waiter has brought Sauternes and she swallows alternate mouthfuls of sweet wine and pudding. The meat and the clouded red-wine glasses are whisked away and forgotten. Perfect. She sighs with pleasure. A third slice perhaps? No. It would be too much. It would spoil it. Paul Parrett is watching her attentively. She lifts her glass to him. Tony looks positively ill with bad temper. If he's enjoying the evening as little as this, Nadine wonders why he bothered to set it up in the first place. It's not going to be cheap.

'Coffee somewhere else, don't you think?' says Paul Parrett. 'What about coming back to my flat? It's warm enough to drink our coffee out on the roof-garden.'

It sounds a great idea to Nadine. The day is turning out well, after such a bad start. They must do it again. If only Kai was more sociable. All he ever wants to do when he isn't working is to stay at home, mostly in bed, mostly asleep. It was so different when they first knew each other. But Paul Parrett is saying something to her. She jerks her attention back to the table.

'. . . all right by you, Nadine?'

'Yes, that's fine. There's no rush – Tony's booked our hotel, haven't you, Tony?'

He nods gloomily. He ought to have shaved before they came out. A man like Tony really needs to shave twice a day. The dark shadow on his cheeks isn't very attractive in this light. Paul Parrett looks so fresh, so vigorous and newly bathed. He smells very faintly of soap and an astringent cologne she doesn't recognize. The waiter comes up with the bill and presents it to Tony, who pays with twenty-pound notes and a faint air of reluctance which Nadine hugs to herself gleefully. Only she understands it. It's not really that Tony's mean, but he does so much prefer to come to an arrangement. Paul Parrett winks at her, a lightning wink. She loves people who wink.

At the restaurant entrance Nadine looks out for a taxi, but the next moment a Jaguar pulls up at the kerb, with a driver in it. I suppose they have to have Jaguars, thinks Nadine. British cars.

'Here we are,' says Paul Parrett. 'Jump in,' and they do, Tony in the front by the driver, Nadine and Paul Parrett in the back. The car pulls away and Nadine leans back luxuriously, breathing in the smell of leather. Nobody speaks. She shuts her eyes for a second. Are they touching, or not touching? She thinks she feels his arm brush against her coat. The car swerves and they lean together, then apart. Tony says abruptly, 'I got to get back to the hotel to make some phone calls. If you drop me, I can get a taxi.' His voice sounds strange. Maybe he's drunk more than she realized – or is he ill? He's been so quiet all evening.

'We could do that,' agrees Paul Parrett calmly. A slight shock goes through Nadine. It's the word 'we'. The coupling of her name with Paul Parrett's. Excitement sparks through her.

'But Tony,' she says, 'I don't even know where the hotel is. You'll have to give me the address.'

Tony scribbles on a bit of paper and passes it back to her.

'Any taxi-driver'll know it,' he says. 'Make sure you get a black cab, not a minicab.'

'My car will take her,' assures Paul Parrett, then he leans forward and tells the driver to pull in where he can. Cabs go up and down here all the time, he tells Tony. The car slides into a gap; Tony opens the door and gets out. He glances into the back of the car, but doesn't really look at either of them. 'Goodbye, Nadine,' he says, and slams the car door. How strange – he hasn't said goodbye to Paul Parrett, after arranging the dinner for him. As the car accelerates away from the kerb, she looks back and sees Tony walking off fast, his head down. Luckily, Paul Parrett isn't in the least bothered by Tony's departure. He doesn't seem to have much interest in Tony at all, which makes the grouping of the three of them at dinner seem even more random now than it did at the time. Of course it's a business connection, not a personal friendship, but even so . . . Paul Parrett leans back expansively in the dusky rich interior of the car.

'Nearly there,' he says. They haven't driven far. They must still be in Westminster. There's the river down there. The car swings in abruptly and dives down into an underground car park. There is a security check, and then they are inside and the driver is parking the car in a brilliantly lit space. He comes round and opens the door for Nadine. She wanders a few yards, as if across a floodlit stage, while Paul Parrett says something to the driver. Then Paul Parrett leads her across to an internal door, past another security man who looks steadily at Nadine, registering her image in his brain for the future. They get into a lift which shoots up to the fifteenth floor in a disturbing muffled silence. The building is new. Even the planes of the lift are beautifully moulded. There is a large print of fish on the wall. She reads the title: *3 Poissons Minces*. A mirror on the opposite wall makes slim vivid fish swim up the building beside them, bright as petals.

When they get out they walk across the corridor to a door of heavy pale wood, with a tiny camera eye winking beside it and a system of alarms which Paul Parrett defuses with what looks like a credit card. Inside the flat it is dark. There's a big, wide, dark space in front of her, not a hall or lobby. Hesitantly, Nadine steps after Paul Parrett into the room. A light springs on, not inside the room but outside, beyond the windows. She breathes in sharply, can't help herself gasping aloud at what she sees.

In front of them there is a wall made entirely of glass. Yet it's framed by the black shadows of leaves, and a small, perfect and formal garden is floodlit just outside, as if floating in the air above London. There are tubs of bay and orange trees, white jasmine trained to wreath round circular frames, glowing troughs of strawberries and cherry tomatoes, roses in tubs, low rosemary and lavender hedges clipped round gravel walks. The leaves move gently.

'There's always wind up here,' says Paul Parrett.

Beyond, there is the wider frame of the city's tarnished orange skies. Headlights crawl up and down choked streets. Then there are bright necklaces of bridges and the dark stain and reflection of the Thames. Paul Parrett goes forward and unlocks the double-glazed french doors to the roof garden. The air is warm but breezier than down on the streets. Vine leaves around the door flicker, and the smell of tobacco plants blows past Nadine.

'Wind is the problem up here,' says Paul Parrett. 'That's why I have all these hedges. They slow it down. Fencing doesn't work as well. It creates currents and the wind force increases. That damages the plants. They burn and they bruise, even if they don't break.'

He touches the petals and leaves of his flowers as he walks, familiar, not needing to look to know where they are. It is like watching him run his hands over the body of someone he's loved for a long time.

'Have a strawberry,' he says. 'These go on fruiting right into September.'

The berry is small, but its flavour is far more intense than the commercial strawberries Nadine knows. It takes her back to the strawberries her grandfather grew by his greenhouse, dark red and brilliantly seeded with yellow. She never dared take one without asking. Crushing Paul Parrett's strawberry under her tongue, Nadine walks after him to the edge of the garden.

'Careful,' he says. 'There's only a low wall,' and he takes her arm to steady her. The wall is below her waist.

'I sleep out here sometimes, in summer,' says Paul Parrett. The words seem to go on moving in her after they've died in the air. *I sleep out here.*

'Is there security out here too?' she asks.

'It's all very safe. Don't worry about it.'

Nadine glances back. Behind, by the french doors, another little TV eye points at them.

'Doesn't it bother you,' she asks, 'being watched all the time?'

He shrugs. 'You get used to it. It's just functional, it's not important,' he says. He's kept his arm round her, but now, aware of the TV eye, she stiffens. At once he lets her go.

'Coffee,' he says.

They return to the apartment and he settles Nadine on a long mole-coloured leather sofa while he goes to make coffee.

'Take a look at the books – they're mostly new. You might find something you like,' he says, gesturing to the table. She wonders if he's read any of them or if they are placed there freshly each month as the bestseller lists come out. There are two novels, a biography and a poet's collected letters. She looks, but does not open any of them. The sight of the books depresses her. On top of them there's a battered book on fruit-growing. There is a panel of stained glass set into the wall dividing the enormous sitting-room from the kitchen. The design is a dense abstract forest of greens, lit from the other side. As she looks the segments of dark and lighter green appear to lap and move, like leaves in the wind. Nadine sits upright on the mole-coloured sofa. She's taken off her black coat. The smell of coffee begins to move through the room. He's taking a long time – what's he doing, grinding it, roasting it? Growing it, perhaps. It wouldn't surprise her to find a small coffee plantation out there in his roof-garden. Nadine yawns helplessly. Her stomach feels empty with tension in spite of the summer pudding.

Paul Parrett comes back and puts a tray of coffee and *petits fours* on the table. It touches Nadine to see a grown man like him keeping sweet things in his house.

'I thought you'd like something sweet. I always get hungry after drinking,' he says.

'You didn't drink much.'

'No, that's true. So there's no excuse. Never mind. As long as you eat some, I can too.'

Greedily they both stretch out for the marzipan, the almond, the dark bitter chocolate. He sits very close to her. Again they touch, or don't touch, as the shaving of space shifts between them. She wonders if he can hear her heart. The coffee is hot and strong, perfectly brewed. She stretches out her legs, slips off a shoe, touches the soft carpet with a bare foot. Does he live alone? There's no marriage as far as she knows, and she doesn't think any children were mentioned in the profiles. You'd think he'd have children. There are no photographs in the room, no notes or letters or clutter, no pinboard, no sheets of telephone messages. She can't even see a telephone. If she didn't know who he was, she'd think it was an empty life. Paul Parrett puts down his coffee-cup and looks at her.

'Light,' he says. 'Miss Light. It's an unusual name. Is it your own, or is it professional?'

Nadine stares at him. 'I'm not an actress,' she says, wondering what lies Tony's told to make her sound more interesting. That explains why he didn't want her to talk about her job. A curious expression flickers on Paul Parrett's face. It's the look of one who wonders how well a new actress is going to perform in a play he knows and loves. His small berry-like eyes shine. All at once Nadine looks behind her. She doesn't know why she's looked round, but she's absolutely sure, suddenly, that they're not alone in the flat. Someone else is here.

'What's the matter?'

'I thought I heard something.'

He tenses, and in one movement reaches behind him and presses something. A second later a voice floods out of the grille above the hatch to the kitchen. She'd thought it was a ventilation grille.

'Is there a problem, Mr Parrett?'

'Not immediately. Has there been any movement tonight?'

'No, sir.'

'Anything over the line?'

'Nothing tonight.'

'All right.'

'Do you want a check, sir?'

'Not now. Run the video through for me, would you?'

'I'll get Archard on to it.'

The flat, matter-of-fact voice stops. There's no click. The line's open all the time. Is it two-way?

Paul Parrett looks at Nadine as if there's been no interruption. He must be so used to this that it's like the water he swims in. Security. She's never seen it in action before, not like this. Smooth and powerful like a current that flows so fast it doesn't break the surface. As long as you're going with it you don't notice how fast the shore is going by. How far out to sea you are. It must be like this all the time for a government minister, especially one who's had to make tough decisions in his time, like Paul Parrett. Nadine's only ever glimpsed the outer flanks of Security. She knows about Underground stations taped off with red and white barriers, megaphoned voices telling everybody to leave the building by the nearest exit, cars racing through traffic lights with dark-smudged figures in the back, square miles of London sealed off for hours and no mention on the TV news that night. But she doesn't know about a set-up like this. Where is she supposed to fit in?

They're probably checking her now. After all, they don't know anything about her. She could be anyone. White silk dresses would cut no ice with his people. They want to see through to the flesh beneath, to brain and bone. They need to know what she is thinking. Paul Parrett takes off his jacket. She smells the cottony scent of his shirt, and very faintly his sweat. He picks up her hand and holds it.

'You have beautiful hands,' he says, stroking the bones and the hollows on the back of her hands. She flashes him a look and their eyes meet in amusement. She could really like this man, if it wasn't for Kai, she tells herself, knowing that she does like this man, in spite of Kai.

'Don't forget I work in a cinema,' she says 'I know all the lines.'

'I was surprised when you said that. I thought you worked with Tony.'

'Tony's just a friend. It's Kai I'm with.'

'Oh? You're with Kai?' A quick look, surprised perhaps, as if this is something new to him. Not altogether a flattering look. Perhaps he doesn't like Kai.

'Yes,' says Nadine. 'Do you know him, or just Tony?'

'Not really. We've met.'

They sit quietly. It's been a long day, thinks Nadine, going back in her mind to the sudden lurch of the train and the noise of the ambulance. When I was thrown forward, that must have been the moment the door hit her head. I wonder what happened to her?

'Has Tony gone into the details with you?' murmurs Paul Parrett, tracing the bones of her wrist.

'Well, no, not really.'

He continues to hold her hand, lightly stroking her wrist. Don't stop, don't move, she thinks. Keep doing this.

'That doesn't matter. We'll go on into my room in a minute. It'll be easier to show you. It's so tedious explaining things, don't you think? Would you like some more coffee? Or brandy?'

'No, I'm fine.'

'Sure? Or the bathroom? It's through behind us.'

'No.'

They stand. He's fractionally shorter than she is. She holds back, dragging a slow bare foot through the thick carpet. He's assuming a lot, but never mind, she can soon put him right. And she flexes her toes in soft wool and lets the dress slither into shape around her and knows she doesn't want to put him right about anything. It's so nice here, so special and cut-off and secret that anything which happens only happens by rules which stop applying the moment you leave. It wouldn't necessarily affect Kai . . . or anyone . . .

'I've been wanting to tell you all evening,' he says, 'what a marvellous dress that is.'

The flat is bigger than she thought. A corridor with several closed white doors leads to his bedroom. A big dark bed, severely made with white sheets and blankets, fills most of the small bedroom. The air is cool, neutral. There are no books or flowers or pictures. She's still looking round as Paul Parrett bends down and pulls what look like crêpe bandages out from under the mattress. She touches one. The material is extremely strong and slightly stretchy when she pulls it. It looks like some kind of orthopaedic apparatus. For a moment she wonders if he has a bad back and wants her to help him with his exercises. Or perhaps he needs support. The high hard bed might be a hospital bed. But it's too big.

One of the bandages is fixed at each corner of the bed and

there are two at the sides of the bed, with a clip-lock at the end of each strap. Paul Parrett touches them lightly, just as he touched the leaves and flowers in the garden. A little more than a touch, a little less than a caress. Nadine stares at them blankly. She must be very tired. All this is brilliantly distinct, but it doesn't make sense.

'Here we are,' says Paul Parrett.

'I'm sorry, I'm being stupid – I must have had too much to drink.'

He touches each bandage in turn. 'It's easy, don't worry. These go round my wrists – these are for my ankles. You clip these over my waist. You'll have to check that they are absolutely secure, because there's a bit of give in the fabric.' He guides her hand. She feels the give. 'The key's in the top right-hand drawer of my bureau. In there. I'll beg you to unlock me but you mustn't give in. No matter what I promise you.'

'And what do I do?'

'You stand there, so I can just see you if I turn my head. But I've got to struggle. You mustn't make it too easy. Pull your dress up but keep it on, so it looks as if it might fall down any minute. You mustn't come near enough for me to touch you. Then just masturbate the way you normally would.'

'I don't,' says Nadine.

'Don't what?'

'Don't masturbate.'

'Come on. A lovely-looking girl like you. You must do. I would, if I were you.'

That twinkling complicit smile again. His white shirt glows in the dusky room. She can't help smiling back.

'A beautiful girl like you,' he amends it, once she's got the joke.

'All the same, I don't. I never have,' says Nadine.

'For me?' he says. 'Surely you could manage?' guying it slightly, turning his hunger into a game. For the first time he moves her. She feels something more than excitement and curiosity. Behind the twinkle and assurance she glimpses

162

humiliation. This is what he has to have. He can't do it any other way. A man like him with all his power and money and charm and warmth. A man at the top of a long slippery slope that lots of people would like to see him go sliding down, arse over tip. It can't ever be easy to ask. Here are my straps. This is what I require. What tact he's had to learn to be able to pass it off like this. He's like a doctor explaining a tricky treatment. And he's a conspirator too, a magician with his straps and his secret garden. How many times has he had to go through it all? And how many of the women have agreed? What about when he was young, before he had all his money? What can it have been like then? Perhaps he had a girlfriend and she went along with it at first, before she realized it was all he was ever going to want. To have her in his arms was never going to be the point.

'What's the matter? Are you worried about cameras? There isn't one in here.'

'No, I wasn't thinking about that.'

He sits down on the bed. It's as if they've just got married. Her white dress, his dark suit and white shirt, the severe hotel-type bed. Their awkwardness. Two people who have got to know one another in fully clothed public daylight wondering, 'Where do we go from here? How do we start?'

His smile is becoming fixed and the room fills slowly with embarrassment and something more familiar, something she wants to wipe out before it can grow any more: pain.

'It's all right,' she says. 'You took me by surprise, that's all.'

'Tony doesn't go into detail with you, then,' comments Paul Parrett, and he bends down to untie his shoes.

Blood shocks up into her face. The room seems to squeeze tight round her as her heart squeezes tight inside her. She stares at him.

'How could Tony tell me anything? He didn't know this was going to happen.'

From a great distance she hears his voice, faintly protesting, faintly mocking, calling her to order. 'Nadine!' he says, like a parent told a transparent lie by a small child. 'Nadine!' It's all still a game and there's everything to play for. Then he looks up and sees her face. His fingers go still on the laces. He gets up from the bed.

'That man's an idiot. He told me it was all fixed up. Is this supposed to be some sort of joke? What he's playing at?'

He's scenting it again, the old spoor of his humiliations. And he's not putting up with it any more, not now. His eyes contract. They are dull and small and dangerous, staring at her.

'I'm sorry,' says Nadine, 'Tony didn't tell me anything.'

'The fucking idiot,' says Paul Parrett.

'You thought I was a prostitute,' says Nadine.

'I wouldn't use that word.'

'Why not? You thought Tony was paying me.'

'And he's not?'

'No,' says Nadine, and then she thinks of the fresh twenty-pound notes, the new knives, the cases of wine, the big house, and she sees herself at the kitchen table, drinking the smooth red wine she could never afford to buy, but she says again, 'No. I don't charge.'

'Then what the fuck was he doing?' says Paul Parrett. 'Letting you come here?'

'I don't know. I don't know what the fuck he was doing,' repeats Nadine. 'I'm sorry.' She is hot with shame. The crêpe bandages hang flaccidly down the side of the bed. 'I'd better go,' she says.

'Hang on a minute,' he mutters. She looks at him. He's amazing. He's back in control. He doesn't want anything now. He's not angry about anything. It's she who feels weak and apologetic.

'I feel awful,' she says.

'He should feel awful, not you, as he'll find out. But he's not worth wasting time on. Whatever are you doing with a man like that?'

'I told you, I'm not with him. I'm with Kai.'

164

Briskly, he smooths down the bedcover which is dented where he has sat on it. He is utterly self-contained now, armoured against her. She feels a pang of regret for the steady warmth of his attention, gone now and never going to return.

'I'd better go.'

'No. Wait a minute. I'm thinking.'

He sits on the bed again, hands on knees, silent. She can sense the energy of his thinking. Like his physical presence, it communicates. She feels it and she begins to be frightened. What if he's thinking of the security implications, now that she knows what she shouldn't know? These days even people who call themselves friends are on the phone to the tabloids for ten thousand pounds. What's to stop her? Is he thinking about how he's going to stop her? The walls of the room squeeze in again. She's closed in by walls, by the corridor, the secure entrance to the flat, the TV eyes and the microphones, the sealed lift, the secure car park. No one knows she is here except people who are employed to look after the interests of Paul Parrett. And Tony. The white dress is sticky under her arms. Don't say anything. Don't blabber that you won't tell, you'll keep it a secret, please –

He turns to her with a warm smile. 'Never mind,' he says. 'Forget it. Let me find your coat, and I'll call my driver to take you to the hotel.'

'That's all right,' she says quickly. 'I'll pick up a taxi.' If only she can get out on to the long dark blowing streets, into a black cab which has nothing to do with Paul Parrett.

'No. My driver will take you. You don't want to be out on the streets on your own at this time. When you see Tony, tell him I'll be in touch.'

His voice is not even menacing, but she feels a stupid impulse to defend Tony. 'I ought to have guessed,' she says. 'I was stupid. I didn't think.' As soon as she says it she knows it's true. Much more than stupid. Wilful ignorance, that's what they used to call it at school. She didn't know anything. But she knew everything, all along.

Paul Parrett doesn't make any judgement. He leads her out of the bedroom, down the quiet corridor with its winking red eyes to the living-room. The roof-garden glows under its carefully placed lights.

'Your garden is so beautiful,' she says. If she thinks only of what is happening now, at this minute, she'll be all right. She mustn't look ahead.

'Yes. It's a wonderful occupation,' he says. 'But you're too young to need occupations.'

The leaves blow around the window, just touching the glass, feathering it. It's well past midnight and the wind is getting up. The weather's breaking at last, not with a storm but with the steady strengthening of a cold current of air from the north-west. Paul Parrett opens the french window and moisture flows in. There's a slick of rain on the leaves. The wind carries a pungent smell of the first rain on city roads and roofs after a long drought.

'I love that smell,' says Nadine.

'It's caused by a microbe reaction, did you know that?'

'No, we never did that at school,' she answers without thinking, and feels him look at her. They move towards the window. The wind and rain in the air plaster Nadine's dress against her legs and damp the short ends of her hair. She rubs her arms.

'I didn't show you my apple trees,' says Paul Parrett, and they move over towards the edge of the roof. They are very high up. The city tilts and wheels under their feet. She looks out. A big plane winks its way westward to Heathrow, lumbering down the sky.

'Here they are,' he says. Sheltered by the low hedges there are six big tubs with branchless apple trees growing in them like fruiting poles. Immature apples cluster on the stems in bunches of six or seven.

'Ballerina,' says Paul Parrett, but the trees have no grace. They are maimed ballerinas with their limbs chopped off. He looks at them with satisfaction.

'They've done very well up here. There'll be a reasonable crop this autumn. See, this is where the fruit comes, near the stem. I'm going to try an espalier peach next, against that wall. With protective screening it ought to do all right.' They stand looking down over London while he talks of his garden. A thin stream of cars races over Westminster Bridge. The night air tastes delicious after the trapped air in the bedroom. If only they didn't have to go back into the flat, down the lift-shaft, into the glare of the car park. It is safe here, with the smell of rain and things growing. He seems to have forgotten what took place in the bedroom. He talks about his garden as if he's in no hurry for her to go. But the intensity of his concentration on her has gone. Nothing will happen now. It wasn't a beginning, it was just something short and stunted which could never have grown. She can't help feeling sorry. In a moment she'll have to go away from his hidden garden, down into London. She'll have to start thinking then.

'Time to go,' he says. 'My driver will be waiting for you at the lift door.'

Again she feels a pang of fear. 'I can easily get a cab,' she says again. Lights spill away down long roads into nowhere, over desolate flyovers, all the blank spaces that connect London. All the quiet places you can take someone you want to silence.

'No,' he says again, inflexibly, taking her elbow and guiding her back into the flat past the steadily recording eye.

'What happens when you're not in office any more?' asks Nadine. 'Can you get rid of the cameras?'

He brushes off lily pollen from his immaculate suit. 'Oh no. They're with me for life, I'm afraid. But, as I said, you get used to it.'

He looks up and smiles and she smiles back. Her fear subsides for a moment, like a wave backwashing to gain power.

'Your coat,' he says, placing it delicately on her shoulders. He reaches out and ruffles her hair. 'You ought to grow your hair,' he says. 'Much too disturbing this way. How old are you, Miss Light?'

'Nineteen.'

'Are you sure? Have you got parents?'

She can deal with this one easily enough as a rule. Explain about Lulu, and most people get deflected. They all have a story about a friend of a friend who's had a handicapped baby, or a child who's made miraculous progress through the Peto Institute. It's just that she's tired tonight.

'I don't see them,' she says.

'Really? That seems a pity.'

Nadine's mouth twists. Stupid weakness.

'That was the wrong thing to say, wasn't it?' he asks. 'I must be more tired than I thought. Losing my grip. In my job what you don't say is as important as what you do say. But it's a pity, all the same. You need someone to keep an eye on you, otherwise you end up with the Tonys and Kais. Someone older.'

Fatherly, protective. What about older people who want you to tie them to their beds with crêpe bandages? 'Keep an eye.' At once she sees Enid's door, half open. Enid watching and listening.

'I've got Enid,' says Nadine.

'Enid? Who's she?'

'She lives in our house. Right up at the top, like you. But it's only a little room in the attic. She'd love a garden like this.'

'Is she related to you? Your grandmother or something?'

'No. Enid hasn't got any children. At least —' She hesitates. It's Enid's story, not hers. But he doesn't know Enid and he'll never meet her, so it can't matter. 'She did have a baby, but he was adopted. It was ages ago, just after the war. So she hasn't got anyone.'

His hand, which has been lightly moving in her hair, goes still. 'What's her other name?'

'Shelton. Tony and Kai can't stand her, but, as she's a sitting tenant, they can't get rid of her.'

'How old is she?'

'I'm not sure. She lies about her age, but I know she's over seventy-five.'

'Over seventy-five.' There's a silence. His hand is quite heavy on her hair. She looks up and sees that his eyes look as they did in the bedroom, but it's nothing to do with her this time. He's a long way away. Tireder than he knows. Then he snaps back to where they were.

'She must be a bit of a nuisance, I suppose, this old woman? Would you like to get her out as well?'

'No. I like Enid. Kai and Tony don't know her like I do. We have a good time. We talk a lot.'

'Do you,' says Paul Parrett. It's not really a question. His bright eyes are intent again and the force of his attention is on her.

'What's she like?' he asks abruptly.

'Who, Enid? It's hard to say. You can't always tell what's Enid being Enid, and what's Enid being old. She gets tired suddenly and it's like a light switching off. But she's not like that, really. She loves bright colours. She wears yellow pyjamas, and she's got a red velvet hat. We go down to the pub in the evenings. She likes that.'

'It sounds as if you look after her.'

'No, if I'm making it sound like that, I'm getting it wrong. It's just as much the other way round. Enid's got amazing energy. More than me in a way, even now. More than most people ever have. She's had an interesting life.'

'Has she? And I suppose Tony and Kai would like to make it more interesting for her, would they?'

'Oh, they wouldn't do anything like that. They've never harassed her. Kai wouldn't do that. It's just that they don't like her being there, that's all.'

'But you do.'

'Yes. I like her being there, up at the top of the house. She doesn't go out much. She's always there when I come back from work. Whatever time it is, she's awake.'

As soon as she starts talking about Enid she knows she loves her. She wants to go on talking about her. And yet she

169

abandoned her and walked away down the stairs with Kai, with the dress rustling in a carrier-bag beside them. She chose Kai.

Paul Parrett has come alive again. He couldn't possibly be more interested in her than he is. No wonder he's gone up through life like a rocket, she thinks, leaving a trail of people behind him dazed and glowing.

'Nadine, it's wonderful talking like this, but you ought to go. You look worn out. I'll call my driver. Where are you going? Not back to the hotel, surely?'

She's not afraid any more. The sense of threat, whatever it was, has dissolved. 'No, I'll go straight to Paddington. I want to get home.'

'Will Enid still be awake? Will you go and talk to her?'

'She might be. I'll probably go up and see. Sometimes she's awake all night, and Kai's away.' He seems fascinated by the idea of Enid, for some reason. He reaches into his breast pocket, pulls out a wallet, extracts a card. It has no name on it, only a telephone number. 'There. You can reach me on that number, if you give them your name. I'll get back to you. I want us to keep in touch. Will you do that?'

She slips the card into her handbag.

'Be careful what you say to Tony,' he says abruptly. 'I'll sort it out with him.'

What a change. Half an hour ago she could have sworn he wanted to rub Tony out like a dirty smudge on paper.

'You mean, not let him know what's happened?'

'Better not, don't you think? Keep him guessing. It would put you in an impossible position in that house. You need time to think what you're going to do. When you know, get in touch.'

'Yes.'

'You might talk to Enid.'

Nadine thinks of the Manchester Ladies. Yes, she thinks, surprised. Enid is the only person I could talk to about all this. She'd probably understand.

'Keep in touch,' says Paul Parrett.

They stand by the lift, in a space full of white windowless light. There's a drone behind the wall, from air-conditioning or other machinery. Nadine smells Paul Parrett's clean skin and cologne. She's exhausted. She'd like to lean against his chest and listen to the strong pump of his heart. It seems as if she's coming closer to him, not going away at all.

Seventeen

London air, bruised by rain, spreads over Nadine's face. She hesitates, one hand on the car door. The driver waits. His body, packed into dark clothes, is tense and athletic. She pushes the car door slightly but it doesn't move. It must be bullet-proof, if not bomb-proof.

'I'll close it,' says the driver, and there's no choice but to get in and let him shut the door on her.

'It's a hotel you're going to, isn't it?' asks the driver. 'Can you give me an address?'

His voice is civilly neutral. There's no hint of speculation in it, no suggestion that he knows what has just gone on in the fifteenth-floor apartment. He'll have had the message: 'No good. She's coming out now,' from some bored observer trained to read clues in voice, body posture, speed of movement, flicker of an eye. Or from another observer who only has to play back the tapes of what happened in the garden, on the sofa, in the bedroom. For she doesn't believe there's no camera in the bedroom. There would have to be. How many times has all this happened before? There must have been other times when it didn't work out. But usually it'll be OK. He'll play very safe, with known girls, known agencies, people who understand what's required. She's a bit of grit in the machine, but the machine's designed to override things like that. She's leaving with more than any of them could guess, thinks Nadine. Her hand is still warm where he held it, and his card is in her bag. There's another story in it, as well as the one the driver knows. 'Didn't Mr Parrett tell you? I've changed my mind. I'm not going back to the hotel. Can you take me to Paddington?'

He nods, looks at her, asks, 'Do you want me to phone through for you? Check the times of your train?'

'No, thank you. I've got a timetable.' And I don't want you to know where I'm going. Even though you're bound to know that the only place I'd take a train to at this time of night is home. Has it been checked already? Has my address come up on the screen, date of birth, place of birth, current residence? Paul Parrett didn't need to ask me for my address. Foggy ghosts of Kai and Tony and me on computer screens.

The air in the car is conditioned and tastes of nothing. He drives fast and skilfully and Nadine relaxes. In a few minutes she'll be out again in the anonymity of the station concourse, the long wait, polystyrene cups of late-night coffee and chocolate croissants which taste of metal and fill in a few minutes of boredom. For now she's safe. Nothing's going to happen, because this is time out of time. If she'd stayed with him, what would be happening now? She'd be pulled into his story, sucked dry and spat out. Or would she? Wasn't there something she ought to have risked, if only for the sake of that moment when she walked into his secret garden hung above London? It reminds her of something else she's heard recently. Another secret door opening. That's it. Enid and the Manchester Ladies. Thank God for Enid. The one person she's going to be able to talk to. Funny how he asked about Enid. And he's not going to tell Tony what happened: that Nadine Light didn't perform. Tony's risk didn't work. *Did Kai know?* She can't ask him. If she says a word to Kai that will be the end. The end of the business, the end of the partnership, the end of the house, the end of her own exemption from the harsh laws by which Kai judges everybody else. And if Tony gets his version in first . . . Tony's clever. Nadine knows how a story can be shaped and slanted. How different it can be made to appear if the storyteller starts at an unexpected place on the web and feels his way in along the thread nobody else would have chosen. Tony's quite capable of that. But he won't. Tony'll keep quiet. Whatever he was planning, it's gone wrong and Tony won't want to advertise that, not when Paul Parrett is involved. You don't want to get on the wrong side of a man like him.

Nadine rolls up her coat sleeves and rubs her arms, which are prickling with gooseflesh. He said he'd make it all right with Tony. That means all right with Kai too. The driver glances back and asks, 'Shall I put the heating on?'

'No thank you. I'm not cold.'

You'd think that he'd need all his attention for the road, at this speed. She puts up her hand and touches the back of her neck, where Paul Parrett's fingers brushed and lay for a moment on her skin. The skin is warm. The car swings left, and into the Paddington taxi-rank.

'This'll be the best place to drop you,' says the driver. 'I could wait while you check that train, if you like.'

'No, it's all right.' He's terrifyingly professional. He makes her feel as if he's there to look after her, even though she knows that's not true. The whole thing has an eerie perfection which she really can't handle. Imagine having someone like that with you all the time, phoning ahead, checking things, making sure there aren't any hitches. That's what it must be like to be Paul Parrett. The driver opens the door for her and she clambers out, twitching her coat over her bare legs.

'Goodbye. Thank you.'

'Mind how you go,' he says, straight-faced. She laughs and waves at him, then hurries away, conscious that he's watching. Maybe he's waiting in case she doubles back and leaps into a taxi and he has to follow her. Maybe he's watching to see if she goes to a telephone. If Enid had a phone she'd ring her, then someone would know that she was on her way home. It feels safer to be expected.

At the front of the concourse she cranes up, scanning the departures. Yes, there's a train, stopping at every stop, going all the way home. It's in already, being cleaned on the platform. A big-hosed machine goes from toilet to toilet, sucking them out. It's late and everything's closed except the fast-food stalls under the departure board, bright striped and nervy with neon. There's a party of late theatre-goers waiting. They've been on to supper afterwards and now they're a small bubble of gaiety, watched by a weary Indian family with two sleeping children, by a group of businessmen, by Nadine. They stand in a circle, laughing together, shielding the pleasure of their evening like a cigarette-lighter flame in the wind.

The train rackets through darkness. Going westward, going home. White faces doze opposite her. They are two young men with lager cans close to their sleeping fists. They don't look as if they belong here in the first class. Opposite, a businessman irritably punches numbers into his calculator, then gives up, leans back, shuts his eyes. The train puts on speed and the businessman's mouth slowly opens as he's sucked down into sleep. Far up the carriage there's the last chink of laughter from the theatre-goers, who have brought wine with them, knowing that the buffet would be closed. The slender threads that bind the passengers snap one by one as they separate into sleep. Nadine can't sleep. She watches foreheads, lips, eyes. All those lonely things going on inside them. That businessman – what's he dreaming about? His lips are moving. If the train wasn't making so much noise she'd hear him talking in his sleep. She wonders if Paul Parrett is asleep now, out on his roof by the maimed Ballerina apple trees, under the jasmine and the rain, trusting himself not to wake and sleepwalk over the edge of the roof so that he wakes for a startled second, then plunges down into London. Are his lips moving too? She wants to lean close and hear the words.

The train cries out, thundering into a tunnel. The ticket-collector walks back up the aisle, having checked all the tickets. He pauses by the two young men, but does not wake them. His eyes meet Nadine's in the unspoken conspiracy of those still awake among sleepers. He goes on up the train and the automatic doors hiss.

Soon she'll be home. No Tony, no Kai. Kai's away overnight, on another business trip. Enid will be alone in the house, and she'll be lying in bed, listening to the house begin to creak as the wind gets up. Enid's never liked Tony anyway. She'll believe anything of him. 'That one', she calls him. Once she said she was sure he carried a gun. That's what you do when you're alone all the time, you make up stories. On and on goes the train, through darkness, past mooning power-station stacks, past orange lamps and platforms rushing by so fast Nadine can't read the names. It bucks and sways and Nadine remembers racing the engines round the track on her cousin's electric train-set, and how the trains flew faster and faster, showering sparks, until they jumped the points or shot into the buffers. They always crashed, no matter how well the train was going, no matter how much she and Rupey hung over the papier mâché tunnels, willing the trains to break their record. They are going so fast that she'll be there soon. Going westward. Stepping westward. Westward. She loves the word. If only she could go on past her station and sleep a little and wake for a second at Dawlish as the sea rocks up to the train windows like a field of wheat, then sleep again through Launceston and Bodmin and Redruth and Camborne, all the way down as the stations get littler and the stops more frequent until at dawn the train comes to the end of the land and there's nowhere to go but the sea.

And then what? Bed and breakfast until the money runs out. Sleeping on the beaches, washing out her underwear in the public toilets and slipping past hotel receptionists to get to the bathrooms for an illicit bath. Eating bread, and bread, and more bread until her stomach is cold and heavy with it. Juggling in bus-shelters while rain lashes the sands. If she's lucky, a tiny part-time job in a tiny part-time arts centre. Or perhaps she could live with a fisherman. She smiles and her reflected smile leans in to meet her from the train window. She shades her eyes and blots out the reflection. There are lights sprinkled over the big dark Wiltshire Downs, like sweat drops on the flanks of a horse. Business goes on, day and night. Some businesses go on better at night. All the invisible deals going on, like cards falling perfectly into patterns. Used, often-dealt, sweaty cards, tumbling like petals. Tony and Kai work late. Places to go, people to see. How easily the words fall into the rhythm of the train wheels.

Trains are lonely places. It's all right in daytime when you can catch somebody's eye as the conductor tells you for the fourth time to place your luggage in the spaces provided, or that a child's green and black bumbag has been found towards the rear of the train. She hadn't heard right at first. She'd thought he said 'bomb-bag'. A child's bomb-bag. Somewhere in the world, in some desperate corner where only explosives have a voice, there'll be a group working in a safe house, making bombs to fit into a child's small zipped bumbag. And somewhere else, in ventilated underground rooms, Security will be learning to identify them. The information will float up on to one of the screens which hedge Paul Parrett. 'Child's bomb-bag, approximately 12 cms by 8 cms, black strap, green and black nylon, no distinguishing marks. Child unidentifiable.'

The computers will be whispering about her still, back in Security, brushing in the last strokes of the multi-dimensional portrait. *Colour of eyes: grey. Colour of hair: dark brown. White Caucasian female, nineteen [?] – possibly younger. No scars or distinguishing marks. White silk dress, black linen coat, black leather handbag, black pumps. No trace on police computer. No previous security record. Fingerprints obtained from coffee-cup. Voice-print available.* Even my own mother wouldn't recognize me. Especially my own mother, fast asleep in her curved wooden chalet above the lake, breathing in the smell of the communal vegetable gardens beneath her open window, listening for Lulu even in her sleep.

'Where's Deenie?' The rasp of Lulu's voice. When she's upset only the family can understand her.

'She's fine, Lulu. She's back in England with her friends, remember? Now go back to sleep. Back to sleep, Lulie-lu. Back to sleep.'

I'll go to Enid. She won't mind me waking her up if she's asleep. She lies awake, with her memories, those memories she's so worried I'm not going to have. She'll make me some tea in the thin china cup, and she'll open a new packet of Rich Teas for us. The tea won't be strong enough and Enid'll call it water bewitched. And the biscuits are flour and water. I'll dip them in the tea – we'll even put sugar in, it doesn't matter for once. I'm so tired. It could be shock. Now, for the final part of our evening's entertainment we present . . . the unshockable . . . the unstoppable . . . the unforgettable . . . Miss LIGHT. He thought it was a professional name. Cathy says it's a good name for a performer. I thought he thought I was on the stage. He thought I thought he thought. My fingers are jumpy, they won't keep still. Or else it's the train that's trembling. I'll go up and up the stairs to the attic, without turning on any of the lights so that even the house doesn't see me. It's Kai and Tony's house, not mine, and I haven't the strength to make it mine tonight, or to call it home. Up and up the dark pillar of the house, away from the rocks and the sea, to where Enid keeps her light on. It's like the beam of a lighthouse. If I follow it, I'll come safe home.

Even the traffic sounds like the sea up there in Enid's room. You can't hear voices, and if you shut your mind the traffic and voices could be waves and seagulls. In her lamplit room Enid's waiting for me. No. That was the witch locking up Rapunzel in her tower. She only did it to keep her safe. She had the right idea. What did Rapunzel think she was going to do with all that yellow hair? I'd tell her to stay in the tower. That old witch knew how to look after her. It's not safe outside. What they don't put in the story is that the witch got too tired and she couldn't take care of Rapunzel any more. That's what the story's really about. Mothers getting tired and bored.

'Go back to sleep, Lulu. Deenie's fine. You don't need to worry about her.'

I can't picture her face any more, only her back. Mother's back turning away from me as she bends down doing something for Lulu. And Daddy's hand stroking Mother's crossed ankles as she lies back on the settee. I'll sleep with Enid all night, and in the morning Kai will come looking for me. He'll say the words that'll magic away what Tony told Paul Parrett. It was just part of the dark, one of Tony's things. Arrangements.

The taxi-driver has been waiting at the station since one o'clock without a fare. Business is bad. He's not really a taxi-driver. He's just driving taxis until he can get another HGV job, but there's nothing going. No vacancies, no interviews. He's rung round thirty firms: nothing. There's not a lot of money in taxi-driving: the rent's a hundred and thirty a week, that's just to get your calls put through, then what with petrol and repairs and insurance you're looking at eighty, ninety quid a week take-home pay. And he can see the drop in the number of fares, even in the nine months he's been driving. When you used to meet the London trains there'd be a long queue waiting for taxis. Now there's half a dozen. Well, there isn't the business. People aren't travelling the way they used to. Day out, was it?

'No,' says Nadine. 'It was a business trip.'

He overcharges her but she tips him anyway. The house is as dark as she knew it would be, and the taxi-driver waits, engine running, as she fits the key into the lock and pushes open the door.

Immediately she smells cigarette smoke. Tony and Kai don't smoke. It might be the stale smell of her own cigarettes. It's nauseating. She really must make the effort to give up. This is an unfriendly house to come back to. She snaps on the hall light and its too brilliant glare shows nothing. She'll go straight up to Enid. No. She'll take off this dress and coat first. She never wants to wear the dress again: its washed silk smoothness feels clammy against her skin. Unbuttoning the linen coat she walks up to the next floor, to their bedroom, and opens the door.

There isn't much light but there's enough. It shows her a tumbled heap on the bed. It shows a shape which is too big to be just Kai. Bodies. A rasp of panic begins in Nadine's throat but she does not cry out. She grips the door frame with her left hand, while her right hand continues automatically to unbutton the black linen coat. Her eyes get used to the dark and she sees

179

more. Kai is on the side of the bed closest to her. He has fallen asleep on his stomach. But he never sleeps on his stomach. One hand hangs, knuckles down, brushing the floor. The other is around the right breast of the naked woman lying on her back beside him, so close that their heads are touching where hers leans into the angle of his neck. The pose is unconscious, and very beautiful. They are both deeply asleep and the woman is snoring slightly, because she is on her back. Nadine pushes the door wider, so there will be more light for her to see them by. Now she knows the woman. It's Vicki, her tanned predatory face smoothed out by sleep. She hasn't taken off her gold bracelet. One knee has kicked aside the rust and gold duvet, and Nadine's linen sheets are tangled between her thighs. Nadine looks at Kai's hand on Vicki's breast. He is not touching the nipple, but the soft shallow curve of the breast, spread sideways under its own weight. The touch looks tender, as if his hands remember Vicki and know she's lying beside him even though he's now deeply asleep. His body is utterly relaxed and his face turns sideways, towards Vicki.

All the buttons on Nadine's coat are undone. She raises her unbuttoning hand to her mouth and bites it hard, but not so hard that she'll draw blood. She bites to stop herself crying out. She mustn't wake them. She daren't wake them. It's like childhood again, standing by Mummy's and Daddy's bed after a bad dream, willing them to wake and take her in with them. But they never woke. They sailed on in their dead-beat sleep. Sometimes Mummy whimpered, dreaming of Lulu.

No. I am not that child. No. You won't make me back into her. I should have known it when you came to the door with your older-woman voice, your experienced face. I was a fool, thinking that you were one. You took me in with that violin lesson patter. You wanted me to think you were the business side of Kai's life. Nothing to do with us. No danger. I kept my eyes shut while yours were wide open.

But even you can't see everything, Vicki. You don't know

180

where I've been and you don't know what I know. Downstairs there's a drawerful of knives. Tony's taken off the plastic wrap and they're as sharp as your eyes were when you looked round my house. But I'm not that sort of a girl.

The way they're lying there, they look like old friends. Friends of the same age. That's where real friendships grow. She'll know all the songs he knows, the ones I don't know.

Kai. Open your eyes. Look at me. She isn't beautiful at all. That tired old tanned skin. Give her two years and she'll look like a crocodile, that's what you said.

But they sleep on, adult, omnipotent.

Enid is only dozing. She sleeps lightly with a book by her bed and the lamp-switch dangling just within reach. Often she wakes and makes tea and reads a chapter or lies there, thinking back into the past. She doesn't mind the night, or long for the dawn. She adapts to the shape of each night, noisy or quiet, sleepless or dream-filled. She wakes easily, so tonight she hears Nadine's light tap immediately, and her bedside lamp is on before Nadine has started to turn the doorhandle.

'It's only me.'

'Are you all right, dear? Is something wrong?'

The girl looks as if she's gone out wearing her slip as she advances into the room, milk-white and pinched, trailing her black coat, her arms crossed over her chest, hugging herself.

'What's happened to that lovely dress?'

'It got dirty.'

'You don't look too good. Shut the door. I'll put the fire on.'

Enid pulls back her nest of sheets and blankets, sticks two frail bare legs over the side of the bed, and toes around, feeling for her slippers.

'Let me lie down on your bed a minute,' says Nadine suddenly, going so pale that Enid thinks she's going to faint. Hurriedly, she pushes aside the blankets and makes space for Nadine. Nadine lies still, looking up at the ceiling. Slowly, her colour returns.

'I thought you were staying in London,' says Enid.

'I was, but I came back.'

'Pity,' remarks Enid. 'Coming back when nobody was expecting you. You look as if you saw something you didn't expect either.'

'Did you know they were here? Did you see them?'

Enid pauses. 'Well, not as such,' she says. 'But I heard her. She laughs so loud I can't help hearing her. They think no more of an old woman up in the attic than they'd think of a nest in the chimney. I don't pay attention to much of what goes on. See no evil, hear no evil.'

'Has she been here before?'

'She has, dear. Once or twice. I didn't like to tell you when you seemed so sure it was only business. Though business and pleasure is all the same thing to your Kai, I don't need to tell you that.'

Triumph in Enid's voice. She's got it right again. Right about Kai, right about the business, right about all of it. I was wrong. She's vindicated herself.

'I wondered if I ought to say something to you when I saw you ready to go to London with that Tony, you looking so lovely and him looking like the cat that'd got the cream. So what happened to your dress?'

'Nothing. It's dirty from sitting on the train.'

'Did he try something on, then, Tony?'

'No. Nothing like that. There was a misunderstanding, that's all.'

'And now there's another misunderstanding downstairs in your bedroom, concerning your Kai, is that it?'

'Oh, Enid. If you knew, why didn't you say? You could have told me. I'd rather have known.'

'No, you wouldn't. You wouldn't have wanted to believe me. You'd have gone and asked your Kai.'

'And he'd have kicked you out, is that what you were worried about? Why didn't you think about me? Why did you leave me to find out like this?'

'You don't understand. It wasn't the right time. Anyway, who was I to interfere? It's not my house. It's not my business where the money comes from. I live here, that's all.'

Enid scrambles off the bed and tugs down her night-dress. Her wispy hair is pinned up with pink-tipped hairgrips and she has rolled a thick yellow crêpe bandage round one knee. She reaches down and feels the knee cautiously, intimately, as if pressing a sponge-cake to see if it's done. All she thinks about is herself, thinks Nadine, why did I ever expect anything else from her?

'I'm going to make us both camomile tea,' announces Enid. 'No sense in losing a night's sleep on top of everything else.'

She really is unfeeling. As far as she's concerned it's no more than if I'd lost my doll or fallen over and cut my knee. She can't begin to imagine – or perhaps she hasn't got any imagination. Nothing shocks her because nothing sinks in.

'So what was your other misunderstanding – the one up in London?'

'Tony's a pimp,' says Nadine.

'Yes, dear, I should have thought that was on the cards. Though they're very high class, aren't they, your Tony and your Kai? You wouldn't catch *them* putting girls out on the streets.'

'*Kai!* No. It was Tony I was talking about.'

'Was it, dear? I thought they were partners? Isn't that what you were always telling me?'

'Well, they call it a partnership, but Kai's the one who's really in charge,' replies Nadine automatically – then hears herself.

Enid says nothing, she just watches Nadine, her light clear eyes friendly and curious. Then she prompts, 'But you must have known there was something up. Where did you think all the money was coming from?'

'You know they deal in property. They have to take some risks – the law's so stupid –'

'Oh, isn't it,' agrees Enid at once. 'Isn't it stupid? Now which law were you thinking of? The one that says you can't put old ladies out on the streets if they're taking up space in a house you want empty, or the one that says you can't put your girlfriend out on the streets to earn a bit of cash for you? Both equally stupid, no doubt.'

She drops a handful of dried camomile into a pot and puts the kettle on the boil. Nadine sits up on the bed.

'OK. Tony's a pimp and Kai's in partnership with him. So, for God's sake, stop calling them my Tony and my Kai. Where does that leave me?' asks Nadine. 'I live with Kai. I couldn't afford this place on what I earn. Not even the food we eat, let alone what we drink.'

'I can't answer that, can I, dear? I live here too. Anyway, it's not as simple as that. Show me the girl who wakes up one morning and decides, "Oh, yes, that's a good idea, I'll go out on the streets. I've always wanted to be a prostitute." No, it's all much more gradual, at least it is the way Kai and Tony do it. She lives with a man, and then one day one of his friends takes her out for dinner, somewhere expensive, and they drink a lot, and they both get carried away and then the next day she doesn't know what to tell her boyfriend – because she's a nice girl and she thinks he's nice too. But she tells him in case his friend does first. What a relief it is when he doesn't take it too badly. He even laughs and tells her these things happen. People get carried away. And then he leaves it for a while. The next thing is he says there's someone coming to town who needs looking after, and can she go out with him, so she does, and this time she gets a present. It won't be money for a long time, it'll be jewellery: a gold bracelet like the one that Vicki's got on downstairs. I've seen it. Later on, when she's got a bit more used to it, they'll start talking to her about money. A proper talk. It's because it's so gradual that it works. They're nice girls from Ruislip, their mums thought they ought to be fashion models, they don't want to know what they're really up to. I'm not talking about street-walkers, but then neither are Kai and Tony. I'm not talking about those poor kids who're on the game by the time they're fourteen either. They're hooked on something they can't get any other way. They're no good for the clients who can really pay. They want something with class. But as for where it leaves you, it doesn't leave you anywhere. Not unless you want it to.'

'How long have you known?'

'I'm like you,' says Enid, and makes a small stabbing jump to fetch down the biscuit tin from its high shelf. 'I know things and I don't know them. And I watch what I ask, if I think I'm not going to like the answers.'

She doesn't care, thinks Nadine, and why should she? Kai's nothing to her, or Tony either. And what about me? Maybe she doesn't need me after all. I was the one who needed her. *I must get back to Enid . . . Oh, Enid's this old woman who lives up in our attic, she's amazing, really interesting to talk to . . .'*

'You still haven't told me,' says Enid, 'what went on up in London.'

It's not a question. It's a space which Nadine can fill or not, as she chooses. Enid is putting out her best china cups, wiping them round with a cloth.

'He reminded me of the Manchester Ladies,' says Nadine. 'He had a garden way up above London. Orange trees and tomatoes and little hedges. You'd never guess it was there.'

'Who?'

'The client.'

'The one Tony took you to meet.'

'Yes, but I didn't know. We had dinner, then Tony had to go off. I thought he was ill.'

'A man like that's never ill unless he wants to be, you ought to know him better. Don't tell me, dear,' says Enid, holding up a traffic policeman's hand. 'Let me guess. You went back to his place for coffee.'

'Yes, but it wasn't like that. He was really nice.'

'What was he, then? Someone with money. Lucky I'm good at guessing. Merchant banker. Judge. Something in the city. Go on, give me a clue.'

'You're getting warm.'

'Tinker, tailor, soldier . . . politician.'

'Yes.'

'They always are. Anyone famous?'

'Paul Parrett.'

Is that sly pride in Nadine's voice? Enid gives her a sharp look. '*Very* discriminating,' she remarks.

'I liked him.'

'Well, that's all right, then, isn't it? You liked him, Tony's happy, Kai's happy, everyone's happy.'

'I don't know why. He just seemed so alive.'

'It's power that does it to them. It's like plugging them in to the grid every morning.'

'No, it was the garden as well. He loved it.'

'So what went wrong? You came shooting back fast enough. You must have been on the train by one o'clock. Not much time for love's young dream.'

'I couldn't do what he wanted.'

'Oh, dear.'

'I wish I had now.'

'That's only to spite your Kai.'

'No – it was him wanting it so much – and it was awful, nearly – only not quite. And I could have made it all right.'

'You can't turn it into your life's work, making things all right for a man like Paul Parrett. He won't have thought twice about it, you can be sure of that. He'd wipe you from his mind like wiping a blackboard.'

'He gave me his number. He said I could reach him, and he'd get back to me.'

'Ooh,' mocks Enid. 'Even though you didn't do what he wanted?'

'Yes. I've got it in my bag.'

'I'm surprised you didn't write it on your hand in biro, just to be sure,' says Enid. 'Well, that's something you'd better keep quiet, hadn't you, dear? Might be useful, though.' She pours the

186

camomile tea and Nadine picks up her cup and sips. It's like drinking hay. It might as well be an infusion of the rushes from the floor. What does Enid think she's playing at? Witch, wise woman, secret-keeper with her herbs and her rushes and her tower room, watching and waiting. Making people talk to her. Nadine puts the tea down.

'Don't you like it.'

'I'm not feeling too good.'

And she isn't. Lack of sleep, the glasses of wine drunk half a night ago, Paul Parrett's *petits fours*, the smell of cigarettes, the sight of Kai's hand on Vicki's breast, all fight together in her stomach. The pain is sharp, like a seam of stitches being ripped open inside her. She leans forward. Her jaw aches with nausea.

'Quick, Enid, I'm going to be sick.'

In a second a yellow plastic bucket is thrust under her head. Kai's bucket, she thinks muzzily, then the slow pulses of sickness speed up, join together and rise in her throat. She vomits up red meat, red wine, dark coffee, marzipan, the jogging of the train, Kai's dark-haired wrist on Vicki's tanned skin. A rush of sour yellow and brown vomit coats the bucket as Nadine retches. She is shaking so much she can't hold the rim of the bucket straight, and then Enid's holding it for her.

It's over. Her head is black inside, she's got to lie down. Enid's light dry hands guide her to the bed, and she lies back, her head singing, her eyes closed. She hears Enid say, 'Just going down to empty this . . .' then the darkness in the room packs together and she lets herself go into it.

Wet cold on her forehead, water dripping down her face. She opens her eyes. It's Enid with a sopping flannel. The flannel isn't clean and the dripping water is musty. Nadine pushes it away.

'Got any tissues?'

Enid has brought up the toilet roll. Nadine wipes her face and hands, then lies still again. She can't possibly move. Her mind races. Enid's hand, like a crisp autumn leaf that's stayed on its twig against all the odds, strokes her forehead. It's nice.

'Nice,' murmurs Nadine.

Enid hoists herself up so that she's sitting by the girl.

'You want to get some sleep.'

'I can't sleep. I keep thinking of things. Everything's going too fast inside my head. Make me think about something else. I know. Tell me about Sukey and Caro. What happened.'

'I'd have to think. I can't remember where we got to.'

'Caro in the newspapers. *You do remember* . . .'

'All right, dear. Wait a minute. I've just had a thought. I've still got those sleeping tablets Dr Govind gave me. They don't go off, do they? I'll give you a couple, then you'll get a proper sleep.'

'But you've got to tell me the story.'

Enid finds the dusty brown tablet bottle and squints at the label. 'You ought to take three, I think,' she announces. Nadine swallows, lies down, shuts her eyes. Enid's voice begins to lull, sing-song.

'Now where was I? You know Caro loved Sukey. And Sukey loved her too, in her way, but it wasn't Caro's way. It doesn't matter, they're both dead now. Sukey's been dead for more than fifty years, that's a long time. Caro didn't die then, of course. They even let her out of prison in the end. Her hair wasn't red any more, it was grey. I went to see her come out. There's only one way out, so you can watch if you want to. She didn't notice me. There was someone with her, a young woman in a fur coat. People still wore fur coats then, when Caro came out of prison. I wouldn't have recognized Caro. She came scuttling out with her head down, but nobody was waiting. Only me, and I was walking towards the gate, as if I was going into the prison. She didn't notice me. All Caro's family had a lot of money. And Sukey's too. I put flowers on Sukey's grave the day before Caro came out. I put my name on them, so Caro would see when she came. I knew she wouldn't be able to keep away from Sukey's grave. It would be the nearest she could get to her. I could just picture her rolling about on the ground and crying, digging her nails into the earth. She'd been waiting twenty years to do it, after all. And Caro never had any dignity.

'Oh, I still hated her, but you can't go on hating someone after they're dead. Not so easily. Once I knew Caro was dead it was like a light being switched off. But I still loved Sukey. You can love people after they're dead.

'Are you still awake? Are you listening? I'll tell you something. It was my fault. If it hadn't been for me, Sukey wouldn't have died, not then. If one single thing had been different.

'Caro killed her, you know. She beat Sukey's brains out with a poker. Then Sukey couldn't think about me any more. That's what she thought. She would beat everything that tormented her out of Sukey's head. But she beat out the sweetness too. All the honey in the comb. What did she think was going to be left?

'Oh, yes, it was in all the papers. They wouldn't have made as much fuss if it'd happened to a girl like me. But Caro wouldn't have killed me. She didn't love me enough. There's lots more but I'm tired. Are you listening, dear?'

What a mess. What a mess. Fancy seeing the pair of them in bed downstairs. Nadine's too young to know about his type. He's always reminded me of Mr Albion; funny, considering I never even saw Mr Albion. That Vicki's well suited to him. If Nadine's got any sense she'll leave him to Vicki.

Enid squints down at Nadine. Her head has fallen sideways and her mouth is open. Her skin is very pale, with a sheen of sweat on it. Her eye-sockets are stained dark brown. Enid can hardly hear her breathing. She leans close. Yes, it's all right. She's breathing. The pills have worked. Fine spikes of dark hair stick to Nadine's forehead. She looks like a sick and ugly child. You'd never believe this was the girl in the white dress who came in to pose for Enid before the taxi arrived to take her and Tony to the station. She looks lost. More fool her if she's been expecting Kai to take care of her. Her family don't sound much good, but then who knows what went on there? Maybe they didn't like the look of Kai. And who could blame them.

189

Suddenly Nadine turns, seizes a fistful of blanket and burrows her head into the pillow, face down. Only the top of her head can be seen. Past four o'clock. Not long now till it starts to get light. Better try and get some sleep while I'm waiting. Waiting for what?

Eighteen

Enid doesn't sleep. She curls herself on top of the bedclothes next to Nadine. It's warm enough for her. She can't stop thinking of Kai and that woman cuddled up together downstairs, dangerous as a couple of Alsatians. You can't tame them, they're always half wolf. They revert. Watch that light in their eyes as they pad back to the forest. What does Nadine think she's playing at? She's seen Vicki sleeping with Kai in her own bed, but what does she imagine is going to happen in the morning? She doesn't even try. She vomits it all up, and then she sleeps. She's only got a few hours left. She ran away from Paul Parrett, that's clear, though he seemed to like her well enough.

'You don't want to get on the wrong side of a man like that,' Enid tells sleeping Nadine. 'You've made a fool of him, and of Tony and Kai too. To crown it all you go and ruin a silk dress which must have cost hundreds of pounds. Daft ha'p'orth. It'll be fit for the rag-bag now. It's a pity you ran off. You could have made something of yourself there. A man like that's got connections. Influence. And he doesn't want trouble. If you treat him right, he'll treat you right. There's enough newspapers waiting for a sniff of scandal. He knows all you have to do is pick up the telephone, so he'll make sure you've no cause to. He's got more to lose than you have, dear. He doesn't want you selling your story to the Daily Whatsit.

'Trouble is, he's got too much to lose. He gave you his telephone number, did he? I hope you weren't fool enough to give him yours. We don't want any callers here. We've had enough of all that, what with your Kai and Tony and their business friends. You didn't see the friends who came along to get rid of Jenny and the rest of them. No. You missed that. Well, they weren't a pretty sight. As for taking the baby out of its cot and dangling it over the banisters, that was just a joke. Jenny didn't seem to get it, though. Ever so upset she was. They told her they didn't think this house was a safe place for a baby. Too many railings missing. 'Course they didn't know I was listening. Jenny stood there, she didn't dare move. One of them had the baby by the feet. He had both the baby's feet together in one hand, the way you'd hold a chicken. He swung him very gently, out over the banisters. The baby was purple, screaming. I'll never forget the sound Jenny made. Like she was being strangled. She was yelling before, saying she was going, she wouldn't even pack, she'd never come back. But they wanted to make sure.

'He gave the baby back to her. He couldn't even cry any more, he just jerked about in Jenny's arms.

'Oh, your Kai wasn't there, don't worry. He wouldn't want to be mixed up in anything nasty like that. He came back later, when they'd all gone. The way that baby screamed. But then you might say it was always screaming.

'I'd've gone for the police, but you can't, can you? If you do, it'll be your turn next. And the police wouldn't pay any attention to an old woman like me. Not if your Kai was standing there in his nice clothes. *"My sitting tenant. Yes, they know her well down at the Prince and Pauper. A bit of a troublemaker when she's had a few. Noisy too."* Oh, they'd be on his side fast enough. They know a nuisance when they see one and they're trained not to take too much notice of old women making wild allegations. And I wouldn't fancy your chances against the word of a government minister, dear. They have to stick together, it's their job.'

It's been a long, long time since anyone turned to Enid for help. Yes, Jenny screamed out her name, but she'd have called for anyone. She must have known Enid couldn't come down and interfere. After all, Enid lived there. Sometimes, when someone needs you, it makes you hate them. You shut your door and turn the wireless on loud so as not to hear the cries.

A bit late to shut the door now, Enid tells herself tartly, when you've let her into your bed. You could say she's not a kid, she's sixteen past. Old enough to know what she's got herself into. No one ever asked her to come here. She walked into it with her eyes open. Anyone could see what kind of man Kai was. The girls these days know everything. They're not like we were. I didn't know anything, till Sukey taught me.

Sukey. 'Oh, darling, you're not *washing* those frightful rags, are you? Sweetheart, you don't need to do that. It's exactly like the Dark Ages. I'll buy them for you every month if you can't afford them.' She was always giving me things. And it was so easy to take from Sukey. It didn't make any difference. She never wanted anything back. Besides, she must have known she had everything already.

Enid scrambles sideways and slips down under the bedclothes next to Nadine. She puts her arms around Nadine and pulls her close.

On the white rumpled surface of the bed the old woman takes the sleeping girl into her arms. She has been waiting such a long time for her. She whimpers and covers the young smooth cold face with kisses, not minding the smell of sour breath. For more than fifty years she has been far out on the ice, waiting. Here is the head: she strokes it feverishly. It is not caved in, not disfigured, not blazing with flies. Here is the hair, short and feathery and fashionable, not matted with blood. Here are the eye-sockets, wet with tears, not empty and unseeing. The fine-grained skin is not torn and battered. The body smells of sweat and stale wine and perfume, not like the entrance to a butcher's shop. The flesh is cold but she can bring it back to life. This time she will not turn her back. This time she will warm, she will warn, she will protect.

'Darling,' she whispers, 'darling.'

Nadine sleeps, her face against Enid's old parched neck. Her smooth skin touches Enid's, which is crazed like a desert, trenched with dry rivers. Enid is small, but she is powerful. Her balding skull is packed with stories of survival. She's been alive so long, she knows everything about staying alive.

'Go to sleep, dear,' murmurs Enid. 'Go back to sleep.'

The ice is cold, so cold nothing human can sleep on it without drifting seamlessly into the drowse of hypothermia, then death. The wind sings across the frozen sea, and the snow-woman walks away contented, to the place where she belongs. She doesn't feel the sting of the snow, or the crusted ice under her feet. She has got her child back in her arms.

The house is empty but for the sleeping wolves, Enid in her room, and Nadine. What are they going to do in the morning? Will that woman have the sense to leave? Or will she hang on for a slow breakfast and the newspapers in bed, knowing that Nadine's in London and can't possibly be back yet? What if Nadine sees them through the door, all toast crumbs and crumpled sheets, handing one another bits of the newspaper? Even worse than seeing them at it. I wonder if Caro ever saw us. I suppose I'll always wonder. She had the key to Sukey's house all the time. We'd never have known if she'd crept in one afternoon when at last we'd fallen asleep. She'd have seen the stains where we'd rolled on the grapes we kept dropping on the sheets. Sukey used to drop them into my mouth, but she always missed. Purple stains, drying to brown, like blood. The wistaria tapping on the glass, and Caro looking, looking, then going away without saying a word. And I saw nothing. I knew nothing. The monkey again. Why didn't Sukey change the lock, or put a bolt on her door? None of it might have happened. The trouble was, she never used her imagination about Caro. She was careless. Just the way Kai's been careless, bringing that woman here.

Enid strokes Nadine's cheek. She's not even pretty any more. Certainly not beautiful. No competition for that one he's got downstairs. Enid looks at her clock. It's nearly six. It's not going to be a nice day today; she can tell from the quality of light coming through the thick dark curtains. They said on the news last night there'd be scattered showers. Nadine's undrunk cup of camomile tea has an oily film on it.

'I'll make her some proper tea when she wakes up. She'll want something. She looks washed out. Bugger it,' she remembers, 'I finished the milk last night.'

Enid has to buy her milk fresh every day, or it goes off. The all-night shop at Texaco will be open. She gets her milk there. Quietly, Enid dresses in her narrow black slacks and a pink Oxfam jumper, crams her beret on her head. Not a sound from Nadine; well, let her sleep it off. Pound coins, raffia shopping-bag, front-door key. An adventure. And someone to come back to and tell all about it. It must be like this all the time when you live with people. Nadine is deep down in the bedclothes, almost invisible. Only the dark top of her head shows. Very gently, Enid eases the doorknob round and sets off down the stairs. Nothing moves.

Nineteen

Vicki and Kai wake up comfortably. Vicki doesn't like sex in the morning: she's funny that way, always has been. What she likes is a pot of really hot fresh tea – Indian, none of your China or Earl Grey muck, a jug of silver-top milk and four digestive biscuits. Yes, she knows they're full of calories, but what the hell. She never eats breakfast, and she's going to the gym later on, with Lila. And Kai, give him his due, does make a really good cup of tea. She nudges him with her elbow, and when he groans sleepy protest she digs hard into the fleshy covering of his ribs. He rolls over.

'That's the way,' she says, satisfied. 'I thought I was going to have to wait all morning for you to wake up.'

He gropes for his watch on the floor beside the bed. 'Jesus, Vick, it's only quarter past six.'

'Yes, but you've got a lot on today, haven't you? Big day. Besides –' She doesn't go on, but he knows she's thinking of the morning train back from London, with a bleary Nadine on it. Vicki handles his relationship with Nadine as she has handled all his relationships with other women. Her tact is perfect. It's as if he's suffering from an illness which will run an entirely predictable course, known only to Vicki. She does insist that Kai wears a condom, but that's fair enough. These days, as Vicki says, you can't be too careful. You never know where people have been. Nadine moving into the house must have been a blow to her, but she kept quiet about that too. Vicki had liked the look of the house herself, and had had plans for interior decoration. She'd come to look round the empty shell with him, and he'd known what she wanted. Nothing was said. Vicki was never one to make trouble, that's why she had lasted all these years with Kai. She just mentioned what she'd do with this room or that, and of course Vicki had a real eye for colour, you had to give it to her. If you liked that sort of thing.

'I know it's nothing to do with me,' remarks Vicki now, obliquely, 'but I still can't help wondering if you ought to of chosen plain brass. Lacquered is nicer.' Kai doesn't reply. His urge to stay in bed curled up against Vicki's neat brown flanks fights his need to pee. And then if he gets up he'll have to make her tea . . . He groans again and swings his legs over the side of the bed, stands up, yawns hugely and scratches himself under the arms.

'Good boy,' says Vicki, snuggling back into her pillow. 'Do you get the paper delivered?'

'I'll go down the corner for you,' he says with conscious magnanimity. '*Daily Mail*?'

'That's right.' She huffs her breath against a hand held near to her mouth. 'Ugh! Ponky! Got any mouthwash, Kai?'

'I don't know. Nadine might . . . I'll look in the bathroom.'

'That bathroom! I don't know how you can stand it, you and Nadine,' she says, her eyes sparkling at him maliciously. He stops scratching and just stands there, looking at her.

'This room's still a bit ponky too,' she says, wrinkling up her nose. 'Smells like cat to me.'

'There were cats in here.'

'My God, must have been those squatters. Some people live like animals. I suppose you had to get rid of them.'

'Yeah – most of them were only kittens, so there was no problem.'

'Oooh, Kai! Poor little things,' says Vicki perfunctorily, scrabbling under the pillow for a comb.

'You wouldn't say that if you'd seen them. They tore my arms to bits. And they could swim too. I thought they were supposed to drown straight away.'

'Of course they can swim! You put them in a bag of stones or something, if you want to drown them.'

'I bought a bucket with a lid on it, and after a bit they

stopped making a noise. But then I took the lid off and they were swimming round and round with just their mouths above the water. They looked like little rats. So I poured all the water out in the backyard and they lay there like those cartoons when the cat gets run over. Flat and skinny. I had to hit them on the back of the head with a stone. They were hard to kill. They wouldn't stop jerking.'

'You ought to take up your squash again,' she remarks, looking at him appraisingly while she combs her hair, 'they've got ever such a good new coach at the health club. Tony's been taking lessons, did he tell you? You've got to keep yourself in shape for a young girl like Nadine. You won't forget my digestives, will you, when you go round the shop?'

'OK, OK.'

Kai stumps out of the room, genitals swinging. Probably off to take a bath first, Vicki thinks, that man's mad about washing. Still, it's nice, when you consider what some men are like. Real shockers.

Kai lifts the bathroom door to one side. He must get it fixed: perhaps this weekend, if Tony's going to be around to help. The smell hits him. Jesus. That woman. Holding his breath, nostrils pinched and angry, he crosses the room. The toilet bowl is streaked with vomit. It hasn't been flushed at all and a curded mass of vomit rolls and floats in the water. The seat is spattered. By the toilet there's a stained yellow plastic bucket. He stands still and swears. It's that old witch again. Too drunk to get upstairs, so she has to do it here. Too drunk to clean up after herself. If Nadine'd been here she'd have cleared it up. She thinks I don't notice the way she scurries round after the old bitch. Next thing the old woman will be shitting herself and peeing herself and expecting us to clean it up. Jesus. They expect you to get rid of rats and mice but a filthy old woman is something else. She must be looked after.

'Oh, no, Mr Toivanen, I'm afraid Miss Shelton is a protected tenant.' Satan take her and her shit where they belong. Nadine's not here now for her to hide behind. If Nadine wasn't so soft I'd have got rid of her months ago. She's nothing but an animal, bringing her filth and diseases into the house. But this time she won't get away with it. Half past six. She'll be up there sleeping it off. Right. She's going to get a waking-up she won't forget.

He can't bring himself to pee into the filth of the toilet bowl. He's not going to flush it either, not before he's rubbed her face in it. He goes downstairs into the bedroom, pulls on jeans and sandals. Vicki glances at him, but his face is averted. From the look of him, there's trouble.

'Going down the shop now?'

'No. The drain's blocked, I have to fix it. Don't go in the bathroom yet.'

Wouldn't you know it? This house. Something ought to be done about the plumbing. She'll take a shower when she gets back to her own place. She doesn't trust the bath here. You never know who's been using it – that dirty old woman upstairs, for one.

Kai goes down to the yard and pees into the main drain. It stinks too. He'll swill Jeyes Fluid down it later. You can't get anything clean in this house. He's beginning to regret buying it. If he'd known about the old woman, he would never have bought it. She's bad luck. As he zips up his jeans, he sees a piece of piping in the corner of the yard. Dull zinc grey, a yard long. Tony was using it to lever off the old taps on the bath. It ought to be put away. Kai picks it up. It might be useful for fixing the drains.

He goes up through the house with fast furious steps as far as the bathroom, turns on the cold bath-tap, then leaves it running so that Vicki will think he is clearing the drain. He climbs the last flight to Enid's attic with quiet elastic steps. He's never counted the steps before. There are fourteen of them, twisting to her door. Her door. Why should she live here in his house? What law allows her? Maybe she thinks he is nice, like Nadine. Maybe she thinks he'll put up with anything. But she's gone too far. This time he'll show her. You try to make a place decent, you work hard, you spend money. She needs to be taught a lesson.

Kai moves lightly now, for a powerful man. His hand is delicate on the doorknob. The only doorknob in the whole house, and the old witch has it. He squeezes it as if he will make blood run from it. He turns it and it responds with a light oiled click. This is going to be easy. The door slips wide.

It's dark in the room. She's got the curtains drawn. There's the bed. It smells in here too. Old stale air, nothing washed, nothing clean. How long is it since those windows have been open? And the smell of vomit is in here too, fainter but unmistakable. There she is. Drunk and snoring in the middle of her bed, with the covers pulled right over her. Like a rat in its nest. Breathing in her own stink. That's her shape under the bedclothes, curled up. Feet, backside, shoulders. Head. All tucked down and snoring. She'd sleep for hours yet if he let her. What a life for an old woman.

He looks away, around the fouled room. Everything cluttered, dirty, untidy. Yes, it's like having an animal in the house. Not a human being at all. There ought to be laws to get rid of such people, not laws to protect them. Oh, she's an old woman, is she? She's got nowhere to go? Then she's lived too long.

He notices that he's brought the piping up with him. Now it's heavy. A bit rough in his hands. Grainy. He swings it, just a little.

They're out of milk at the Texaco garage when Enid arrives. But the milkman will be along soon, the assistant tells her, folding back the pages of his Terry Pratchett. She waits. It's nice having shops that stay open all night long. If you go out, you know you'll find someone to talk to, even if it's only to ask for a box of matches or a loaf. Not that she wants to talk now. Save it for later, when Nadine wakes up. There'll be plenty to talk about then. What a bloody mess. The assistant looks up at her. She must have said something aloud.

'Must be a long night for you,' she offers companionably. Look, I'm normal just like you.

'Oh, it doesn't bother me. I like reading, see. And now we've got the automatic doors you can keep trouble out when you see it coming.'

Enid nods agreement. A good citizen, she is, on the side of Texaco against trouble.

'Here he comes. You didn't have long to wait,' says the assistant. He lays the book face down and goes to help pack the cartons of milk into the fridges. Enid selects two, and waits. She's in no hurry. Something else, perhaps, to make a nice breakfast for Nadine? She looks around the racks for inspiration. American blackcurrant muffins. Sounds interesting. The assistant returns to his desk, tots up Enid's purchases and offers a plastic bag.

'They nice, are they?' he asks, indicating the muffins.

'I've never tried them before. It's for a friend. A little treat. She's staying with me.' He nods, cautious in case she gets talking, and gives change. Enid goes out, saying goodbye separately to the assistant and to the milkman, and trots away across the forecourt with her shopping. It's no distance back to the house. Just a nice walk. And the day's perfect. New-made, grey and cool. Much better than all that sun they've been having lately. It'll brighten up later, you can tell. Only a few cars about, and no one else walking. A young boy on a paper round skims by on his bicycle, hurls a paper over a hedge and skims on. Well. Enid's surprised anyone puts up with that. Papers just dumped on the front path, even if they are wrapped in plastic. It must be some new American fashion. All Americans are mad about speed. It's like a disease with them. A good strong cup of tea, and then the muffins. That'll settle her stomach. Then we'll talk.

The birds aren't frightened this time of the morning. Sparrows pecking and fluttering nearly under my feet. Swallows'll be going home soon. Think of them going all that way. And knowing where to go. We think we know a lot of things, but we don't know as much as a swallow. Those swifts were making patterns round the house last night. Cutting the air with their wings. Imagine going on and on, flying, never stopping to sleep. They even mate on the wing, apparently. Oh, it's been a beautiful summer. Never mind the flies in the ointment. And then there's autumn to look forward to. This year I'll try beech leaves in glycerine again. It makes a lovely decoration. Those rushes weren't much of a success. I shan't try that again.

Enid tiptoes up through the house. She doesn't want to risk waking those buggers up before their time. Let sleeping dogs lie. Even when she's past the bedroom and on to her own stairs she makes sure no one can hear a footfall. At the top the door's open. Funny. Nadine must have woken up. She ought to've slept for hours yet, with those tablets. Still, perhaps it's as well.

It's not a sound or a movement that alerts Enid. It's a change in the shadows: some bulk where it shouldn't be. She stands at her threshold, slowly makes sense of the broad blocking back of Kai, bent over her bed, his hand with something in it, stirring, starting to swing.

She could get away. Back down the stairs. He hasn't seen her.

'*Why, Caro, darling,*' comes Sukey's voice, protesting, humorous, not yet afraid. And then the black hiss of the poker.

'Look behind you,' quavers Enid, singsong.

He swivels, fast as a heavy man can be fast when he wants, and sees her. What does he think he sees? The ghost of her, to judge from his colour. Better make things clear in case he goes and does something silly.

'It's not me in the bed,' she whispers. 'It's your Nadine.'

She's never seen a bull charge but it must be like this. He runs at her and she's lifted with him, the butt of it thwacking out her breath. The air is tearing around her: everything's so fast, so much stronger than her. Suddenly he's close, his breath in her face, his eyes glaring at something she wants to say isn't in her, isn't here at all. But she has no breath. He's got her, she's in the air, lifted high by his arms so her feet dabble against the floor. For an overwhelming second she's a child again, flooded with it, helpless. Her mouth creaks but it won't scream or talk. She sees her doorknob whip past, her heavy door, and then he hurls and she flies but she doesn't know where she's going as the air hisses in the white downpour of her falling.

Before the fall there wasn't any noise at all. Barely a scuffle. When she fell it made a sound like a broom falling down inside a cupboard. A small, dull sound. Now there's only one person on the stairs. He looks down at the sprawled figure beneath him. It's all wrong. The geometry of arms and legs isn't right. That's not how a head goes. Not even a child would draw it like that. Gently, he goes down the stairs towards it. She has fallen face down but with her chin touching the floor in a way which shouldn't be possible. There seems to be some movement going on in her mouth still. Her eyes are open but they are not looking at him, and anyway they certainly don't recognize anybody. A little bit more sound, a sad chuffing noise, then silence. It was air coming out of her lungs, not real breathing. Jesus. Nadine. What if she's woken? He listens, but all he can hear is the cold water running into the bath. Vicki, stay in the bedroom. Drains are difficult things.

The piping. Where did he put it down? Cat-light, he mounts the stairs again. He's getting sick of going up and down them. It's surprising she wanted to stay here with all these stairs. The old woman in her big, dirty bed. The black top of Nadine's head. What is Nadine doing here? She should be in London. Really she's got to be more careful, she might have got hurt. No. This isn't the time to think about it. Let her sleep. He stiffens, listens. No sound from upstairs. She hasn't woken.

Stepping carefully over Enid, he goes down to the bathroom and turns off the tap. For a moment it feels hard to move again, but he manages it. Once he gets going, it's easy. He goes on down to the bedroom.

'Vick.'

'Got it fixed, have you?'

'Vick, there's been an accident.'

She looks up sharply, measures his expression, gets purposefully out of bed and pulls on her neat white lycra panties and bra. 'Chuck me over my top, Kai, would you?' A minute later she's dressed. 'Right. Is this something I want to know about?' she asks.

'The old lady fell.'

Lady, notes Vicki. Never heard her called that before.

'Let me have a look at her. I did do my first aid, you know.'

'She doesn't want any first aid, Vicki.'

She sits, straightens, stares. 'Oh, my God,' she says.

'You better get right out of here.'

'OK.' Her fingers crisp the duvet frill, squeeze it convulsively, let go. 'Are you sure?' she asks.

'Yeah. You look yourself if you want to.'

'No, thanks.' She shudders. 'You're right. I'm getting out of here.'

He stands in the doorway, big and heavy and dark. He's in her way. Poor old Kai. Why did this have to go and happen? It's the house. You always get trouble in a place like this. She's never liked the atmosphere.

'Listen,' she says. 'You come over to my place. You've got to go careful. It's the shock.'

'No,' he says, shaking his head. 'There's things to do here. Police.'

'You don't want to go getting the police,' she says automatically. 'What've they got to do with it? Get the doctor.'

He thinks of the doctor. He thinks of bruises, marks. Postmortems. He sees Vicki from a long way off. He needs to be alone. He needs space to think.

'You go,' he says. 'I'll come later.'

He doesn't need to urge Vicki. She's already crowding her things into her overnight case, smoothing the duvet.

'You will change the sheets, won't you? Don't forget, now. Or shall I do it before I go?'

'No,' he says. 'You better go, before something else happens.'

She is quick and deft, at the doorway already, yellow-pale under her tan, bag in hand.

'Phone me,' she says. 'Soon as you get it sorted out.'

'Yeah,' he says, but it's no good. There's no time for any of that now. She's going. She wants out. Thank God, Vick's the type who'll keep her mouth shut.

The click of the front door behind Vicki releases him. Things to do. First, something to cover his hands. He'll never cram them into Nadine's rubber gloves. Two tea-towels will do. He wraps them round his hands, fetches the length of piping from the bathroom and replaces it carefully in the backyard. Fingerprints. A flash of heat goes through him. He washes, rubs, dries the piping, dirties it again with dirt from the green-coated brick walls, tugs forward a wreath of ivy. The piping looks as if it's been there for ever. He looks at the digital clock in the kitchen. A new second bubbles up on its plastic display. It is 7:11 and 23 seconds. 24. 25. The sky is clearing and it's going to be sunny again after all. Kai jerks away. The tea-towels are coming loose and they've got dirt on them. He binds them tighter.

The hall and stairway are filling with early sun. Later, he'll take Nadine her coffee. No. The gentle sun hasn't wiped away anything. More things to do. At the bottom of the attic stairs she'll still be there, the old woman, awkwardly folded together. A bag of dirt and blood. Face half turned from her, he feels for her and gathers the dense, heavy body. It flops, rolls out of his grasp. He fixes the tea-towels tight and spoons his arms under the body. Holding in his breath, he carries Enid through to the empty room next to the bathroom. The spare room, Nadine calls it. He lays the body on bare boards behind the door, curled as it was at the foot of the stairs, and shuts the door. He breathes out.

There's a stain at the bottom of the stairs. He will need mop and bucket. First, he'll have to clean the bathroom. Have it all clean before Nadine wakes up. The clotted vomit is hard to shift with cold water, but he daren't use the geyser and wake Nadine. He fills and empties the yellow bucket, swills the sides of the lavatory, scrubs it with the brush. The smell is awful. A small sound seeps out of his mouth. He gags.

The bathroom is clean. The boards are clean. Now, the towels. He hesitates, then goes down to the kitchen again, finds a plastic rubbish bag, drops in the tea-towels and seals them with a wire tie. He carries the bag upstairs to the bedroom, where he slides a leather suitcase from under the bed and tucks the rubbish bag into its corner. He leaves the suitcase lying open on the bed.

He makes coffee, and thin white toast with Marmite for Nadine. He butters it carefully so that there will be no lumps of melting butter on the toast. She doesn't like them. He heats her milk and pours it into a jug, puts two big cups and the toast on a tray and carries it up all the stairs, spreading the fragrance of coffee and fresh toast through the empty house. The smell of coffee often wakes Nadine. He wants her to wake up now. He wants someone to talk to.

'Nadine. Nadine.' He puts down the tray, pulls back Enid's curtains, opens a dirty window. It shudders in its frame. 'Nadine!' He pounces at the bed, suddenly frightened. He can't hear her breathing.

But when he tears the covers back he feels her warmth. She groans and twists away from the light. He shakes her shoulder. 'Nadine! Nadine! Wake up!'

Groaning, white and puffy-eyed, she wakes. Her eyes are bewildered slits against the light. She doesn't know where she is. Slowly he sees everything come back to her as she looks round Enid's room, taking it in.

'Oh, God, I feel terrible.'

'Drink your coffee.'

He holds the cup carefully under her mouth so she can sip. She drinks it with her eyes shut, holding her head as if it hurts her. When half the coffee is gone she flops back on the pillow. Her eyes are clear, narrow, accusing.

'Has she gone?'

'She's gone into town. I met her going out,' he says steadily.

'I don't mean Enid. I mean that woman. Vicki. Has she gone, or is she still in my bed?'

Jesus. Vick. At once knows what she has seen.

'I thought it would be a nice surprise for you when I came back early,' says Nadine.

'I made you toast. It will get cold,' he says stupidly. His head rings. What does she know – what does she not know?

'I'm going to get washed,' says Nadine.

'Darling –'

'No. I'm going to get washed. I need a bath, really.'

She gets out of bed very carefully, holding on to the bedstead. Her dress is rucked and spoiled. She pulls it over her head, drops it to the floor, kicks it aside and steps unsteadily towards the door.

'Be careful! You'll fall.'

Kai follows Nadine down the stairs, watches her bare feet pad down each stair, follows her into the bathroom. She bends down, rinsing the bathtub with cold water, then lights the geyser pilot. It coughs, roars into flame and begins to spurt white-hot water.

'I can never get this bloody thing right. I wish Enid was back, she's much better with it.'

She leaves the bath to fill and bends over the washbasin, scrubbing fiercely at her teeth. When she stands up again, she turns dizzy and catches at Kai's arm. 'Go and make me some more coffee, Kai. I feel awful. Enid gave me some sleeping-pills.'

Once he's out of the room she feels better. She runs in cold water and steps into the bath. The hot clean bath feels delicious.

She'll wash her hair. It smells of trains and drinks and stale nights. She'll wash it all away.

When Kai carries in the coffee, she's lying in the bath, her back arched, dipping her hair. She puts out a wet hand for the cup and he sits on the dirty-linen basket by the bath. He watches her tensed, bare body, streaming with water, the stomach muscles flat and tight under her skin, her breasts going shallow. How young she is. His hands remember the dead weight of Enid. Nadine sits up, pours shampoo into the palm of her hand and massages it into her hair.

'I'll move out,' she says, shampooing hard.

'But why – there's no need for you to do that. Vick's a friend, an old friend, that's all. There's nothing in it.'

She stares straight out at him from under her cap of white bubbles. 'A friend,' she levels at him.

He puts his hand on the side of the bath. It is trembling. He watches it, watches her noticing it.

'Darling Nadine, she is a friend. She is one my business friends, you know that. She should not make you unhappy.'

His English slips, making her tender. Or does he know it works like that? She glances at him sharply.

'I am sorry,' he says. 'I love you.'

There's sweat on his forehead. He looks very ill – why didn't she notice that before? His fingers are tight on the rim of the bath.

'You aren't well, Kai,' she says. 'It's all this running around. It's destroying everything.'

'Yeah,' he says eagerly. 'Yeah, you're right. This business is killing me. Let's go away, Nadine.'

His words pour through her, sweet as victories. He has never looked at her like this before. There's something seriously wrong and he's confiding in her, not Vicki. Maybe he's telling the truth, there was nothing in it, just two old friends and too much to drink. He looks – frightened. She thinks of the wads of new money, the phone calls, the men Enid talked about, the ones who got rid of the squatters. Business. If things aren't going well, he might have good reason to be frightened.

'Darling Nadine, why don't we go away now? Straight away? We can go to my country. I know a place there. Just us together. We can pack and go today. Tony'll look after things here.'

She pats the lather on her hair, thinking. Time for ourselves. Time to be together. Just us. Darling Nadine. Her veins are warm with his words. And if we have time together we can sort things out. All that business in London – Tony – Paul Parrett – we can talk about it.

'I'll take you to my friend's summer-house, Nadine. We can stay as long as we like. We can go now – we can go today. Say you'll come.'

He doesn't touch her, but he leans close, his face closing out the world, full of hunger. Of course she'll come.

'But won't we need a lot of things? What about tickets? Do I need a visa?'

He shrugs, relaxing. 'We've got money. What else d'you need?' A touch of the old Kai.

'Right.' She leans back and sloshes water on to her hair. 'Did Enid say what time she was coming back? I'll have to say goodbye to her.'

She'd been going to talk to Enid. But Enid's never liked Kai. Nadine knows what she's going to say, and knows she doesn't want to hear it now. The frowsty night, the witchy secrecy of Enid's room: her clear statements; her stories; that stretching memory; no, Nadine doesn't want any of that now.

'You know what she's like,' says Kai. 'She'll have wandered off somewhere. She might not be back all day.'

Nadine frowns. It seems odd that Enid's gone off like this, but never mind. 'I'll get ready. You go and pack.'

He smiles, kisses her wet head and goes out. Joy rises in her, coming from nowhere. As long as she doesn't look outside the frame of now, she's safe. Concentrate on now. Clean hair, clean jeans and top, leather jacket. Her face looks exactly the same as it usually does in the mornings. No one would guess all that had happened the night before. They are going away, she and Kai, the two of them. No Tony, no Vicki, no house, no cinema, no business. Only Kai and a wad of new money that will fly them through the air, fill them with food, whisk them into taxis, hire them cars. All they'll hear will be the noise of money making things happen.

They stand outside the house with their two expensive leather bags at their feet. The sun is warm and gay on the steps and pavement, but already there's a crisp edge to it. Autumn's on its way. The plane trees above them rustle. Kai has ordered a taxi and it'll be here in a minute.

'Fuck,' says Kai. 'I forgot to write a note to Tony.'

'You could ring from the airport.'

'No. I must leave him a contact number in Helsinki.'

She doesn't question anything. She stands in the sun, drinking in the air which tastes like cider, smiling dreamily downwards and watching for the taxi to appear round the corner of the square.

Kai walks past the notepad and pen by the telephone, leaps up the stairs to the spare room and opens the door. She is still there. He grips the body under buttocks and shoulders and carts it out to the landing. Looking up the attic stairs, he gauges the angle of fall. He can't remember exactly how she lay. Now he has to look at her: the nodding flopping head, the skinny shoulders. And yet there seems so much of her. He puts her down at the foot of the stairs and begins to arrange her, hands forward, foot skewed to one side. She still moves quite easily: she hasn't started to stiffen up yet. There's something dark dribbling out of her nose. It smears the back of his hand and he wipes it off frantically, then steps back. She seems to subside a little, like an artist's model relaxing into her pose. He backs off, goes into the bathroom and washes his hands hard, turning them over and over, applying soap to each finger. Then he leaves the bathroom and goes down the stairs without looking at Enid, though he can't quite get the shape of her out of the corner of his eye. It's like something lodged there.

The breeze is blowing up Nadine's freshly washed hair. She waves to him, points to the taxi turning at the corner and backing to their kerb. She picks up her bag, but he takes it from her and smiles, opening the taxi door, pushing in their bags, letting Nadine step in first. The taxi whirls them away on its practised wheels, and the last thing he sees is the sun glinting on his shut front door before they leave it all behind.

Twenty

So here we are. Here I am, alone with Kai, the way I always wanted to be. There is no telephone and nobody will call. It's eight o'clock in the morning, cool and quiet. Here, autumn is coming fast. When we left England it was late summer and the air was warm. It was months since I'd needed to put on a jacket or a thick jersey. Now I'm wearing a cable-knit oiled wool jumper which Kai found packed away in a wooden chest in the bedroom here. It's all right for me to wear it, he says – this is just old stuff which the Linnas keep here all year round. A couple of heavy jerseys, two pairs of waterproof trousers, a pair of fisherman's waders, a long coat. It was all neatly folded and the clothes smelled of pinewood as we shook them out. I pulled the big jersey on over my leggings and wondered what the people were like who last wore these clothes. The jerseys had been washed before they were put away. The Linnas were old friends of Kai, he said, but he hadn't seen much of them for years. Matti was a teacher and Marja was a paediatric nurse. Good people. Kai knew Matti when they were students. Marja probably bent down, filling the chest, while the children skipped round the veranda waving the buckets they'd been told to put in the car. There's a photo of the children on the wall. Their skin is smoothly tanned and their hair is white.

The summer-house was packed up for the winter when we arrived. Matti and Marja wouldn't be coming back until spring. The place looked as if it had been put to bed, to sleep for months under the snow. We drove for hours and hours to get here. We'd flown from London to Helsinki and spent the night in a hotel there, then we flew on to Tampere the next morning. Kai bought a car in Tampere. He paid cash. He changed a lot of money at the airport. He didn't want to go to a car-hire firm, but he knew a man in Tampere who sold second-hand cars. We went to his flat, and his wife told us we'd find him in a bar near by. It was full of men and smoke: short grey men in bright jackets with sports logos on them. They stared at us. We went round to the man's garage and there was a yellow Saab with 100,000 kilometres on the clock. Not at all the kind of car Kai usually drives, but he gave the man cash. It must have been plenty, because he shook my hand as well as Kai's, and wanted us to come for a drink with him, but we didn't. I was prickly with irritation, not knowing what people were saying or even what their names were. But another side of me relaxed into Kai's shadow and was glad not to think of anything.

The Saab was a good car, built for rain and blizzards. You could see the point of it as soon as we got out of Tampere. We kept driving north-east, and soon there wasn't much traffic on the roads. All the summer visitors were back in the cities, Kai said, and the summer-houses were shut. I was tired because I hadn't slept well in the hotel in Helsinki. It was too hot in our room, and some engineers came back drunk at two o'clock in the morning and made a row in the corridor. I wanted to look round Helsinki the next morning, but Kai said he'd had enough of cities. 'Let's get away from everything,' he said. It seemed a pity not to stay and look at the harbour, and the boats leaving for Tallinn and St Petersburg. I'd always wanted to go to St Petersburg. It was hard to believe that now it was only a hundred and fifty miles away, and if we got into a train and headed east we'd soon be in Russia. Kai bought me a map of Finland so I'd know where I was, and where we were going. It kept shocking me slightly when I heard him speaking Finnish, even though it was only to the hotel receptionist and the waitress at dinner and people like that. I'd never heard him talking his own language except on the telephone. I couldn't understand a word of it. It wasn't like not understanding German or Italian, where some of the words swim out of the blur because you know them from war films or operas. There weren't any handholds at all. It wasn't till then that I really understood how brilliant Kai's English was. He could walk in and out of the two languages as if they were rooms in his house.

I've never seen such quiet roads. Sometimes a track led off into the forest, to a logging camp. Otherwise it was just forest, dark and quiet. I kept falling asleep, jerking awake, falling asleep again. It felt as if we'd been driving through the forest for ever, not speaking to each other. Kai had the radio on and it played long mournful songs with plenty of accordion. His favourites. He sang along in Finnish some of the time.

The tan on my feet looks yellow in this morning light, not brown. It's too cold for sandals, and there's been a heavy dew. Lucky I packed my Doc Martens. If I knew which ones to pick, I could go into the forest and gather mushrooms for breakfast; but I only know field mushrooms. Kai says that people here take mushrooms into the chemist's for identification, if they aren't sure what they've picked. There isn't a chemist anywhere near here, though. No shops, no lights, no litter blowing along the ground, no advertisements, no sound of traffic. Just forest and water. We stopped at a town about twenty-five miles from the summer-house, on our way, and bought our stores in the little supermarket. It was a tiny town, more like a village, centred on the railway station. A group of kids was hanging over the railway bridge, gazing down the tracks until they disappeared into the forest. It was a quiet grey afternoon and the kids stared up at us, long and slow, then back down the track again. The girl on the till in the supermarket kept looking at Kai's leather jacket until he said something to her which made her laugh. She was asking where he got it, he said. She liked the design. She had a good eye, I thought, remembering what that jacket had cost. I had my own leather jacket in the back of the car, slung over the seat. The wind ran over my arms and I thought I'd put it on, next time we stopped. It was nice being in the car. It was our own world with nobody else in it. I didn't even want Kai talking to the girl on the till. Once we were alone, really alone, we'd work out everything that'd been happening.

Kai bought a trolleyful of tins and packets, and a sack of potatoes. He'd bought beer and vodka back in Tampere. I went and got some fruit: little scaly apples and grapes which had been in their plastic nests much too long. We dumped everything in the car and set off again. I felt as if I was going on holiday with my parents, the way you do when you're a kid, not knowing how long the journey is going to be or where you're going. Not really believing that the journey will ever end, and not really wanting it to. Just being taken.

'When will we get there?'

'Soon.'

There's a small double bed and two bunks in the bedroom. The Linnas and their kids sleep all in one room when they're at the summer-house, though Kai says they sleep out on the veranda too, if the mosquitoes aren't too bad. There's timber stacked under a tarpaulin behind the house, so I think they're planning to build an extension, perhaps another bedroom. Marja and Matti built this place themselves. It's the kind of little house in the forest which you think you could live in for the rest of your life. You know it so well, because of all the fairy stories about little houses deep in the forest. But in fairy stories something happens. A witch or a prince knocks at the door and everyone's life changes. Here, nobody knocked. No one would come here until spring now, except for the hunters.

The bed is too small for us. Kai isn't sleeping well. He tosses and kicks off the duvet. He groans and I try to wake him because I know he's having a nightmare, but he throws me off and I have to listen until he starts making little sounds in his throat as if he's choking and then he wakes and grabs for me. He's sweaty and trembling. I think he's ill. It's cold at night and later on I wake up too, time after time, because he's been throwing himself about in the bed again and the duvet's fallen on to the rug.

I've moved across to the bottom bunk now. It's tiny, but fine for me as long as I don't sit up suddenly and crack my head on the slats of the top bunk. I curl up against the pine walls. There are knots in the wood, and I expect the Linnas' children trace out patterns of eyes and noses with their fingers before they go to sleep. Or perhaps one child stays awake later than the other, and he shuts his eyes and smells the wood and listens to the wind in the birches by the house and pretends this is a ship sailing through the forest. I used to wonder what Lulu imagined at night, what she dreamed, but she could never tell me. Sometimes she whimpered and cried. Perhaps the boy dreams of wolves. Kai hasn't seen the Linna boys since they were babies. I don't know when he telephoned the Linnas to ask if we could use the summer-house. The key was under a stone by the sauna door, wrapped in a plastic bag, and Kai knew where everything was. We'll pack it all away again, when we leave.

You can't see far from the veranda. There are no horizons. Just trees, and water. It's an area of small lakes, nothing like Lake Saimaa in the east, Kai says, but the lake looks big enough to me. And it's deep; it has that slaty shine you only get on deep water. There's a little path down through the birch trees, from the summer-house to the lake's edge. The Linnas have their little jetty there, and there's a grey sandy bit of beach. The kids have been digging castles. The sand has nearly collapsed back into shape, but not quite. In the mornings the grass and moss is wet with dew. The Linnas keep a boat, but that's put away for the winter too. There are a couple of rods, and when we first came Kai said he'd do some fishing, but he hasn't. I'd like to fish. Birch leaves are falling into the lake already, very slowly, one by one, so that you find them floating there in the mornings, then they sink down. There's a sharp smell in the air, the smell of autumn. In the middle of the day it still gets quite warm, and I spread out some cushions on the veranda and shut my eyes and let the sun run over my face. There are big dewy cobwebs on the veranda every morning. Sometimes I sit for a long time and watch the spider working her way round the web. Some days it is so still that every twig and leaf is reflected upside-down in the water. You can watch and watch until it feels as if the water and the forest are talking to each other in words you can't quite hear and would never understand anyway. They lean close to one another, brushing against one another with sounds I'm too human to catch. I've never been anywhere so still. In England there's always machinery operating far off, or a road not quite out of earshot, or the RAF splitting the sky overhead. But here every birdsong has its own space.

Two days ago Kai went out without me. I listened to the Saab's engine dying away down the track. I could hear it for a long time. Then I sat there on the veranda. It was too quiet to play the radio, and a little too cold to sit for long. I went indoors and made myself coffee. All the sounds were distinct, as if they were part of a percussion piece being played in front of an audience which didn't even dare to cough. I imagined people leaning forward in their seats to listen as my spoon dug into the coffee granules. Freeze-dried coffee is noisy stuff.

I leaned on the veranda, looking down through the trees at the steady grey shine of the lake. A fish plopped, way out in the water. I thought I would like to go out with one of the Linnas' rods. I would sit on the end of the jetty all morning with only water in front of me. Lakes in England always have people watching them, saying how beautiful they are, catching fish in them or sailing on them. They reflect back all the eyes which have looked at them. Of course people fish and swim and sail here, but there are so many lakes you couldn't ever use all of them. You can't even count them. Miles from anywhere – except that after a few days you forget about anywhere. Anywhere is here.

I stood and thought of the lakes and forests going on all the way to Russia, and then straight on without taking breath, because borders don't make any difference to the pattern of water and trees. What if Kai didn't come back? I used to be so afraid of that in England. Now I just wondered how long it would take me to walk the twenty-five miles to the town. I knew I could do it. There must have been neighbours living nearer, in the forest, but I wouldn't be able to make them understand what had happened. I had money, though. I could speak that language.

I took money from Kai, the third day we were here. He was drinking a lot already. The first two or three hours each night he slept heavily, before he started his nightmares. While he was sleeping I took Finnish money and English money, and hid it under the sauna inside a plastic bag, the way the Linnas had hidden the keys. He must have known it had gone, but he never said anything. I felt as if he was afraid of me, though I don't know why. That day Kai went out and I realized how hard it was to be in the same room with him now, or even in the same house. There were too many things we couldn't talk about. He knew I knew about the business. Often I'd catch him watching me, and his eyes looked small and hurt as if I was in the wrong, not him. I hadn't trusted him. I didn't believe him about Vicki. Not that Vicki seemed important any more. I wondered why she'd been so powerful. I couldn't even be bothered to think about Vicki here.

He tried to explain about her again, but I stopped him and said I didn't want to talk about it, it was better to forget the whole thing. I was standing quite near him. He was at the table drinking and doing a crossword, and he reached out and pulled me close to him. He pressed against me, grinding his face into my stomach and we stayed like that for quite a long time, me looking down on the top of his head and him with his arms wrapped round my body. He hadn't washed his hair for a few days and I could smell that warm dirty smell. There was so much grey in it. I looked over his head and saw the forest through the open door, and wished I was out in it. It was easy not to think about Vicki, but I did think about Paul Parrett. I wanted to see him again. It wasn't finished.

I keep dreaming about Enid. I expect it's being alone so much. They are long dreams, like conversations. I wake up wishing I'd said goodbye to Enid and told her where I was going. She must think that I don't want to see her because she knows too much about me and Kai, and that I ran away because I didn't want to cope with all that. Perhaps I did. Once I dreamed of Enid in the bath, feeling around for her soap and not finding it, and calling out for me before she remembered I'd gone. 'Nad-een! Nad-een!'

But that's stupid. After all, Enid managed for years before I came. And she's got things I haven't got: all that past. I only know a bit of it. I keep thinking of the Manchester Ladies. They are like a childhood photograph that I've looked at so much that I can't tell the difference between the memory I've built around the image and a real memory. Sometimes it is as real as if it had happened to me, not Enid. I can hear Sukey's voice. I can smell her hair. Sukey the rescuer; that's what Enid thinks she was, but I'm not so sure. There's something frightening about Sukey too. I can hear things about Sukey through the gaps in the story, the things Enid doesn't say.

I wrote a long letter to Enid while Kai was out. It was easy to write. I told her about the summer-house, and the lake, and swimming alone in the cold water. I could have made it sound like a wonderful holiday, just the two of us together, in the middle of nowhere, but I told her other things as well, about Kai drinking and us not talking about Vicki or the business, and about the money I'd taken. I couldn't imagine when I'd be able to post the letter, but it was good to write it. I hadn't written anything for a long time, because of the way the words fuzzed out of shape, but this was easy. I didn't need to read it back.

Kai came back in the late afternoon. It was a shock when I heard the car engine: almost frightening. For a moment I wanted to run off and hide in the trees. He came in smiling and looking much better, and he said he'd got a surprise for me. 'Come out to the car, Nadine.' Then he gave me that small furtive look again. I went out to look, though I didn't really care what he'd brought back. The boot of the Saab was tied down with rope and there was a bike in it. A mountain bike, a really good one. Kai untied the rope and got the bike out. It was brand-new, a beautiful heavy machine with twenty-one gears. Just the kind of thing I'd always wanted. But it was frightening too. Kai stood there beaming like a daddy who'd just bought his little girl her birthday bike. I knew he'd done it because I told him how frustrating it was not to be able to drive, and asked him if he'd teach me. There wasn't any traffic here and it would be perfectly safe. But I sensed that he didn't want to teach me, and once I saw the bike I knew.

'You'll see something of our Finnish countryside now,' he said. His English was getting more stilted. I hadn't been sure at first, but it was really noticeable now. I thought it must be deliberate. Kai'd always boasted that he spoke English better than any Finn he'd ever met. If people thought he was anything, they thought he was American, because his teacher had been American. He was peeling it off, all that language, all that knowledge, and I didn't know why. I thought maybe it was because he felt safe back here in his own country. He wanted to retreat deeper and deeper into silence. Sometimes I wondered where he really wanted to go.

I looked at the bike and felt quite depressed. You can get out on a bike, but not very far. I wanted to go miles and miles. And in the back of the boot there was a cardboard box full of beer, and three bottles of vodka. Jesus, Kai, I said to myself. I looked at his belly under his t-shirt. He didn't feel the cold, because he was so much heavier than me. Kai has this thick warm flesh which means he can go out in the frost in a shirt.

I hooked my feet into the pedal straps and cycled off. The broad tyres felt very safe. It was perfect for riding on tracks and paths in the forest. It felt powerful too, with all the gears and a strong, lightweight aluminium frame. A bike like this would cost five or six hundred pounds in England. Maybe more. I pedalled on, waving a hand to Kai and calling back. 'I'm just going to try it out.'

The summer-house is a couple of miles off the road, but the track is quite good because it's also a forestry vehicle track for the first mile and a half. They're not logging now. I wish they were; I'd like to hear the whine of a saw and the slow tear of trees coming down. I rode carefully, wobbling a bit, getting the feel of the bike. Soon I was out of sight of the summer-house. When I got to the road I thought I'd turn left, up the road I didn't know. The road was as quiet as before, with no traffic or sound of traffic. The trees that lined the road weren't birches. These were commercial evergreens, waiting for harvest, dark and bare-trunked, leaning in slightly. They had a watching look. I couldn't see too far into the forest. It was so dark, and the trees were close together. They didn't look as if they were trying to grow upwards into the light. They looked as if they preferred the changeless, barren dark they'd created. Nothing much grew under them. There was a carpet of needles and a dry sour smell which stuck to the back of my throat.

I thought if I looked back, I would see the trees move. They would spread out across the road, covering it, barring my way. Anything could happen here, because this wasn't somewhere, it was anywhere. The trees loomed and shrunk me to nothing. I might have been an insect crawling through the stiff fur of a black bear. The branches round me looked like bristles. I was breathing quite fast and I knew I wasn't far from panic. I was out in the open, but I was getting the kind of feeling I get in lifts or in the Tube. I did what I've learned to do: I shut my mind, blinkered off my senses, breathed deeply, pedalled hard. I was going to ride this bike.

The trees went on and on, a tunnel there was no getting out of. I'd made my point. I hadn't gone scurrying back at the first flash of panic. I must have cycled about four miles or so, and I didn't want to go too far the first time. I didn't like the idea of having to stop and rest here, listening to the trees whisper.

Kai was already drinking when I returned. He wouldn't try out the bike, but he thought I ought to explore the forest on it every day. I wouldn't have to stick to the roads. This bike was tough enough to handle tracks. He'd bought a helmet too, to protect my head. It would be better exercise for me than swimming in the lake, which was much too cold. Kai would never admit that my swimming in the lake made him uneasy: not so much because it was dangerous, but because I think he couldn't swim. He didn't like me going where he couldn't go. I swam every day, when the sun grew warm.

'Have you eaten?' I asked. 'I was going to make something.'

'No, I'm not hungry. But I bought some vegetables for you. They're in the car.'

'Let's go out,' I said suddenly. I couldn't face another long grey evening with Kai drinking and me flicking the pictures in magazines or listening to endless weather forecasts and tango music on the radio.

'Go out? Why do you want to go out? It's nice here. Besides' – he swallowed the rest of his drink – 'besides, I have taken too much alcohol. You know our laws about driving and alcohol.' He looked at me smugly.

'All right. Tomorrow. There must be somewhere we could go. What about the bar in the town?'

'There is something,' he admitted. 'There's a dance in the town hall on Friday. But you won't like it, it's all the type of music you don't like.' A flash of frustration went over me, as powerful as the earlier flash of panic. I couldn't understand the posters for coming events, even if I'd been able to drive into town. Kai wouldn't have said anything about the dance if I hadn't asked. He owned the language now. He was in control, driving the car, telling me what he wanted to tell me.

'Of course I want to go. I'd like to meet some Finnish people. Otherwise I might as well be anywhere.'

'OK. We'll go.' He poured more vodka, filled a saucer with peanuts and began to crunch them between his front teeth. I went to fetch in the vegetables. He had bought fruit too, those acid Spanish plums you can buy in England nearly all the year round. Bright red, tight-skinned plums, not melting and sweet like Czars or Victorias. Just carrying them set my teeth on edge. When I came back, Kai was singing to himself. I listened. The song gave me exactly the same feeling as I'd had in the forest on my bike. As if something was closing in on me.

'What does it mean?' I asked.

'You mean, what does it mean in English? Nothing. It only means something here.'

'Tell me the words anyway.'

Kai hummed, as if to catch the tune again. 'It says:

> Karelia moon
> daylight is dying
> and you are sleeping
>
> Karelia moon
> daylight is dying
> tonight you can't climb
> close to the stars
>
> tonight you sleep
> sleep in the dark
> close to my heart.'

The words finished, but Kai kept on humming quietly. Moths were banging around the lamp, hurting their wings. I wanted to get on the bike and ride to the nearest town where there'd be a hamburger bar and order a triple cheeseburger and double fries and a thick shake and relish and bright red tomato sauce and put money in the jukebox until the music drowned everything. Instead I went into the kitchen and began to make a grated carrot salad with French dressing. I'd cook potatoes and sausages with it. Kai needed something to soak up the alcohol. I'd made Jansson's Temptation yesterday, from one of Marja Linna's cookery books. Kai had translated the recipe for me, but he hadn't eaten any of it. There was a cold wodge of it in the fridge. Still, we were going to the dance on Friday.

The front door of the house opens and Tony drops his overnight bag in the hall. He's tired and sweaty. The air is greasy and much too warm. It's going to rain. There's thunder in the air. His shirt itches, even though it was clean on that morning in London. He'll take a bath and change. But first, coffee.

A really good trip. He'd made some new contacts. And he'd telephoned Paul Parrett at ten that morning. Paul Parrett had thanked him for the dinner.

'It's a pleasure,' said Tony. 'A pleasure. I knew you'd like Nadine. She's a really sweet kid.'

'Yes, we had a good time,' said Paul Parrett.

'Yeah, Nadine's got something. Fantastic looks, someone ought to photograph her.'

'I expect someone will.' There was a short silence.

'Nadine's got loads of potential,' went on Tony, gabbling a bit, but then it was always tough talking to Paul Parrett. He left so much silence for you to fill up. 'She's a sensible kid too,' he added, his relief that everything seemed to have gone OK making him feel quite warm, for a moment, towards Nadine. It'd been a gamble doing it on his own, but it'd paid off. Kai'd been ready for something to happen, but he hadn't been ready to make it happen. He was going to be pleased.

'You don't get a lot of girls like Nadine,' he went on. Tony liked this type of chat. Getting the message across, not saying too much.

'Yes,' said Paul Parrett. 'It was good to meet her.'

Another silence, OK, but Tony judged it wasn't the time to say any more. No need anyway. Kai'd been through the terms with Janice. Tony drew a chain of interlocking daisies on the hotel telephone pad. Then, 'Well, I got to get on,' he said. 'Busy man, eh? Not like you, though, Mr Parrett.' He paused, letting the idea of public life fill the silence. In his mind he saw the big black car draw up, the security men hold open the door, the car pull away with Paul Parrett in the back, already talking on his car phone. He saw the gates which would open, the saluting policemen, the big desks and carpets which soaked up the noise of footsteps. The Palace of Westminster. Once you'd got all that, you'd do anything to keep it. And there was always someone ready to put a ferret down your trousers.

'I'll let you have a note,' said Paul Parrett, 'about that business we were discussing last night.'

The daisy grew bigger and tiny sharp teeth appeared on its petals. 'Yeah, that's right,' said Tony. 'Take the figures we were working with before, and we'll go from there.'

'That's fine. And we must fix up another of those dinners.'

You got to give him credit, thought Tony. Cool as a cucumber. You'd think he was paying his fucking Access bill. Funny how some people got their kicks. Like driving right on the edge of the cliff when there was a fucking great four-lane motorway going your way.

'Yeah,' said Tony. 'We'll be in touch.' He yawned luxuriously, booted a hotel towel off the floor with his foot and kicked it into the air. A good start. Now to check out and get on that train and tell Kai what was going on. Or maybe leave it a bit. Wait till it was all fixed up.

The house is quiet. He's got it to himself, and he'll cook a good meal before going to visit Clara's *nonna* in St Thérèse's Hospice. Everything is working out well there. That little misunderstanding with Paolo is all sorted out. There, the rain's coming, just as he thought. Big separate drops. The summer is breaking up. There's a grumble of thunder, far off. He picks up his mug of coffee and goes upstairs to the bathroom. He isn't really looking at anything, and when he first sees Enid it is only as a blotch which shouldn't be there on the everyday lightness of the stairs.

Boiling black coffee slops over his hand. He swears, not at the pain, but at the still bundle at the bottom of the stairs. 'Jesus, Jesus,' he says aloud. Just when everything is going so well. The old woman. Fuck it to buggery. He puts down the coffee and wipes his hands carefully. The way she's fallen he can't see her face, so he kneels by her head. She's a terrible colour and a black thread of blood has gone solid and stuck under her nose. He checks her ears, but there's no blood coming out of them. Very lightly, he touches her cheek with the back of his hand. It is cool but not cold. Not dead cold. He reaches out for her left wrist and feels around for the pulse. He's not quite sure where this ought to be. The angle's all wrong. The arm is floppy, not stiff. How long's she been here?

Kai must've gone over to Vick's for the night. Again Tony fumbles for the pulse, but can't tell if what he feels is his own blood bumping in his fingers or the old woman's. Jesus. This is going to mean trouble. He shouldn't've touched her.

Tony sits back on his heels, eyes black and blank. No one knows he's back from London. He could walk out again right now and leave someone else to find her. It won't make any difference to the old woman. She'll die anyway. She's been lying on the boards for hours. Why did it have to happen now, just when everything was going so well? And why should he have to deal with it? Police and doctors coming to the house. Questions.

Carefully and almost tenderly, Tony rearranges Enid's arm as it was. Perhaps he can fetch a cushion so her head won't be on the hard wood. His shirt is sticking to him again.

Enid groans. It's a small sound. Nobody would hear it unless he was right by her, kneeling down, almost touching her. Tony jumps. He stares at Enid and a thread of sweat runs down inside his shirt. No more sound. Maybe he imagined it.

Why is she doing this to him? Any other old woman would have been killed right off by the fall. It's unnatural. What if she opens her eyes and looks at him? Does she know he's there?

He sits back on his heels, very still, thinking. After all, he argues against himself, what harm can it do? Why not? There's nothing here. The house is clean. Even Kai can't be that paranoid. It's not as if it's involving anyone else. She's just fallen downstairs, that's all. It's not a crime.

She moans again. Now he knows. It's a sign.

Tony stands up, steadying himself, and looks down at the old woman's body. Yes, she's alive. Only a pinch of life but it won't let him go. Then he turns and goes down the stairs to the telephone and dials. Controlling a natural impulse, he gives the correct address to the placidly inquiring voice on the other end, then wipes sweat off his face. There won't be time for a bath before the ambulance arrives, but he should still be able to go and see Clara's *nonna*, who will be expecting them. Jesus.

Less than fifteen minutes later the ambulance whoops into the square. The ambulance-men are gentle and reassuring with Tony, even though he doesn't seem to be listening when they tell him he can go with them to the Infirmary in the ambulance. From his sweaty pallor they can tell that he is in shock.

Twenty-one

'There's bruising on her upper arms; do you think it ought to go on her notes?' suggests the sister discreetly. The young houseman flushes. He hadn't noted the bruises. He's been on duty for twenty-three hours and he's running between six serious emergencies beside Enid. She's just one case and he's already spotted concussion, suspected skull fracture, shock, hypothermia and a broken arm. Accident and emergency is packed. He takes the notes from the sister and writes. His fingers are sweaty and they leave a soft place on the paper.

After the head x-rays they make Enid comfortable for the night. Her arm's been set. She'll have a night in intensive care, but she should be on a ward by the morning. The bruises are inspected. The staff have had a training course on abuse of elderly people by their carers but there's no next of kin on Enid's form. The ambulance-men said that the young man who called them hadn't been in the house when the fall occurred. He gave what details he could, but he didn't accompany the patient to hospital. The police will have to get in touch with him to check the facts. The bruising doesn't look consistent with a simple fall downstairs. Very upset, he was, apparently. Let's hope they send a tactful policewoman.

Everyone calls her Enid. They talk to her all the time, even though she's unconscious. They know that patients can hear even when they give no signs of awareness. Hearing is the last sense to go and the first to return. On the operating table, anaesthetized patients have been known to twitch at surgeon's jokes. So staff are careful now.

'You're doing fine. We'll soon make you more comfortable. You've had a fall and hurt your arm. You're just going to have a little injection now, and then we're going to pop you down to x-ray. Donald's taking you on the trolley, you'll be all right with Donald, won't you?' Enid's jaunty pink sweater is cut and peeled from her body. She dreams of being swung through space, then stops dreaming.

It is mid-morning on the ward before Enid regains consciousness. It's nothing dramatic. The slow and intermittent process is noted by the ward sister, who came on shift when Enid was transferred from intensive care. There is eye movement under Enid's lids, then she begins to stir. Her head moves slowly to one side.

'You're in hospital, Enid,' says the nurse distinctly. 'You've had a little accident, but you're getting better. Don't worry now. Just relax.' She checks the drip, takes Enid's blood pressure and records the figures. For a couple of hours Enid remains with eyes closed, twitching slightly, occasionally moaning. A doctor on his ward rounds lifts her eyelid, shines a light in, tests her reflexes. She's a fighter, she's doing well.

Enid is aware of something yellow and kind in front of her. For a long time she doesn't know that it's the sunlight on the wall opposite. When she's worked this out, she closes her eyes. Everything hurts. 'It's dark inside my head.' Who said that? A little later she is awake again, and thirsty. Her mouth is very dry. She tries to run her tongue over her lips but it sticks. Anyway she's too tired. Pain comes in pulses but she won't let it wash her away. Each time she holds it back. Then she sleeps. A blurred dark shape has settled close to her. She squints but it hurts her eyes. She understands that the shape is a face with dark hair round it.

'Nadine,' she says, 'Nadine,' and her fingers pull at the crisply boiled sheet. The auxiliary nurse pats her hand and reassures her, then goes back to the nursing station.

'Enid's waking up. She said something just now.'

'Did you catch it?'

'I think it was a name. She's asking for someone.'

'Better tell sister. There was a policewoman in just now. She wants to sit with Enid once she's awake.'

The drinks trolley butts its way over polished flooring, between lockers and beds and slow-creeping patients with drip-stands attached to their arms. The air fills with smells of Ovaltine and hot chocolate. Sunlight plays warmly and gently on hurt flesh and on the skin which forms quickly on the drinks of patients who are too tired to lift their cups. The nurses move to and fro, bare-armed and strong, coming on duty with the smell of outdoors on their clothes and hair.

The car park outside the town hall is full of young men when Kai and Nadine arrive for the dance. They are wearing jeans and leather jackets, and they sprawl against cars or stand under the two lamps, drinking cans of strong lager. It's dark already and electric light streams invitingly from the dance hall windows. They can hear the music. There's going to be a band tonight; it tours all round the countryside, Kai says, playing in one small town after another. It is quite famous in the Finnish countryside, he says. Older men are on the veranda, drinking from a bottle of vodka. Kai isn't going to drink tonight: he's promised. He's got to drive them back, and once he starts drinking these days he doesn't stop until his head drops on the table, or, by sheer luck, on the pillow. It's grim drinking, with no pleasure in it. Sometimes he gets up and walks steadily, heavily, to the veranda where he can hear the night noises of the forest and smell the water.

The hall is bright but bare. On the stage the band is warming up, but nobody's dancing yet. Men congregate on one side of the hall, women on the other. There are some tables.

'Can't we sit together?' asks Nadine.

'No, this is your chance to meet some Finnish people,' says Kai with satisfaction. He leads Nadine over to a table where there are three matrons drinking orange squash and mineral water. They are packed tightly into pink, bright blue and shiny black dresses, and their hair is permed into tight colour-rinsed frizzes. They are the jailers of their hair, thinks Nadine. They waft a strong warm smell of make-up and perfume. Kai explains Nadine to them in Finnish. Broad smiles are turned to her, hands are shaken and Kai leaves. Then there is nothing to say. The smiles cannot go on for ever, and none of the three ladies speaks English. After a polite minute they turn back to their conversation and orange squash, nodding and smiling at Nadine from time to time. Nadine sits still, very conscious of her short tight dress and of having nothing to drink. A few moments later Kai comes back from the bar with an alcohol-free lager for Nadine. He points to the red illuminated panels at the end of the dance hall.

'When the top one lights up, it is men's turn to ask women to dance. When the bottom lights up it means women's turn to ask men.'

'Oh, God,' says Nadine. 'What do I do if I don't want to dance with somebody?'

'Just dance with him for one dance. You were the one who wanted to come.'

'But I won't be able to say anything.'

'You'll be dancing, not talking.'

Nadine waits in dread for the lighting up of the panels. The band is playing more vigorously now, one of Kai's sad endless songs. The accordionist pumps, and a man in a dark blue suit comes forward, seizes the microphone and begins to sing, his eyes half shut. His voice is beautiful, sonorous, resonant. Suddenly the song makes sense. Nadine leans forward to watch and listen. She has not noticed the lighting up of 'men's turn', and is surprised when a moment later a young man with very short and much gelled hair blocks her view and stands there unsmiling. The three matrons beam encouragement and explain to the young man that she is English, a foreigner, but keen to dance. Nadine stands and is taken into the young man's arms. The dance seems to resemble a foxtrot, which she more or less knows how to do. They dance past Kai, who is deep in talk with a group of heavy middle-aged men. They dance past the singer and his voice vibrates through Nadine, making her close her eyes with pleasure. The young man holds her and does not attempt to talk. Soon they are back at the table. She smiles and says one of the few Finnish words Kai has taught her: '*Kiitos.*' Unsmiling as ever, the young man nods, then heads off outside for another beer. Nadine relaxes. But the next moment the light is on 'women's turn'. The three matrons get up purposefully and head off across the room. One of them spots that Nadine is missing her chance. She pulls her up, points vigorously at a likely partner on the other side of the room and shoos Nadine towards him. Nadine veers sideways to a quiet older man in a suit. She likes the look of this one. In a moment they are dancing. Nadine is triumphant. She has done it, she has coped in spite of Kai. The man even speaks a bit of English. He thinks she is very clever to understand 'men's turn' and 'women's turn'.

'Our Finnish dances are difficult for foreigners,' he remarks, pronouncing the *g* firmly.

'*Elämä on vaikea,*' she ripostes, using the only Finnish phrase Kai has succeeded in teaching her, through constant repetition. Life is hard. Her partner beams approval. He is small and rotund, with shiny peat-coloured eyes. He reminds her slightly of Paul Parrett.

After several dances Nadine glows with confidence. She has cracked Finnish social life successfully. None of the young men she has selected has refused her. Then a man comes to the microphone and begins to talk without stopping in lugubrious tones. Everyone in the hall roars with laughter. The matrons even have to get out their handkerchiefs to wipe off mascara which is smudged by tears of laughter. Nadine fixes a smile on her face and looks across at Kai. He doesn't notice her, he is laughing so much. She sees the wet red inside of his mouth, laughing.

Then the dancing begins again and it's all right. The three ladies buy orange squash for Nadine and she buys them alcohol-free beers. The men dance energetically now, fuelled by drink. Then there is a long, slow number. Nadine is clasped against her middle-aged partner again. He becomes sentimental, strokes her hair off her forehead and tells her he always wanted a daughter. He has two sons, one at Helsinki University, one at Turku. But why doesn't she grow her hair long? Perhaps he is a distant cousin of Paul Parrett, thinks Nadine. The evening is turning out well, though she cannot see Kai anywhere. And those men he was talking to – they've gone too. Everybody's in couples, except for the matrons who are beating time and smiling from the side of the hall. Where's he gone? God, what if he's drinking? She stiffens inside her partner's embrace. She excuses herself, leaving him smiling in confusion, not liking to admit that his English isn't up to following what she's just said. She scoops up her bag from the table, smiles again, shakes hands with the matrons, and goes.

Yes, there he is, under the lamp-post with a whole group of them, passing vodka. He watches her with unfriendly eyes as she approaches. He's been drinking, all right. He is shoulder to shoulder with the men, and he stares at her with deliberate blankness. He's a different man from her English Kai.

'How are we going to get home?' she whispers fiercely. 'You can't drive in this state. If you get caught you'll go to jail.'

'Go to jail, go to hell. One of my friends will take me,' he says, lordly, dismissing her.

'They're all drunk too,' she says. She spots another bottle going round. Kai turns back to the other men and begins to talk in Finnish.

'No, Kai. I want to go now.'

'Then you drive, Nadine. You drive us home.' He hands her the car keys, capitulating, challenging. The men laugh. They are used to this sort of thing. They don't know that Nadine can't drive. Kai shrugs and smiles, playing to the gallery.

'Right,' says Nadine. 'Right. I will. Get in the car.'

Luckily the Saab is parked on the edge of the car park, not

locked in among other cars. She'd never be able to reverse out. Kai gets into the passenger-seat and sits there with a smile on his face, watching to see what she'll do. He thinks he's called her bluff, does he? Thank God, it's an automatic. She ought to be able to manage.

'You'll have to direct me,' she says sharply. 'We don't want to end up lost in the forest.'

'OK, OK, I know the way.'

She puts in the key and turns it. The engine ignites, then stops. She turns it again and this time it's OK. Gently, she eases the gear from PARK to DRIVE and presses the right-hand pedal. Nothing happens. She's being too gentle. She tries again and then she remembers the handbrake. The car creeps forward, then suddenly jumps. Kai reaches over and the lights spring on. The car moves down to the road. She knows she's got to turn right here. The car jerks and jolts as she accelerates too much, then too little. It's OK, she tells herself, you'll get the feel of it in a minute. It can't be that hard. All sorts of idiots drive. She sits bolt upright, tense, gripping the wheel. The speedometer wavers on twenty kilometres an hour. She'll do it. She'll defeat Kai, she'll get them safely home. The car's lights probe forward into a dark tunnel. They are past the last houses of the village and into the forest.

'You've got to stay awake,' she says, 'I don't know where we turn off.'

On and on they go, mile after mile. She is driving, she's doing it. 'Go faster, Nadine,' grumbles Kai, but she daren't. Twenty-five kilometres an hour, thirty. She can't take her attention off the road for a second. She is alone with the road and the forest, more alone than if the seat beside her was empty.

'We turn off here,' says Kai out of long silence and darkness.

She panics, wrenches the wheel too hard and the Saab judders across the entrance to the track, nearly hitting a post. Stones bounce up and tang off the side of the car.

'Maybe I'll drive now,' says Kai.

'No. I'm going to drive all the way home.'

And she does. Very slowly all the way up the pitch-dark, rough forest track, flinching at moths in the headlights. And there is the unlit bulk of the summer-house, and they are home. Kai gets out, walks slowly past the house, and takes the path to the lake. Nadine switches off the engine and sits still in the seat. Her hands are trembling. It's only because she's been gripping the wheel so tightly. She looks at her watch. The journey has taken well over an hour, and here she is. She's got them both back safely. Her stomach hurts. She's got to have something to eat.

Kai stays outside the summer-house for a long time. She wonders what he's doing, but she's glad he's out of the way. The little wooden house feels more claustrophobic than ever. It will be unbearable with the two of them in it tonight. The living-room smells of the tinned leek and potato soup she has heated. The thought of another day of silence and forest, broken only by meals, drinking and staring at old copies of Finnish women's magazines, fills her with nausea. Kai has changed, or else she's changed. The money in his pockets is paper. He can't help her, and she can't help him. He is not the rescuer.

When he comes in she asks him where he's been. He tells her he has been looking at the lake. It's dark, she says, what could he see? There isn't any moon tonight, and there's so much cloud even the stars don't show. Why doesn't he have something to eat, to soak up the vodka? He's drunk enough of it. He yawns and drops heavily on to a chair. He is red-eyed and his shirt is dirty.

'Go to bed,' he says. 'I'll stay up a little.'

He's going to start that joyless drinking again. She stands up, gathers her magazines and an apple and a glass of water, then stands holding them, looking at Kai.

'Go to hell,' he says, looking back at her smooth, young critical face.

She'll leave him to it, climb into the little bunk, turn to the wall and abandon him altogether in her dreams.

*

His mumbling wakes her. He's sitting by the bed, saying her name over and over. 'Nadine. Nadine. Nadine. Are you OK?' The door to the living-room is open and the light is still on in there. She blinks and sits up.

'What's wrong, Kai? Why don't you come to bed?'

His weight comes at her. For a second she thinks he's going to hit her. Then she feels him shaking. He wants her to hold him. She braces herself against the hard wooden wall and puts her arms round him. It is ridiculous, the two of them crushed into this child's bunk. Any moment now the slats will give way. She rocks him feebly, oppressed by his heat and weight and the smell of drink. Girls at school used to say it was OK to drink vodka in dinner-hour because no one would smell it on your breath in the afternoon. Well, now she knows that wasn't true. It's seeping out of Kai's skin. Funny how you learn things. She feels herself smile helplessly, stupidly, over his dark bulk. He is burning. His rough, hot, prickly face scrubs against her neck. Her lips tighten.

'Go to bed, Kai, you'll feel better in the morning,' she says, and smiles to hear herself say what her mother used to say, hovering in the doorway, wanting to leave Nadine.

Kai turns his head against her shoulder and begins to tell her what he's been waiting to tell her since that morning when she lay in the bath, her back arched and water sluicing off her body. And Enid lay upstairs curled round on the boards of an empty room. It's growing in him and he's frightened. He can't get the dark of it out of his head. The vodka doesn't work. His hot whispering voice fills the space of the child's bunk and runs off through the knots in the wood, away into the forest. He tells Nadine what he has done to Enid. He tells Nadine that the Enid she writes to is not there any more. There is nothing and nobody there. His words run like insects over Nadine's body before they find freedom. He is hot and tight on top of her and she cannot move him. Her smile has peeled away from her lips like wax.

Twenty-two

'Enid's dead. Enid's dead because of me. I'm only alive because Enid's dead. No, Enid's dead because I'm alive. No. Enid's dead –'

Pedalling fast, Nadine shoots out of the forest on her mountain bike. Here the road straightens and its verges widen. Heavy spruce gives way to a scrub of birch. Here there's light, movement and a flurry of birds. She slows down, her bare brown legs straining to push the pedals. She's come a long way, and now the forest is at her back, a big shadow, soughing, full of hush, broken by sudden creaks and cries. Soon it will be winter. The long sweeping wind from Russia flexes itself and strokes the crowns of spruce and pine until they moan in anticipation and then are quiet again.

Nadine doesn't turn round or look back. She can feel the forest like a cold wind behind her. She's got a long way to go yet, and her legs hurt. She'll have to stop and rest. She brakes and gets off the bike clumsily. She'll push it for a while, then she'll sit down. She won't look behind her because there's nothing coming and anyway she'd hear the car miles off and have time to drag the bike off the road into the scrub and hide. She's sure Kai won't be capable of driving for hours yet. He'd crash into a tree if he tried. Also, she's hidden the car keys and it'll take him a long time to find them. She should have thrown them away, deep into the forest or the lake, but she couldn't do it. He'd never be able to get to the town without the Saab. He'd collapse on his way through the forest, and lie vomiting on the moss. She looked at him in the grainy first light and then she left him. All she took was a few clothes in a backpack, and the wad of money from under the sauna. If only she had a mile-ometer so she could tell how far she's come. Two hours' riding:

say thirty kilometres? No, much less. The track from the summer-house to the road was so rough that she hadn't dared go fast, even with thick tyres. A puncture would have been fatal. After that it was uphill quite a lot of the way: one of those long gentle slopes you scarcely notice when you're walking, or in a car. She hasn't got to the lake with the island yet, and she remembers that the road curves round it and then back into the forest before it reaches the town. A black, still, reed-circled lake. Very deep, Kai said as they drove past it. The town isn't much of a town, with its dance hall where people come from miles around to dance tango, its little supermarket which is also a bar, its school. You wonder where all the houses are, and where the people come from. The dance hall was packed last night. The express trains going south and north stop there; she's made sure of that. She doesn't know the times, and there might be hours to wait. It's not so easy to hide in a town. She'll have to dump the bike. She won't need it any more. Kai can pick it up and take it back to the summer-house. He's bound to go straight to the station to look for her, once he finds the keys. He'll guess where she's gone. But not in time. She'll be gone. At first he'll just think she's gone off for a ride. Yes, she'll have to get rid of the bike. It makes her much more conspicuous. People will remember her. 'Have you seen a girl with a bike? A mountain bike? An English girl?' Kids would notice the bike because it's the kind they all want. Aluminium frame, twenty-one gears, quick-release saddle. Kai would question the kids who hang round the dance hall or the railway station in the fag-end of after-school.

Will Kai remember what he said last night – what he's told her? What she knows? And what will he do if he remembers?

Wind shivers through the birches, turning over their leaves. They are dry, beginning to rustle. Their colours are changing. Soon they'll turn to brief gold and then wind and rain will tear them off their branches and they'll be mashed brown by storms before the first snow falls. The sky is a low, cool grey. It rained heavily last night and the bog at the edge of the forest smells sharply of autumn. She listened to the rain while she lay for hour after hour, keeping herself awake, while Kai moaned in his sleep and cried out in the language she didn't speak. Time for cutting firewood for winter and gathering mushrooms. A perfect autumn day, still and mild and smoke-scented.

Nadine plods on, one hand on the saddle of the bike, one on the handlebars. Kai says this is the correct way to push a bike – this way you don't get backache. Not that she ought to need to push the bike: with so many gears she should be able to pedal up the steepest slope. But even though she's much fitter than Kai, she's never been any good at cycling uphill. It makes her legs shake. Ahead of her, dark Sitka spruce are marching towards the edge of the road again. The road's going to twist back into the forest. She doesn't like walking between those dark, airless flanks of trees which crowd out the sky. Better to ride and blot out silence with the swish of tyres. She's had a rest. She mustn't lose any more time.

But as Nadine cycles round the next bend a flood of light makes her eyes sting. There it is – she's reached the lake. It's huge and pale, spilling out before her, rimmed on one side by the whitey-grey thread of the little road, on the other by black bog and forest. It's a lonely place. Kai's told her that hunters come here in winter, to shoot in the marsh. There are pike in the lake. Black overhanging rock in a shape like a head and shoulders above the water rears up on the opposite shore. But here, on this side, there's a little beach facing an island only fifty metres or so out in the water. It's a tiny island, the kind you dream of discovering when you're a kid. Short, tufty grass, one birch tree, a fallen branch. A perfect place to put up a tent. It even has its own miniature beach of grey sand, fringed with reeds. The autumn breeze has dropped again and the reflection of the island is flawless, a dark, polished outline on the water. Nadine bumps her bike off the road and down the grass to the beach. It's small, perhaps ten metres across. There are no footprints but her own. No one comes here. There are no summer-houses, no fishing rods, no walkers or cyclists. This is just an ordinary lake, nothing special, one of tens of thousands. The sphagnum moss just off the road is spongy and deep. It sucks around her boots, then she steps on to the dry, crunchy beach which is edged with fading rushes. Pebble and sand shelve shallowly into the clear water. Something flickers around the base of the reeds. Tiny fish. There'll be frogs too, and water-snakes. Nadine leans on her bike, peering into the water.

Then, from behind the island, there sails one swan followed by two cygnets. The cygnets are well grown, brown and grey but with a speckle of white feathers beginning to push through. The cygnets paddle behind, eager and dingy against the parent swan. Another swan glides round the island, followed by three more cygnets. Nadine can't tell which swan is the male, which the female. They sail towards the beach, leaving long rips in the silky lake surface. It is so still that as they come near she can hear their webbed feet plashing under the water. They are close now, and they slow down, watching her. One cygnet drifts off to dive among the reeds. It gives out a frail but confident cry. It is much bolder than the others. The grown swans spread their beaks down flat along the water and sweep from side to side, bills combing the surface. The cygnets bob and imitate, dredging the shallows. The bold cygnet climbs up the beach, its legs awkwardly hinged at the thighs, clumsy out of the water. Its short, stubby wings would never fly. A parent moves in behind it, watching Nadine and the bike. The swan puts down its head and hisses. They can break your arm with a blow from their wings, Nadine remembers. She is miles from anywhere. The swan watches, protecting its young. The other parent bird swims out with two cygnets in its wake. They mate for life, thinks Nadine. They are faithful to one another even if their partner dies. She stands there, watching the swans with extreme atten-tion. The swan stops hissing at her and moves off, plucking at grass. Nadine keeps still, holding the bike upright. It is the bike that frightened the swans, she thinks. When they've moved off a little she'll lower it on to the grass so it won't bother them. There they go now, slipping back into the mineral quiet of the lake. Its surface is dark as graphite. They float back across the lake, their powerful feet working beneath the water. The sound of them thins and disappears as they go back behind the island. They must have their nest there.

She ought to get on. She's wasting time, but the small beach and the small island hold her. It's one of those places you feel you've seen once before, tantalizingly, from a train or a speeding car. If only you could stay and explore, find at last the template that makes the perfect pattern of water, island, sky ... She crunches across the beach and carefully puts down the bike so it is supported against a low bank of stones. She looks across at the dark spiky top of the forest. It is like fine handwriting which she cannot read.

So much has happened. She can't make sense of it. Kai says that Enid is dead. He says that he has killed her. She stands still, hearing those words in his drunken mumble. Fine hairs stand up on her upper arms. Summer's over now. Everyone's gone back to the cities, back to jobs and apartments and to starting to think about Christmas.

'Enid liked Christmas. She said she would show me the place on the Downs where she cut holly to decorate her attic. No one else knew about it.'

Kai can't go back to England. No more city for Kai, no house, no business, no wads of new money. Only the summer-house in winter, the sky going yellow with snow, the wind feeling its way through knots in summer pine. Kai tells Nadine stories about the winter war, and men on skis gliding through the forest dressed in white, their silent knives in their hands. He'll hunt, he tells her. As long as there's a cupboard full of colourless vodka, he'll be fine. They'll never find him – why should they look here?

'Enid, darling ... I couldn't help it. What could I have done? I wasn't there. I didn't look after you. *I didn't know it was going to happen.*'

Nadine unlaces her boots and puts her socks neatly inside them, pulls her red t-shirt over her head, takes off her shorts, her bra and pants, folds them by the bicycle and walks down to the water's edge. It is cold. Kai has told her not to bathe anywhere unless she knows the water. Some of these lakes are very deep. She should never swim alone. There's always the risk of cramp and sudden exhaustion from cold. Kai can be very protective. He didn't like it when she swam straight out from the summer-house jetty, a hundred metres or so, then lay on her back drifting and watching the clouds while the water lapped her face. She was perfectly safe. She knew how far it was safe to go. Kai never came in the water. Summer was over, he said, it was too late for swimming, but she began to think that perhaps he didn't know how to swim, even though he'd grown up by the sea. Or perhaps it was because he knew, long before she did, that they hadn't come here to swim and boat and fish, like summer visitors. He was drinking so much, more than she'd ever known. She wouldn't have thought anyone could drink so much every night. He was slow in the morning, red-eyed, not clumsy but heavy and unnatural in his movements as if he had to remember painfully how to get out of bed, how to dress himself, how to swallow. He wasn't eating. She made bland porridge for them both but he said his stomach was a ball of acid. Towards evening he might make an omelette. Sometimes he'd vomit up the food.

Every day she swam, even through the rain, far out on the water where she couldn't see him or know what he was doing. She didn't know how late he stayed up at night. She went to bed early, tired out by walking and swimming and chopping wood and making easy food for herself: soups and black bread and cheese and apples. There wasn't anything to do in the evenings, once it was dark. She couldn't read. Instead she gorged on sleep. She'd sleep ten hours or more and when she woke he'd be at the rickety card-table, a little glass at his right hand, working out calculations on a piece of paper. Something to do with business.

Now she knew what those figures represented. She never knew if he'd been drinking all night, or if he'd started early, unable to wash or make their coffee without it.

The cold still water licks at her ankles. Kai's right: it's really too cold to swim. But she's used to it. She's got tough. She tenses, hearing an engine, then relaxes as a high, lonely aeroplane crosses above the clouds. She bends down, kneels on the coarse sandy bottom of the lake, sweeps the water up over her arms and shoulders. The water is very soft, cold, close-grained. It draws her in; she wants to be deep in it, embraced by it. She gets up and walks forward, covering waist, breasts, shoulders. She wades until she is almost floating, then kicks off and glides. Beneath her are weeds and small red and grey pebbles, beautiful in their wetness. Weeds wave up from the lake shore, frighteningly distinct. The water is delicious on her naked body. There are no waves, only her own rippling disturbance. In front of her everything is smooth.

She keeps swimming out. Now it's deep underneath her and she doesn't want to look down for fear of what she might see. The pike in this lake are huge, Kai says, but she guesses that the water here is too clear for them. They are fresh-water sharks. They hang in their holes in deep reedy water, waiting for movement. She's beyond weeds, and the lake is deep and dark all around her. She rests, sculling with her hands. But she must swim farther. She can't swim round the island because of the swans. Now that she is naked and in their element, she'd have no chance of fighting them off. She heads out towards the crag, laying her face against the water at each stroke. The cold lake is seductive. It washes away Kai's voice, and the smell of his body metabolizing alcohol all night. It's an acrid smell that comes out on his skin and breath. The lake is pure. Her solitude in the middle of the water is dizzying. No one is here; no one who knows her; no one to call her back. No Kai. She lets herself sink until her head is just under the water. Now there's nothing on the surface to show that she's here. If Kai drove past all he'd see would be the lake looking back at him, smooth as an eye. She's a small disturbance, quickly ironed out. Her breath tightens and red spots thicken in front of her closed eyes. Her lungs hurt. She comes up, lies on her back, looks at the sky. The lake is beneath her, supporting her and drawing her down, caressing her, so cold that it leaves her with scarcely any sensation but the one of opening herself wider and wider against the body of the water. She belongs to the lake. The bike and her pile of clothes and the scuff of her footsteps in the sand are drifting farther and farther off.

Nadine flips over, pushes back her wet hair and looks at the crag opposite. She might swim to it. That would be the deepest part of the lake, where the rock goes down sheer into the water, and down and down to its haunted floor. She's not much more than a hundred metres offshore, and how wide is the lake here? About two hundred metres. She can swim a mile. She has swum a mile before.

'In this cold? Some of these lakes go down to a thousand feet, remember what Kai said?'

She isn't swimming fast. She knows better than that. These are slow strokes that will carry her over the water. She watches her hands push through the water. This is all she has now: herself. Her arms and legs, her heart beating hard against the cold. What does the little heap of clothes and the bike add to that? Kai wouldn't think she could do it. He says she hasn't got enough fat on her to go swimming in cold water. He loves telling her what to do. If he was here now, watching . . .

But he isn't watching. She's sure of it. He couldn't even find the road, he's so drunk. When he wakes up he won't remember anything. He won't remember the things he said, the things he told her. What she knows now and can't stop knowing. But once he finds that she's gone, won't he guess why? No reason why he should, unless he remembers last night. He'll think she's got tired of it all: his drinking, and the summer-house in autumn with winter coming fast. He knows she doesn't want him to touch her any more. Perhaps he thinks it's because of the drink or the way he doesn't bother to shave, or the smell of his breath, or because the bunks are narrow and uncomfortable, made for children. He's got plenty more bottles. Maybe he'll light the sauna, if he can be bothered. After all, it's Friday. Friday night, smoke going up, smelling sharp in the autumn evening. No one to smell it or watch the line of smoke go straight up between the trees.

She stops swimming and looks back. The shore is as far away as the rock. The swans have come out from their island again, and are fanned out across the bay. It wouldn't be safe to swim back through them. They'd attack her. She'll have to go on. No use deciding now that she never meant to go to the crag, no chance of coasting slowly back to the sandy safe shore. She'll have to climb the rocks.

The lake is getting colder, or she's getting colder. It's pewtery on the surface, black underneath. Her arms are moving quite slowly and they look thin and weak in the water. She hears her gasping breath. She kicks hard. Her right foot is beginning to trail. It's never been as strong as the left since she twisted her ankle when she was twelve. Another rest. No. She's getting too cold. She'll shut her eyes and swim thirty strokes, then the rock will be much closer. And again. She counts aloud. The rock is getting near. It's bigger than she thought, and shiny and steep. There's got to be a ledge somewhere for her to climb. Otherwise she'll have to swim round to the bog and she might not be able to get out that way. She daren't risk getting stuck there. Not far now. Count another thirty strokes. The rock is so dark she's frightened to swim under it. What if there's a current? What if the water pulls her down?

The thing is not to panic. Think of numbers. Twenty, nineteen, eighteen . . . The rock is quite close now. It's not as smooth as it looked from a distance. There are cracks – yes, and shelves. If she can just get her foot up . . .

But she's so tired. Her breath is creaking and her arms are

very slow. Her legs drag in the water. They aren't even kicking any more. She pants and scrabbles at the lake like a dog.

'The thing is to come alongside the rock as if I'm a boat. Then I'll find a handhold.'

Her right hip bangs hard against the rock. She looks down and sees blood fanning out into the water, but she can't feel anything. No. No. Don't look down. Try again. This time she sculls in on her back, her feet towards the rock, feeling for projections. The rock won't let her cling. It's like a big un-friendly body shaking her off. She isn't going to be able to get out. A bubble of panic rises, trapping her breath. No. No. Try again. This time her feet catch a slight shelf under the water. Now, a handhold. She scrabbles again, but it's wet and slimy and she falls back into the water. Try. Try. This time hold it harder. The handhold lasts for a couple of seconds and she kicks desperately, flings herself upward, wedges one foot in the crack in the rock and spread-eagles herself, leaning in against the cold crag. She's up. She's out of the lake. The water only reaches her knees. Her fingers are numb on the rock, dead-white. She's going to fall back. She'll never climb to the top. Her legs are shaking too much. Then she sees that she doesn't have to climb, because the crag is seamed with ledges. She can follow this ledge round until it's safe to step down into the scrub. Inch by inch, she moves around the crag until there's earth below her, not water. She unsticks her hands from the ledge above and lets herself roll into the rough grass. She lies still, looking at the blades of grass criss-crossing in front of her eyes. She can't see the water. She's done it.

Cold. She's got to get up. She rummages, tears off a clump of grass and rubs herself as hard as she can, all over her body. It would be stupid to die of exposure after managing such a swim. And she's done it. She hasn't drowned. Kai would have been sure she'd drown. The cut on her hip's not so bad after all – already it's slowed to a rusty trickle of blood. It's on her side. She's won. She's done it. After this everything's going to be easy. She can get back to the beach if she keeps to the edge of the trees and doesn't cross the bog. Any idiot can avoid that sharp, deceptive green. It's not far, and if she moves fast she'll get warm. She's got her dry clothes to put on, and a sweater in her cyclebag, and she can eat her chocolate. At the station buffet there'll be hot coffee and sausages.

Thank God, there's no wind. She scrubs harder with the grass, triumphantly, feeling the blood sting its way to the surface of her body, feeling her skin hurt and tingle. The lake is glassy. It settles as placidly as it would have done if she was twisting down and down through pleats and currents of cold, head over heels, slowing as the current tilted her pale body over and over like a starfish doing cartwheels until it bumped and settled in the silt. But she is alive. She's made it.

'I've done it. I'm alive. Enid's dead. Enid is dead, but I'm alive. No. It doesn't have to be like that. Enid is dead, and I am alive. Enid's dead, and I am alive.'

Enid. She sees her, walking away in her black reefer jacket and those black trousers with a strap under the foot which she calls slacks. She walks away quickly, frail and jaunty, the beret on her head hiding her grey hair and the delicate pale scalp which shows between its strands.

'Enid,' whispers Nadine, but she can't make the figure walk less quickly, or turn, or show her face. 'Enid, I'm waiting for you.'

Nadine stands. She is naked. Her nipples are puckered like blackberries, her breasts taut in the cold air. Streaks of mud and grass slime run down stomach, buttocks, thighs. Her feet are black with mud which has oozed up through the crevices between her toes. She smells of lake water.

Nadine looks down her body. She's lost weight over the past couple of weeks, and there are concave shadows on the insides of her thighs. Maybe her breasts have shrunk too. She will not be worth as much now. If she put on her white dress again it would not cling and slide over her flesh, giving glimpses of breast and thigh. It would hang a little loose on her, wrinkling disappointedly, sexless as her mother's wedding-dress.

It doesn't matter. This body is for her. It is not for looking at, unless she chooses. But it's cold here, much too cold to stand. The water shivers, pulled by a breeze. A bird she doesn't know calls from the marsh with a sound like winter. The hunters will soon be here, in their greens and browns and greys, with their guns over their shoulders. Already they are oiling their guns, putting dubbin on their boots, buying cartridges. Nadine moves. Close to the wet ground, weaving her way, she works along the reeds. There's the little beach, its sand bright although there is no sun on it. Suddenly three ducks take off from the reeds in a long skittering launch off the surface of the lake.

Twenty-three

The policewoman who sits so long at Enid's bedside is kind as well as patient. She knows all about Nadine now. She reassures Enid that Nadine is bound to come and see her soon. She's probably gone away for a few days, that's all. Gently, she continues to probe. Who else lives in the house? What about visitors? And the landlord, Mr Toivanen, isn't it? Has Enid seen him recently? Enid probably notices the comings-and-goings, living alone, doesn't she? The policewoman is young, but she is not inexperienced. She catches Enid's small, cautious glances. She knows there are gaps in Enid's story, though she isn't yet sure where they are or why they are there.

Enid is feeling so much better now. It's over two weeks since her accident. At first she couldn't talk for more than a minute or two because it hurt her head and muddled her. But every day she manages something new. She graduated to a commode, then to the slow shuffle down the ward to the toilets. Her arm is mending. It'll be a long time healing, but what can you expect at her age. Doctor is very pleased with her, says the nurse who has made a pet of Enid, crouching by the bed and hugging her after a sick, dizzy, successful walk right down the ward and back. Enid gets bad headaches, and she can't remember things very well yet, but that's only natural, the nurses say. Once she starts eating properly things will get better. Enid prods Rice Krispies, composted with All-Bran, and gives a small, disbelieving sniff. Once she's got her strength back, she'll soon put these nurses right about what constitutes a healthy diet. No fruit to speak of, and when she asked for a vegetarian meal she got a four-egg omelette and banana custard.

The policewoman suspects that Enid's memory is under better control than Enid will admit. There are things she doesn't want to tell them. After all, she has been living in that house all the time. She must have seen things; heard things. God knows there's been enough going on. Several people are very interested indeed in Mr Toivanen and his business associates. Patiently the policewoman accepts another cup of tea and continues to talk and listen. Enid seems very fond of this Nadine. Nadine Light, aged sixteen. Another person whom the police are anxious to interview. The bruises on Enid's upper arms are fading, but they have been photographed. They are the kind of bruises caused by hands, gripping hard. Something has happened in that house. From all directions the floodlights of inquiry switch on to the confused night and morning which Enid can't quite remember. One old woman has fallen downstairs. The flood-lights throw shadows and fling up patterns.

'Who else was in the house the night you had your accident? Can you remember?'

Enid's hands move on the sheets. She crisps a corner of sheet between her fingers. Her lips move. In a feeble whisper she gives Vicki's name. The policewoman leans forward and writes in her notebook. Enid's eyes are half shut, but her fatigue and weakness don't prevent her from giving a photographically accurate description of Vicki. Then she appears to sleep, limp after her effort. What else swims in the sea-cavern called memory? Far down the ward a door slams, a cry comes once and is cut off. It floats, lost in the white disinfected air above the beds. Nadine in her bed. Kai on the stairs – or was that another time? Nadine was crying. Enid sees the dark shadow of Nadine's hair on the pillow.

'I hope she hasn't gone off with her Kai,' she says aloud. 'He's no good to her. Just like Caro.'

'Who's that, Enid? Can you remember?'

'They didn't hang Caro. She went to prison,' whispers Enid, and shuts her eyes. They are there again, Sukey and Caro in the beautiful fields of summer grass. Soon the mower is going to come and cut them all: cocksfoot and quaking grass and Yorkshire fog. It might be tomorrow. The weather is perfect for mowing. A cottage door opens and a man comes out, walks down the stone-paved path lined with tufts of pinks and cherry-pie, and leans over his back gate looking down the fields. He is the mower. His scythe is whetted. He looks at the red streaks of sunset and the clear green evening sky with one star budding in it. He smells the air.

The ripe grasses bow and dip in the summer wind as if someone is stroking them. Sukey comes first, Caro after. Sukey's dress blows against her body and her beautiful tanned round arms. She shields her eyes against the sun and laughs. The soft welcoming wind cups her cheeks, which are rosy under their tan.

'Darling,' murmurs Enid, lying in her plain white hospital bed. Classic FM leaks from the Walkman of the woman in the next bed. 'The most beautiful music in the world . . .' The bed rocks too, gently, not quite anchored on the glassy floor.

Someone is standing over her. A nurse with a big red-faced smile.

'There's a friend of yours here to see you, Enid,' she says, delighted to be bringing good news. Enid hasn't had a single visitor yet, apart from the police. Enid opens her eyes. The policewoman seems to have gone. And there, coming down the ward –

'Nadine!' says Enid. Nadine sits on the policewoman's chair, leans forward and kisses Enid. Her young soft lips press into Enid's dry cheek. She smells of a new perfume, and she's wearing clothes Enid hasn't seen before. She looks elegant, older, thinner.

'Silly girl, you went off with him, didn't you? After all I told you,' she grumbles. Nadine smiles and takes Enid's hand. Enid goes on, 'Where is he, he's not with you, is he?' and her face is suddenly shrunk and panicky.

'No, he's not with me. He won't be coming back to England.'

'But you came back.'

'Yes.' Nadine hesitates, folds Enid's hand between her own. The bed has steadied again. Enid knows where she is. How funny people's faces look upside-down, even Nadine's. 'The thing was, Enid, I heard you were dead. I came back because I thought you were dead.'

'You heard about my accident,' says Enid.

'Accident,' says Nadine. 'I know about all of it. I came back to tell the police what really happened.'

'But I'm not dead, dear, am I? You don't want to go telling all that to the police. You know how they get muddled up if you start telling them things. Anyway, you were asleep. How could you have known what was going on? You'll never get rid of them. There's a policewoman round here all the time, ever so nice she is, but she's got her job to do. She'll be listening somewhere.'

'The sister says you're much better.'

'Oh, well, she should know, shouldn't she, dear? You ought to have seen me when I first came in. You'd have thought I was dead, all right. I was unconscious for a whole night and a day, you know. I was in intensive care.' Regret that Nadine can't now see her at her worst and appreciate the miracle of her recovery crosses Enid's face.

'Don't make me sorry I missed it,' says Nadine. She strokes Enid's forehead. Enid's hair is brushed straight back in tight strands over her scalp. The liver-coloured age spots on her cheeks stand out against the whiteness of her pillow. Her Viyella night-dress has a demure high collar, buttoned up. She looks like a small, well-looked-after child.

'Where did you get that night-dress, Enid?' she asks. 'What happened to your pyjamas?'

'Oh, there was no time to think of anything like that, dear,' says Enid proudly. 'I was an emergency.'

They smile at one another. It's another beautiful day, and Nadine has brought a big bunch of bronze chrysanthemums which she lays down on the bed in a sheath of crackling white paper. Their smell excites Enid. It makes her think of autumn, and things beginning. There's nothing like a touch of frost to get the blood running in your veins. Nadine delves in her carrier-bag and gets out a bag of russet apples.

'I'll have to get the nurse to cut them up for me,' fusses Enid.

'Can't you manage them? I'd have got grapes, only these looked so nice.'

''Course I can manage them. That young nurse over there, look, don't let her catch you staring – that's Jackie. She's a good girl. She'll do anything for me. She'll peel them if I ask her.'

'You've got her where you want her, I can see that.'

'Oh, well, I'll be home soon,' says Enid and sighs. Her eyelids droop and her fingers tug fretfully at her high collar.

'Don't you want to leave the hospital?'

'It's nice in here. They're all very good to me, but I'm better off in my own place. A social worker came to talk to me about sheltered housing.'

'Is that what you want?'

'It's not what I want,' says Enid with the first touch of her old sharpness. 'It's what I can get. I can't go back *there*, now can I? With that Tony about, and, for all you say, your Kai likely to pop up again like a jack-in-the-box. What with air travel these days, who can tell? I don't think I should feel comfortable.'

'Tony won't stay. He'll be gone before you're out of hospital. He wants to move back to Manchester.'

'No doubt he's got business there as well, dear. Still, give him his due, he *was* the one who called the ambulance. Otherwise I'd have been lying dead on the floor, that's what the doctor told me,' invents Enid. 'You wouldn't have thought it of Tony, would you? It just shows you should never judge people too harshly. He hasn't been in to see me, though.'

'He told me you were in here. I went to the house first.'

Oh, yes, thinks Nadine, Tony was more than ready to leave for Manchester, but the police had told him to stay put for the time being. Until they'd finished their inquiries. He had been on the phone when she opened the front door. He looked at her, pressed the silence button, then thought better of it, cut his conversation in a couple of words and turned to Nadine. His face was yellow and tired. He looked older than Nadine remembered, and somehow much worse, as if lots of small changes which were just about to happen in his skin and eyes and expression had happened all at once and together. Or maybe she was the one who'd changed.

He was suspicious of her. He wanted to find out what Kai had told her, and how much she knew. He padded round her with questions like a cat. It was the business he was thinking about, of course. Always the business. That wasn't dead yet. He was going to go back to Manchester, he had contacts in Manchester, as well as all his family. There was no end to it. If only he'd just go. Vicki would be on her way too, no doubt. Whatever happened, she'd bob up somewhere, with her tan and her gold bracelets and her good advice. Vicki was waterproof.

'What about the house?' Nadine asked Tony. 'What's going to happen about it?'

'We'll get rid of it. It'd never've worked out. We bought at the wrong time.'

Tony got up from the telephone table and stretched himself. A big shadow stretched itself out too, on the opposite wall, and from the plane trees in the square Nadine heard a wood-pigeon coo in its throat. The sound bubbled into the house and made it quieter and emptier than ever. Suddenly she realized that there was no Enid upstairs, watching and waiting for her. Tony and Kai had got what they wanted: vacant possession. Except that now they'd got it they didn't want it any more. They wanted to get shot of the place, and everything to do with it.

And of everyone. She watched Tony's shadow yawn across the opposite wall, almost touching her own shadow. Here she was in the empty house with Tony. He smiled. And now she was frightened, more frightened then she'd ever been in the summer-house with Kai, miles from anywhere. But it was stupid to be afraid of Tony. They'd lived together, eaten together, gone to London together. And he'd called the ambulance for Enid, hadn't he? He could just as easily have left her on the floor. Nobody would ever have known. She'd never actually known him hurt anyone. Yet she saw knives. She saw that the day in the kitchen when he bought them and the way the veal fell into ribbons under dull razor-edged steel. The colour of a sea-anemone. Her skin prickled and she moved back towards the window which was open a little at the top. She glanced down into the square but no one was passing. It was the dead middle of a cool afternoon. Tony stood by the telephone, looking at her and still saying nothing. But it was all right. She'd been in the house on her own with Tony dozens of times.

'Empty, empty,' said the attic overhead.

Her body tensed. A little grey breeze ran from the top of the window and feathered the back of her neck. *Go now. Go now*, thudded her heart.

'I talked to Paul Parrett this morning,' she lied quickly. His face changed. Now he'd got to guess how much she'd told Paul Parrett. Play for time.

'Did you?'

'Yes, he wanted to know how I was. He's really nice, isn't he?'

'What'd you tell him?'

'Oh, you know. This and that.'

'About the police? Did you tell him that?'

'He asked how you were. I said you were fine. I told him I'd be seeing you today.'

'You want to watch what you say to him. He's got contacts. Influence.'

'I wouldn't say that, Tony,' said Nadine. 'He doesn't need influence, does he? I mean, he's the one who makes things happen.'

'Yeah. You could be right,' said Tony.

'I know I am,' said Nadine, watching him. 'That's why I had a chat with him. I shan't be coming back here, Tony. I'm getting a flat. I'll be fetching my things in a few days.'

'OK,' said Tony. 'OK. If that's the way you want it. Remember me to him.'

'He remembers you,' said Nadine. 'He's good at remembering.'

'What about Kai? When's he coming back?'

'I don't know. I'm not with Kai any more. I expect he'll be back,' she said, walking past him. The prickling in her flesh was gone. She turned her back on Tony and he watched her go out and up the stairs.

She went up to the bedroom which had been hers and Kai's. Their rust and gold duvet still lay plumply on the bed. She wouldn't take it with her, or any of the other things. Not the linen sheets, none of it. In the end Vicki'd been the last one to sleep with Kai in that bed. The sheets were still rumpled where the two of them must have tossed the bedclothes back. They hadn't had time to think about making the bed. They would have been in a hurry.

There were her clothes and a few books, and that was all she wanted. Not much to show for her time here and everything that had happened. It was less than she'd brought with her, because she'd left so much of her stuff at the summer-house. If she'd brought a case, she could have taken everything she possessed now. The bedroom door had been closed for two weeks, and the room smelled of cats. You never got rid of the smell of cat's piss once it had soaked into the wood, no matter how hard you tried to scrub it away. She looked upstairs towards Enid's room. She'd have to go back there too and help Enid pack, but not now.

She would ring Paul Parrett soon. She would ring with her credit card from a call-box. He'd told her it might take a long time to be put through to him, but if she waited he was always in reach of a phone. She must give her name. A powerful man. A man with a midnight garden high above the city, and ballerina apple trees, and a car to take him anywhere he wanted. There were worse things to want than what Paul Parrett wanted. His crêpe bandages were starting to look as innocent to Nadine as the handcuffs children wear to play cops and villains. He'd liked her, she was sure of it. And surely she'd be safe with him, if she was ever going to be safe with anyone. If it mattered, thought Nadine. If safety mattered so much, after all. Because when you thought you had it, it was already gone. The cold lake is in her. It has gone through her skin, penetrated blood and bone, left her immune. She wants to see him, that's all.

'So someone told you I was dead, is that it?' asks Enid in her hospital bed. 'And that's why you came back? That's the only reason?'

'Yes.'

'It was Kai who told you, wasn't it? I thought so. Still, they say a bad conscience is its own punishment, don't they? Even for your Kai. Think how Caro must have felt.'

'He drinks all the time. He wants to cry but he can't. It's not just about you, it's other things. I can't do anything about them.'

'So you came away.'

'Not just because of that. I wanted to see you,' says Nadine. 'Even if you were dead. And now you're not, I'll come every day.'

'Would you, dear?' says Enid eagerly. 'You know how the nurses like you to have visitors. I've just kept having that policewoman.'

'I've got to look for somewhere to live,' says Nadine. 'I've got enough money for a deposit, and I'm going back to work.'

'But they won't keep me here for ever.'

'I could look for a bigger flat,' says Nadine. 'If you liked. If you'd be all right without a warden and things. You know, all those bells. I'll have to be out at work.'

'Oh, I don't need a warden, dear,' exclaims Enid. 'Bells you ring if you fall over and buttons you push if someone you don't know comes to the door. I can't be doing with all that. I'll have my pension, I won't be a burden on you.'

'I'll start looking, then. I'm staying in a guest-house at the moment, just till I get fixed up. I'll leave the number on your locker. I've still got some money. We can get all your stuff out of the house once we find a flat.'

Enid's eyes have closed. She looks very tired and there are marks under her eyes. Nadine bends down and kisses her again, gently, on the fragile, papery temples. She smells of hospitals, not of herself. She would never have chosen that night-dress. One of the nurses must have gone out and bought it for her. She hasn't had any visitors.

'Goodbye, Enid darling,' she says. 'I'll bring you some grapes tomorrow.' Enid smiles slightly but doesn't open her eyes. 'Get black ones,' she murmurs, 'I like those.' All she wants now is a nice sleep. She can relax at last. She can smell the bronze chrysanthemums Nadine has left on the bed.

Half-way down the ward the policewoman sees Nadine move away from Enid's bed. She steps forward purposefully and intercepts her. It's all very undramatic, think the watching patients disappointedly. A nod, a gesture. Sister's office door closes behind them. The low murmur of voices goes on and on, but even the patients nearest to the partition can't make out any of the words.

Paul Parrett's telephone rings three times. The quick, immaculate tones of Security answer it. Nadine gives her name, and then there's a long pause while money is steadily drained off her credit card. She stares down the bank of telephones, imagining other people's conversations. A girl leans into her receiver, smiling. What's making her smile like that? She finishes her call loudly: 'I've got to go, Mum! Meet me off the 7.40, all right?' Nadine turns away and taps the glass rhythmically, then Paul Parrett's voice comes through on the line, fresh and vigorous.

'Nadine! I've been wondering when I was going to hear from you.' Not if, thinks Nadine. When.

'I've been away,' she says.

'Did you have a good time?'

'Not really . . . Listen, I'm moving, that's why I'm in a call-box. I'm getting a flat with a friend of mine. I'll let you have the address once we've found a place.'

'A different friend? Not Kai?'

'A different sort of friend. I'm going to share the flat with Enid, she's the old lady in the attic I was telling you about. We don't want to stay in the house any more.'

There's a slight pause. Then his voice again, 'Well, it sounds as if a lot's been going on. So you'll be sharing a flat with Enid. Tell me about it – can I call you back, if you're in a call-box? This must be costing you a fortune.'

'It's OK,' says Nadine. 'I've got a credit card.'

'The thing is,' says Paul Parrett, 'when am I going to see you again?'

'Soon. Really soon. But I've got to get Enid settled in first. She hasn't got anyone else, and she's had an accident. She's still in hospital.'

'Is she all right?'

'She's getting better. But any fall's serious at her age.'

'Who's looking after her? Just you?'

'Well, there's all the nurses. But I will, when she comes home. When we get the flat. They said at the hospital that she was doing really well. The sister said she was going to make a complete recovery.'

'Good. Good.' Then suddenly, his voice urgent down the line, 'What does she look like?'

'Oh, well, pale. But you'd expect that. Her arm's in a sling.'

He is silent. The line hangs dead between them. 'Does she need anything?' he asks. 'Money?'

'She's got her pension. But it's a bit complicated – the accident. Listen, is it all right to talk – I mean, on this phone?'

'Yes.'

'It's to do with the accident, Enid's accident. The police are involved, but Enid's not saying anything. That's why I wanted to talk to you. I mean, it's one of the reasons.'

Silence. Then, 'Yes. Go on.'

'You know she was the sitting tenant in our house. And she was around all the time. Maybe she saw things. You know. Things to do with Tony and Kai.'

'I can imagine.'

'Or she heard things. The reason I phoned you, one of the reasons, is that I don't want there to be any more accidents.'

'You think there might be?'

'I'm not sure.'

'That it might happen again?'

'Yes. Not just to Enid, to both of us. But I don't think it would, if people knew I'd been talking to you.'

'People being who?'

'You sure this line is OK?'

'Sure.'

'Tony. Kai. Maybe others.'

'Right. So the thing is, to make sure that these people do know?'

'Yes. I did talk to Tony a bit today – I wanted to make it seem as if I'd already talked to you.' Her voice is thin, breathy.

'He frightened you.'

'Yes. A bit.'

'OK. That's no problem. I'll get in touch with our dinner host and I'm sure he'll pass the word on to all his friends. They've got a bit big for their boots,' says Paul Parrett. 'Starting to act as if they're in the big time. But they're not, you know.'

'Aren't they? How do you know?'

He laughs. 'Oh, Nadine. They're a couple of amateurs, your Tony and Kai.'

'Don't call them that.'

'Anyway, they can be taken care of. No need to worry.'

There is more silence, then in a quite different voice he asks, 'How old are you really, Nadine?'

'Why do you ask?'

'No reason. Only, perhaps, people sound younger on the telephone.'

'I'm sixteen.'

'Sixteen,' he says.

'Yes. Yes.'

'You've got enough money?'

'I'm all right for money.'

'Let me have your new address as soon as you know it. And if anything worries you, anything at all, ring me up straight away. But it won't. It's all going to be OK.'

'I dreamed about you last night,' says Nadine.

'Did you?'

'Yes, you were on a liner, we both were. It was dark red, you know the paint that stops rust? That colour. We had to sail down a street. The river ran between the houses and it was steep, like a street in San Francisco or being on a switchback.'

'Did we get through?'

'I don't know. The front of the liner reared up out of the water, then it went down. We went so fast everyone was screaming. Like on a rollercoaster. That hanging bit at the top and then you plunge.'

'What colour was the river?'

'Bright green. And little white clouds in the sky. And people were looking out of the house windows and waving. We could have touched their hands.'

'Oh, Nadine,' he says. 'Nadine.'

'I know. Silly, wasn't it?'

'No. No, it sounds wonderful.'

They say goodbye. Nadine hangs up and leans against the transparent plastic hood of the booth. She is smiling. Really, what he wants is so little compared to what he is able to give. The way he makes her feel alive. How funny, Tony was right after all. He said she'd like him. What a long time it seems since she was on that train, going to London. And the girl jumped out of the train. He makes her feel twice as alive. Where's she going to find that anywhere else? Compared to Paul Parrett, Kai's half dead. Anything could happen.

That's what Enid was talking about, what she found at the Manchester Ladies when the doors opened and she saw the lights and the mirrors and the flowers and flames leaping against their reflections. And Sukey made all that happen. Sukey's energy. Sukey lapping Enid round with it. And it was love, argues Nadine, though the newspapers had a different word for it.

Hundreds of miles north the wind sifts across the forest. The birch grove by the lake grows lighter daily as leaves fall. The forest is getting ready for its yearly transformation, when light pours upward from the snowy ground. The birches strip themselves and stand naked, ready for the snow. The evergreens darken as pale grains of sun hit the forest floor. Wind ruffles the lake, fish sink into its silt for the winter, and grass, leaves and rushes are tinged with brown. It won't be long before the marshes freeze. In their apartment in Tampere, Matti and Marja Linna plan the extension they will build to their summer-house next spring. The children are getting older and they need more space. Marja hopes that the doors and windows she fastened so carefully on their last visit will remain secure against the winter storms. Neither of them thinks of Kai Toivanen. He was a friend once, but they haven't heard from him for years and he has gone out of their address books. Their friends are parents of young children, like themselves.

It is cold now. The birch leaves that remain are yellow, and the sap is sinking in the young pines. Soon summer-house and sauna will be under the snow. The lake by the summer-house will freeze until the ice could support an army of skaters, but no one will set foot on it. The lake where the swans nested and

Nadine swam will freeze too, until it's possible to walk safely to the island and to the black crags which are shaped like a head and shoulders. Snow will cover the ice, and the wind will blow it into stiff peaks and curves. It will harden, then new soft snow will fall, covering the scar marks of birds' feet and falling branches. There will be footprints too: perhaps a dog, perhaps something more savage and lonely, looking for company. In the long, silent, lightless winter a wolf could become a man, or a man could become a wolf. A man can burn with vodka until he doesn't feel the cold, and when at last he does it's only very slowly, like sleep. A child stands for hours on the snow crusted ice, waiting for the snow-woman to find him and cradle him to her cold heart.

READ MORE IN PENGUIN

In every corner of the world, on every subject under the sun, Penguin represents quality and variety – the very best in publishing today.

For complete information about books available from Penguin – including Puffins, Penguin Classics and Arkana – and how to order them, write to us at the appropriate address below. Please note that for copyright reasons the selection of books varies from country to country.

In the United Kingdom: Please write to *Dept. EP, Penguin Books Ltd, Bath Road, Harmondsworth, West Drayton, Middlesex UB7 0DA*

In the United States: Please write to *Consumer Sales, Penguin USA, P.O. Box 999, Dept. 17109, Bergenfield, New Jersey 07621-0120*. VISA and MasterCard holders call 1-800-253-6476 to order Penguin titles

In Canada: Please write to *Penguin Books Canada Ltd, 10 Alcorn Avenue, Suite 300, Toronto, Ontario M4V 3B2*

In Australia: Please write to *Penguin Books Australia Ltd, P.O. Box 257, Ringwood, Victoria 3134*

In New Zealand: Please write to *Penguin Books (NZ) Ltd, Private Bag 102902, North Shore Mail Centre, Auckland 10*

In India: Please write to *Penguin Books India Pvt Ltd, 706 Eros Apartments, 56 Nehru Place, New Delhi 110 019*

In the Netherlands: Please write to *Penguin Books Netherlands bv, Postbus 3507, NL-1001 AH Amsterdam*

In Germany: Please write to *Penguin Books Deutschland GmbH, Metzlerstrasse 26, 60594 Frankfurt am Main*

In Spain: Please write to *Penguin Books S. A., Bravo Murillo 19, 1° B, 28015 Madrid*

In Italy: Please write to *Penguin Italia s.r.l., Via Felice Casati 20, I–20124 Milano*

In France: Please write to *Penguin France S. A., 17 rue Lejeune, F–31000 Toulouse*

In Japan: Please write to *Penguin Books Japan, Ishikiribashi Building, 2–5–4, Suido, Bunkyo-ku, Tokyo 112*

In Greece: Please write to *Penguin Hellas Ltd, Dimocritou 3, GR–106 71 Athens*

In South Africa: Please write to *Longman Penguin Southern Africa (Pty) Ltd, Private Bag X08, Bertsham 2013*

BY THE SAME AUTHOR

Zennor in Darkness

As U-Boats nose the Cornish coastline, the village of Zennor is alive with talk of spies. It is a world of call-up and telegrams, secrets and suspicion, and no one is immune. Not Clare Coyne, nor her beloved cousin John William, who is home on leave from the trenches, shell-shocked. Not D. H. Lawrence and his German wife Frieda, who have retreated from London war-fever and censorship to a cottage in Zennor. In this, her first novel, Helen Dunmore has written a passionate story of love, betrayal and self-discovery in wartime.

'We believe in Clare's intelligence, talent and passion, and it is something of a triumph that the dense pleasure of landscape and texture never overpower our involvement in her story' – *Independent on Sunday*

'Her touch is subtle, delicate … The opening scene of three girls laughing as they slip down the warm sand dunes will haunt us as we read of soldiers drowning in mud' – *New Statesman & Society*